THE CAPTOR CAPTIVATED!

He had lain with naked women before, but never had he felt a desire like the one that overpowered him now. He wanted to kiss and caress every part of her, and yet he knew that he wanted her too strongly to have her when she was not ready for him. Deprivation had long been part of his training to be a man, and now this was no different. While she slept he kept his lips from her, and he kept himself from going inside of her, but gently he caressed every part of her anyway, and the lightness of his touch and the continuance of her sleep was the sweetest agony he had ever known.

"LOVE, VIOLENCE, MYSTICISM AND SUSPENSEFUL ACTION SET AGAINST AN AUTHENTIC INDIAN BACKGROUND... A HAUNTING STORY OF LOVE!"

—*Burlington Free Press*

Nakoa's Woman

Gayle Rogers

SOJOURNER
PUBLISHERS, INC.

To
The American Indian

Sojourner Publishers, Inc.
23119 19th Drive N.E., Arlington, WA 98223
360-435-4622 • www.sojournerpub.com

ISBN: 0-9723078-0-X
Library of Congress Control Number: 2002111954

Previously published as The Second Kiss.
Sojourner Publishing softcover edition.

Cover art & design by Holly Smith.
Drawings by Dorothy Bowles.

Printed in the United States of America.

The Second Kiss

For every man there are two kisses.
The first kiss is of the mother, the earth,
With her food and warmth and light for growing.

The second kiss is the golden kiss.
It is the kiss of the self,
And its fire and light and warmth
Is greater than all of the suns in the sky!

With the second kiss, the mother is needed no longer.
She is for the children yet crawling upon her surface.
With the second kiss darkness has light,
Coldness has warmth,
And all strangers are accepted.

Blessed be the dead. Blessed be the receivers
     of the second kiss.
They feel not with hands of clay,
But with the beating of the universe.
If they remained in our shadow,
We would hear them wailing for us
From the Wolf Trail itself!

Chapter One

Nakoa looked out upon the morning with new vision. Celebration burst within his soul and his only response was stillness. He had become a part of the complete, moving now in a force so beautiful, so powerful and beyond imagination that he was awed just standing in its outskirts.

Prairie grass lay all around him, shimmering and green from the winter's snows. It was life; it was an extension of himself and of the miraculous flowing of every living thing. He wanted to kneel and weep. He wanted to lose himself in his recognition that he was an eternal part of an eternal whole. Napi, Napi, giver of all and receiver of all, had flooded his heart and soul. His body was a vessel to bear His wine.

Nakoa had found his Nitsokan, the vision that made him a man, a sacred sign from the sun. For days he had deprived his body of food and drink, and finally he had melted into the morning mists and had found not an animal for his Nitsokan, but a woman! He had never known a man's sign to be a woman before; but she had come to him so clearly that there was no mistaking her. She was the other part of his incomplete soul. Her face had been as pale as the mists around them, her lips as red as if she had just eaten fresh berries. Her breath had warmly touched his face. When he looked deeply into her eyes he knew that she was a part of him that had been taken away long ago. She had moved seductively against him and when he felt the touch of her bare flesh he shuddered with an ecstasy he had never known before. She had been a white woman, the first white woman he had ever seen.

Now he moved noiselessly and dreamlike into the morning. All of the night's shadow was gone. The prairie grass hummed in full sun, its pungent odor making him smile with pleasure. He stopped and looked toward the east. There the whites lived, beyond the land of the Crow. Suddenly, he knew that this white woman had been more than his Nitsokan, more than a mystical vision. She would come to him again from the white man's land, and he would possess her, and what had been joined from the first would be joined again in the endless circle of reality.

Tears ran down his cheeks as he walked through the tall bunch grass toward his home. Near him came the sound of a meadowlark calling out sweetly, a benediction.

The Indian moon faded into the Indian sun, and as year after year passed, word from the white man's settlements in far-off Oregon reached Americans east of the Mississippi. Fires burned in the smithies day and night. In the red shadow of the bellows, men pounded and hammered and sweated to outfit the wagons, horses, and mules that would carry them out into the silent prairie.

May of 1845 was budding green and warm with the promise of an early summer. To Maria Frame the whole world responded to the joyous calling of her own youth, to the singing of the blood within her veins. She was aching to move out into the great American desert, because it was unknown, and to her spirit, the unknown was a thing to conquer.

But to her sister, Ana, two years her junior, the Oregon Trail portended disaster. She had grieved at the selling of their farm in St. Louis; her mother's grave had been too new for other feet to have trod her orchards, for other hands to have prepared food upon her stove. Still, she could not hold back her father, or Maria. It would have been like trying to stop the rushing waters of the swirling river that had carried them up from St. Louis, or like trying to silence the lusty shouting of the emigrants camping along the shore. To Ana, the whole world had become awry, with everything tilting as crazily as their boat had, as it made its way past treacherous sandbars and snags. But her father and Maria had not noticed the dangers of the river or the discomforts of the constantly flying water, the smell of the horse and mule dung, the cramped quarters of the boat. For them, this trip had been only the beginning of an adventure, a new life, which they anticipated with growing enthusiasm.

By the middle of May they were on the trail to Fort Leavenworth where they were to join a large wagon train leaving for the Oregon Territory. The Indian apple was in full flower, the maples already in red bud, and numerous little streams crisscrossed their path. The woods were deeply shadowed and filled with bird song. But still Ana felt an inner chill, a quaking that even this beauty failed to dispel.

"There are two thousand miles ahead of us," she said to Maria.

"That we have never seen." Maria's voice was brimming with excitement.

"But there are only four small trading posts."

"For us to discover!" Maria almost laughed.

"How can you be so happy?" Ana asked sadly. "You know that there is a war between the Snake and Dahcotah Indians. And the Oregon Trail crosses their warring grounds!"

"We will be all right," Maria said firmly, and then looked tenderly at her little sister. "Father and I will never let anything happen to you," she said. "Life will be beautiful for us, Ana." She looked ahead at the cool ribboned trail and began to hum.

Ana frowned and turned away, wanting suddenly to weep. The beloved and familiar land was sinking irrevocably from her sight. Sensing Ana's growing pain, Maria stopped her humming and became silent. "We should have stayed on the farm," Ana whispered.

"Our life lies at the end of the trail before us, Ana, not behind us."

"For me, this trail will end in the sky," Ana whispered.

The train they joined was a great one, its one hundred wagons stretching across the prairie for over four miles. The day it first moved out, Maria was in a frenzy of delight. The first slow turning of the great wheels, the dust from the bawling oxen, the excited shouting of the children—even the cursing of the men prodding the mules made Maria ache to get rid of her dragging skirts and be out in the midst of the dust.

"It is beautiful! Beautiful!" she cried.

"It is hardly a painting," said Ana.

"It is better than a painting because we are in it!" Maria's eyes shone with joy.

For three hundred and sixteen miles the wagons struggled through the flat land. Then the Oregon Trail met the great Platte, and the wagon wheels cut into the Pawnee trail. Game became plentiful; small antelope came boldly up to the creaking wagons and watched them curiously, their white throats and soft black eyes just showing above the rank grass. Buffalo were seen, first a few lone bulls against the sky, and then a bull leading a few cows single file in a stately and deliberate fashion. The tall grass stretched ahead without end like a hungry sea.

In time the wagon just ahead of the Frames' was emptied of all of its children, one at a time, but so quickly that they all seemed to have died at once. Then the mother who had held the new baby next to her breast was gone too, buried farther along the trail, beyond the graves of her children. The land devoured them. There were so many mounds freshly dug and left to the lonely sky and the hungry white wolves. But in the end it would make no difference, for the land would devour the wolves too.

Mary Ann
Age three
Died June 20, 1845

Willie Walker
Age eleven
Died June 20, 1845

Bertha Johnson
Age twenty-four
Died June 22, 1845

Maria saw the markings and grieved with Ana. She had not

known Bertha Johnson. Had she been pretty? Had she been much in love with her husband, and he with her? Had she been happy? What might Willie Walker have become? Would he have been a pride to his father's heart? And Mary Ann, who died at the age of three. How many more days might she have seen the sun?

And so the wagons were emptied of children, of men, and of women, and deeper and deeper in despair, Ana waited to die. From the high wagon seat she saw pieces of furniture that the wagons ahead left behind, a child's chair, a woman's bureau, a table once carefully waxed and rubbed, and now left to crack in the hot sun.

In July they reached Laramie. Ana looked at the fort's high bastions and perpendicular walls in disbelief. She was still alive. They were all alive, she, her father, and Maria. They had survived the green sea. If they had lived to reach Laramie, they would live to reach Oregon, and now she was as confident of living as she had been of dying.

Maria was delighted with the fort and the tall mountains that loomed behind it. She traveled happily among the wagons near them, joking with the men and talking with the women as the cooking fires started to burn out. She loved to see the evening fires winking out in the darkness; she loved the smell of fresh bacon and coffee in the late dusk. Now there would be wood for their evening fires, and relaxed conversation without fear of the Indians. Serenity swelled in Maria's heart. The worst of the trip was over. Someday Oregon would have cities and then Ana could have her wish of spending her days in the peace of an elm-shaded street.

Edith Holmes was well enough to leave Laramie by the spring of 1846. The fever and even some of the nausea had passed, and she and Jim and the boys could move out with the next train without her losing the baby.

"How do you feel now, Edie?" asked Jim. They were in bed together, husband and wife, married five years. Edith stiffened, as his hand touched her back. "Are you well enough; are you really well enough for us to leave the fort?" he asked plaintively.

"Of course," Edith said sharply. "If any families go on, we'll go with them."

"I don't know whether it would be right," Jim said uncertainly.

"If you sit around waiting for things to get right, they'll never be," Edith answered.

Her husband sighed, and placed her head upon his shoulder. For a moment he was still, and then his hands moved softly across her stomach, and up to her breasts.

"No!" Edith said impatiently.

"You said you feel all right."

"I don't want that!"

"Damn it, Edie, you are already pregnant! When you aren't you are afraid you will be, and when you are, you're always sick! You aren't going to have one of those spells now. It's been too Goddamned long!"

Edith shuddered. His coarse hands were rough against the tender nipples of her swollen breasts. "You're hurting me!" she said furiously, but she accepted his embrace. Then satisfied at last, he gave her a rough and affectionate pat and fell into immediate sleep.

Edith lay awake beside him. He was snoring now, his mouth wide open. He was satisfied. She was the one seven months' pregnant with a swollen belly and a baby inside of it that flopped and turned all night long.

One of her boys cried out from under the wagon, and, alert, she realized he was calling her in his sleep. Even in their sleep they called her. Three boys she had had in five years of marriage, and now probably another on the way, and they all wanted her every minute. This was not what marriage should be: a snoring husband, the bone exhaustion, the nausea and having to cook, cook, cook anyway. How could she ever have let herself get pregnant again? She had been so pretty everyone had said—was she still pretty? She had been so little —little—and now she sobbed at her bigness, the coarseness, the sickness with it that probably never would end until she died.

Jim turned to his side and stopped snoring. Edith looked at the shadow of his back. Jim Holmes was her husband, but he was not a man. He was a moth that fluttered through life, without any purpose but just to flutter. He had never earned a living in his father's business. Even before the panic of '37 he was just too indecisive to work for himself. In Oregon he said it would be different, with good land just for the taking, and with the boys to help him. If only they had gone on to Fort Bridger last year, Edith thought. They had reached Laramie too late to go on, even if she hadn't caught the fever that had almost killed Ana Frame. She thought of Ana Frame jealously, for Ana was seventeen, and slim and beautiful. Maria Frame was nineteen, and she was beautiful too because she was unmarried. What would it be like to be Ana's age again, and go to bed, and sleep all night long, and not have to wake up to the feeding of a baby? What would it be like to sit down and to eat and feed only yourself?

In the spring of 1846 there were only twelve families of emigrants at Laramie. Four wagons had remained behind the train that had gone on to Oregon in the summer of 1845. There had been sickness among them, and they had elected to stay at the fort, although there was no doctor or medicine within its walls. But there was more comfort in dying with a roof over your head than out on the prairie beneath the open sky. Eight more wagons had arrived in October to wait for an early start the next spring, and, if possible, the twelve wagons were to travel together. It would be a small train, but there had been smaller ones. Now the snows were melting; there would be an early and long summer. The men who had been confined to Laramie for so long were restless and kept looking out over the land. What was there, after all, that waited ahead for them? The prairie was quiet, the sun was warm and the grass was growing. Why not jump off early and beat the summer heat? Why not be in Oregon planting new orchards when the next wagons from Leavenworth were choking on trail dust?

Edward Frame wandered away from the fires and the voices of the excited men talking around them. What kind of a bastard was he to bring his girls out into a wilderness like this? Ana had been so ill. In her he had seen his wife's face, still and white upon their bed, still and white in her coffin. If Ana had died, he would have believed himself forever branded for what he had done with Meg. He sat down and covered his face with his large rough hands. "You were already gone, my darling," he said to his dead wife, and felt tears flow unchecked against his beard.

He remembered when Meg first came to cook for them. His wife already lay indifferent to food and drink, and he was in wild rebellion at her dying. She had revealed no regret at leaving him, at doing what made him rage against his God. When he sat with her and touched her forehead, stroking her beautiful black hair away from her face, he remembered all of the times they had made love. He remembered their joys and their sorrows, and how she had almost died when she was having their daughters. He wanted to talk over this terrible calamity; he wanted her to share his agony as she had always done since their courtship, but she was silent, and gave no sign to his suffering. Her long lashes remained motionless against her cheeks, and when he kissed them, it was as if she had already died. He had wanted just one look, one glance into her soul; he wanted her to know his soul too, now at this time of departure.

Shaking, he finally left her and went down to the kitchen to the girls. It was then he saw Meg as if for the first time, her black hair shining against her white flesh, her large breasts straining against her bodice. He watched her breasts and imagined them naked, and he neither saw nor tasted the food she put upon the table. Meg's lips were sensuous and full. He imagined kissing them, and kissing the naked swelling bosom, and he thought of her thighs, and in this sad autumn night with his life's love dying above him, he made up his mind that those warm thighs would envelope him and bring him life.

Just before dawn he went to Meg's bedroom. She knew his feelings and was waiting for him. He had never been so wild with a woman; all of his rage against death drove him into Meg again and again, and when she became frightened, he held her helpless until he was exhausted, but unsatisfied. He left her then and went out in the barn to milk the cows. Because he had been so rough with her he expected her to be gone before breakfast, but she did not leave. And when he brought her wood for the stove her eyes met his in new seduction. Her new dress was even tighter across her bosom, her voice was lower and more musical, and a scent had been placed at the base of her throat. With his own throat growing hot and dry,

Nakoa's Woman

he tried to eat with his daughters.

Later Meg went upstairs to tend his wife. Ana and Maria went to sit with her, but he could not. He sat by the fire with his head in his hands. Then much later, Maria gently touched his face. "She is just sleeping," she said softly, and went to bed after Ana. The fire burned itself out. In the cold he shivered and stiffly rose to his feet. He went to the kitchen to sleep where he had slept since his wife's illness. Taking off his shoes, he stretched out his long frame, and thought of Meg. He went back to her bed that night and returned in the morning, and even when he was with her in front of his daughters it was all he could do to keep his eyes off her breasts.

His wife regained consciousness, and when she first opened her eyes, she gave him such a long and overpowering look of pure love that he wanted to moan in agony. She was dying in holy grace. He felt unable to touch her flesh again. He was hollow inside and was slipping down a void that had no bottom. His daughters could weep, but he could not. For what he had done and wanted to do again and again with Meg, he was denied even the solace of being able to weep. His wife soon sank into a deep sleep, and she remained this way for weeks. She would sleep and rally, and after seeming to gain strength, slip into unconsciousness again. All of these dismal days the skies were darkening, and more and more rain streamed against the small windows.

Now Meg sought him as much as he sought her. Neither one of them was satisfied just to meet at night, and when they met they were like savages. He thought her the lowest kind of bitch, for she would do anything to oblige him, but his wildness did not abate, and grew equally in her. It was a nightmare. But his only touch with reality seemed to be when he was with Meg.

One afternoon the girls were upstairs with their mother, and before he could go up, Meg came to him. She led him to her room and their intimacy had already begun when he heard a noise. Yet he could not leave Meg for his own life, nor would she give him up. Later he rested with his lips against her breast, and then he dressed and went into the kitchen. There wasn't a sound in the house. He walked into the front room, and Maria was huddled, shivering and wet, in front of the fire.

"Where have you been?" he asked her, astounded that she would go outside in the driving rain.

"I went to the orchard," she replied softly. "Mother is dead," she said matter-of-factly. "I thought you might like to know that she died calling for you." The way she looked up at him, he knew that she was aware where he had been.

Remembering, Edward Frame sobbed openly, his hands clenched into tight fists. Now he was alone with their daughters, and God, oh God, he did not know what to do. Were twelve wagons enough? Oh, my love, do you know? Do you know that all of the time it was you, and the loving and caressing that could be no more between us? Or do you look coldly down, unforgiving, because I am still mortal? Or do you know at all? "I don't know what to do!" he whispered. "I don't know what to do!"

In early April the twelve wagons moved out from Laramie. The great wheel by Ana's side drove lizards and snakes from its path. Prairie dogs watched the wheel pass and then went back to sleeping in the sun. Ana felt Maria's serenity, and ahead of them Edith Holmes pressed the life she felt moving in her womb. Clouds gathered and made the prairie ahead shimmer in sunlight and become somber in shadow. "Come into the world of light and darkness, my little love," Edith whispered to her unborn child. Dust from the moving wheels rose ahead and behind them, but now there was not the safety of their wagons stretching from horizon to horizon.

Roll on, oh great wheels; nothing can stop the path you are making to the shining sea! The prairie wind is strong and behind us now are the still hands and the molding furniture; ahead lies the future. Time is pressing! Why wait for the other wagons? Why wait?

Anson Frederich returned Maria Frame to her wagon. He spoke briefly to her father and Ana and left her with them.

"I don't like you out with Anson at night," Maria's father said crossly.

"When else can I see him?" Maria retorted. "The only time the train isn't moving is when the sun goes down."

"Why do you stay out with him so late?"

Nakoa's Woman

"We have a lot to say," Maria said sarcastically.

Ana gave her a disapproving look and then retired to their wagon.

"Ana thinks I am naughty again," Maria said wearily.

"No. She thinks you are deviling Anson Frederich, and so do I," her father replied.

"What on earth is that?"

"You know damned well what it is!" Her father lit his pipe and studied her through its smoke. "It is all promising and no giving!"

"Father, what would you know about that?" Maria asked, suddenly bitter.

Her father looked at her shrewdly. "I mean you are making him want you and you have no intention of marrying him."

Maria felt a rage building against him, a rage that she hadn't felt even when she had seen him in Meg's room. "I didn't know you cared so much for marriage," she whispered.

"I just don't want you alone with Anson—so late at night," he answered.

"Why not, Father?" she lashed out. "Are you afraid I would do for him what your little Meg was doing for you the afternoon my mother was dying?"

Her father recoiled. "Maria!" he breathed, as if the wind had been knocked from his body.

"That is my name!" Maria panted. "That was also her name— do you remember? That was my mother's name too!"

"Maria, Maria!" he repeated brokenly.

"She called you too, when she was dying. I am sorry you were so busy!"

He lashed out and slapped her across the face, sending her reeling away from the fire. "Daughter" he choked, "do not judge me! Never—never—can you judge me! I am my own executioner! Do you hear? Do you hear?"

Maria got to her feet and walked toward the wagon where Ana apparently slept. "I will never hear you again," she said grimly.

"You do not know anything!" he said. "You do not know any thing!"

"I know what I saw! I know what made me so sick that I had to go to mother's orchard to throw up!"

"Mother's orchard?"

"Her orchard! It was her touch that brought the fruit to your marriage! Not yours! You would bring blight—blight!"

"You do not understand," Edward Frame said, close to weeping. "You will never understand."

"She wasn't even dead—she wasn't even dead!" Maria began to sob. "With everything that was left—she called for you! She wanted you so! She wasn't even—dead!"

"That is why," her father said, turning to her with tears touching his face. "When she was gone, Meg became like cardboard to me. To me—then—Meg was your mother—I can't speak my feeling, I don't know why I did what I did—but it was not because I didn't love your mother!"

Maria shuddered and hid her face in her hands. When she looked up, her father was walking away from her, his form bent against the light of the fires. Pity and revulsion for him combined with her overwhelming love drove her to the ground. She clawed the roots of the prairie grass with her fingernails, crying desperately.

From somewhere in the camp came the sound of a fiddle, and as she lay upon the earth and wept, hands clapped to a dancing tune, and the fiddle played gaily on and on.

When Edward Frame walked away from his daughter, he knew spring would never come to him again. He wondered if he had ever known spring at all; it must have been only a fleeting dream.

It was very late when he returned to their wagon. A coldness stayed within his heart, though the night was warm. A full moon had risen, and it shone serenely now upon the camp with all of the great wagons dark and quiet, and the Snake River flowing by so peacefully.

A white wolf called out from the hills, as if it knew something they did not. Edward Frame sighed, his troubled spirits sinking lower. There had been no new sickness, and they were just two weeks out of Fort Boise. The worst of the trip was over. They had made it; they were all alive.

He made his bed under the tarpaulin, but could not fall asleep. Something of danger seemed to be building all around him. He heard the two o'clock watch return to the wagons, calling out that all was well.

He tossed and turned, his mouth becoming drier. The four o'clock watch returned, calling out that all was well. Finally he dozed, still conscious of how restless the horses were in-the bright moonlight. And so it was that on the night of May 19, 1846, the twelve wagons bound for Oregon rested upon the silver prairie, rocking gently in the growing wind; twenty-nine men, seventeen children, and eighteen women all slept, and for all except one of them it was their last night upon the face of the earth.

Chapter Two

At dawn Edith Holmes began labor. The pain came like an enemy bent upon her life, lustful and torturing from the very beginning. How could she have forgotten for one moment how terrible the birth was? Why hadn't she remembered back in that soft twilight when she had wanted to seduce and be seduced?

Jim sent the boys to the Frederichs' wagon because she could not control her screaming. Every time she shrieked, Jim wrung his hands and wept.

"Edie! Edie!" he sobbed.

"Go away!" she said, for suddenly she couldn't stand his crying.

"I can't leave you, Edie," he moaned piteously. "I can't leave you!"

"What good can I do you now?" she flung at him bitterly, even when she did not have the strength to say it. He cowered at her side, covering his ears against her cries.

"Damn you! Go—to boys! No—get me rag—to pull on— something to pull on!" Why did all of the pain in the world have to come to her all at once?

"I'll get Mrs. Bentley—and Maria," he said.

"No! Not—yet. Just a rag—a rag—damn you!"

He handed her one of her dresses to pull on. She tore it, as she was being torn.

"It never happened like this before!"

"Didn't it?" she gritted. "Didn't it?"

"Edie, the whole train can hear you screaming!"

"Then let them—have your baby—instead of—" She could not go on. She had started to vomit now. At first she had the strength to vomit on the floor, but then she became too weak and vomit began to soak her pillow and hair.

"Edie—Edie—" He was clumsily trying to clean her up, and he placed something dry under her head. Time blurred and became red and swollen. A haze deepened in the wagon so that she could not see past Jim's face. There were no contractions. There was just one giant pressure, and she bore down and pushed and pushed, but the baby would not move, and neither would the agony. She saw that the blood was bathing the lower part of her body; bile continued to mat her hair, and Jim could not keep her cleaned up.

The sun began to shine strongly upon the wagon. They seemed to be moving. Jim must be driving the team then, for a woman's voice was with her now, but where was the woman? There was a whisper, not meant for her to hear. "She won't stop bleeding!" Cool hands kept putting dry cloths under her hips. Then she remembered what she was doing, that she was giving birth, and she suddenly pushed again. "My God!" someone said. "She is being torn to pieces!"

Well, she was tearing up the dress, the silly little dress, with its tiny silly waist and pretty blue eyes. Who would need it again, the vain calico with its bright colors?

Someone began to weep softly. "I can't stand it!" a voice said.

"Leave, child, and get some air!" another voice answered.

"No!" came the reply.

Yes! Yes! Why not? The dress is already rent and cannot be patched up. All of the color was leaving the dress now, that is what it got for trying to be so pretty and being vain about it too. Now they would throw the dress out upon the prairie and it would be hidden in the grasses with all of the other useless things, the empty cribs, the claw-footed chests, the useless tables.

Someone began to cry again. "Shouldn't we call Jim?"

"No no! Not—yet."

Jim. Her husband. Where had he gone? Out of the red air two hands wiped off her forehead, and another pair of hands held her own, her far-off dummy hands that remained attached to the blue calico dress. The voices belonged to Maria Frame and Mrs. Bentley, but how, oh Christ, could just two women save her from the white wolves? They were tearing at her insides. How could Jim have left her upon the prairie to be eaten like this? Didn't he want his little baby? Didn't he want his wife? What would her boys do without her in the years ahead? Oh, God, where was Jim?

Maria left the wagon, weak and sick, and stepped into the fresh air and sunshine. All of the wagons had stopped, and she leaned against the wheel of the Holmes wagon and cried bitterly. Ana walked to her and put her arms around her shaking shoulders. "She is dying!" Maria sobbed. "She won't stop bleeding and she won't have the baby!"

"Isn't there anything anyone can do?"

"No no, nothing!"

Ana went into the wagon, and Maria finally straightened up and saw Anson Frederich riding toward her. She wiped her tear-streaked face. Anson pulled in his lathered horse and looked down at her. "Is she worse?" he asked, nodding toward the Holmes wagon.

"She is dying," Maria said, starting to cry again.

Anson bowed his head. "I am sorry. Have you told Jim?"

"No. I will have to tell him now." She suddenly noticed Anson's horse.

"Where have you been?" she asked.

"We have been looking for Lon Jacoby. He was riding lead and is missing. We can't find him anywhere."

Maria searched his face. "Is it Indians? Is the train in danger, Anson?"

"If it is Indians and a small band of them, they would not attack."

"But we are a small train," Maria said. They looked into each other's eyes.

"Maria—Maria." He had trouble forming his words. "If there should be an attack, remember that yours is the end wagon today, and that fresh horses are tied behind it."

"Anson!"

"I will come to you—but if I can't—if we are lost—you could escape the train on a fresh horse!" He bent from his saddle and clasped her hands. "Maria, you could escape at the first sign that the train is lost."

Nakoa's Woman

"No! What could there be for me escaping?" Their touch upon each other tightened. "Anson," she said suddenly. "I would be a good wife for you."

"Maria," he said, his expression changing, and making him almost a boy. "Would you marry me ever?"

"Anson, I will marry you! And now—oh, Anson, how could we die?"

"We will not!" He smiled warmly. They kissed, and controlled the world. "There will be a life for us together!" he said. Then he rode away from her, and Maria watched him until he and his horse were hidden by the wagons waiting ahead.

Far ahead, the men gathered and talked together in low tones. Danger had suddenly menaced them everywhere from the silent prairie. All sound had stopped, as though the heartbeat of the earth itself was no more. Every man was afraid. What had happened to the lead pilot? Was Lon Jacoby dead? Had he been killed by the Snakes? If he had been, where for Christ's sake were the Indians now? Should they go on and try for Boise, or should they circle the wagons and wait? Wait for what, oh, God? If they moved on would they invite attack? If they stayed would they invite attack? If the pilot had seen trouble, why hadn't he signaled? Where was he for God's sake? Where was he?

Lon Jacoby lay near them, across a swell of the prairie, a gently sloping little knoll that hid him so well that the men searching for him had ridden by him several times. He was dead because he believed what most white men believed. He believed that the loading rifle was superior to the bow and arrow, and when he met a group of Indians he felt safe behind the shadow of his gun. When he saw trouble he immediately fired, and the sound of his one shot was not heard by the wagon train so far behind him.

It takes thirty seconds and sometimes longer to prepare a muzzle loader for reuse. The powder of the loading rifle has to be measured and poured, a ball pushed down the barrel with a ramrod, and the tube primed and the cap or flint adjusted—and in thirty seconds an Indian could aim and shoot ten arrows. If a man took one minute to reload his gun, he had to stand against twenty arrows, and the

Indian could ride three hundred yards closer all of the time he was firing. But Lon Jacoby did not know this, and that is why he lay dead in the waving grasses near the men who were arguing about what had happened to him. He lay dead with only four arrows in him, but he was just as dead as if he had twenty.

Now Edith Holmes knew she was dying. She watched the sunlight shining through the canvas of the wagon. It must be a bright beautiful day, the feel of the sun was so warm. She reached for it. If she could hold it, she might not have to go. Had she had the baby? Would there be then, another child for Jim to care for alone? Poor Jim, poor helpless Jim. He must get a wife right away, a good wife for her boys. She prayed that he would do this. She was so tired and so sad. She could not even move the poor little blue calico arms. She could never hold one of her babies again.

She had always heard that a woman dying with birth went to heaven, but how could there be heaven when she would worry so about her boys? And she had been bitter at having each of them; she had cried because she had lost her pretty little waist and the free time of her girlhood. She had wept and stormed at all of the golden moments, a creature burrowing away from the sun.

Mrs. Bentley was gone. She and Maria had probably gone for Jim so that she could give him their last farewell. She hoped that she didn't look too bad. She wanted him to remember her as pretty. She wanted just to touch him, and to touch her boys—and in her touch to tell her love and her sorrow.

Finally she dozed peacefully. She drifted softly into a warm sleep, heavy with the scent of the earth warming after a first rain. Near the garden, Jim came to court her again. His hair was slick and smelled of oil. He was so sweet and so shy. She was as gentle with him as he was with her; she soothed him and caressed him tenderly. Her dainty hands touched his rough ones. "Remember me gently," she whispered to him. Joy was in his eyes because she loved him, and her boys appeared, and she touched each one with her love. Bright flowers bloomed all around them, and there was sweet flowing water, too, in the sunlight and the shade of that garden.

Nakoa's Woman

"Mamma!" a frightened little voice called in all of the beauty of that garden. Yet, she sighed happily, the small voice's sorrow hidden in the petals of new flowers.

"Mamma! Mamma!" Again and again it was, and even in her own serenity, she knew its pain. She was jerked from her haven, torn between warmth and biting cold, and she became a chilled shivering thing. She gasped to breathe. The wagon was rocking crazily, wild shouts and running horses stampeded around her, and always came the cry of "Mamma!" and the tugging, tugging, the pull upon her of the barren earth. Why were they destroying the wagon? Wasn't she dying fast enough? In the last convulsion of life she opened her eyes and looked up into the tear-streaked and terrified face of her youngest son. Lucid, she reached out to comfort him in his terror, but her little blue calico arms could not respond to her will.

There is a different death for each life; there are as many deaths as there are lives. Upon that day in May of 1846, the wagon train died a separate death from all of its people. It died quietly when the Snakes first attacked; only a long sad sigh, not apart from the prairie wind, traveled from one helpless wagon to the next, as death so swiftly and silently swept down upon them. The Indians came from a green and innocent rise, scarcely more than a knoll, and the later shouts, the screams and the frenzied cries of the men to form a circle with the wagons, were all the convulsions of death, for the corpse had already been formed.

The Indians were everywhere. The blue of the sky had been shadowed with their arrows. Amid the screaming of the women and the crying of the children, the pounding of the horses' hoofs and the firing of the guns, the painted men darted, flashed, disappeared and appeared again, ten times as strong.

"Oh, Maria! Maria!" Ana sobbed. "We are going to be killed!"

"No, oh, no!" Maria said. "We will not die." She grasped Ana's hand. "Quick!" she said. "Get under the wagon!"

Their father was riding down upon them, and he reigned in his horse with difficulty. He gestured them away from the wagon, and Maria saw with horror that blood was running from his mouth.

"Take horses—and go," he gasped. "Train gone lost—lost." His words ended in a new torrent of blood, and Ana clapped her hands to her ears and screamed. Edward Frame looked down upon his terrified daughters with an agony upon his face that burned Maria's soul.

"I'll cover—go," and then he could speak no more but weakly clung to his gun and his horse.

"Father," Maria's agony cried, "Father—please forgive me. Dear God, forgive me," but she spoke not one word to their father and led the protesting Ana to the horses tethered behind the end wagon. Tears blinded her, but somehow she cut out a bay for herself and a roan for Ana.

The horses were wild; the smell of the Indians, the smell of death, the rising clouds of dust, the shooting and the screaming had them white-eyed and dancing sideways in terror. Mounting, Maria glanced back at their father. Tears were streaming down his face and he looked at them both riding away without a gesture of farewell. Maria heard two horses pursuing them, and then heard two rapid shots. Their father had covered them and they had a chance to escape to the hills.

Out upon the prairie they rode, with the tall grass whipping at their skirts and the wind blowing all of the pins from their hair. Ana's braids loosened and her hair billowed out behind her, brilliant and yellow even in the light of the fading day. She was riding behind Maria, hugging the neck of the roan in terror, and Maria remembered Ana's fear of horses.

"Catch up!" Maria shouted back at her, for the gap between the two horses was increasing. "Kick him! Kick him!" Maria shouted, but Ana paid her no heed and did not even look ahead to guide the animal.

Behind them, Maria suddenly saw dust clouds rising, and could see five Snakes riding after them. "Hurry! Hurry!" she screamed desperately to Ana, and kicked her own horse so viciously that his quick response almost threw her from his back.

On and on their two horses raced, but the blue hills in which they could hide seemed to be as far away as ever. She glanced back at Ana again and was stunned to see how the Snakes were gaining upon them, and how far behind her Ana had drifted. Her sister was looking at her pleadingly, her face completely drained of color. She looked so innocent, so sweet, and so terrified, that Maria wanted to ride back to the Snakes and give her life so that Ana might escape. But while she watched, the roan stumbled and threw Ana to the ground. Maria tried to turn the bay back, but horse and rider fought each other in mounting terror, the bay wheeling and thrashing and refusing to be turned back. Sobbing, Maria beat him without mercy, choking upon clouds of rising dust and the agony tightening in her throat.

"Maria!" Ana screamed.

Around and around the bay turned as if he were pursuing some mad game of chasing his shadow.

"Maria!" Ana screamed once more and when Maria looked toward her she saw the Snakes brandishing the locks of her golden hair.

There was a woman's scream. Maria heard it clearly. It had no beginning and no end, as if it had always existed in its own horror. The earth shatters the living and gives the living an end, cover, burial, but this thing, this scream, could never end, could never be shattered into even an echo. Its sound had torn her into pieces, and fragments of herself clung stubbornly to the bay that was once more racing for the hills.

Behind the thundering hoofs of the bay, flames from the wagon train and prairie grass licked the sky. The bloody sunset generated its own force; the prairie wind was quickened and its low sad sound reached her ears, its breath touching her face and stretching out across that broad land in the split second before the bay plunged into the shadow of the forest.

In the early darkness, Maria saw branches of the dense trees sweep down at her. A blue jay screeched excitedly. Suddenly a limb hit her upon the side of her head, and she was swept from the horse. She lay stunned upon the ground, and when she opened her eyes, she remained inert, watching the patterns that the branches above her made against the sky.

The bay stood quietly by her and remained even when there was the sound of the Snakes' horses moving toward them. With effort, Maria got to her feet and held onto the horse for support. Blood rushed from her head wound and even began to cover a part of her bodice. Everything became blurred and indistinct. It seemed as if two Snakes had found her, and one swiftly dismounted and seized her. She struggled to see his face and met his eyes. They had no expression. They bore no hatred for her, no lust, not even an expression of mild anger. Yet he was going to kill her, as swiftly and silently as possible. In a great roaring he was strangling her, and she put up a tremendous struggle to breathe.

Suddenly the iron hands loosened their hold, and air burst into her starved lungs. The Snake looked at her in amazement, his hands clutching desperately at her shoulders. He made a low cry, almost indistinguishable, then slid to the ground. An arrow had been driven deep into his back. Maria looked up at the other Snake; amazement was upon his face too, and he slid swiftly from his horse. He drew his knife, his eyes searching the darkness all around them. There wasn't a sound. The bay then moved slightly, and the silence returned.

With her heart hammering in terror, Maria began to inch toward the bay. She had just touched the horse when there was a sudden flashing of movement, and almost before she could see it, another Indian, a giant of a man, had come and had broken the Snake's neck. Just as swiftly, he bent and cut and seized the Snake's scalp. As she watched him in horror, he kicked over the corpse at her feet and just as neatly scalped it. The ripping of the flesh, the smell of the blood brought Ana to her mind, and she screamed. The Indian stifled her cry and threw her to the ground, covering her body with his own so quickly that she did not even have a chance to take a fresh breath. He would suffocate her. He would strangle her as surely as the other had almost done.

It was now completely dark. There was no light beneath the thick trees at all. Maria heard the approach of other horses. The rest of the Snakes were calling out to their companions. The Indian's grip upon her tightened. His weight crushed her breasts and tortured

Nakoa's Woman

her throbbing head. The Snakes rode all around them and finally went away. Still, the Indian held her in the vise of his strength.

When he finally released her, she was too numb to sit up. He picked her up and put her roughly upon the bay, mounting behind her. Without a sound, he guided the bay through the thickest recesses of the forest; like fellow phantoms his and the Snakes' horses followed, and Maria felt that she was living through a nightmare of silence.

The Indian held her closely. The bloody scalps at his belt dampened her dress, and she strained as far away from him as she could. But he would give her no leeway. The pain in her head worsened, and each step that the bay took grew to be agony.

After more than an hour's riding, they reached the forest's edge. The Indian stopped the horses. He dismounted, looking up at her and studying her in the starlight. He then seized her and stood her before him, as if he were measuring her height and the contours of her body. The terrible paint upon his face drove her from looking at him, and she turned away. He touched the side of her head, either seeking the seriousness of her wound or trying to see her face again, and all Maria knew was the smell of fresh blood upon his scalps.

Suddenly dim shadows of mounted men appeared at the forest's edge. They stopped, looking at Maria and the Indian. "*Ok-ye*," someone called softly.

"*Ok-ye*," the Indian replied, and four men rode toward them. They were staring at Maria in amazement. "*Pyeeteokweeweewa waapeakesiwa!*" one said in disbelief.

They, too, were painted. They all looked terrifying, and Maria uttered a low cry of fear in spite of herself. Her captor immediately gagged her, doing it so roughly that she became dizzy with pain. He bound her hands behind her back and placed her upon the bay. Once more, he mounted behind her and led the others out upon the prairie. The grasses were wild and thick and from a distance looked like a carpet of silver. But when the horses began to travel at a steady gallop, the grasses became cruel, whipping at her through her thin skirts and hiding deep and treacherous ravines that the bay took unknown, stumbled upon, and started fresh blood running down her neck.

Maria spun in and out of fainting spells. The fire of the wagon train had not burned itself out upon the prairie; it was searing yet in her brain, and there would never be enough blood in her body to quench it.

On and on they rode, their pace quickening, the flying hoofs of the horses following the path of the prairie wind. They rent soft land, leaped ravines and plunged unheeding through the deepest of rivers. Cold water made her skirts cling to her shivering legs; hot blood coursed eternally down her neck and congealed thickly between her breasts. She slumped against the savage behind her, but in no way did he know her pain, her weakness, her womanhood.

At daylight they changed course and sought the shelter of the hills. The Indians talked in low voices and then Maria was lifted from the bay. From out of old mists the painted face came before her again, this mask of this most hideous of men, and not ungently she was laid upon the ground. As she was covered with a buffalo robe the bloody scalps brushed against her and in them she saw the scalp of Ana. Strangling, she fled to a sanctuary deep inside of herself where this most agonizing of all days had never dawned.

Maria

Nakoa's Woman

Chapter Three

Maria awakened, and pain was still violently upon her. She opened her eyes and looked up into the clear blue sky and prayed for help. She was still bound and gagged. She tried to move and nausea came, and she began to strangle on vomit. Quickly her gag was removed, and when she had vomited, she lay weakly back and felt someone untie her arms. She was nothing now, for where were all those who had loved and cherished her? With nothing to love and cherish in turn she was not even a seed upon empty winds. She moaned in agony, and someone touched her and raised her to a sitting position. Two strong hands held her head and applied something cool and comforting to her wound. The burning in her head lessened, and with relief she opened her eyes. It was her captor; she knew this although he now wore no paint. The hideous face that had come at her from the mists was gone. In the morning sunlight she saw before her a handsome man. Here was a new strength too, more masculine than she had ever seen before. His black eyes were fierce with pride, and she wondered at the fact that he was Indian. He held no resemblance at all to the poor begging savages that she had seen back East.

She was staring at him, and she soon became conscious that her appraisal was making him angry. He stopped treating her wound and just as boldly studied her. His eyes traveled from her own to her lips, to her breasts and waist and hips and then back to her breasts. Fear of him made her heart hammer, and she dropped her eyes and felt her face grow hot. He said nothing. When she looked at him again, the boldness upon his face was gone. He knew her fear.

Slowly he raised his right hand in front of her, palm out and even with his shoulder. He rotated it a few times, trying to tell her something. She looked at him in perplexity. He placed the fingers of his right hand against the palm of his left, sliding his right off as if he were cutting meat. "*Iksisakuyi?*" he said.

He was asking her if she wanted food. "Yes," Maria said. "Please! I am hungry." When she nodded her head he understood her meaning. He handed her a calfskin bag in which was a mixture of meat and berries that she began to eat greedily. He signaled that she was not to eat so fast, and when she persisted, he angrily took the bag away from her. He then motioned her to get up and when she refused, scowling because he had taken away her food, he pulled her to her feet. "*Menuah,*" he said, pointing into the forest. He made sign that she should follow him, and she meekly walked behind him. She now saw the other Indians, and when they passed them, one of them called out something, and her captor laughed. Deeper in the forest, she lagged behind him, and impatiently, he reached for her again, holding her at his side for the rest of the way.

They came to a river, and he indicated that she was to drink. When she had quenched her thirst, he made sign for her to remove her clothing. Maria refused, and he again signed that she should bathe. She gestured for him to leave her alone, and he shrugged his shoulders, walking away from her. Watching the trees for a sign of him, she removed her dress and washed it, but she would not take off her chemise and stand where he might see her naked. When she had bathed, she lay upon a large rock and waited to dry her wet chemise. Birds called happily from the trees, and the water rushing by her made such a sweet and melodious sound that for a while she forgot grief. The air was pungent with the smell of warming pine and spruce. The sun was so warm that she could feel her chemise drying and the gathering of perspiration between her breasts. Still exhausted, she began to doze, with the water continuing to murmur contentedly at her.

Two hands touched her face, and then lips fiercely found her own and held her in a long and agonizing kiss. The Indian's eyes were closed, and his face was even darker with passion. She gasped and began to struggle against him, but he effortlessly removed her chemise from her entire body. Maria felt an agony of terror and embarrassment. When she tried to cover herself, he held her hands, and then his lips went back to her own, down to her throat, to her breasts, and his hands caressed her hips. His excitement was so intense that he shuddered in his postponement of raping her, but rape her he would, and Maria now knew this was why he had taken her to the river and away from the others.

More than terror made her weep. More than the humiliation of being stripped and appraised, assaulted where she never had been touched before. His rape would be not just the destruction of her innocence and her virginity but the destruction again of the wagon train, dying in its own horrible and bloody sunset. Ana fled from her again; her mother died in the dismal rain; the Maria and Anson of just yesterday burned under orange pillars of smoke. Edith Holmes lay white and ashen and blood seeped and seeped from beneath her thighs.

"God! God!" screamed Maria.

He struck as if he had come in a nightmare from the dark and lustful core of her own being. But he stopped with her. At the beginning of his penetration he stopped, and suddenly the pressure of his whole body was gone. She turned on her stomach, hiding as much as she could from him, not able to bear looking into his face. She wept in hysteria.

When she was drained and could cry no more, she felt a cool little breeze ruffle her hair and pass over her naked body. Her dress had been brought from the rocks and placed beside her. Numbly she reached for it, and after she had put it on and fastened every button of her bodice, she looked up at him. He stood towering and mute, almost blocking the whole sky. Here was the shadow that had come to make her die.

He touched her arm, indicating that she return with him to the others. She started to walk with him, hiding her face from his own. Before they moved, he cupped her face in his hands and kissed her lips. He could not have been more tender. His black eyes were filled with a new light, and she noticed the sweetness and sensitivity of his lips. He yearned to speak with her but did not know how to convey his thoughts. He closed her eyes and kissed her lashes, and then searched her face to see if she understood: in his new gentlemanliness, she was to close her eyes to what he had done. She understood and looked at him mutely. He moved away from her, indicating the distance between them, and she read this to mean that he would never again attempt to rape her.

As they left the river, Maria glanced back at her torn and ragged chemise. Its white lace was soiled with the mud of the riverbank, and for a moment she felt as if she was walking away from herself, the girl who had been a virgin to life. In his gentleness, the Indian had penetrated her as deeply as if he had succeeded in raping her.

When they returned to the others not a one gave any sign of noticing them. Her captor gestured for her to lie down, and when she did, he lay down beside her. Her face became crimson with humiliation at having to lie beside him upon the ground. He fell almost immediately into an easy sleep, and when the others slept too, Maria studied them all.

They wore shirts, breechcloths, and leggings, and across their shirts and leggings ran strange black bands. Their clothing was tanned more darkly than any skins she had seen on Indians, and because of their dark clothing, the dyed hair that fringed their shirts and leggings showed up brilliantly. Every one of them carried a knife sheathed in his belt, but Maria noticed some difference in the dress of her captor and the others. He alone wore an ornate pattern of quill bands that ran the breadth of his shoulders and down the length of his sleeves and leggings, and he wore his hair in one queue rather than two braids as the others did. He was clearly the leader of the band and Maria took him to be a chief, but of what tribe she did not know.

The sun moved its slow course across the bright sky. Maria lay upon her back and watched it, and watched the slow moving of the shadows upon the ground. In time she became drowsy and slept deeply. When she awakened, it was with a start of horror. She had dreamed of drifting down into the depths of an endless sea, and she became crazy in its darkening shadow and wanted to embrace it, forever become a part of it, and never see the sunlight again. She shuddered, gasping for air, savoring its sweetness in large gulps. She lived. She yet lived, and swift and terrible tears came for Ana and her father who did not.

The Indian beside her still slept. Again Maria studied his handsome face with its tender lips, so incongruous to the complete man. He had no facial hair; she remembered that Indians kept it pulled with tweezers. In his sleep, the Indian's hand moved, and she studied his fingers. They were long and slender. His nails were clean, pink, smooth, and tapered without any bluntness. As she was watching his hand, it moved and brushed against her. Swiftly, she sat up, and he sat up too, his dark eyes meeting her own.

"*Kisipenae—lantamen hec?*" he asked her.

"I don't understand," Maria said. "How could I know your language?"

He held both of his hands before her. "*Kewaapami,*" he said, and repeated the word again. This was his word for hands, and he waited for her to repeat the word after him. Suddenly the indignity that she had suffered from him that morning came back in overpowering force. A few hours before he had tried to rape her, and now she was supposed to sit meekly by his side and learn his language!

"*Nhikas,*" he said, indicating his fingernails. "*Nhikas,*" he repeated, still patient with her.

"*Shtinkas,*" she said stupidly.

"*Nhikas!*" he said, frowning.

"*Pinkas!*" she answered promptly.

He pointed to his fingers. "*Ohkitchis,*" he said.

"*Rinkas!*" she said. He frowned. "*Rinkas!*" she repeated belligerently.

"*Ohkitchis!*" he said furiously.

"*Shtinkas!*"

"*Nhikas!*"

"*Shtinkas!*" They glared at each other, and the language lesson came to an abrupt end as he got up and left her.

Maria smiled to herself and stretched out upon the ground. It did not take her long to go back to sleep. When she awakened it was late afternoon, and she was very hungry. She thought gleefully of all of the ways that she could vex the Indian; let him see what an idiot he had found for a wife! A strong wind was building in the pines; the night would be cold. Shivering, she looked around for him. To her amazement, she saw that the Indians were eating. Well, savages would eat before a woman did. She had always heard that a wife to them was not as valuable as a horse. Getting colder in her thin dress, she watched them consume their meal, and she thought that they would never stop. They ate on and on and on; her captor seemed to be relishing his food. He saw her watching him, and bringing his food, sat down by her, and continued eating.

Her stomach began to growl. Saliva gathered expectantly in her mouth, and she had to swallow again and again to keep herself from

"Oh, I am the belle of the ball!" Maria said to herself bitterly. She looked beyond the shelter of the trees. How many more nights would they ride? Where, oh God, could he be taking her?

Her captor suddenly touched her arm, and she started away from him violently. He moved like a cat, without any noise at all. He had placed another robe upon the ground, and upon it he had placed an assortment of food. "*La lematahpi,*" he said, indicating that she should sit down.

There was the mixture of meat and berries, but there was something else that looked crisp and delicious, some kind of meat that had been cooked and smoked by itself. Almost joyous with relief, she reached eagerly for the food. He restrained her hands, and she stared up at him, dumbfounded. "You told me to eat!" she said. Was he going to torture her again? The idea of starving herself to death had vanished entirely. Stubbornly, she reached for the food again, but he slapped her hand smartly with the back of his knife. Murderously, she flew at his face, aching to claw its smooth surface, but he slapped her own, sending her spinning away from the food. Like a whipped animal she crept back, and sitting by it, began to weep. How could an Indian be smart enough to be such a tyrant?

Between sobs, she saw him waiting patiently. He had not touched the food, so it was meant for her. Wiping her face, she quieted and looked at him.

He held his hands before her face. "*Nhikas*," he said quietly. The language lesson! *Nhikas*, the word for fingernails. Maria swallowed hard, and after studying the food carefully couldn't fight any more.

"*Nhikas*," she said sullenly.

"*Kewaapami*," he said clearly, again showing her that the word meant hands.

"*Kewaapami*" Maria repeated.

"*Nkitenenc*," he said for fingers.

She repeated the word and learned the rest of the words he wanted her to. The lesson went on and on, and for the words she learned, she was tested and retested. Satisfied with her progress, he at last indicated that she could eat, and while she did so, he never took his eyes from her face.

She ate everything that he had given her. When she finished, he signaled that water was nearby by cupping his hand, putting it to his mouth, and pointing to a meadow a short distance from them.

She got up and left him, and he made no move to follow her. At the spring she drank thirstily. All of the Indians remained at their camp, giving her privacy, and in spite of the miserable morning, she bathed herself. When she returned to the Indians, her captor was riding away with two of them. Two were left to guard her and one of them indicated a crude bed that had been made for her. She lay upon it, falling to sleep almost immediately. When she awakened finally, it was later, much later. It was now raining hard and water was dripping down upon her face from the thick branches overhead. But it was not the rain that had awakened her, and remembering what it was, she gathered the robe around her, and got up with wild hope racing in her heart. She had heard the firing of a rifle.

Chapter Four

These Indians didn't have guns; even the Snakes hadn't had guns. The firing of a rifle could only mean that a white man, or several white men were near! "Dear God, let it be! Let it be!" Maria prayed wildly. White men were close enough for her to hear the firing of their rifles! Clutching the robe to her, she raced to the bay.

"*Hai-yah!*" one of the Indians shouted, but she ran on anyway. He came after her, caught her, and when she screamed he gagged her with his palm. She struggled against him desperately, hampered by the clumsiness of her robe, as it slipped away from her shoulders.

"*Ah-meeteh!*" a voice said low and savagely. Maria looked up into the enraged eyes of her captor who still sat upon his horse. His knife was drawn and upon it beads of water collected and fell off like colorless drops of blood. Rain was streaming upon Maria's hair and naked breasts, and she drew the robe hastily around her. His face was wild. She looked up at him, dumb with fear and blinking through the driving rain.

Her assailant started to speak, but his leader leaped upon him, driving him helplessly down upon his back. Immediately, the other Indian who had stayed with Maria intervened, talking rapidly to Maria's captor and holding back his knife hand. In time, that awful hand stilled its struggle, the rage and savagery left the awful face, and Maria's captor released the Indian he had held helpless beneath him. Not one word did he say. Instead, his black eyes swung to Maria and she was overwhelmed with fresh terror of him. How could she have fought him in anything? How had she defied a beast so hungry for the letting of blood, so quick with a knife, so eager to kill even one of his own kind?

Fearfully, she went to her bed, and hid her head under her robe, listening to the rain beating against the skins and her own heart beating in terror. She felt his presence, felt him lie beside her in their bed and take a part of the robe that covered her nakedness to cover himself. She was facing away from him, cringing and desperately trying to keep from shaking. He did not touch her. He was quiet and seemed to sleep, and at last she relaxed, and stretched out her cramped legs. He suddenly turned her upon her back, and taking the robe from both of their heads, studied her face. She made no struggle for she knew what he sought. He wanted to know if she had seduced the man he had almost killed, and Maria knew with certainty that if she had, her captor would know it, and if he saw this upon her face, he would probably kill her. She was his and in his awful way he would have her and she would be possessed in his darkness or would die. Maria met his eyes without flinching. She had sought only escape. Without a word to her then, he turned away, and finally they both slept, their bodies bringing warmth to each other.

In sleep they met, and while Maria remained in drugged sleep the man awakened and saw in her body a desire for total consummation that made him nothing beside it. He had lain with naked women before, but never had he felt a desire like the one that overpowered him now. He wanted to kiss and caress every part of her, and yet he knew that he wanted her too strongly to have her when she was not ready for him. Deprivation had long been part of his training to be a man, and now this was no different. While she slept he kept his lips from her, and he kept himself from going inside of her, but gently he caressed every part of her anyway, and the lightness of his touch and the continuance of her sleep was the sweetest agony he had ever known.

And while she slept, Maria again sought the waters, but now they were golden green, and much closer to the sun she had always known. She drifted happily in them, but not crazily. She could go to their depths, but ascend at will, and in union with blackness she was free and was nothing and everything. Lightly the waters caressed her breasts, her throat, her lips. Her long black hair floated out lazily behind her. She circled and dove and came joyously up behind it, her lovely black hair floating so happily in the warm waters. The winds were all still. Shadows of cool caverns were far below, where she might go some day, if she so wished. But here the lips of the waters were sweeter than wine, than flowers in the spring; and here she would linger and let the wondrous lips find all of her, and in a miracle, find and meet them. She could draw the waters inside of her too. She would lie upon her back and accept them as a woman lies upon her back and accepts a man; and in accepting she would be nothing, for she would accept so much that she herself would be gone.

The man who had held her so gently felt her response, the swelling of her breasts, the quickening of an excited heart, and he kissed her mouth long and hungrily, only to see her eyes open in startled and wounded fear. The heat that had flashed over him at the touch of her lips beneath his own left him weak and shaken, and the terror upon her face made him sick. In real pain, he left her in the warmth of the robe and sought her dress. It was dry enough for her to wear, and taking it to her, he left it there for her to put on. He watched her as she struggled to dress under the robe and smiled in spite of himself. When she was dressed, she lay down and pretended to sleep. He knew that she did not sleep, for he detected tears upon her cheeks. He fought a trembling within himself again, so desperately did he want to go to her and kiss them away.

And so I live, Maria thought bitterly. My heart beats, and my stomach accepts food, my lungs seek air, and all of this allows me to live so that animal can rape me today, tomorrow, and forever, or as long as I shall live.

Remembering the sound of the rifle she thought that if a white man had been in this area, he was gone now, and so was all opportunity of her escape. She knew now that the remainder of her life rested upon the discretion of this one man, this Indian, godless, and to her even nameless, whom she would be reluctant ever to defy again.

For twelve more nights they rode toward the great North Star, and for twelve more days they slept hidden in the protective shelter of the woods. They crossed a chain of mountains and then took to the prairie once more.

After the third night the Indian allowed her to ride the bay alone, and never again did he tie her hands. He gave her strict privacy when she bathed in the streams and rivers, but she was forced to go on with her language lessons or she would not receive food.

All day, they continued to sleep side by side, and with this contact, a change grew between them. He and the others bathed as much as she did; they dispelled for her the myth that all Indians were dirty. His hair was always neatly oiled, his nails clean. Lying beside him, she remembered the clean masculine smell of Anson and how she had thrilled at being kissed by him.

The Indian grew more handsome to her each day. When he studied her in his intent way she felt her face color. She had been master of Anson with all of his strength, but here was a new strength that she knew she could not control. Yet, she wanted to look at him seductively; she was secretly glad that her breasts were full, her waist was tiny and her hips softly rounded. She suddenly was overwhelmingly glad that she was beautiful. Her mind returned to the morning that he had tried to rape her, but in her memory his assault became more gentle, and she felt a wrenching inside of herself.

Yet, as attraction grew between them, he became reserved and distant with her. He could have forced her a hundred times already, but he didn't even attempt to kiss her again.

Upon the next to the last morning of their travel she walked to their bed when she had finished bathing. Long before she could clearly see his face, she felt his eyes upon her, and she felt a violent hammering of her heart. Hot color suffused her face and traveled down to her throat. When she got closer to him, the intensity of him made her feel the most seductive woman in the world. She lay down beside him. He is a savage; why doesn't he act like one? her whole soul cried out in anguish. If he would seize her this time she could still pretend it was against her will and have the ecstasy of his caress and the superiority of her civilization too.

They were alone; the others had gone. Their eyes met and held, but she couldn't read the depths of his. She could feel her breasts straining against the tightness of her dress. She lay perfectly still and yet surrendered to him as the summer earth turns to the first rains. A squirrel fled noisily from one tree to another; birds were singing happily and excitedly. She half-closed her eyes and saw his lips near hers and then they kissed. One kiss, and now she did not struggle against him at all, but closed her lashes tightly and savored the hard lean pressure of him. She ached to embrace him, to touch him with her hands, but she could not abandon the role of a captive and so she remained passive though her heart leaped wildly with her body's desire to hold him to herself until they had satisfied their longing with each other.

He drew away from her gently, and when she opened her eyes he placed his hand over her fast-beating heart, then he took her hand and held it to his own breast so they both would know the effect of their kiss upon each other. His eyes smiled and they were shining with new light. They lay together under the robe, and almost immediately, he fell into his tranquil and easy sleep. Anson Frederich, sweet, gentle, civilized, and well bred, was a dear memory, but his masculinity had faded as if he had been killed years before.

Upon the thirteenth day they did not rest, but pushed on through the vast green land that stretched ahead of them. The prairie rippled under the wind like the flowing of green water. Bees hummed thickly in the air. In the wooded valleys, elk and deer suddenly bounded from the shadows and glinted for just a moment in the sunlight before disappearing again. Out upon the open plains once more, they rode through miles of wild flowers, purple lupines, yellow sunflowers, and white shooting stars. The earth exuded a warm fragrance and Maria was caught in it, every throbbing part of it, and when she looked back at the Indian, his eyes instantly met hers.

At dusk they reached the Indian village. Maria's joy fled with the light of the vanishing day and terror began to fill her heart. The mountains loomed behind her with a terrible foreboding. She was suddenly a gnat trapped into nothingness against them. She was a

Nakoa's Woman

white woman, a captive of Indians whose savagery she did not even begin to know. Drums began to beat from a distance, or was it the pounding of her helpless heart?

They had halted their horses upon a butte overlooking two rivers that gleamed with the light of the paling sky. Not far from the south bank of one of the rivers lay two circles of tipis, one circle inside the other. From them, Maria could hear the faint tinkling of bells and the sharp cry of a baby. To the southwest of the camp lay a large lake and it, too, reflected the twilight. Maria began to shiver. It was the time that the wagon train had died, the time of day before the awful night when all the wagons were burned away.

Her captor rode to her and then mounted behind her upon the bay. She turned back to him, and tried to bury her face against his breast. Firmly, he faced her forward. "*Wambadakka*," he said to the Indians and led them slowly down the butte. The bay struggled with rolling rocks and loose dirt, but kept his footing. Suddenly there was the beating of many horses' hoofs. More than forty Indians rode toward them shouting excitedly. "*Awksee!*" they said, and then seeing Maria said no more. They looked up at her in disbelief.

"*Waapeskesiwa!*" said her captor.

"*Waapeskesiwa!*" came the answer, and then, "*Pyeet eok weeweewa o wayawashtay!*"

Maria tried to turn away from them all, but again her captor kept her facing forward.

"*Essummissa!*" her captor said, and gestured to the Snakes' horses and his own riderless mount.

"*Sakah-pi!*" one of the riders shouted and they all rode away, taking the riderless horses with them.

Now they rode slowly toward the village. The drums were beating with a quickening excitement. Swiftly now, night came and the tall tops of the tipis glowed eerily in dancing firelight. The wind from the mountains was strong and smelled of pine and spruce. It was an awful wind that made her shake uncontrollably in her thin dress. She tried to cling to her captor, but he would not let her be dependent upon him in any way. He was anxious that she show no sign of weakness, but suddenly she had no strength to grasp, and she bowed her head, weeping wildly.

He stopped the bay, and signed for their companions to enter the village without them. When they had ridden from sight, he swung from the horse and lifted her to the ground. She continued to sob, and all the while felt his hands brushing her hair back from her tear-streaked face.

"*Culentet*," he said over and over, his voice tender and filled with love. When she stopped weeping, he gently touched the sides of her cheeks. "*Cho hetta ke tesistico?*" he asked, indicating the vast land around them. She could only stare at him mutely. "*Culentet*," he said again, in the same loving voice. He then bent and kissed her lips, brushing them lightly, and then kissing her more deeply.

At the touch of their lips the stars sent shining sparks of themselves down from summer skies. Here was the man, the warmth, and the protection. Here was fire in darkness, food in hunger, and water in thirst. She began to caress his face with infinite tenderness. She wanted his lips upon her breasts again so that he could take all of the sustenance that she had to give. "I love you! I love you!" she whispered, covering his lips with kisses of her own.

She was consumed with passion. She pressed her body against his; the fire in her sought to turn the fire in him into a raging holocaust. The clean buckskin smell of him, the iron strength, and the will that fought her possession, made her almost mad with desire. She pressed herself almost painfully to him and was riding the swelling crest of her passion when he suddenly tore her free from himself. He held her at arms length and studied her face with a deep compassion.

Why were his eyes so deeply sad? Did he see her frenzy as not for him at all? "I love you," she had told him. Ana's blue eyes gazed sadly and lovingly into her own and vanished. Her father, struck with an Indian arrow, wept openly at the impotence of his coming death. Love—an Indian? Love an Indian with *their* hands stilled forever upon the prairie? Shuddering, Maria buried her face in her hands. Her thoughts were darting swallows and she reeled after them.

His lips softly brushed her forehead, and rage suddenly leaped within her. "Indian! Indian!" she screamed, lashing his face as hard as she could. Stunned, he recoiled wordlessly away from her. His face became an expressionless mask.

He wouldn't even give her life, as the savage Indians hadn't given her father and Ana life!

Silently, he gestured for her to mount the bay. He made no attempt to help her, nor did he mount the horse behind her and shelter her from the bitter mountain wind. Every fire in the world had gone out and she felt as if she would never be warm again.

Natosin

Nakoa's Woman

Chapter Five

When the Indian led the bay into the village, it seemed to Maria that all sound stopped. Drums were muted; talking ceased; there was only a dog barking frantically, and then, with a loud yip, he too became silenced. People had gathered where she and the Indian would enter the village, and more and more were quickly coming. Their black eyes were all upon her, as if she were a strange thing apart from themselves. Had they never seen a white woman before? The reflection of the firelight shone upon their unwavering gaze.

Without a word, the Indian led his horse past them all, and then Maria could hear them quietly following, now not so hushed or awed, and their voices beginning to murmur. Maria began to pick out separate words. "*Essummissa! Essummissa!*" she heard over and over. Was that their word for white? A child darted up to them, looking up at her closely, and then ran away only to return and search her face again. A crowd was following them now, and more throngs lined the route that they seemed to know the Indian would take. "*Makto mahxim!*" a man shouted, and then another said, "*Ksiksi num-ksiksi num!*" and still her captor answered none of the voices.

Maria felt sick; she concentrated upon holding herself erect and on keeping any fear from her face. Dear God, where was he taking her? Did he have to display her to everyone in the village? She wanted to call out to him, but she did not even know his name, so she looked proudly ahead, and refused to look at any more of the eyes watching her.

They were now approaching the inner circle of tipis, and here the crowd collecting behind them stopped. "*O wayai—ashtay!*" a good-humored voice laughed. "*Tsumah tsi tsi? Ninow?*" There was laughter in answer from the others, and then the Indian led her away from them.

The inner circle consisted of only nine tipis, and apart from them stood one of tremendous size. It was over twenty feet in height and was supported by at least thirty lodge poles. It was at this lodge that her captor stopped the bay and gestured for her to dismount. When Maria swung to the ground a pack of dogs came yapping furiously at her feet, and the Indian kicked them away from her. "*Piintwike*," he said, telling her to enter the door of the tipi. Maria hung back. "*Piintwike*," he repeated impatiently, and slowly Maria entered the door. She had to stoop to enter the lodge, and as she did so, she glanced pleadingly back at the Indian, but he gave no sign of encouragement.

Inside the lodge Maria straightened, and her captor took her by the arm and led her to eight or nine men who were sitting around the fire. The Indian who had prevented her from escaping on the bay already stood before them. Maria looked at him in surprise. He was arguing, and without looking at him, the seated men listened, and as they listened they smoked from one pipe that was slowly being passed from right to left.

Her captor plainly grew enraged at what this man was saying, and again Maria saw the killing wrath come to his face. She shrank against the wall, but her captor jerked her roughly back to him, and she stayed by his side, looking at the seated men fearfully. Her assailant at the meadow finished speaking, and then there was long silence.

The fire burned steadily in front of them all, and wearily Maria moved her weight from one foot to the other. She noticed that the fire pit was neatly lined with stones; that the interior wall of the lodge was covered with cowskins upon which were painted crude scenes of battle; she saw that the lodge was so large that the fire did not light its shadowed corners. Her captor now began to speak, and for the first time the eyes of the seated men swung to her. She was the subject of this conversation—this bitter argument!

Directly across from the doorway they had entered sat a man

who held her gaze. She had been mistaken in believing her captor to be a tribal chief; clearly here was the leader of these Indians. There was a familiarity about him that Maria could not place, and she met his searching gaze and was struck more and more by it. Where could she have seen this man before? He was probably in his early fifties. He wore his hair long; it was streaked with gray and fell unbound to his shoulders except for one lock, about two inches in width, that was cut short at the bridge of his nose. He was very large, muscular, and flat bellied. He had the body of a much younger man; it was only his gray hair that made him look older. His eyes were fierce in their pride— but his mouth—his lips—and . . . Startled, Maria glanced swiftly from him to her captor, and then knew that these two men were father and son.

As his son talked, the father still watched her intently. How was she so positive that he was the tribal chief? Only an elaborate necklace of elk teeth and bear claws, and the way he wore his hair, distinguished him from the others. Yet it was the dignity, the awful dignity and pride, and a majesty that even his son did not yet have, that made her know. She was spellbound by the eyes. In them she saw truth, the answer to questions unknown, and there was temperance, and Maria felt safety in his presence. She sighed, breathing more quietly, and then the chief looked away from her at last, but the glances of the others still remained. The son had finished speaking, and again came the silence, with the pipe still wordlessly passed from one seated man to the other.

The fire shrank in size, and fell to hissing at a wet piece of wood. It hissed like an old witch whispering of dark nights and evil winds, and then it bit into a pitch pocket and spewed venom out in a scalding stream of pitch. It leaped brightly into new life, and having devoured the pitch, sank back and resumed its monotonous hissing at the water spot.

Maria felt pains of fatigue. She had ridden over twenty hours without sleep and she despaired for rest. Each of the seated men spoke directly to her captor, and when they had finished, the father nodded in agreement. The Indian who had been arguing before them shouted angrily. Her captor leaped at him in a fury. "Nakoa!"

the chief called sternly, and her captor reluctantly and slowly released the man he had again attacked. Mother of God, these two were fighting over her! She saw in humiliation that every man in the room was looking at her, and finally the chief motioned for his son to take her from the tipi.

Outside the night air was cold and blew her hair back from her damp forehead. The Indian signed for her to mount the bay again, but she could not. She pressed her head weakly against the animal. "I am sick!" she whispered. "*Estse no stum,*" she repeated in his tongue.

He lifted her upon the horse, and this time mounted behind her. "*Neet akkse,*" he answered, but she had forgotten these words. They rode back to the outer tipis, and he stopped the bay before a lodge that was dark and silent. He went inside and started a fire, and she followed him timidly, standing at the door. Suddenly a huge shadowed bulk emerged from nowhere, and almost knocked her down at the entrance. It was an old woman, shouting at her captor excitedly. She pulled Maria into the tipi, and tried to study her face in the firelight. She smelled of grease and sweat and her stringy gray hair was standing almost on end. "*Essummissa?*" she asked and belched.

"*Essummissa,*" her captor answered. The old woman belched again in wonderment. She squinted her little black eyes into Maria's face. God, what a smell! Maria thought.

"By damn!" shouted the old woman. "By damn!"

"You speak English?" Maria asked her immediately.

The old woman gave no indication of understanding. She pulled Maria closer to the fire and when she still couldn't see her well enough, angrily threw more wood on the flames. In the growing light she looked at Maria bug-eyed. "*Hai-yah!*" she exclaimed, scratching herself, and Maria saw with horror she wasn't particular where she scratched. "*Neek? Neek?*" the old woman asked her captor, but without answering her, he left the tipi. Maria looked numbly after him. Why had she been brought to this old hag?

The old woman put her hands on her hips and then pointed to herself. "Atsitsi," she said proudly.

Maria nodded. "You are named Atsitsi," she said. She saw some water in the lodge and asked for it by cupping her hand to her lips. The old woman handed her the buffalo paunch, and when Maria had finished with it, gave her a cold stew of some kind. It was horrible, but Maria ate it anyway, and all the time she was eating the little black eyes never left her face.

When she had had enough, Maria went to one of the two couches in the lodge, and without an invitation of any kind, lay down upon it to sleep. "Good night," she said to her absorbed hostess.

The next morning the first thing Maria saw was the old woman still watching her. "My goodness," she said to her, "didn't you close your eyes all night long?"

The old woman bared her gums, and began to scratch under her breasts. She offered Maria more of last night's stew, and Maria forced herself to eat some, and thanked Atsitsi when she had finished.

The old woman grinned happily.

Maria looked around her, running her hands through her tangled hair. If only she had a comb and could bathe and put on a clean dress! She went to the water pouch and was preparing to wash with its contents when the old woman almost knocked her down. She led her to the door and away from the outer tipis to a river. She pointed to the water and then looked at Maria as if she were crazy to bathe at all.

Maria strove for privacy while bathing, but the old woman seemed to be peeping from every bush so Maria tried to resign herself to her staring. Maria called her names, and the old woman nodded in agreement.

Returning to the village, Maria found crowds waiting for her arrival. Food and fires had been left unattended. Children had abandoned their play to stare at her; dogs left their gnawing on bones to yip and snap at her heels. She was frightened, and she kicked at the dogs savagely. Panting, she felt tears sting her eyes and she ran and hid herself in the old woman's lodge.

Maria lay down on her couch and buried her face in shaking hands. "Why didn't he just kill me?" she moaned to herself. "Why did he save me at all?"

The old woman had entered, and she sat down upon Maria's couch. "Ha!" she exclaimed in English. "You not know why you saved?"

"You speak English!" Maria said, at once astonished and overjoyed.

"I no say I not."

"But last night—"

"Last night I look."

"Are you the only person here who speaks English?"

"Yes. I work once for white man. I the white man's word for good Indian woman. I whore. I whore at Laramie for many suns!"

"Oh," Maria said, feeling pity for the old woman.

"I no like sweet look," the old woman said angrily.

"I am sorry," Maria whispered. "You worked for whites. You know my tongue—won't you help me?"

"Why need help?"

Maria felt her lips tremble. "I am a prisoner. I am here against my will!"

"Ha!" the old woman leered.

Maria felt growing discomfort. "Why do you say that?" she asked.

The old woman moved closer to her, her stench making Maria sick. "You virgin—before Nakoa?" she asked.

Maria recoiled. "I am still a virgin," she said without thinking.

The old woman got up and stood over Maria enraged. "You lie!" she shouted.

"I do not!" Maria replied heatedly.

"You lie and insult Pikuni and whole by-damn Blackfoot nation!"

Maria looked up into the little hate-filled eyes. "Blackfoot?" she repeated. "You are Blackfoot?"

"Pikuni of the Blackfoot nation. And you tell by-damn lie about Nakoa!"

Maria was stunned. She was a prisoner of the Blackfoot who were known never to trade with the white man and never take whites as prisoners. She had heard that no white man ever had been allowed in a Blackfoot village. "Oh, no," she moaned, pressing her arms against her stomach.

"Go toilet again if sick," the old woman growled.

"Where am I?"

"Sitting on tipi couch, fool!"

"I mean, where is this village?"

"In Blackfoot land. Where else, by damn?"

Maria sighed. "Who is Nakoa?"

The old woman rolled her eyes and batted her eyelashes. "Who is Nakoa?" she mimicked, mincing her words.

"Is he my captor?"

"What this by-damn captor?"

"The man—I will be forced—to marry."

"Oh, oh." The old woman smiled and sucked at her gums. "That a 'captor'. Make poor white virgin marry bad Indian. How old is sweet white virgin?"

"I am nineteen," Maria said stiffly.

"Why men stay away from nice virgin? Not all pale and sick like most white woman. And have nice big breasts. No understand."

Maria's face reddened. "Don't worry yourself about it," she said angrily.

"What little virgin's name?"

"Maria. I would like to be your friend. How did you happen to work at Fort Laramie when you are Blackfoot?"

"Husband not Blackfoot. He Dahcotah. Dead now, thank God. I come back to my village but no man want me because I sleep with whites. Big sticks here leave me alone, so I no bathe any more. It make village unhappy, but I Pikuni and I stay here until I die."

"When do I have to marry Nakoa?" Maria asked.

"You no want marriage with Nakoa?"

"Certainly not. I want my freedom. I want to live with my own people. How could I live the rest of my life in an Indian village?" Maria's voice shook. She thought of this woman at Fort Laramie and she pictured the lonely Laramie hills and heard the birds calling again from the ruins outside its gate. The thought of Ana and her father made tears spring to her eyes and she rocked back and forth in pain. "Help me! Help me!" she whispered.

"Not bad for you now," the old woman said happily. "Get bad when Nakoa give you away!"

"What do you mean?"

"You think Nakoa save you to have as pretty wife?"

"Yes. Don't I have to marry him?"

The old woman threw back her head and laughed. All mirth was gone from her face and her expression was one of mockery. "Little white virgin no use brain! Do you know Nakoa the most important man in this village? Nakoa son of head chief. Nakoa head of the Mutsik, greatest society of Pikuni braves. Now you think Indian man like this would marry a white woman?"

Maria bowed her head.

"He screw pale woman for a while and then sell you for a horse! How you be such a fool! Screw one thing marry another! To marry you—insult to his father, to the Mutsik—to the Pikuni—to me!" The old woman was screaming with rage. "You nothing but—white woman! White woman!" When Maria looked up the old woman spat into her face.

Woodenly, Maria wiped the spittle away. "He will sell me?"

"Siksikai next. Already ask at council of head chiefs."

"Who is Siksikai?"

"He rode from Snake land with you. You saw him asking for you last night." Her face was gloating.

Maria shuddered at her expression. "What is wrong with Siksikai?"

"He hurt women, all women he take to his couch. Maybe he not like you and trade you off quick!"

Maria hid her face in her hands. She thought of the tender way the Indian had kissed her outside of the village, of how he had not raped her. "Nakoa—" she whispered.

"Nakoa can't help you even if he wanted to keep you. He pledged to marry Nitanna this summer in sacred ceremony between the Kainah and the Pikuni. Would Nitanna want white woman around? Siksikai no have woman. No Pikuni woman go near him. That is why he want you."

"You are animals!"

"All men animal! White man animal with Indian woman—Indian animal with white woman. All men have sticks, little white virgin."

"I am no whore."

"But soon to be. Then two whores in Pikuni village—you and me. Nice old Indian whore and nice white whore!"

Maria leaned back against the skins of the lodge, sick. She clutched at her stomach. The image of the Pikuni head chief came suddenly to her mind.

"What is your sun chief called?" she asked.

"Natosin. You think you get to sleep with him, too?"

Maria closed her eyes. Natosin had had an innate dignity, a face of wisdom and of compassion. She would go to him for help.

Maria walked away from the old woman's lodge with her heart hammering in her throat. Atsitsi had not restrained her, or even bothered to ask where she was going. Maria walked by tipi after tipi. They all looked the same, with the blackened area painted at the top and black bands at the bottom broken by two rows of white circles and an upper row of triangles.

Two braves passed her, secretly looking at her, and she shuddered. God, she might be used by both of them, or any man around her if he could afford the price! She ached for Anson Frederich to come and save her, for her father to come and save her. But there was no one to help her but herself, and she wondered how long her strength would allow her to live.

A dog rushed at her, tearing at her skirts, until a woman working a skin called him back. The noon sun shone down upon her relentlessly. The bodice of her dress became drenched with perspiration; her hair hung damply to her neck and still she walked grimly on, the inner circle of tipis appearing just as far away as ever. More riders passed her, but so feverishly was she seeking the inner lodges, she did not see the look of amazement upon their faces. She saw a little girl peer at her shyly from the interior of a lodge and her heart pained with envy. If she could be a child in that cool shadow and lie down to afternoon sleeping with life kind and comforting all around her! If only she were a child—if only they had never heard of the Oregon Trail!

Not once did Maria think of the uselessness of her actions. If she could find Natosin, what would she tell him? How could she speak to him? Even if she could speak his tongue, who was she to thwart the wishes of his son and the decision of the high chiefs? But her mind churned with fierce rebellion only.

She remembered the way she had embraced the Indian outside the village. She thought of the soft lines of his mouth when he saw her pain or fear; she remembered the tenderness that could come to his eyes. When she had slept by him in the sunlight and had kissed him under the stars, a strength had come from him that made pain bearable. The clean buckskin smell of him, the scents of the warming prairie with its carpets of bright wildflowers, the smell of the mountain pines in the wind—all of these had seemed a new atmosphere in which she could live and grow. But she had been reaching toward nothing; how she hated her foolish mind and her unclean flesh for yearning for something that never was!

At last she reached the inner circle of tipis. There were nine of them, with all of their doors facing east. They were different from the lodges of the outer circle. They had the same black border at their base and top, but between these borders were designs in brilliant colors.

Maria looked around her, seeking someone to speak to. A woman came out of one of the lodges, and seeing Maria, stopped in her tracks in amazement. She hastily retreated, even lowering the flap of her tipi. Maria wondered if she had done something terribly wrong in coming to these lodges. Now moving cautiously, she walked slowly toward the council lodge. Two women came out of another tipi and silently watched her. Their faces, too, reflected surprise.

The council lodge was empty, so she had to seek the tipi of Natosin, for surely it was here in the inner circle. She passed a tipi with its skins decorated with a yellow cross, another painted with the figure of a black buffalo. A young girl sat by its door, quilling moccasins. She looked up at Maria with large frightened eyes. "*Weekw?*" she asked softly.

"I am seeking the lodge of Natosin," Maria answered, using the Indian tongue she had learned and the sign language too.

The girl immediately pointed to a tipi decorated with an eagle which stood across from them.

"Thank you," Maria said in Pikuni, and walked toward it. It was the most beautiful of the inner lodges. Its whole top was a brilliant red with yellow bands below it in varying hues, and it looked as if the eagle flew against a sunset sky.

Maria's hands grew cold and she began to tremble. Dear God, what had she done? She approached the lodge, and then timidly walked away from it and stood by another decorated with a beautiful blue star. She could hear male voices coming from Natosin's and then the sound of pleasant laughter. The young girl and the two women were staring at her but she had gone too far now to turn back. She went to Natosin's lodge and boldly drew aside the doorflap.

"*Nakaa-lo!*" her captor exclaimed in surprise and immediately came to her side. His forehead was creased in anger, and he began to shake her shoulders.

Directly in front of her, opposite the door, sat Natosin. Maria called his name, struggling to get to him. Nakoa held her back. "*Keleoene—*" he said furiously. Maria suddenly stopped fighting him and looked up into his face. Here was the man who had kissed her tenderly and soon would trade her for a horse.

"*Weekw?*" he asked her now, more quietly. What is it?

"What is it indeed," Maria answered in English. "Why, you have found yourself a wonderful little whore!" With these words she raked his face as deeply as she could with her fingernails. She watched his blood follow her imprint and heard excited exclamations of amazement. "Liar!" she screamed at him.

He did not even touch his face and no longer showed signs of anger. He gestured to two men in the lodge. "*Mahto hahxim.*" he said softly, and the two Indians forced her from the tipi.

Outside Maria struggled and screamed again for Natosin and was in such a frenzy that she was dragged like a madwoman through the village. "Help!" she cried hysterically. Dogs became wild; children shouted with her and followed the sad spectacle; men and women left their lodges and watched her silently.

Nearing Atsitsi's, Maria quieted. She was released at her door and Maria ran into the tipi, throwing herself down upon her couch and sobbing as if she never intended to stop.

Atsitsi was eating and looked at Maria sourly. "All by-God noises ruin good food," she said. "Why not eat and shut up?"

Maria pounded the buffalo robe with her fists.

"Animal already die once. You mad robe no cry with you?"

Maria turned her head to the wall. She would die. She would hold her breath or starve until she died.

"Oh, we all sad. Robe sad, walls sad, stew sad. All cry for baby white woman. I cry later when stomach full."

"Shut up!" Maria screamed.

"Just tell big sadness of everything. You cry little self away, nothing left to wash at river! Nothing left to keep virgin!"

The afternoon sun moved slowly. Flies buzzed against the lodge skins. Maria kept her head to the wall. In time the lodge skins darkened and the smell of food cooking upon the evening fires grew stronger. Her stomach began to cramp. With her soul still twisted in pain, the will of the flesh triumphed and Maria left the lodge for food.

Chapter Six

Two days passed. Maria knew that the village was talking of the way she had scratched Nakoa's face, and she was glad. No matter how much she had hurt herself, she had shamed Nakoa more.

Toward Atsitsi she maintained a stony silence. The old woman raged at this. "Now why you no talk? You think sweet words too good for Indian tipi? You filled with yourself twice! Big mess! Why not Nakoa take you to his by-damn lodge? Why leave you here to eat up all my food?"

Atsitsi in fact was trying to eat all of the stew herself. She had eaten four bowls of food and was going for another. "Man fool!" she said, sucking at the meat noisily. "What good it be for man to go through Sun Dance, kill for coups when just become crazy before titty of white woman?"

Maria looked at her in contempt. Atsitsi belched loudly and scratched between her thighs.

"You are like a dog," Maria said furiously. "You draw every fly upon the prairie!"

"At least I don't wash self all time like body one big disease! Ha! Wash hands! Wash face! Wash hair! Fool!" She scratched again.

"You don't mind if I have a little food?" Maria asked wrathfully, filling her bowl. When she had filled it, Atsitsi kicked all of its contents upon the floor. "Well, that was nice!" Maria said.

"You no need meat. Go and eat petal of prairie flower! Or no eat and go quick to white man's sweet heaven!"

But Maria did eat, and afterward they walked to the river for water and wood. "Now water in paunch for drink!" Atsitsi said "Not for sweet little hands and face! And stay close; Nakoa say you to stay in my sight."

"I'm walking out of smelling range. At least out on the prairie I can breathe fresh air!"

When they came to the river, groups of women were already bathing in it. Maria found that with the unhappy exception of Atsitsi, the Blackfoot women were very clean. They washed in the river or the lake every day; their clothing, nails, and hair were always well groomed. Maria bathed and sunned herself as far from Atsitsi as she could get, lazily watching the many women around her. They laughed and talked softly as they swam and gathered their scrub wood and water paunches. Their faces glowed with good health and the recent touch of the cool water. They neatly slicked and braided their hair, some touching the part with vermilion. Most were tall and slender, moving with a lean muscular grace. Their dresses were of the soft skins of elk, deer, or antelope, their skirts coming about halfway down their legs, with leggings as high as the knee. Their blouses had short wide sleeves, fringed at the elbow, the hems and sleeves alike decorated with brightly colored quills. Beautiful pendants were worn as earrings, and shining white elk teeth as necklaces. All of the women wore knife cords that hung from their belt to the length of their thigh.

Now none of them bothered to look at Maria. It seemed as if no one desired to interfere with what Nakoa had elected to do with a captured white woman.

"Well, leave now!" Atsitsi shouted across the moving water to Maria. "Go back to lodge! Water like you, never shut up!" she finished in sarcasm. Maria reluctantly approached her, shaking her still wet hair in the sun. "Fires of evil in hair," Atsitsi observed. "Much red." She looked deeply depressed. "Body—face—all nice." Suddenly she brightened. "Nitanna better. Nitanna more beautiful."

"Tell me of Nitanna."

"Nakoa's woman. Most beautiful woman in Blackfoot nation. White woman nothing by Nitanna! Nakoa love Nitanna and marry her in moon of Sun Dance. She come with Kainah then. She daughter of Kainah head chief."

"How nice for both of them."

"Not nice for you. Then you go to Siksikai."

"I don't want to talk about it."

"By damn—there Anatsa!" Atsitsi had picked up the water paunches and now she quickly put them down. "I no want to go now. I not see Anatsa for long time and now I look." She was staring at the young girl who had started to bathe by herself in a quiet and secluded cove of the river.

"What are you staring at?" Maria asked crossly.

The girl in the cove left the water and for a moment revealed herself to them. She was piteously frail and thin.

"See?" said Atsitsi.

"See what?" Maria asked impatiently.

"No woman! No titty! Nothing!"

"You old fool. She is just thin. Look, she is putting on her dress. Now, can we go?"

"See closer. Wait until she pass." Atsitsi settled her great hulk and waited for the Indian girl to walk by.

"Do you want to carry the wood back or the water?" Maria asked her.

"Paunches. They don't scratch."

"Where do the men bathe?" Maria asked.

"Here. In afternoon. You want to hide in bush to peep at Nakoa?"

"Please! Be quiet!" Maria said sharply.

The Indian girl had finished dressing, and after gathering some scrub wood, walked toward them with great difficulty.

"Why, she's crippled!" breathed Maria.

"Ugly. Always ugly like that!"

"Being crippled isn't ugly."

"Leg dragging like that damned ugly."

"Why don't the others wait for her?" asked Maria.

"Hurry back to husbands after bathing. Sleep together in afternoon."

"She has no husband?"

"Now who screw that?"

Maria shuddered at her cruelty.

The girl reached them, and as she passed, Maria gave her a warm and friendly smile. She smiled shyly back and Maria saw with surprise that this was the same girl who had directed her to Natosin's lodge.

"See what mess," Atsitsi hissed. "Own brother-in-law won't sleep with her."

"You have no heart, do you? Don't you know she suffers for what she is?"

"Better she suffer than Atsitsi. Still big mess."

Furious with the old woman, Maria began to gather the scrub wood. "Why don't you help me?" she asked Atsitsi impatiently.

"You carry wood. You gather wood." She reached for the paunches that Maria had filled. "Now why so much by-damn water? Can't leave any for poor river?"

"Don't spill any on yourself," Maria answered. "You will die." Carrying the wood, Maria walked rapidly toward the village.

"Wait for me, by damn!" Atsitsi shouted.

"Move your by-damn feet!" Maria shouted back. Ahead of them, the crippled girl was nearing the village. Two men rode out to meet her and while they were talking to her, Maria could see that she kept her face shyly averted.

Maria's heart went out to this Indian girl, Anatsa. They were both in an alien world in which there was no compassion for either of them. The two men were now riding toward her and Atsitsi. It was her captor and his friend. Nakoa glanced at her only briefly and then rode on to Atsitsi. The old woman put down the paunches and bared her gums in a grin. Nakoa spoke to her and she began to scratch in delight. She suddenly stopped scratching and looked at Nakoa in astonishment. Nakoa and his friend rode toward the river, and Atsitsi stared after them.

Maria walked back to her. "What is the matter?" she asked. "Did he ask you to marry him?"

Atsitsi kicked over one of the water paunches. She was going to kick over the other paunch, but Maria shoved her away from it.

"Leave that water alone!" Maria said. "That one is mine!"

"God damn!" Atsitsi screamed.

"What is the matter with you? What did he tell you?"

"He say you to stay with me until I teach you Pikuni! You no learn—you no eat! Now why this? He crazy! Why you have to learn Pikuni? You screw in Pikuni? You make baby with Pikuni words? What Pikuni have to do with white woman?" Atsitsi turned and looked mournfully after Nakoa.

Anatsa walked ahead of the white woman, wanting all the time to turn back and speak to her in her own tongue. "I feel pain for you," she wanted to say. "I feel pain that is deep for what Nakoa is doing to you!"

At the river, Anatsa had studied the white woman. She was so vivid and vibrant with life. Naked, she was slender and yet voluptuous; her softly rounded hips and beautiful breasts made Anatsa despise her own frail body. Every part of the woman was beautiful: her full red lips, her straight nose, the lustrous dark hair with its flashes of red in the sun, the long-lashed eyes. How could Nakoa take a woman of such beauty and make her unclean? The white woman did not want him. Anatsa had heard her frenzied attack upon him and had seen her forcibly dragged away from Natosin. Nakoa loved Nitanna—why did he have to make this white woman unclean?

When Nakoa slept with the white woman no man in the village would marry her and she would be traded from one to another until she died. She would have no place among the women of the village either, for the unclean were avoided, were not invited to any gatherings, were even denied the right of prayer at the Sun Dance. Tears came to Anatsa's eyes. She had known Nakoa all of her life, and since Natosin had lost all of his wives in the sickness from the Mandans, she had prepared all of Nakoa's food. Around him she had always felt at ease. He had always been so gentle with her; understanding had always flowed between them. He was the only man in the village who made her forget her crippled body. He was even a part of the world she had made for herself where everything was beautiful and where she was accepted.

Anatsa reached the inner circle of tipis with her wood and since it was too early to start the cooking fire, she sat outside her brother -in-law's lodge and began to dream quietly in the sun. She had no family except her older sister, Apeecheken, her brother-in-law, Onesta, and their child, Mikapi. Anatsa's touch with reality was through them, but her own world lay deep in the shadow of the mountain where she had her own place. Here was a glen with a magical stream that was balm for the wounds of living. When the struggling and grieving of the prairie became too intense, she had the cooling waters that sprang from the earth's breast. Early in the morning when Apeecheken, Onesta, and Mikapi all slept, and the firepits were still warm with the ashes of the night before, she would steal from the village. Sometimes the late moon would still be in the sky, a pale silver thread when the eastern horizon was streaked with color. All would be quiet and still. Not even a dog would bark as she walked quietly past the tipis.

In the shadow of the mountain forest she would reach her glen, when the tips of the tall trees around it were orange and the air yet night-cold. Here she would quake and shiver as if she had just been newly born, uncrippled. She would linger in the glen until afternoon. Then the forest would be hot, slumbering, and lazy, and she would breathe deeply the scent of warming pine needles. Birds joyously called back and forth above the motionless ferns and the cool moss that seemed so indifferent to the vibrant sounds around them. In all of this beauty she would lie still and sleep a sleep as golden as honey, and in the touch of the wind and the shade of the trees she would feel deeply loved, deeply blessed. In return she loved all she could see and all that she could not see. She would awaken and walk in wonder back to the village, and she would look down upon the tipis and the cooking fires and want to bless them all with the ecstasy she had felt.

She had waited many years to be a woman. She had waited patiently for her breasts to form, for her eyes to have something in them that would make a man love and want her. If her face could become beautiful then her deformed leg would not be seen; surely radiant beauty would put her leg in shadow. But she did not change. Her pale reflection in the river showed she remained too thin, a bud that would not open, a flower that had no sweetness with which to grow.

Suddenly, this afternoon, Anatsa no longer wanted her glen. The stream and its shadowed ferns were not enough. She wanted to be in the village with Apikunni even if the prairie was scorching under the sun. Water flowing from the beginning of life itself was not the earth where the animals crawled to mate. The glen and its pond and stream did not bear the image of the man she loved, Apikunni, as close as blood brother to Nakoa. He was the man she wanted, and yet he was the one to whom she could not speak a sensible word. Dogs and horses and even the worm beneath the moss could feel and desire and unite—but not she! Not she! She loved Apikunni tenderly; she loved him passionately, she loved him purely and she loved him lustfully, but never once had he seen her! Anatsa put her head in her hands in despair. Her own suffering was enough for the whole world—why should the white woman be treated like a dog bitch?

The moon was rising, silvering the prairie in poignant serenity. Anatsa thought back upon how many lovers yearned for each other in its magical light, and then she made herself turn away from its face. It was late and she should have started the cooking long ago. Her sister, Apeecheken, was pregnant and couldn't stomach the preparing of food, so it fell upon Anatsa to do all of the cooking. Anatsa built her fire near Nakoa's lodge and as she boiled meat, she watched his tipi thoughtfully.

Nakoa's Nitsokan was the voice of the west wind, the woman of the west wind who had appeared to him in a vision when he had fasted and sought his sign as a youth. What had she been like, this foreign woman who had traveled from distant seas and brought to the dry prairie the touch of water? She had been seen only by Nakoa, for most of the boys who sought their Nitsokan in lonely and dangerous fasts in the woods had seen signs of animals—the eagle, the bear, the white wolf; no brave had ever ridden into battle protected by a human sign before. Yet his was the most powerful of medicines, gaining him the most coups among the Blackfoot, and bringing him the chieftainship of the Mutsik society.

Upon the skins of Nakoa's lodge was a brilliant blue star and a yellow pine cone. Nakoa had not allowed the woman to be painted. Her touch stretched from the pines to the North Star, but like the winds themselves, she had to remain invisible. What would Nakoa's woman of the west wind think of him now? How would she give him strength and protection when he would destroy one of her sex and beauty in blind lust?

Anatsa took the cooked meat to her sister and Onesta and Mikapi. She could eat none of it herself and went back to sit by the fire near Nakoa's lodge, feeding it with new sticks. At last she heard the sound of his horse.

Nakoa picketed the animal, and quickly walked over to her. He smiled and accepted the food she offered. "You will not eat?" he asked her.

"I have no taste for food tonight," she answered shyly, and then determination made her look boldly into his face. "I would like to talk with you," she said.

He looked surprised at the tone of her voice. "I am here," he said.

"My words come hard."

"Words have never been scarce between us before."

"I want to speak to you of the white woman!" she blurted.

Immediately he looked wary. "Why should you speak of her?"

"Because I should not, and if it is that I should not, then no one else will speak of her as I will."

"If you are afraid of your words then do not utter them."

"I must. I will say them and not keep them silent within myself where they will fester and grow in power."

"Then speak what you will."

"I feel sickness at what you are doing with this white woman."

"Why?"

Anatsa felt her face burn but she went bravely on. "It is what you *will* do, then."

"What will I do?"

"You have told the high chiefs. You will use her as a mistress and then trade her to Siksikai!" Anatsa was appalled at her bold words. "I am sorry—" she said timidly. "I know she is yours—I know—but I cannot see such a woman done this way!"

"Such a woman? She is white!"

"She is clean! She is the most beautiful woman I have ever seen!"

"You are pained for her just because she is beautiful?"

"I am thinking of you!"

"No. I want to lie with her. I want her for a mistress."

Anatsa began to tremble, suffering an anguish of embarrassment. "She does not want this."

"I do."

"When you are through she will be dirty like Atsitsi!"

Nakoa looked at her earnest face, and putting down the food, took her thin hands and held them in his own. "Anatsa," he said gently. "My heart is warm toward you. I have known you since you were born and have lived near you in this circle of high chiefs—but Anatsa—you are not of this village!"

"Why?"

"You cannot grow in the mud of a prairie river! You have always been so frail—"

Anatsa thinking of her leg tried to draw her hands from his.

"It is as if you were a flower that needs the sweet water of a more gentle stream—the shadow of protecting trees, Anatsa. This white woman is not like you! She—it does not matter what she is! I am a man," he said somberly. "I am of the earth and of the mud where you gather the scrub brush for your cooking fires. I have desires and I live to meet them. I have fought for the coups I have; I have bled my blood for them, not the blood of my father, nor the blood of the high chiefs. I am not as you. I am of this village—this world. I do not have time for dreams. I do not live to scatter sunbeams!"

She bowed her head sorrowfully.

"Anatsa, I do not mock you. Be kind and gentle. Dream what you will in the mountain place you seek. Give others your touch of the sun. I am not a woman. I am a man. I have hot desires and I satisfy them. If my father and all of the head chiefs had said that I could not have this woman, I would have her anyway!"

"Why do you wait?" Anatsa whispered. "Why is she still at Atsitsi's?"

Nakoa stretched out his long legs and looked at the fire.

"I am sorry," Anatsa said quickly, "I deserve no answer."

"Why do I wait?" Nakoa asked, speaking more to himself than to her. "She will accept me. I wait for this."

"You wait for this?"

"To make my pleasure deeper."

"Nakoa—"

"She has her life! If I had not wanted her I would not have saved her from the Snakes! Why else would I care whether a white woman lived or died?" He was getting angry. "And yet this woman has touched me. I see her face—and her body—when I am not with her. Why would it make my pleasure greater to have her accept me? Why would I care when I can take her by force any time?"

Anatsa shivered.

"I do not know my actions! For the first time in my life, I do not know my actions!"

"You feel pity?"

"No! Why would I feel pity for a woman I saved from being killed? I want to see her naked again. I want to hold her with nothing between her flesh and mine." He suddenly realized Anatsa's embarrassment. "My words are ugly to you," he said. "They are coarse because you are a virgin to life. I am sorry, my little Anatsa."

"You have always been so gentle with me," Anatsa faltered. "You are not animal—mud of the river of earth . . ."

"We are all of the earth," Nakoa said softly. He looked at Anatsa with tenderness. "But you are not. Anatsa, you are a note of a bird song." He looked musingly into the fire, his handsome face even more tender. "But the white woman is of the earth and she fights the call of her body. I wait for her to listen. With an Indian she will still have to be the woman and—accept."

"Your face is filled with love," Anatsa said. "You speak tenderly of the white woman."

"I am touched by her beauty."

"It is more than that."

"She will bring me pleasure. Do not be blind to what I am. Near her I know the heat of my blood. That is all."

"That is everything," Anatsa said gently and left him.

At her sister's they were all asleep and the last of the lodge fire flickered faintly upon the ceiling. Soundlessly, Anatsa stretched out upon her own couch. Her despondent mood was gone. She knew the white woman to be blessed with Nakoa's desire. Mikapi giggled in his sleep, his boyish face pure and innocent in the firelight. When did innocence flee at last? When did baseness come and rule the flesh?

Before sleeping, Anatsa thought lingeringly of Nakoa's words. If she were but the call of a bird's song, for her there would be no life, just a flashing of melody as brief as a spray of foam flung from a stream, quaking for a moment upon the earth before being dissolved by sun and wind.

Chapter Seven

"Nakoa important man," Atsitsi said to Maria savagely.

"That is all you have been telling me for two weeks," Maria retorted. "I think that you are in love with him, Atsitsi. Are you going to take him away from Nitanna?"

Atsitsi scowled. "You laugh at fatness. Atsitsi not always fat. And when was fat still white man like to screw with me."

"I imagine it was your quiet delicacy and gentle refinement. And also you were probably the only woman west of the Mississippi!"

For two weeks, night and day, Atsitsi had been teaching Maria Pikuni. Pikuni was easy to learn; the language was beautiful in expression, moving in images.

"Tell me the Ikunuhkahtsi," Atsitsi growled, beginning to eat again.

"The Ikunuhkahtsi is the tribal police," Maria said wearily. "I know all of this!"

"I hear all again. Nakoa say, no repeat my word, no food, no eat."

"All Blackfoot men enter the Ikunuhkahtsi, and advance from one society to another all of their lives."

"Tell societies."

"You just don't want me to eat!"

"Shut mouth about food."

"You old whore!"

"You young one. You be whore longer I bet! Now tell societies."

"Boys enter the Little Birds, where they learn how to fight. When a boy has been to war three times he goes on to the Pigeons."

"Give Pikuni name."

"Kuk-kuiks. Then, when he is accepted as a tried warrior he goes on to the—Mosquitoes."

"Pikuni name!"

"Tuiskistiks. Then if a man has led this society in coups and he is no longer mortal but is all God, he may join the greatest society of all because it is led by your old wished-for lover, Nakoa . . . This society is the Mutsik."

"This—our greatest warriors. Nakoa leader."

"Yes, yes, yes! And most young men do not make it, but go on instead to the—Knatsomita, the All Brave Dogs, the Mastahpatakeks, or Raven Bearers, the Issui, the Emitaks, and the Bulls. Now that I've named more men than even you've probably slept with, let me eat!"

"No. Tell where tipis."

"Your tipis are arranged in two circles with the chiefs of the Ikunuhkahtsi camped in the inner circle. The outer tipis are arranged according to blood genes."

"Not enough on lodges of high chiefs. Arranged according to age advancement of chiefs society."

"All right. I agree. Now can't I have some of that delicious food that you and the flies are fighting over?"

Atsitsi belched. "Why?"

Maria looked away and suddenly noticed two riders heading rapidly toward the inner circle of tipis. A crowd excitedly followed them.

"Something wrong," Atsitsi said. "Something happen." She stopped scratching, and got clumsily to her feet. The crowd waited at the fringe of the inner circle, staring at Natosin's lodge.

"I go see," Atsitsi said.

"Me too," Maria answered.

"You to stay by my lodge!"

"I'm to stay with you, so you'll just have to take me along!" They both walked to the crowd where Atsitsi listened a minute to the talking. "Strangers have come to village," she said to Maria.

"Who?"

"Enemies from the south. Blackfoot have no friends to south."

"Is this a war party they are talking about?"

"Yes. I hear now. They are Snake. Snake party come to challenge some of the Mutsik in battle."

"The Mutsik?"

"The Mutsik always meet war parties. Now shut mouth, so I listen."

The crowd was growing; Maria and Atsitsi were jostled about, and the old woman furiously shoved anyone who tried to take her place. Soon Maria thought that the entire camp was in the inner circle, but then she saw five riders approaching them, followed by a group of excited boys. The riders were painted. "Are those the Snakes?" she asked Atsitsi.

"Yes."

"Can your enemies just ride into your village—like that?"

"If come in open challenge, yes! Now shut mouth, I listen."

The murmuring of the crowd around them grew. Maria heard one name repeated in awe and fear. One of the Snakes had been recognized and was obviously a great warrior. The Snakes rode near them, forcing some of those around Maria to move out of their way. The Snakes were so close to Maria that she could smell the sweat on their horses, and see their features under the paint on their faces.

"Damn, damn!" Atsitsi whispered. "Nakoa get it now!"

"What do you mean?" Maria asked instantly.

"Listen! Maybe you read the Indian talk with hands."

The Snakes had stopped before Natosin's lodge, their horses forming a straight and unwavering line. Maria watched them spellbound. They were armed with bow and quiver, and the sunlight flashed from the long lances that they held before them. Each man held a shield close to his breast, and each wore a headdress of eagle feathers that the wind ruffled out. Scalp locks danced on their lances. They stood in stillness and silence.

"What are they waiting for?" Maria whispered.

"This," Atsitsi said, and Maria saw Natosin, Nakoa, and a brave ride to them from the outer tipis. They were not painted for battle, but both Nakoa and his father wore a headdress of buffalo horns that Maria had never seen upon an Indian before. The three Blackfoot stopped, facing the Snakes. After a moment of stillness, one of the Snakes prodded his horse out from the four Snakes behind him and raised his arm high in sign language.

Instantly the brave with Nakoa and Natosin prodded his horse forward and signed back. A hush settled on the group around them. "What are they saying?" Maria asked Atsitsi anxiously. "Tell me what they are saying!"

"The Snake who gestures is Shonka, the greatest of Snake warriors. He has come for the scalp of Nakoa. He is the brother of Eeahsapa, who lies dead by Nakoa's arrow. Nakoa's arrow is known in Snake land because it has been found in friends and relatives of Shonka and the men who have ridden far to Blackfoot land with him. Shonka will kill Nakoa, and the four men with him will kill the four Mutsik who went into Snake land with Nakoa. The taking of Snake hair and Snake horses will end with the death of Nakoa and these four Mutsik." Atsitsi was translating directly now.

The Blackfoot signed rapidly back, and Atsitsi had difficulty in keeping up with him. "The great Shonka does not tell that it is already seven times that Nakoa has ridden into Snake land and taken Snake hair and Snake horses! What will Shonka, who is both a woman and a coward, do about it?"

"Shonka will kill Nakoa tomorrow morning when the sun first comes to the sky, and the Snake warriors with him will kill the Mutsik they have challenged!"

"Nakoa and the four Mutsik will accept the challenge, and will be glad in their hearts to take yet more Snake scalps."

"Good! So it will be!" Shonka signed, and then looking past the Blackfoot who had signed to him, looked directly at Natosin. He gestured again. "I talk to the man who wears the headdress of the Blackfoot high chief. I talk for my brother and for all of the Snakes who move restlessly in the ghost hills without the peace of the dead. Tomorrow your son, the man who has done this, will lie dead by my knife, and I shall wear my war shirt decorated with his hair. Tomorrow this ground will ring with his death cry, this cry of your only son, and his life blood will run at my feet."

Natosin looked at the Snake without any change of expression, his eyes as deep, calm, and tolerant as they were the first night that Maria had seen him. Angrily the Snake signed again. "I have no words from the great Natosin. Does he tremble like a woman without speech before Shonka's awful words?"

Slowly and with indescribable dignity, Natosin raised his arm and signed back. "I do not shake and I do not tremble at words that boast of such courage. When the courage is in the words, the man is empty. If tomorrow Shonka of the Snakes wants to die, he shall have his wish. If it is that my son will die I will remember that I did not tremble at his birth, and so I will not tremble at his death."

The Snake looked at Natosin for a long moment. Maria and all of the Blackfoot looked too, drawn to his majesty. Like the greatest of kings he sat his horse, royal with his crown of ermine skins and buffalo horns, thin, polished, and gleaming in the sun.

Shonka seemed changed; some virility was now gone from his face. "Tomorrow," he signed, "the four Mutsik warriors will lie dead too, and their lodges will be emptied and burned. Your village will weep with the wailing of their women and the weeping of their little children! I am Shonka, of the Snakes, and I have spoken!" Fierceness was in the words but no longer in the man. Slowly he led his war party from the inner tipis, through the outer lodges, and Maria could see that they would camp that night out by the guarded horse herds.

Natosin and Nakoa turned their horses and rode away too, and then the crowd dispersed.

"He will not kill Nakoa," Maria said to Atsitsi as they walked to her lodge.

"No," Atsitsi answered. "But if Nakoa die tomorrow you go to Siksikai, and then it bad. Siksikai might take you for wife and you not lucky to be good whore!"

"Oh be quiet!" Maria snapped, not hiding her concern at what she had just seen.

"Whore lucky woman. My words are straight. Whore accepts all. Whore no fool!"

Nakoa's Woman

Maria went to bed early that night, suddenly numb with exhaustion, but the premonition of coming doom made her restless. Late at night she heard the beating of a drum.

"What is that?" she asked Atsitsi.

"Prayer song of Ahkiona, one of Nakoa's Mutsik, Snake to kill."

"Oh," said Maria and tried to go to sleep. Did only one of the five challenged Mutsik think it necessary to pray? Did only one have the desire to seek help?

A chanting began with the drum, and, tossing and turning, Maria heard it all night. The stars glittered coldly through the smoke hole of the tipi, and as Maria lay upon her back and watched them, they paled and disappeared with the coming of the dawn. Maria rose, shivering. The east would soon be touched with color, and would that mean that his blood would run as red as the eastern sky? She thought of his gentle beautiful mouth; the day had dawned already when he would kill, or be killed.

To the beat of the ceremonial drums, all the men, women, and children of the Pikuni village walked to the inner circle of the high chiefs. Maria and Atsitsi went there too, and all around her Maria saw eyes that were alert, shining, dark with excitement. For the first time since her captivity Maria was unnoticed, and she was quick to see also that there were no morning fires. A wildness was growing all around her, restrained now, but bursting to be unleashed.

When the drums commenced, people pushed to reach the high chiefs first and when they approached the inner lodges they formed a circle. Murmuring grew louder as Natosin appeared with all of the high chiefs except his son. Maria and Atsitsi stood near the crippled girl Anatsa, and Maria saw that the girl was twisting her hands as if she were suffering a terrible pain. "*Weekw?*" Maria muttered to her softly, but Anatsa only looked startled and tried to smile. She shook her head to indicate that nothing was the matter, but after awhile went back to twisting her hands again.

The sky in the east was red now, and for a moment the black forms of some flying birds showed darkly against it and then vanished. The early morning was cruelly cold. A shout suddenly went up from the spectators. Turning to where they all looked, Maria saw Nakoa and his four Mutsik warriors riding slowly toward them. In the terrible chill they were stripped for battle, wearing only breechcloths and moccasins, and their bodies and the bodies of their horses were painted. They came to the spectators and entered the circle where room was made for them to pass. For a moment they held their horses still, and except for the constant drums a silence settled as the crowd became worshipful and reverent.

The warriors were facing the rising sun. This was prayer; the cry for blessing. Then, a woman's voice began chanting to the drums, and called out Nakoa's name. He separated from the others, and walked his horse slowly around the inside of the circle, and the woman began chanting again.

"What does she do?" Maria asked Atsitsi.

"She count his coups. She tell why he is head chief of the Mutsik." Maria listened intently to what the woman was singing, but she could not decipher the words. Then the spectators chanted, singing the praise of the man who rode before them, and as they chanted, young boys in the crowd walked proudly in the path of his horse. Nakoa's cheeks were covered with vermilion paint, his arms and back bore bright gashes of color as if he were recently wounded. He was on display, the sign of Pikuni valor and courage, this man painted and dressed for fresh killing. On each face of each boy walking behind his horse was worship, idolatry, not for just the man who rode in front of him, but for the man he himself hoped to be.

When Nakoa had finished, Apikunni rode around the inner circle, his open boyish face obscured completely by its paint, and then came Siksikai, Ahkiona, and finally Opiowan. These were the men who had brought Maria back from Snake territory; familiar and yet so strange. Now, with no sign of nervousness, they were to fight for their lives. Nakoa alone wore the horns and ermine skins; the others wore feathers, but singly, not in the magnificent war bonnets of the Snakes.

When the coups of Opiowan had been recited and finished, the drums suddenly changed, and the boys following their chosen warrior quickly scattered. Faster and faster beat the tempo, and the challenged men rode together, chanting themselves.

Nakoa's Woman

"What is it?" Maria asked, tugging at Atsitsi's sleeve.

"Wolf song. Now they fight!"

"What do you mean?"

"Sing Wolf song just before battle!"

The warriors nudged their horses into a wild run, and their ponies' hoofs kicked dust at the spectators who stood oblivious to it. Enraptured, they listened to the warriors' chanting, the lust to kill intoxicating them all. Wildness, savagery, pounded above the drums. Faster and faster went the horses beaten into a new frenzy, and with a sudden and wild shout, their riders urged them on, and broke from the circle. The spectators scattered in all directions, then ran frantically after them as they raced toward the waiting Snakes.

Row to row, man to man, horse to horse. Blackfoot and Snake stood upon the prairie facing each other. Panting, Maria reached the rest of the spectators, and when Atsitsi came and shoved her way to the front, Maria followed her. She saw Anatsa, and saved a place near them.

The girl stood watching Nakoa's friend. Maria saw that her eyes were filled with tears.

"Anatsa—" she said gently, and took the crippled girl's hand.

"*Apikunni,*" the crippled girl whispered. "Father—the Sun . . ." She did not go on.

"Why she loves him!" Maria thought, and within her own hand, Anatsa's grew cold.

At last the Blackfoot drums became silent. A meadowlark called out near them. "Bet forget white titty now!" Atsitsi said, still watching Nakoa.

"Shut up!" Maria hissed, shaking in spite of herself.

"Dumb man might be killed and not get to hear you talk Pikuni," said Atsitsi.

"*Keepetahkee!*" Nakoa shouted to Shonka who shouted the word back, and kicking his horse into a run, made a wide circle away from Nakoa and his Blackfoot warriors. Thirty yards away he turned the animal, and rode at a dead run toward Nakoa as if he meant to ride him down. Nakoa's horse began to plunge in terror, and when Shonka threw his lance almost at his feet, Nakoa had difficulty holding him down.

A soft sound came from the Blackfoot spectators. Nakoa kicked his horse and riding a similar circle, plunged his lance before Shonka's horse. Instantly Nakoa and Shonka rode away from each other, turned, and came back upon each other as fast as their horses could skim the rank grass. Maria hid her face within her hands and in a second heard the awful twanging of bows, a sound that made her sick with terror.

"*Haiyah! Haiyah!*" the Blackfoot were shouting excitedly. Maria looked up and saw that the Snake's horse had taken an arrow and was thrashing upon its side in agony. A woman screamed, "*Initsiwah!*" The crowd around Maria repeated the word excitedly. "*Initsiwah!*" Kill him! Kill him!

Shonka worked free from his horse. He faced Nakoa and held his quiver high so that Nakoa could see that in his fall it had been emptied of all his arrows. Nakoa pulled in his horse, and in spite of the frenzied shouting did not ride the Snake down. Swiftly, he dismounted, and holding his quiver high, threw it and the arrows it contained away from him. The Blackfoot moaned in fury. He then cast aside his bow and his shield. Shonka drew out his knife, and stripped to just his knife too, Nakoa went to meet him. Disgruntled silence settled upon the Blackfoot.

Nakoa's hand moved toward his knife belt and came away empty.

Maria cringed. He had lost his knife! He had shown the Snake mercy, would not Shonka do the same for him? But Shonka would not wait for Nakoa to find his knife or get a new one.

The Blackfoot moaned again. Would not Natosin stop this, and see that his son was armed to fight? "*Niikassi! Niikassi!*" shouted some men to Nakoa, but his father made no move to help him, and Shonka came at him for the kill.

Maria could not see Nakoa killed. She could not accept his death. Oh, God, what good the prayer drum, the paint, the forlorn chanting. The crippled girl began to look at her closely.

Maria could not turn away. The dawn was red. Red sky burned all around her from the pitiful wagons, and now another would die that she loved.

Nakoa was backing away from Shonka. He stopped suddenly where he had thrown his bow and, with an incredibly swift movement, grasped it, parrying with it the knife thrusts that Shonka now dealt furiously upon him. Retreating all the while, in a magnificent gesture of surprise, he felled Shonka with one swipe of the bow and leaped upon him. Lying upon the earth, twisting, turning, thrashing, the two men struggled for the knife, and its blade slashed both of them, and each lay colored with the other's blood. Nakoa was the stronger; wresting the knife finally away, he plunged it into Shonka's heart. A long sigh traveled out from the Blackfoot; air rushed into Maria's lungs; color returned to her face. Atsitsi began to scratch with relief.

Maria turned away. Nakoa was scalping Shonka, and when he had finished, he stood and faced the mounted Snakes, silently holding their leader's bloody scalp.

Bloody sunrise was gone, and a golden morning rested upon the still grasses. A meadowlark called out sweetly. Now it was that Shonka lay dead in Blackfoot land. Now it was that a Snake lodge would hear the wailing of grief and useless despair, and the wandering soul of Easapa would know no peace.

The four Snakes looked down upon their leader's hair held in Nakoa's hands and spoke no words, and made no sign. The long black locks seemed to move with their own life. Silent upon their painted horses, they were but four men alone in the land of their enemy, four men alone and without even the protection of their medicine now. Even the great Shonka's medicine had not been strong enough to save him from an unarmed man!

Slowly, one of the Snakes turned his horse to the south, back to where their villages lay. Another followed, and in time another, and when the first three were small upon the prairie, the fourth turned away from the waiting and silent Mutsik too, and not one Blackfoot spoke a word, or called anything after him. Now all of the Snakes were gone except Shonka who rested behind them with his hands outstretched, still reaching for the knife that had been taken from him.

With terrible difficulty, Nakoa mounted his horse, and rode

slowly toward the spectators. Silently, the Blackfoot made room for him to pass, and Maria went to where his horse was picking his way through the crowds. Unthinking, on blind impulse, she blocked the animal's way. With tears touching her face, she looked up at him, wanting to tell him that she loved him, that in these last moments she had learned that she wanted life with him, and could not bear life without him. "Nakoa," she whispered, but this was all she could say, for she could not think of one word in his tongue.

His right arm was horribly mutilated, and dangled uselessly at his side. Blood welled yet in his chest, and at his side, and when Maria saw his bleeding, she shuddered against his horse. Without a word to her, he moved the animal around her, and then the crowds following him hid him from her sight.

He had looked at her without any expression of recognition. She looked back once more at Shonka. She would rather be dead than alive. In this awful world she was all alone, for the man she loved did not even know her.

Chapter Eight

The celebration of Nakoa's victory went on for weeks. There was feasting in all the lodges. When the cooking fires were going, the flaps of all of the tipis were left open and anyone could enter and eat. Atsitsi was everywhere. Her own fire was dead; she was tired of the dried meat she had in store, and wanted the fresh game that the hunters brought to their lodges. Their women received her coldly, but this didn't bother Atsitsi. She went from one lodge to another, eating constantly, and only stopped long enough to torment Maria when she too entered a lodge for food.

"Sweet little thing tired of own company?" she would ask Maria in English. "You die on own sugar?"

"I have come to see how long these women can stand you," Maria snapped back.

"I much too good for them," Atsitsi said. "Big damn fools. But fresh meat good. This good about men. Bring fresh meat and always have big stick."

Maria shuddered. Her hostess looked concerned, as if Maria had found the food bad. Maria smiled at her, and told her in Pikuni how well the meat was prepared.

"Her husband good hunter," Atsitsi commented in English. "Hunt all time for fresh meat and fresh girl. Find both. That's why so strong. Exercise all the time."

"Why don't you say this in Pikuni?" Maria hissed to her.

"No. Let dumb wife sit all time on sweet ass. Why keep unmarried girls in tribe from good time?"

Maria decided to ignore her and turned to the Indian woman be side her. "I am called Maria," she said in Pikuni.

"I am Sikapischis," the woman answered. "I live two lodges from this one. I live with my son Siyeh, and with my father who cannot see with his eyes."

"You have no husband?" Maria asked.

"My husband is dead. He went into Snake land for coups and did not return."

"He went for coups and stayed for . . ." Atsitsi started, and Maria responded with an anger that startled everyone in the lodge.

"I know what you were going to say! You are not going to insult this woman's dead husband to me!"

Sick with Atsitsi, Maria got up and left the lodge. They did not speak that night but the next morning resumed Maria's language lesson and their bitter battle.

"Hurry up and fill brain," Atsitsi said disgustedly. "Learn all by damn words so can screw in Pikuni. I tired of you around."

"I don't find you exactly charming."

"Now how can you sit here in hot sun? You sweat in heat. Why not go quick and jump in river?"

"I have already bathed. But you haven't, so I prefer it outside."

Maria rose and walked away, her hands pressed to her ears as Atsitsi's words followed her. She became dimly aware that ahead of her a large crowd was watching a horse race. She quietly joined the spectators. Across the circle she saw an Indian watching her. It was Siksikai. Other men began to glance at her. If they thought it rude to look a person full in the face why did they all stare at her? She closed her eyes in helpless anguish, and when she opened them, she saw that two men, with their backs to her, talked to Siksikai. It was Apikunni and Nakoa, and when they turned toward her, she could see that she was the subject of their conversation. Her senses tightened, and her mouth became suddenly dry. What was happening was not good for her; she could feel it with certainty. Talk built everywhere around her now. Women were staring at her too. There was a sudden agitation as someone shoved toward the front of the crowd. It was Atsitsi.

"Now what I hear?" she shouted. Her little black eyes darting wildly around. "Ha! Siksikai and Nakoa talk!" She slapped her thigh, and showed her gums.

"Why do you always have to follow me?" Maria snarled.

"Like bee to sweet little flower," Atsitsi chirped. She grabbed a woman standing near them and shook her roughly. They talked in Pikuni and Maria could not follow their words, but gathered that Atsitsi was asking her questions. "Ha!" she said again with such glee that Maria felt panic. "Why are you so happy?" she asked her.

"Good world now," Atsitsi answered. She began to scratch happily.

Maria felt a chill, and the perspiration upon her body felt like ice. "What is it?" she asked. "Why is everyone staring at me?"

"To see if when you sweat, sweet bird song come from your body!"

Siksikai and Nakoa walked to the starting line of the racers. All talking around Maria stopped.

"They are going to race!" Maria said stupidly.

"No!" hissed Atsitsi back, pretending surprise.

"You old devil, Nakoa can't race—he's still wounded!"

"Nakoa doesn't race. His horse does."

"You're so smart!"

"All Indian smart. Even Nakoa now!"

"What are you talking about?"

Where Nakoa and Siksikai had stood mounted, there now appeared two bursts of dust, racing toward the crowd at the finishing line. Nakoa's horse had gained the lead and kept it, but as they approached, both quirting their horses savagely, no one shouted or cheered as they had done in the previous race. At the finish, both riders dismounted, and Siksikai silently handed his horse over to Nakoa.

"They bet their war horses!" Maria exclaimed in surprise because she had learned how valuable these animals were to the Indian.

"Siksikai bet horse. Nakoa not so stupid. He bet you!" Atsitsi said in triumph.

There it was again, in all of its terrible clarity. To Nakoa she was an animal to be traded for a horse. With black rage came darker despair. That night Maria paced Atsitsi's lodge like a caged animal. She hid her face in her hands. "To him I am a dog—a lowly dog!"

"No. He just like horse better! Now why you so mad?"

Maria picked up a piece of wood. "Don't speak to me! If you say another word I will kill you!" Tears coursed down her cheeks in spite of herself. She flung herself upon her couch.

"White woman fit all of time!" Atsitsi moaned. "Why not go outside and have fit? More room!" Atsitsi began to eat, and finally Maria quieted. From the inner circle came the sound of drums. "What is that?" Maria asked.

"Mutsik dance in council lodge; celebration 'cause you finally shut up."

Maria turned to the wall, a plan beginning to form in her mind. She remained quiet and pretended to sleep. Much later she cautiously turned over and saw that Atsitsi had fallen asleep, her mouth slack and spittle running from its corners.

"She must be having a good dream," Maria thought. "Atsitsi!" she whispered. "Atsitsi!"

The old woman started slightly, scratched and began to snore. Maria noiselessly left the lodge.

Laughter and singing were coming from the inner circle, and Maria walked toward it. The cool night air brushed her face, smelling as it always did of the pine from the mountains. Nakoa would be in the Mutsik lodge; the thought of seeing him in a few minutes made a tumult in her mind, a pounding in her blood.

"Who is this?" a voice asked suddenly.

Maria looked up at a tall shadowed form. "The white woman," she faltered. "I do not know you," she continued slowly in Pikuni.

"I am Siksikai."

Maria drew back in fear.

"Why is Nakoa's white woman walking alone at night without Atsitsi?"

"She fell asleep. I wanted some fresh air."

"You speak our tongue well."

"Atsitsi spends all day teaching it to me! That is, when Atsitsi is not eating."

Siksikai did not smile at her humor. Maria could see him better now, and he was studying her intently. "Has Atsitsi told you that Nakoa is to give you to me?"

Maria bowed her head. "Yes."

"I do not want to wait," he said suddenly.

"What do you mean?"

"You know my words. Come to my lodge with me now. Nakoa will not know."

Maria began to shake in fury. "It is to be that easy? From one to another?"

"I have looked at you." She started to back away from him, but he held her closely. One hand held her wrists and the other brushed her hair, her lashes and finally her lips. He kissed her mouth. "I have watched these lips," he whispered. "I have seen your breasts— naked—beautiful—and I will see the rest of you."

With a tremendous effort Maria broke away from him. "Move toward me, and I will scream!" she panted. "Nakoa almost killed you twice because of me!"

He remained still.

"You do not know that he will not keep me!"

"He will give you to me. Nitanna would have it no other way. What you do now will determine the way you will be treated as long as I have you."

"I have no choice. You will have to wait your turn—like the others—after you." In spite of her intent, she had begun to cry. She walked away from him, toward the inner lodges, and he made no attempt to restrain her.

"Remember my words," he said quietly, but she neither answered nor turned around.

Near the council lodge, she stopped to wipe the tears from her face. Inside there was loud laughter, and the drums began again.

"Maria!" a feminine voice called softly. "Maria!" It was Anatsa; Maria could tell by the crippled girl's walk as she came toward her. "Maria," she said, very agitated. "What are you doing here?"

"I am going to a dance," Maria said bitterly.

"It is for only the wives and sweethearts of the Mutsik!"

"Well, aren't I everybody's sweetheart?"

"What do you mean?"

"I know you have heard. Everybody in the village has heard. Anyone can be my lover. In your tongue I would be unclean. In my tongue I would be a whore. In either tongue, I am to be another Atsitsi!"

The little Indian girl took Maria's hand. Maria fought tears, and was surprised to see them spring into the Indian girl's eyes. "I know your pain," Anatsa said simply. "Come and sit with me before Onesta's lodge, and we will talk."

Wordlessly, they seated themselves before the darkened and quiet tipi, both watching the lighted council lodge so close to them.

"Where is Atsitsi?" Anatsa asked.

"Asleep. She won't get up until she gets hungry."

"Why did you walk here alone? This would make Nakoa very angry."

"I—hoped to see him. I want to talk with him."

"Inside there tonight there will be sacred ceremony. This night the women of Mutsik choose their lovers—the men they will accept."

"Do the women do the choosing?"

"In this dance they do. If a man does not want to be the woman's lover, he does not meet her in the Kissing Dance." Anatsa's slender hands began to twist again in her lap. She had been sick all day at the thought of a woman choosing Apikunni and his accepting her. Maria saw her hands.

"Anatsa," she said gently, "I think I know what is in your heart."

Anatsa looked startled. "What is in my heart?" she repeated.

"Yes. You love Apikunni."

Anatsa bowed her head.

"Why do you bow your head at love?"

"Because I am nothing before it. Love brings agony, but loving alone brings death. No there is not even the peace of death. There is just emptiness. Emptiness—with expectation gone."

"Why should expectation be gone for you?"

Tears now rushed suddenly down the thin cheeks. "How can

you ask this when you have seen me? Have you not seen that I am crippled and ugly, a thing that can never even grow into a woman? It is only a woman that can produce a son!"

"I see a beautiful young girl who has the most beautiful eyes that I have ever seen. I do not see just a crippled leg."

"If I existed for him at all—that is all he would see. But I do not exist for him—I cannot!"

"Little fool!" Maria scolded tenderly. "Little fool. You do exist, and you cannot destroy yourself by saying you are nothing. Does he know your love? Does he know your feelings? Does he know that you would take his face within your hands and kiss his lips and know nothing else in the world but the need to do it again and again?"

Anatsa looked at Maria strangely.

"Does he know that you would lie with him and in your love have all of the beauty of all of the women who ever loved a man? You can be drink that he will have to have—yes, you!" Anatsa looked into the beautiful shadowed face. Maria stood, feeling a strength that shook the prairie. "Such is the power of the woman who loves," she said softly. "It is as strong as the tide of the oceans—the pull of the earth. Anatsa," she said. "Get up. We will go to the sacred dance!"

"I have no sweetheart," Anatsa said.

"I give you one of mine!"

"Maria, it is serious ceremony!"

"And I am serious. Anatsa, I saw my father and sister die. My old life is dead, but I am not. I am living now, with each beating of my heart, and there is no place upon this earth for the living to hide. I will not hide, Anatsa, and neither will you."

"I cannot."

"Then I will go there alone."

"Maria, you cannot, you have been told not to leave Atsitsi's alone."

"Inside of the lodge I will be with the whole Mutsik."

"All right," Anatsa whispered, getting to her feet. "I will go with you."

Outside of the council lodge, Maria hesitated before she opened the doorflap. She saluted the sound of dancing and laughter within. "To our sweethearts," she said soberly.

When they entered the lodge, all of the drums stopped as if a magical wand had suddenly willed silence.

The men had been dancing, two rows of them facing each other. They stood still and looked at Maria and the trembling Anatsa. The women seated upon the sidelines looked at them too, and no one said anything. Maria saw Nakoa right away, and an amazed Apikunni. After the first long silence, Nakoa did not favor her with another glance, but signaled for the drummers to commence again, and the dancing was resumed.

"What ceremony is this?" Maria asked Anatsa.

"This is the dance for warriors who have never fled from a battle."

"Well, one just fled now!" Maria said.

Anatsa smiled, and Apikunni saw her smile and wondered which one of the Mutsik was her lover.

The women were slow to turn back to the dance of their husbands and sweethearts, seeming to find Anatsa and Maria more interesting.

The dance finally ended, and two more followed, the dance for men who had never been surrounded in battle, and the dance for men who gave most freely of their possessions. Nakoa was in both. "That is a good dance for him!" Maria said of the last, thinking of Siksikai, the horse race, and the way Nakoa had held her once and ignored her now.

Anatsa caught Apikunni's eyes upon her, and blushing, tried to move behind Maria. "Where are you going?" Maria asked angrily. "We haven't asked anyone to dance yet."

"Maria," Anatsa scolded. "These dances are sacred to the Indian. Do you see the stripes a man wears upon his leggings? Each one stands for an enemy killed in battle."

"Or that he is a skunk," Maria said.

"The cut pickets upon their shirts stand for the coups of stealing an enemy's horse. Stealing a great warrior's horse is as great a coup as stealing his scalp."

"And a lot more valuable than stealing his wife."

"Yes."

"Of course." He didn't even look at her. For forty days he had held her captive, and had branded her as a whore for the rest of her life, and now was even too godly to give her an angry glance! His complete indifference was the one thing she had never expected. When the drums finally stopped she was choking with rage. If I were chief of this village I would make him sleep with Atsitsi! Every night—and twice a day! she thought.

The men had gone back to their side of the room. "Now what are they doing?" Maria growled.

"They are preparing for the Kissing Dance. Oh, Maria, what can Apikunni think of my being here?"

"That you have a lover—I hope!"

"Maria, that is a lie!"

"So are all of them!" she said wrathfully, nodding at the men. At last, very softly now, the drums began again. Some of the women stood, and moved forward from the others still seated to watch the dance. They moved slowly and beautifully to the beat of the music. A solemn hush fell over the room. The women danced toward the line of men, and the men who responded to them with feeling rose to meet them. Anatsa's face became suddenly radiant. Apikunni remained seated!

Now the line of men approached the dancing women who began to sing sweetly, moving their hands and arms gracefully toward them. When the women had danced close enough to their men to touch them, the first woman touched her lover lightly upon the shoulders. He immediately drew her to him, and they kissed, and then the two of them danced between the lines of men and women. When they had gone from one end of the line to the other, they parted, each returning to his own line. The next woman chose her lover, with the singing and dancing resuming after they had kissed.

"Nakoa has remained seated," Anatsa whispered.

"He's probably tired from being so mean," Maria replied. She saw the dance as a moving and a beautiful ceremony in spite of herself. "Now which one will I choose?" Maria asked Anatsa flippantly.

Anatsa clutched at her arm. "Maria, you are pledged to Nakoa. A woman can have only one man. Adultery is severely punished!"

Behind her, Maria felt someone enter, and turning, saw Siksikai. He smiled at her, and hoping that Nakoa would see her, she smiled eagerly back. Anatsa began to stir uneasily. "I think we should leave," she said softly.

"No," Maria replied. "We have Apikunni stealing all kinds of looks over here. Now we can work on stone-mountain Nakoa next to him!" She glanced at him wrathfully as she spoke. From the men's line Siksikai caught her attention.

Rage made her sick. If Nakoa had lost his race this afternoon, Maria would have been forced to bed with Siksikai. She darted for the woman's line. Let Nakoa pretend not to see her now!

Behind her, she dimly heard Anatsa gasp, "Maria!" Blindly she went to Siksikai and touched his shoulders. Standing on her toes she kissed him upon the mouth. Let him not see her—now!

Her breath was knocked from her lungs. She had been flung to the floor with killing force. Blotting out all light, Nakoa stood over her again, his knife drawn and facing Siksikai. The drums had stopped. The singing had stopped. There was no sound, as though all of the world was dead and they were bloodless shadows in a frozen twilight.

Anatsa came swiftly to her and helped her to her feet. "He will kill me!" Maria sobbed.

"No," Anatsa said.

Maria hid her face against Anatsa. How could she not have remembered his awful wrath?

"If you ever touch this woman again before I am through with her, I will kill you!" she heard Nakoa say. "If you ever allow even her touch before she is yours, I will kill you!"

"Kill him now!" Apikunni shouted. Maria looked at him aghast.

"Kill the woman!" another said.

Maria moaned and with terrible effort faced Nakoa. He came to her and grasped her roughly by the arm. *"Akai-Sokahpse!"* he said low and savagely, and forced her toward the door. Terrified she

Nakoa's Woman

looked at Anatsa, and then Siksikai, and Nakoa saw her pleading.

"There is no one to help you now," he said and forced her outside of the lodge.

Chapter Nine

Hardly away from the lodge, Nakoa seized her and shook her by the shoulders. When she cried out, he slapped her across the face. She screamed in rage, and he slapped her again. She sprang at him like a wild animal, but was powerless against him.

"Fool! Fool!" he raged. "Are you so crazy to have a man inside of you that you have to come to my tribal society to straddle them all?"

"How dare you! You unspeakable despicable . . ."

"Speak my tongue!"

"Savage! Savage!"

He slapped her again. She bit her mouth and blood came to her lips.

"I know that word," he said low and ominously. "You will never use that word for me again." His hands had tightened upon her flesh. He shook her again. "Answer me!"

She hung her head, her long hair covering her face, blood running unchecked to her chin.

"I know the word for you that the white man gave Atsitsi. Harlot. Harlot. If you are a harlot, why did you fight me at the river? For what were you crying when I started to enter you? You have made me a fool, waiting to take you as my wife!"

"As your wife? You are marrying Nitanna!"

"As my second wife! I have waited—when now I will not wait! I have wanted you to keep."

"Siksikai—I am to go to Siksikai—and then everyone else. Atsitsi said—"

"I can change that."

"You told the high chiefs—"

"I am the high chief. I am next to my father. You are mine to do with as I will. If I decide to keep you, I can. If I decide to kill you, I can." He forced her to walk with him, toward his darkened lodge.

"Where are we going?"

"To my lodge."

"Why?"

"To lie upon my couch. I will sleep with you tonight. I will try you and see how many more nights you will stay with me."

She began to sob. "You did not weep in there," he said. "You did not weep when you invited Siksikai to your bed tonight and told the whole village that you are a harlot!"

Maria looked up at him in a rage. "You will not be called a savage by me; I will not be called a harlot by you. I cannot beat you, and I cannot kill you, but don't you call me a harlot again!"

He pulled her inside his lodge, and built a fire. He looked at her as she crept close to it, trying to control her shivering. "Isn't this the time for you to take off your dress?" he asked her quietly.

"I will not take it off," she said. "You can do it for me—like you did my chemise!" She would not cry again, but she would not look at him either. He turned her face toward his.

"What did you want tonight, Maria?" he asked.

"To make you angry," she blurted.

"Why?"

"For over forty days you have ignored me! You have not looked at me, spoken to me, and yet you have told your people that I am to be your mistress and the village whore when you marry this—Nitanna!"

"I have kept from you—to make you my second wife. I have kept you clean so I wouldn't have to trade you!"

"Why couldn't I have known this?"

"Because I didn't know it myself until tonight!" he said. "Maria," he added, studying her face, "do you want Siksikai?"

"No. Dear God, no! I will not be raped by any man!"

"You will accept me," he said fiercely.

They looked at each other angrily. Suddenly tears came into Maria's eyes. "Can't you show me kindness—some tenderness?" Close to him, Maria felt the strength and buckskin smell of him again. "Are you going to take me without one kiss?" she asked him.

His black eyes searched hers. "I kissed you outside the village, and you met my feeling of tenderness with hatred. No, I will not kiss you. And I will not use you as a harlot. I cannot make you my first wife, Maria, but I will make you my second wife. I cannot give you up."

"If you will not kiss me, then I will kiss you," she breathed, kissing his lips. Immediately she was held in his embrace and the wildness and the wonder came to them with the same potency that it had the first time, outside the village. When he finally restrained her, they were both shaken.

"Maria," he said, "what you did tonight was a blind and dangerous thing. Stay away from Siksikai."

"I could tell him the dance had no meaning to me."

"Tell him nothing! I will have it announced that you are to be my second wife. That is all he needs to be told!" He was becoming angry again.

"Nakoa, would you have traded me?"

"Yes." He made no attempt to avoid her eyes.

"From the very first, did you want me just for a mistress? Is that all?"

He smiled. "Wasn't that enough?"

"Because you saved my life? No. If you had done what you intended, it would have been better for me to have been killed."

"Not for me!" His eyes went to her lips and breasts and back to her own gaze. "You are a beautiful woman. I knew you would bring me pleasure, and I was there to capture you."

"Did you not think at all of what I would feel?"

He took her in his arms again. "I will say what we both know. At the river—when I held you naked—when never was I so mad to enter a woman—"

"There have been several?"

He ignored her question. "I did not. I did not do what I wanted

Nakoa's Woman

to do, so I knew your feelings. I have known them ever since."

"Then after that morning you didn't ever intend to trade me?"

"I will not give you up, and so I will not make you my mistress now. I do not want to give you up when I marry Nitanna." At the mention of Nitanna, Maria kissed Nakoa again, but he resisted her embrace. "I will take you back to Atsitsi's" he said gently. "I should not have kept you here so long."

At the outer tipis the fires had died and the village was in total darkness. At Atsitsi's lodge, Maria turned to Nakoa and huddled against him. "I do not want to leave you," she whispered. "Can't we stay here and talk?"

He touched the thinness of her dress over her shoulders. "You are cold. Maria, you will have to start wearing the dress of an Indian woman."

"All right." She sat apart from Atsitsi's lodge, and he sat near her, putting his arm around her shoulders and shielding her with his warmth. "That is why a man is born," he said, smiling.

"Why?" Maria asked.

"To keep coldness from a woman."

"A woman?"

"His woman," he said tenderly. "Maria," he continued, "you have come to a new life. Hear my words, Culentet, with your heart."

"Culentet? What does that mean?"

"My little white bird. It is an expression of . . ." He stopped.

"Of love?" Maria asked.

He kissed her hands and then studied her face gravely.

"Maria, hear my words. When the flame burns, it does not always give warmth. Darkness comes at the end of every day, or we would not know the beauty of the sunrise or of the sunset."

"What are you saying?"

"I am saying that you are in Indian land and your path will be strange and hard. This is the beginning, and pain seldom starts in the beginning. You will have to accept."

"I can accept you! I want you!"

"Maria, you will have to accept much more! Culentet, that is why we live! To accept the joys and burdens of the body. In our flesh we live to accept the will of the Great Spirit. We accept, and we move with the will of the Great Spirit, for we cannot move against it. Whether you walk in the Indian's way or the white man's way, you will have to accept. Strange paths are harder to follow and there is an undying loneliness in the soul of every man and every woman. That is why we are seeking— seeking—but in our endless seeking we still must accept!"

"Nakoa . . ." She tried to touch him tenderly again, but he held her hands stilled.

"Accept not through me, Maria. Your old life is gone, and I cannot replace it. I can warm you now, but you will be naked in the wind until you accept a new life."

"I eat your food, I have learned your tongue. I will wear the dress of an Indian woman. I will be your wife."

"Culentet! There is more than just accepting me or my people, for when you do this your old life will be gone and there will be nothing left but yourself. You will be alone! What is it that you bring to me? Are you bringing the innocence that wept in terror at rape, or the harlot who went to Siksikai and asked to be his mistress so I would make her mine this evening?"

Maria hung her head sorrowfully and made no reply.

"Do you think that I do not know the touch of a woman's lips? Do you think that I don't know when a woman wants me? Maria, you wanted this before we even reached this village!"

"I know it. I know it," she said sadly.

He tenderly touched her face. "And now the sadness is back at feeling this—for an Indian. Yet when your dead are truly accepted in your heart, and your past is really buried upon the white man's trail, then you will come to me as neither virgin nor harlot, and you will accept me as a man."

"It has been so hard for me," Maria said. She saw Edward Frame dying and shuddered convulsively.

"It is too cold for you here," Nakoa said. "It is time for you to go to your couch and dream long dreams." He kissed her once more. "Perhaps in our dreams we will meet," he said, and left her at Atsitsi's door.

Atsitsi still slept by the cold firepit, and Maria left her there. She stretched out upon her couch looking up at the stars through the smoke hole of the tipi. His lips were still warm upon hers. He had said he loved her.

From a nearby lodge came the sudden wailing of a medicine man. "Listen Sun to what I say! Hear the wailing of this mother! Take pity upon the sickness of this child!"

Speak the voice and cry the heart. This is still the most tender of nights and beyond all of the suns is someone who does care.

"Maria," Anatsa said, "I do not like Siksikai. He is shadow and darkness to me, the coldness of the deep earth where the white men are said to bury their dead."

Maria and Anatsa had gone to the lake to bathe, for there they had privacy. They had walked the extra distance because Atsitsi did not follow them there. They had bathed, and after dressing, were lying in the morning sun.

"If you had chosen any man—any man—but Siksikai!" Anatsa went on.

"I am sorry for what I did. I was someone else, someone that comes into me and does these terrible things, as when I scratched Nakoa's face. It is as if some part of me is not hurt enough and wants to suffer more!"

Anatsa sat up, and shivered. "I am cold, yet the sun is still warm upon us. Maria, there are voices in the wind, and in the sound of the little bells moving on the ears of all the tipis at night. I hear this, and I know."

"Anatsa, Anatsa!"

"Those that have moved here before us, for all of the years passed and long lost on the Indian time stick, still talk of the circle of their lives. The roundness of living is repeated and repeated." The frail girl shivered, and her beautiful eyes were luminous with the strange expression that Maria had seen in them the first day they had met. "My body is weak," she whispered, "and so there is a different strength within me that you—and many others—do not have. I know things, in waking dreams, in pictures and in sounds that you cannot know."

"Anatsa, do not be so upset at my foolishness!"

"The coldness that has touched me does not come from across the lake," Anatsa said, still lost within herself. She grasped Maria's hands, and looked searchingly into Maria's eyes. "Siksikai is your death, Maria," she said quietly.

"Anatsa, he will not bother me. He is afraid of Nakoa."

"You have committed your body to him. You have asked for his possession."

"I did not mean it! You know this!"

"Your actions have started the circle and every circle has to meet its beginning."

"You talk strangely too, like Nakoa."

"Nakoa is a wise man, like his father. Natosin is far wiser even than Isokinuhkin, our medicine man, because Isokinuhkin thinks only of the body and the beating of the heart. My body is nothing, but I know that I go far beyond its frailty."

Maria squeezed Anatsa's hand. "Love your body, Anatsa, for no matter what you believe about death and life, now you are your body."

"No! No! All of me is not—crippled!" The girl shook in anger.

"I am sorry," Maria whispered. "Everything I do and everything I say in this village is wrong."

"Nakoa has told me," Anatsa went on, slowly, "that I am the song of a bird. Do you know what such words from Nakoa mean?"

"You are the song of a bird? Why he thinks you are sweet and . . ."

"How lasting is the song of a bird? The bird comes from the earth and goes back to the earth, but its song trembles sweetly in the air and becomes nothing, and is no longer even part of the bird."

"Anatsa, you cannot think like this!"

From the trees above them came the call of the gambel sparrow, echoing in three notes twice repeated, and six plaintive little sounds came down from the tall pines and then were gone. Anatsa looked up. "Six notes," she said softly. "Six notes falling slowly with sweet sound. Now they are gone, Maria, and did we really hear them at all?"

"Anatsa, I will not listen to you talk such nonsense. How can that bird singing have anything to do with you? Maybe you hear the wind at night moving the bells of the tipis, and the sound of them makes you dream something. But what is a dream?"

Anatsa looked at Maria strangely. "They are my dreams," she said. "The Indian has always listened to the speaking of his dreams. Every brave seeks his medicine in a dream. If the bravest warrior dreams a bad dream before battle, he will not fight. The voice within him is a sacred voice, and is the voice of the Sun."

Maria looked away. "I will not argue with you if this is part of your religion—your talk with the Great Spirit."

"We all walk our own path," Anatsa said, "and every path leads to the sun."

Maria sighed. "I do not follow your words."

"About Nakoa," Anatsa said, "I cannot ask, if it is not in your heart to tell me."

"He did not hurt me last night," Maria said. "He slapped my face in great rage, but his touch was not strong, and when we had finished talking, our talk with each other was not angry." Hotness came to Maria's face, and she clasped her hands tightly. "He is not taking me—the way he was. He is going to make me his second wife."

"Maria! Maria!" Anatsa exclaimed softly. "You can have a good life with us now! Maria, you will not be unclean, and as Nakoa's wife . . ."

"Second wife," Maria said, her voice bitter.

Anatsa heard the bitterness, and some of the gladness left her face. "You will be under the protection of Nakoa," she said. "You will be kept clean. You can have a voice to speak to the Great Spirit! Nakoa will always be rich, Maria. Any girl in this village would give deep thanks to be Nakoa's second wife!"

"I do not want to be farmed out."

"I do not know your last words."

"I do not want to be used by every man in your village, but I do not want marriage with Nakoa either. I do not want to be—"

"To be what?"

Two other women had come to the lake, and Anatsa whispered

so that they wouldn't hear.

"I do not want to be a second wife," Maria said.

"You will have to accept this," Anatsa said. "Accept this and be thankful in your heart that you are being taken in marriage. When it is announced that Nakoa will marry you after he marries Nitanna, Siksikai will not harm you. He is afraid of Nakoa, for he knows Nakoa would enjoy ending his life."

Maria looked affectionately at Anatsa. "Why do you think of death and killing and shadowed dreams when your thoughts should be on marriage and children?"

"I will not marry," said Anatsa.

"There were six notes even to that bird's song. If you are the song of a bird, you have to take six steps, too!"

Anatsa smiled.

"You were born . . ."

"And I was crippled."

"And you were crippled, and you fell in love."

Color came to Anatsa's thin face.

"There are three steps already!"

"And I have grown in friendship with a white woman."

"Then you must take the fifth step, little bird! You must marry!"

"Maria, Apikunni does not know me."

"He looked you full in the face at the Kissing Dance. Is this usually done?"

"No."

"Then you will take the fifth step and marry Apikunni."

Anatsa laughed, the first time that Maria had ever seen her laugh. Her eyes shone. "Tell me how! You worked your magic on Nakoa. Give me some of the magic that you brought from the land of the rising sun!"

"I will! I will tell that you have a lover in the Mutsik, and you must tell no one that this is not true. I will tell the whole village this."

Anatsa laughed again. "And how can you tell the whole village this?"

"By telling Atsitsi of course!"

Anatsa smiled, then shook her head. "I do not want it thought that I would go to a man's couch without marriage!"

"Of course you do not. I am sorry for what I said."

"I walk in the shadow of those who are whole, but I am not only my body. If I could, I would not give the body that I have to a man —to a man that . . . No, I speak with straight tongue— not even to Apikunni!"

Maria understood her faltering words. "I know that you wouldn't," she said. She looked at Anatsa and heard a soft Spanish lullaby, and then saw her mother's face cold and waxen in her coffin and the white naked breasts of Meg Summers. She shuddered.

"Why do you tremble, Maria?" Anatsa asked.

Maria looked out at the lake. "It is those women in the water. They must be cold." The two women were swimming. The Blackfoot were strong swimmers, and the women used a stroke that Maria had never seen before. They did not use the breaststroke of the white man, but drew one arm at a time entirely out of the water and reached forward and pushed back with it. They seemed to move faster with much less fatigue.

"That is not why you shuddered," said Anatsa.

"Your words made me think of my mother. You are a lady, Anatsa. A true lady. I have only known two of them. My mother, and Ana, my baby sister." And they are both dead. They are both dead, but the breasts of Meg Summers are alive and warm.

They walked slowly back to the village. Anatsa left her, and went toward the inner lodges, and Maria saw her nephew Mikapi run to meet her. Anatsa ruffled his hair affectionately, and then placed her hand upon his shoulders, as the two of them talked excitedly. Maria watched them until they were out of her sight, and then turned toward Atsitsi's.

Apikunni and Anatsa

Chapter Ten

The spring of 1846 had been unusually warm and mild. Summer came early to the prairie; it touched the columbine, gaillardia, and the mountain golden rod, and they all bloomed before their time. Because the warmth of summer had come early, the running time of the buffalo, usually in the moon when the leaves turn, came in the moon of the flowers. Less than thirty miles from the village their shaggy forms blackened the prairie for miles around, and so it had to be the time for their hunting.

All the societies of the Ikunuhkahtsi, except the Knatsomita and some of the Mutsik, left with their women for the buffalo grounds. The warriors that remained behind were to guard the village. For in this year, known on the Indian time stick as the sun of early spring, there had been seen sure sign of an enemy.

The Blackfoot nation with its three tribes of Pikuni, Kainah, and Siksikauwa, and their two allies, the Sarcee and Atskina, protected their lands with studied vigilance—but their land was vast. Their holdings stretched from the northern branch of the Saskatchewan River in Canada, south to the mouth of the Yellowstone, and from the western summits of the Rockies east into the land of the Crow and the Dahcotah. Beyond this land was the Blackfoot enemy, the Crees to the north, the Assinoboines to the east, the Snakes, Kabspels, and Kutenais to the southwest and west. But most dreaded and hated of all was the Crow from the Badlands. For the Crow alone came boldly into Blackfoot land in the eternal Indian search for coups. To the Crow, a woman's scalp, taken within sight of her village, counted as a coup equal to an Indian male's, or the stealing of a great warrior's horse.

In that moon of the flowers, in July 1846, at the time of the great buffalo hunt, came the first sign of the Crow. There was a stray dog found near the village with a pack of Crow moccasins tied to his back, bruised grass made by a camp was seen in a mountain meadow, strange moccasin markings were discovered in the mud of a mountain stream bed, and so it was clearly known that a Crow war party was waiting in the mountains for the taking of scalps. The Mutsik who remained in the village rode out on patrol of the camp's surrounding territory, and when they rode back, they were met by the Knatsomita, who did not return to the village until daybreak. Separate war parties rode to the mountains. Braves, mounted on warhorses, wearing war shirts of two thicknesses and carrying skinning knives for the lifting of scalps, became a common sight to Maria. She saw at close range the ash war bow and the war quivers filled with barbed arrows, glued so lightly to the shaft that the point of the arrow would remain in the wounded man even after the shaft was removed. Each warrior's quiver contained one hundred arrows; he could fire from fifteen to twenty in one minute.

During the new vigilance the women were told to use the lake and to walk to the river only in the light of full day. They were to travel in groups, and to follow only the paths guarded by mounted Mutsik. Anatsa and Maria went to the lake together, but when Anatsa's sister Apeecheken became ill in her pregnancy, it fell completely upon Anatsa to bring wood back from the river. At first Mikapi accompanied her, but with the inconsistency of a child, he became bored, and let Anatsa go with the women while he rode with some of the men, or gamboled with the other young boys of the tribe. Even with the other women, Anatsa hated going to the river, because across from it were the Pikuni burial grounds, with their dead buried openly on platforms high in the trees. She had been to the grounds only once, and she would never go again. There the sky had a different color to her, the wind a different sound, and the sky and the wind were both hungry to imprison her there forever. She could not remember when she had started fearing the dead sleeping across the water. She must have been born afraid of their

Nakoa's Woman

shadow.

On the second day after the hunters had gone to seek the buffalo, Anatsa walked to the river, lagging behind the other women. Maria was not with her, and walking in the hot sunlight, she began to feel terribly alone and lost from the village behind her and the women ahead of her. If the Mutsik were patrolling the path she did not meet them. Anxiously she struggled to catch up with the women.

The banks of the river were cool, and deeply shaded. Anatsa gathered the scrub wood from among the willow thickets and snowberry bushes, listening to the murmuring voices of the women working to her right. The river rushed loudly through the groves of aspen and cottonwood that bordered it, and its noise made her unaware that the other women had gone.

She straightened, and listened intently for their voices. There was no sound of them above the water. Hastily, without even enough wood, Anatsa turned to go back to the village. She passed a bush of serviceberries, now ripe and ready for picking. She could have gathered some; Apeecheken could eat berries if she couldn't eat meat, but Anatsa was too afraid to stop. All of her body listened for a strange or an alien movement, and her heart began to beat frantically with the feeling that she was not in the thicket alone. Would the scalp of a crippled woman count as a coup? Why would it not? she thought. Her scalp would bear no mark of a crippled leg!

Through the shadows of the trees she walked quietly, trying to move without any sound at all. In the willows ahead of her she saw a slight motion, but it was so slight that it could have been just a movement of the wind or the quick touch of some light-footed animal. Anatsa stopped and hugged the wood that she had gathered to her breast. Someone stood behind the willows; she knew this. Her heart struck at her in terror. Minutes passed, and she still remained motionless. The wind moved suddenly through the aspens, making them glitter with the sunlight they hid from her, and then the cottonwoods moved too, more slowly and lazily. The river rushed monotonously on, washing the shore of the dead, its water keeping the restless spirits of the ghost hills from the Blackfoot camp. Oh, if she were dead, she would travel the great Wolf Trail and never come back to stir unrest among the living! She would never speak through the air and the wind that another would come soon to rest beside her.

Something ahead moved again, and Anatsa saw a tall man in buckskin. She screamed and dropping her wood, tried to run from the thicket. "Anatsa!" someone shouted, and she stopped running, panting wildly. Apikunni walked to her. "Why are you here alone?" he asked her angrily. "Why have you come for wood at all?"

Shaking violently, Anatsa looked down. "There is no one else," she said finally. "Apeecheken is sick with her baby."

"You could come with the other women," he said sternly.

"I cannot keep up with them."

"I could have been Crow," he said, still angry. "This morning their prints were found across the river, in the burial grounds."

With her head averted from him, Anatsa walked slowly back to her wood. He followed her, watching her limp, seeing her drag her almost useless leg. She knew that he watched her leg, and her face became hot with misery.

"The Crow do not enter a burial ground at night either," he said. "They have been there when women were here, gathering wood."

"I am sorry," Anatsa whispered.

"You can't even run!"

She looked up into his face for the first time. "Or walk," she said quietly. Their eyes held for a moment.

"Tomorrow I will come with you, and I will see that you return safely to the village. Do not ever come here alone again!"

"All right," Anatsa said softly. She started through the thicket, and on the prairie, she saw Apikunni's horse. He followed her and mounted his horse, riding slowly beside her. For a while they didn't speak, Anatsa becoming more and more aware of her dragging walk. "I do not want you to wait for me!" she said suddenly.

"I will ride with you every day like this," he said shortly.

The wood began to scratch Anatsa's arms. When she had learned that Apikunni had not gone to the hunt with Nakoa and most of the Mutsik she had felt joy, but now that he was so close beside her, and spoke to her, she fervently wished that the earth would open up and swallow her. The wood was miserable. If she stopped and shifted it so that she would be more comfortable, she would be with him longer, and she couldn't bear it. Her growing misery was broken by the sight of Maria walking toward them, followed at a distance by the sweating Atsitsi.

"You get by-damn wood!" Atsitsi was shouting.

"If I get the wood, I'll have my own fire!" Maria shouted back.

"Full of big Maria now because Nakoa take you after Nitanna! He never marry you, no matter what he say! He never marry you—big fool Maria!"

"Oh, shut up!" Maria shouted. She saw Anatsa and Apikunni and smiled. "Tonight Atsitsi and I are going to have two fires," she said.

"Hers and mine! Now that I am going to be wife to Nakoa, she can get her own wood!"

Atsitsi had caught up with her. "White woman full of Maria now," she said.

Apikunni and Anatsa looked puzzled, for they could not follow Atsitsi when she broke into English.

Atsitsi scowled at Apikunni and scratched herself. "Why do you ride with Anatsa?" she asked him.

"Crow have been at the burial grounds. Do not go to the river by yourselves. After I take Anatsa to the village, I will come back and ride to the river with you."

Maria laughed. "No Crow, no matter how ragged and starved for coups, would get near me with angel Atsitsi protecting me. That is all she has to do just smell for them!"

"I protect you for hell!" Atsitsi raged, and sat down. "We wait," she said in Pikuni, and Maria sat down too, but a good distance away.

Apikunni smiled at Anatsa as they left Maria and Atsitsi alone. "They have their own language," he said. "Nakoa's woman is very beautiful," he added.

Anatsa felt like nothing beside the incomparable beauty of Maria. The wood had scratched her arm, and shifting its position, she scratched herself again. Her arm was bleeding.

"You have hurt yourself," Apikunni said. He reached down suddenly and took the wood. She was so thin; he had never before known that she was so delicate. He had heard that she prepared skins for lodges and clothing faster than any woman in the village, yet how could she even flesh a hide and soften it when she was so frail? She looked terribly unhappy. "What is the matter, Anatsa?" he asked her gently.

"You should not carry my wood."

"That is not why you look at the ground and act afraid to meet my eyes."

She said nothing, and he saw the hot flushing of her cheeks.

"You are friends with the white woman," he said, trying to put her at ease with him.

"Yes," she said briefly, still averting her face.

"She is beautiful, but she will bring no happiness to Nakoa."

"Why do you say this?" Anatsa asked.

"She is white."

"What reason is that?"

"She will always want her own people. She will not accept the people of Nakoa, and if she cannot accept them, she cannot accept him."

"Why couldn't a white woman accept us?"

"We do not walk in the white man's way or wear his dress, and because we do not he thinks of us as animals, no better than the buffalo that he destroys without reason on our prairie."

"How do you know this?"

"Natosin has talked to me of the white men. He used to travel to the Mandan villages and visit with his friend Mantatohpa before the sickness brought to them from the white man killed them all. The white man came to the Mandans in trade, and because the Mandans accepted them, sickness from the white man's boats killed every man, woman, and child in their village. Natosin was there when they died. That is when all of his wives and children except Nakoa died with the sickness too."

"Did Natosin see the white man too?"

"Natosin met only one white man, a medicine man who came among the Mandans to draw the Indian. He lived among the Mandans and the Dahcotah and persuaded some Indians to go back with him to the white man's land, and there the white man looked upon the Indian with mockery and set him apart from men. The white medicine man had accepted the Indian with open heart, but the whites don't listen to the voice of their medicine men."

"Maria does not look upon us as something apart from men."

"Maria is held as Nakoa's captive. She cannot be free in her thinking."

"Maria does not think with the mind of others! This is done by people with fear in their hearts, and Maria knows no fear!" For the first time Anatsa completely forgot herself and was fully communicating with Apikunni. Her beautiful eyes were flashing in anger and Apikunni looked at her strangely. He had never seen her before.

"Why do you become angry?" he asked softly.

"The white woman knows no fear," Anatsa repeated stubbornly.

"Or wisdom. What did she think Nakoa's feelings would be when she scratched his face and went to the Kissing Dance and chose Siksikai as her lover?"

"Who has thought of her feelings? She is white, but she has the feelings of an Indian! He should not even force her to marry him!" Apikunni looked at Anatsa in astonishment. "She is his!" he said. "She is his!" Anatsa mimicked furiously. "She is his!"

"He saved her life. He wants her and she is a white woman!"

"Oh, oh! So she should be destroyed—like the white man kills the buffalo?" Anatsa was shaking in rage. Apikunni watched her wordlessly. Her face was flushed and she met his eyes fearlessly. Why had he thought her pale, a shadow of a woman? He began to smile down at her thin outraged face. "What should Nakoa do with this woman?" he asked.

"He should set her free!"

"How? Where would he take her?"

"To the Nez Perces! They trade with the white man."

"But they are our enemies!"

"It makes no difference."

She walked indignantly ahead of him, her head held high. Grinning to himself, he followed her all of the way through the village, from the outer tipis to the inner circle of the high chiefs, and everywhere they walked, women stopped working and stared in astonishment at a brave carrying a woman's wood. They came finally to Apeecheken who stood wordlessly at the door of her lodge. Never had she seen her little sister so haughty. When Apikunni handed Anatsa the wood, she refused to touch it, dropping it disdainfully at his feet. She then went inside, and Apikunni looked after her, still smiling. "The little flower has thorns," he said, and rode his horse away.

Apeecheken angrily flung open the doorflap. "Now what is this? Is this what the Mutsik is to do for us now—carry a woman's wood? What would he have done if he had met Crow, defended you with a serviceberry twig?"

The next morning Apeecheken became violently ill. She began to vomit and did not stop. She grew so weak that she could not leave the tipi. Isokinuhkin was sent for and said that she would lose her baby. Onesta would not leave his lodge, but sat outside of it, his face drawn and suffering. "I am afraid she will die," he told Anatsa. "If she can not eat, the baby will die, and when a woman's baby dies within her she dies too."

Anatsa stirred food she was cooking for Onesta and Mikapi.

"She has to have food," Onesta said despairingly.

"I have boiled her beard tongue, and gray leaves and apoksikim. The only thing left that could make her eat is otsqueeina. The berries are ripe now, but they are in the mountains."

"Does not Isokinuhkin have the berries?"

"No. I have asked him. No woman in the village has any either."

"Do you know where they are in the mountains?"

"Yes. I have gathered them with the women."

"Then you will ride to the mountains today. One of the Mutsik can go with you. I will go to tell Natosin." Onesta left, and Anatsa and Mikapi ate hurriedly and in silence. From the inside of the lodge came the sound of Apeecheken's vomiting.

"Anatsa." Apeecheken called weakly, and Anatsa went to her.

"I would like water," Apeecheken said, wiping her face. Anatsa held her head and helped her drink. She heard Onesta's voice, and the sound of the Mutsik who was already waiting for her.

"I am going to the mountains to get you otsqueeina," she said to her sister. "You will eat by tomorrow."

Apeecheken lay back on her couch exhausted. The Mutsik was talking to Onesta now, his voice clear to Anatsa's ears. It was Apikunni! She stood still, and then with shaking hands hastily changed into another dress.

Apeecheken began to watch her with interest. Anatsa had selected a dress she had never worn before, and around her neck, hidden in the dress, she wore two little bags of meadow rue berries. She combed and braided her hair carefully, and then brushed it with the oil of sweet pine.

Apeecheken sighed. "You tremble, and your face glows, and you wear meadow rue berries and scent your hair with pine—all so you can be like this!"

Anatsa was silent, and Apeecheken looked at her tenderly. "Do not look so stricken, Anatsa. You are no different from the rest of us."

Anatsa clutched at the meadow rue berries, her eyes filling with tears. "Oh, if only I truly was not different," she said softly, and went outside.

Apikunni smiled at her, his face warm. He held a horse for her, a light-footed mare, already blanketed and bridled. Anatsa smiled shyly back at him, and mounted the mare. Apikunni gestured to Onesta and then led Anatsa from the inner circle of high chiefs.

They rode without words through all of the outer tipis. Anatsa hung her head, and clutched her hands. Why hadn't she spoken to him? Would all of the long day find her tongue dumb?

The smoke from the cooking fires rose in a haze over all of the tipis. The smell of burning wood and cooking meat was all around them, and curious eyes followed them from sight. Why would Apikunni be with her? the eyes would say, and then the voices would speak and the tongues move and say, "Anatsa is a cripple! Anatsa is a cripple!" Maria said that I am not my leg, Anatsa thought fiercely to herself.

They rode out of the village, and on the prairie the horses pranced spiritedly through the tall bunch grass. They passed the lake, calm and unruffled with no bathers or swimmers. In the shadow of the mountains they rode into carpets of pink loco weed, blue and white phacelia, and meadows colored with bluebells and Indian paintbrush. Their trail suddenly became steep and unmarked. Anatsa had given Apikunni the general direction they were to follow, but he picked their trail himself, avoiding both hilltops and ravines. He looked back at her when they entered the forest and smiled. "Your eyes do not flash fire this morning," he said briefly, and said no more, because talk on the trail could be dangerous.

Anatsa watched him as he rode ahead. She knew that he studied every clump of trees, every group of tall ferns for any movement, any flashing of color. The mountains near the village were searched constantly by the Mutsik; she knew this and told herself that patrols were near the trail that Apikunni chose, but still she watched his exposed back and began to feel anxiety. She shivered. The sky seemed to her to have suddenly changed color, to be blue no longer. Yellow light gleamed evilly through the forest; she sensed that death followed them with pale eyes, like a killer cat. If only she were riding behind him on his horse and could protect his back with her body! Her hands grew numb, and when from the trees about them came the two toned cry of the curlew and then the soft notes of the myrtle warbler, she became convulsed in terror.

Apikunni turned and saw her face. He stopped his horse, and in silence they both sat among the thick trees, listening. Slowly Apikunni's glance traveled all around them. Gradually the yellow light lifted; evil slipped into the shadow, and the sun came and made the sky above them blue again. He saw the change in Anatsa's face, the fear and the terror were receding. Looking at her curiously, he prodded his horse onward once more.

They came to the higher reaches of the mountains, the region of pine and spruce. Their path hit shale, white and barren, burning now in the hot sun. They reached a shadowed stream, the horses walking up against its current, fetlock deep in its rushing waters. It was this stream that led to the meadow they sought.

"Here is your meadow," Apikunni said, and Anatsa dismounted and started to gather the otsqueeina. Anatsa looked back at Apikunni. He had set the horse grazing on the summer thistle of which they were so fond, and was studying the grasses all around them. A black-tailed deer moved suddenly across the meadow; except for it, there was no sign of animal or man. Hastily, Anatsa filled her parfleche bag with cool, moist berries. It was a beautiful day. She looked at the shining green of the meadow, at the deep sky and softly moving clouds. She would never forget this day—the day she spent alone with Apikunni.

When he saw that she had filled her bag, he led the horses to where she stood and silently helped her mount. With Indian caution he chose a different route down the mountain, and soon they followed the course of another stream. Branches slapped ruthlessly at them; the horses slipped and stumbled on rocks and pebbles, brushing them sharply against the banks, and they rode on and on in the ribboned sunlight with not a word between them. They were nearing the foothills, for Anatsa recognized the vicinity of her glen. She began to feel some of its power, and wondering at herself, Anatsa signaled Apikunni to leave the stream and follow her. He looked amused, and motioned her ahead, for now they were close to the prairie and the Blackfoot camp. Smiling, she set the trail, and for a while they traveled in the hot sunlight, and the horses began to sweat. Ahead of them two mountain slopes came together and here was her glen. Here was a smaller stream, gently moving; for a while the water was caught in a pool, a shadow of refuge in the summer heat. By it, Anatsa halted her horse, dismounting and looking up at Apikunni with shining eyes. "This is my place," she said softly.

He slid from his horse. "It is beautiful," he said, captured by her eyes. He sat with her at the edge of the pool. The stream had been caught in a beaver dam and as it moved away, ripples pushed out at its mossy banks.

Her luminous eyes held him enchanted. They held deeper

serenity than the water. Outside their refuge the forest hummed with life and heat. He felt a hunger he had never known. He studied her face soberly, and when she shyly turned away, he reached for her thin shoulders and brought her lips to his. At the feel of her frailty he burned to take more of her and was torn between the desire to seize her entirely and the need to shield her innocence. The confusion of his emotions made him dizzy. When he looked at her again, she was stretched out upon her stomach, lying upon the soft moss.

"Why is this—your place?" he asked her, his heart still pounding enough to keep him aware of its agitation.

"This glen nourishes me," she said, smiling up at him. A bed of wild strawberries lay near them, and she plucked a berry, putting it into her mouth, making a wry face.

"I hope it feeds you better than that," he answered with a boyish grin.

"Oh, it does," she answered quickly. "Here, I could even accept your kiss."

"Was that so hard for you to do?"

"Yes."

He looked deeply hurt. "You do have a lover! I could not believe it; I could not believe that you have accepted a man!"

"I have!" she flashed angrily, thinking he mocked her leg. "I have met him here, I have met him here many times!"

Now he looked away from her, deeply depressed. "Do not speak to me of it."

"I will. I lie here with him, and upon this moss we sleep through many afternoons together. He kisses me and I kiss him."

"Stop your words. They are not for me."

"And here I also have the forest people that I have created, that live in those great ferns, and when I come here, they sing happily, and talk lovingly and tell me that I am—I am." She stopped, tears rushing down her cheeks. "Apikunni, it is all created by me. The people, the songs—and you as my lover! That is why it was so hard for me to accept your embrace."

"Why?"

"Because it is wrong for me to love you! I am crippled, and I cannot even crawl like a baby! This is my secret place just for dreams. I have no right to bring you into them."

Trembling within himself, he covered her shaking hands with his own.

"Do not pity me," she whispered.

He gently wiped away the tears that were still falling from her closed lashes. He took her in his arms and kissed her again, warming her whole body with his. He kept embracing her until she relaxed. He kissed her until she forgot about herself and knew only his rising passion. He kissed her until she met him with a passion equal to his own. Finally, in exquisite tenderness they separated, and looked into each other's eyes. He then picked some swamp laurel that bloomed near them, and handed her the pink flowers. She smelled them, and with her large eyes luminous with feeling, held them to her lips. She was the most beautiful of women.

Outside of the glen, the touch of the sun was warm and untroubled. A wisp of cloud moved against the blue sky. High above them she could see a curlew circling, and then its shadow skimmed the earth near them and it landed in the next valley glade, calling back to them sweetly.

He touched her face with his hands, loving the look of the pink flowers against her vivid coloring. "Anatsa!" he said wondrously. "Anatsa!"

Suddenly the curlew flew from its shelter in alarm, circling in great sweeping strokes and refusing to land. Anatsa looked up at it and saw the color of the sky change to the waxen look of flesh after life has left it. She felt the coldness of the Wolf Trail that stretches across the night sky.

"What is it?" Apikunni whispered, dropping her hands. He looked around them.

The forest had become deadly still. More birds had flown away. Apikunni crouched and drew his knife. A gentle wind came for a while to the pines and then fell to silence. Their horses turned toward the opposite bank, their ears cocked.

"Sahpos!" Apikunni hissed, and using the bank as shelter, rapidly crossed the pond and disappeared in the direction in which the horses were looking.

There wasn't a sound. Anatsa clutched at the moss in agony. Napi, let your power be within him!

The little pool lapped at her legs. With her heart in her throat she watched its widening ripples, like an eye that widened to vanish, so swiftly, so silently. What did it see? What, besides the face of the deer, the elk, the mountain goat, or the white wolf? Did it see those who came for its sustenance? Did it know her ugliness—her weakness? So swiftly the little images came and disappeared, what mattered was that the eye was unchanging. You could agitate the waters, but not the final image. Reality ultimately reflected itself in its own mirror of perfection, so she would never feel imperfect again. Her glen had sustained her, and this magical eye of the mountain had made her see beyond her frail flesh. When Apikunni returned, he returned to her, and she caressed his face with a wild abandon that even their caressing before had not aroused.

He smiled in deep pleasure. "We are alive!" she whispered over and over.

When they mounted their horses, and started home, Apikunni studied the trail frowning in perplexity.

"There was sign of only one Crow," he said. "I could not follow him and leave you alone, for he must be part of a larger war party. If he is lost, why would he stay alone here, in our land?"

"He was watching us twice," Anatsa replied. "He was watching us on the trail, too."

Apikunni said no more and rode ahead, constantly alert to an attack. The afternoon light was going fast. The sun only shone on the peak of the mountain, and the tall tips of the pines. Where they rode was already deep in shadow.

Near the village they rode abreast. Smoke from the evening cooking fires clung wraithlike over the tipis, and in the last strong light of the day their eyes met. To them both, the day ended golden and shimmering, and Apikunni felt as if he had parted some bunch grass, long familiar to him, and had discovered the most precious flower in the world.

The memory of their day together haunted Apikunni as he rode with the Mutsik the next morning. He saw Anatsa's image in the rippling pool; he saw her as beautiful and as fragile as a spray of foam that trembled upon the earth, yet was as indestructible as the sun.

They could find no fresh sign of the Crow. His prints of the day before disappeared into hard shale, but the thought of how close he had come to Anatsa made Apikunni feel terror. The thought of the light ending in her eyes made him quake in his soul. He wanted this girl whom he had lived near all of his life, but had just discovered. He wanted her to prepare his food, to lie with him on his couch; he wanted her to bear his sons.

That evening he walked across the Pikuni camp toward the inner circle of high chiefs, to where Anatsa lived with her sister and her brother-in law. A light wind blew from the mountains, moving the little bells on the ears of the tipis. The night was magic; mystical medicines from the wise men long dead came from the stars and fell gently to his shoulders.

His new recently dressed buckskin gleamed in the night, and from a distance Anatsa saw him coming, and saw the sober look of his face. She was working quill bands into Onesta's shirt; inside the lodge Apeecheken was still sick, still vomiting, for the otsqueeina had not helped her yet.

When Apikunni stood tall and silent over her, Anatsa could only look down at her own hands.

"Anatsa," he said. "You watched me as I was walking toward you. Why do you take your eyes from me now?"

"I do not know," she whispered, looking at the shirt she held as if it would be the last thing she would ever see upon the earth.

He sat beside her, gently taking the shirt from her hands. "You have a good name for your sewing," he said, "but do not sew now. Look at me, Anatsa. I have come to ask you something."

She forced herself to meet his gaze.

"I have come to court you," he said. "Would you ride around the camp circle with me tonight?"

She looked at him in disbelief. "What?"

"Would you ride with me tonight in sign of courtship?"

Anatsa's eyes became pained. "You have not changed—from yesterday?"

"No."

"You do not come to me and ask this in jest?"

"Anatsa! Why would I do this as a joke? Why, Anatsa, why?"

"Because no man has ever come for me before!"

"What does any other man in this village have to do with me? Do I think with the minds of other men? Do I seek coups, the buffalo, with the minds of other men? Why would I follow them in the seeking of a wife?"

Anatsa felt a violent beating of her heart. "Do not mock me!" she almost sobbed.

"Why do you act like this? Didn't you tell me at the glen that you loved me?"

"I do love you!"

"Then why would you weep at becoming my wife?"

"I am afraid that it is pity that has touched your heart."

She tried to hide her face in her hands, but he grasped her hands and held them firmly within his own. "I am a proud man," he said. "I would take no woman because of pity."

"All my life," she said to him, "all my life I have dreamed of being your woman and living in your lodge. Yet never did I believe it would happen! I thought that we would live and die in this village together, and you would never know me."

"I want you to ride with me tonight, and every night, until you become my wife," he said tenderly.

"All right," she said, her voice unsteady. "But know your words. I am crippled, and our sons might be in my image, and not in yours. Think of this now, Apikunni, in long silence."

"I will not think of this," he answered, and taking her in his arms, kissed her long and lovingly. From inside the lodge, Apeecheken began to retch again. Love came sweetly and softly, and love came darkly and violently. Sometimes the seed of love grew and sometimes it died.

"Anatsa," he said. "It is beauty that is crippled; the rest of the world is different!"

"I will not speak to you of my leg again," she promised. "I will ride with you tonight, I will be your wife!"

She went inside the lodge and told her sister, and came outside with the little meadow rue berries at her throat again. She mounted his horse, and sitting before him rode through the village, and every one who saw them knew that they had announced their marriage. The children of other loves watched them solemnly. Wives long married looked after them too, and before their fires of boiling meat and vegetables from the prairie, remembered other times; through long years either bitter or sweet, they were virgin-young once more, when the first kiss was followed by the second, and the moment of union trembled ahead in its own wonder.

In custom as old as their tribe, Apikunni and Anatsa rode around the outer circle of the Blackfoot camp, and around the horse herds that grazed quietly out upon the prairie. They met other betrothed couples, whom they passed without sound.

Anatsa looked up at the great form of the mountain that obscured half of the night sky. "Apikunni, when the glacier fields above us melt next spring, when the ice breaks and feeds all of this land with the winter snows, I will have your son! Apikunni—I will have borne your son! Think of the wonder it will be! My heart and your heart will be his!"

He kissed the side of her face, remembering an old Blackfoot song. "From whence did I come?" he whispered. "Does our son know—is our son blessed even before the meeting of our bodies?"

Her face became serene. "How I love this night!" she said. "How I love this world—my life—my body that has given me this transport!"

Back at the village the campfires died out. So deeply in love, Apikunni and Anatsa could not bear to part for sleep. They watched the slow moving of the stars, and only when the seven brothers of the north sky had dipped toward the prairie did they ride to the inner tipis. At Anatsa's sister's lodge they clung desperately to each other. When Apikunni rode away at last, all of the fire pits were cold and deep with white ashes.

Chapter Eleven

Pikuni men go crazy!" Atsitsi screamed at Maria. "Apikunni marry ugly Anatsa and Nakoa keep you!"

Maria, quilting some moccasins for herself, ignored the old woman.

"Why man ever want ugly thin woman like Anatsa?"

"Anatsa like boy. Without crippled leg already a mess. No man want Anatsa."

"Apikunni does," retorted Maria.

Atsitsi got up abruptly. "I go see why."

"Oh, no!" moaned Maria. "You can't ask Apikunni that!"

"How else I know, fool?" Atsitsi grunted and waddled away.

Maria looked after her, so fat, so old and bent, and sweating in the hot sun. Pity for Atsitsi smote Maria's heart. Here too was a creature who suffered. Sitting, suddenly desolate before an Indian tipi, she heard voices speak to her, voices from within herself. Love Atsitsi they said, love all things of the earth, for all things feed the earth, and it is the earth that feeds you.

Maria got up and walked, and some dogs barked at her heels. She shook her head, weak and dizzy. Was Indian superstition affecting her reason? Love Atsitsi? Fat, loathsome, filthy Atsitsi?

Nakoa, Nakoa, her mind called. She had thought of him every day and every night since they had been alone after the Kissing Dance. She could not erase his image, the memory of his overpowering strength.

She had not seen him again since the night of the Kissing Dance, but before he went with the others to the buffalo hunt he had had it announced that she was to become his second wife.

"My daughter," a voice said quietly, "where do you walk?"

It was Natosin, and in his face she clearly saw again the face of his son.

"I do not know where I walk," Maria said sorrowfully.

"All of life is a strange path," he answered.

"Natosin! Natosin!" she exclaimed, not knowing if she should have called him by name. She hung her head. "I feel more pain than I can bear."

"It is sad that the young have to bear youth," he said. "They have not had the time for it!"

Maria looked up into his eyes. They were kind and filled with compassion; so much of Nakoa stood before her that she wanted to bury herself in his arms. "No," she whispered, "I did not have the time to be young."

"You wear the dress of an Indian, and speak Pikuni. Is this what is destroying you?"

"I am captive of your son," she said. If only he knew how captive she was! "Since I have been here, a part of me that I have never known is growing—haunting me."

"When you are aware of a stranger, do not weep, my daughter, but feel blessed!"

She studied his face again. Once more this king of savages struck her with his great dignity, and now she was fascinated by his words. "Why should I feel blessed with feeling a stranger to myself?" she asked.

"We are all part stranger to ourselves."

"But this part of me that I feel now—never existed before!"

"You know it exists now, so it is not strange. Someone has come forward who always was you, but was in shadows. Keep her in the light; accept her and use her strength!"

"Wait!" she said in Pikuni. Maria met his searching black eyes. "Natosin, you have called me daughter, but you do not want me to marry your son."

He looked at her steadily and lost none of the compassion for her that remained upon his face. "No, my daughter, I do not want this marriage. I think such a marriage will bring my son sorrow. I would prevent his taking you for a wife if I could!"

"Can't you?"

"My son will walk his own path. Life was not given him to follow mine."

"Then why do you call me daughter? I am captive—white—you are the chief of the Pikuni."

"It is a truth that all of the land in the world is surrounded by sea. If water surrounds all of the land, then it is the same water that nourishes us all."

He walked away from her and as Maria watched his proud carriage, a small voice wailed over and over within her, "I love your son! I love your son!" She walked on. What did Natosin mean when he said the seas fed the earth? It was the other way around. And how could he say that the young did not have the strength to bear youth? Youth was the spring song of life and only the vigor of youth could deal with its treasures! What wisdom could Natosin have when his words were opposites?

She did wear the dress of an Indian woman, but she still refused to braid her hair like the other young girls of the village. Was wearing her hair loose her last symbol of being a white woman?

Around her was talk of the hunters. When would fresh meat from the hunt be brought to camp? Had they not found the herds yet? Dried meat and stews had lost their taste; the feasts of the running days when fresh steaks could be broiled over coals, or meat could be roasted, were one of the main delights of the village.

Like the Indian women, Maria went to the river for wood and got coals for their cooking fire; she gathered the prairie turnip, cow parsnip, wild potato, onion, smart weed, and bitter root; she slept upon an Indian couch and spoke the Pikuni tongue.

Maria used the Indian rooting stick and wore the little buckskin bags of balsam fir or meadow rue berries for their fragrance. Anatsa had taught her how to sew skins, for these were necessary for clothing and shelter, for the men's pipe bags, paint bags, tobacco paunches, knife cases, and the parfleche bags used for the storing and carrying of food. Thread was sinew or dried tendons pushed through holes made in the skin with a bodkin, and Maria had her own sewing kit of bodkins, shredded sinew, and a sewing knife all in the traditional bag of buffalo skin.

Maria was also taught the Blackfoot art of fashioning bowls and dishes of sheep or buffalo horn by boiling, splitting, fitting, and sewing them together with sinew. She had learned to make spoons and ladles by scorching a horn over a fire, shaping, then boiling and shaping again.

With Anatsa, she gathered the herbs used by the Blackfoot for healing. She could identify bear grass used to stop inflammation, purple loco weed chewed for a sore throat, the wind flower burned upon coals for headaches, black root for coughs, sixocasin and grape root to stop bleeding of the stomach, and big larb used by the men in their ceremonial smoking.

The land around them was raw and wild and the Blackfoot lived upon it and cherished its wildness, but it was hard for Maria to accept. There was no cultivated field, no orchard planted in stiff design, no road filled with the dust of moving wagons and carriages. There were only the narrow paths through the tall meadow grass, the vast and quiet prairie, the towering shadow of the west mountains. There were no church bells to peal on Sunday, the sound sending birds scurrying from the belfry, no humming of barter and trade, never the whistle of a boat or a lonely train. Instead, in Indian land, the geese, ducks, and swans returned silently from warmer regions and heralded the time of the great Sun Dance.

There was sweetness for the body: wild rhubarb to be roasted over hot coals, the pulp of the cottonwood tree, not unlike maple syrup in flavor, the sweet camas gathered and baked in the earth in the fall. But there was no milk and no salt and no sugar.

As Maria walked on through the village a woman called her name. It was Sikapischis, the widow who lived with her blind father and her little son. Maria went over to where they sat in front of their lodge.

"You look like an Indian woman now," Sikapischis said to her kindly.

Maria smiled and sat upon the ground with them. She noticed

that Sikapischis's father held a deerskin flute in his lap. "We have other music besides the drum," Sikapischis explained. "My father teaches my son the skills that he has known. He teaches Siyeh how to hunt and to fish and to approach an enemy unaware, with no sound at all. (Maria smiled, for the boy could not have been over eight.) And when they have finished with these things that a man must know, they come back to my lodge in the evenings, and my father teaches Siyeh how to sing with the flute. Siyeh can play the flute, too, and now when one plays, the other sings the flute's song."

"What is your father called?" Maria asked looking toward the blind old man. "I am sorry," she said, remembering that this information was never asked of one Indian by another, but was always volunteered. Sikapischis smiled.

"My father is called Mequesapa, and I am glad to tell his name to you. He was a Mutsik and a very great warrior known deep in Crow land for the number of his coups. It was in fighting a Crow that he lost one eye, and then a growth came to the other and left him blind."

"I know my grandfather's coups!" Siyeh interrupted. "I know them all! Would you like to hear them?"

"No, Siyeh," his grandfather said quietly.

The round little face and shining black eyes lost none of their eagerness. "I am proud to walk with my grandfather," Siyeh said.

"Of course you are," Maria answered, looking at the little boy affectionately. A beautiful light came to Sikapischis's eyes as she looked at her son. "I am deeply blessed," she said. This was the second time Maria had heard the word today. "I was blessed with his father, and I am blessed with our son."

Siyeh began to fidget. "Grandfather, would you play the flute?" he asked. The old man hesitated. "Please," Maria asked, and for the first time Mequesapa's sightless eyes turned toward her.

"The white woman's voice is a gentle one," he said to his daughter.

"She is a gentle woman," Sikapischis answered.

"But it is still that Nakoa is foolish," he said sadly, and Maria looked away from them all. In the long silence, the old man finally picked up his flute and began a haunting tune. "It is filled with sorrow," Maria said. But she was held spellbound by the music, and Siyeh's young face shone in rapt worship. Others in nearby lodges came to gather around Sikapischis's tipi. As the last note slipped away, it seemed to end more than just a melody. "It is like a prayer!" Maria breathed. "Are there words for it?"

"Yes," Sikapischis answered. Her father began to play the tune again and Sikapischis sang its words.

I accept.
The love and the pain; the sunlight and the rain,
I accept.

The day and the night; the blindness and the sight,
I accept.

The love and the glory; the end of the story,
I accept.

From winter's deep snow, spring waters must flow,
The body and the heart, is the beginning and the start,
I accept!
I accept!

Sikapischis finished. "It is an old song," she said. "It has been sung in Blackfoot camps as long as their tipis have been pitched upon the prairie."

"It is beautiful," Maria said. "I thank you, deep from my heart," she said to the old man. "Your notes have given me peace, and so did the words they carried."

"Can you be given peace?" he asked her softly.

"I have found peace this morning," she answered.

"Are you a beautiful woman?" he asked her.

"I don't know!" Maria stammered.

"She is beautiful," Sikapischis said.

"She is very beautiful, except her eyes are a different color!" Siyeh added and then flushed in embarrassment.

"I have asked the white woman!" Mequesapa said sternly. "She is the only one who can answer this!" His sightless eyes were seeking her, one eye a hollow pit and the other covered with a white growth.

Maria met the dead eyes. "I would like to be beautiful!" she said.

The old man's face softened. "When a woman asks for beauty and does not think she has it, she wants it for a gift, and the woman who gives is the rich woman and blesses the earth!"

Maria said nothing. Why did they all talk in such a strange way?

"Would you like your beauty for a man?" Mequesapa asked. "Would you trade its heart away?"

"Yes," said Maria. "I have! I have!"

Mequesapa closed his eyes. "There has been no light for me so that I could have sight for Siyeh. But I have had as much for him. Without the light of the sun its warmth is as great. Beauty is a small gift, but if given in trade, becomes a great one."

Maria looked warmly at the three of them, at all of the Indians who, when the song was finished, had begun to go back to their own lodges. "I do not know all of your words," she said, "but this morning has been a rich one for me. Good-bye," she said, rising, and thinking that she would go to the inner lodges and seek Anatsa. The two of them could walk to the lake and swim and sun the rest of the afternoon.

"Talk with us again," Sikapischis said. "You are always welcome, even to share our food."

"Thank you," Maria replied. Sikapischis was her friend; Anatsa and she were becoming as close as sisters. Natosin may not have wanted his son to marry a white woman but he liked her; Mequesapa liked her too. Her only enemy in the Blackfoot camp was Atsitsi, and on Atsitsi Maria did not waste one thought.

Another Maria she did not know had come to her out of the shadows, and she was strong and could bear anything. She loved Nakoa and would be his wife, and from the Indian prairie would come milk and honey. Near the inner tipis, Maria began to hum happily:

The love and the pain,
The sunlight and the rain,
I accept!
I accept!

Atsitsi was talking to Anatsa and Apeecheken. "Anatsa, you are good girl, but how could Apikunni sleep with you?" She had respect for Anatsa and watched the usage of her words.

Anatsa smiled. "If you have love for someone the eyes see differently," she said.

The talk turned to Apeecheken's baby. Apeecheken smiled. "I hold my food now. I do not believe that I will lose my baby."

"When you have your baby, big Maria?" Atsitsi asked, spitting out the meat she didn't want to swallow. "When you get big belly with big red Indian baby inside?"

Maria shuddered. "You even make having a baby horrible!"

"Having baby horrible!" Atsitsi said. "Big price for big passion!"

Maria suddenly saw Edith Holmes dying, and she bowed her head. Edith had been so pretty and proud of her little body.

Atsitsi's shrewd little eyes read Maria's face. "Ah! Big Maria see bloody kicking of birth and wonder if it so good to let Nakoa between . . ."

"Atsitsi!" Anatsa said, shaking in anger. "We—are women!"

"Fool white woman think she different! Big Maria think she get baby from cloud in sky!"

"Atsitsi, why should you care what she thinks!"

"Because she think me fool! That is why! She think me big fool like big Maria, and Atsitsi not fool! Atsitsi fat, and Atsitsi whore, but Atsitsi not fool!" The old woman's face was lit with passion, her voice shaking.

Maria stood up to leave, her face pale. "Anatsa," she said, "would you go the lake with me?"

"Little bird song go to wash nasty Atsitsi away!" Atsitsi jeered, helping herself to more stew.

"I hate that woman," Maria said to Anatsa as they walked away. "I hate her!"

"You are too close to her in your heart to hate her," Anatsa said. "Hate is heat, and not the coldness of indifference."

Maria was thoughtful. She had hated Meg passionately too. Was she ever close to her heart? What did this mean, close to your heart? Was it the bitch in her that was close to these two women? She had thought of sleeping with Nakoa, and the thought of Edith Holmes dying had driven the desire from her. "Why do you keep Atsitsi in this village?" Maria stormed. "Why don't you drive her away, and let her die a . . ." She stopped.

"Atsitsi is unclean," Anatsa said quietly. "She bears the shadow of the rest of us, and this is a sad burden for her to carry."

"I don't understand! I never understand!"

"Atsitsi is dark, and she makes us look lighter, and cleaner, and more gentle. She is unwashed, and she makes us look clean. She is ugly, and she makes us look beautiful, even when there is no beauty at all! Mothers can tell their daughters to stay clean, or be like Atsitsi! Wives can tell their husbands that if they become unclean they will be Atsitsi, and the men will look upon Atsitsi scratching and Atsitsi belching and be thankful in their hearts for their wives! I am sorry for Atsitsi's words to you, but I like Atsitsi, and I feel in my heart that Atsitsi bears my burden."

"All things feed the earth," Maria said softly. "And it is the earth that feeds us, so that when we stand on the ground, we can reach toward the sky."

Anatsa looked at Maria strangely, in the manner that Natosin had studied her that morning when she had told him that she did not know where she walked. "Where did you hear these words?" she asked Maria.

"They came to me this morning, and they frightened me, and I walked through the village, a stranger to myself. I met Natosin, and he saw my tears and stopped and talked with me."

"This is strange for Natosin. He does not talk with many people."

"I told him why I wept; that strange words and thoughts unknown to me before had made me see that I was changed; that the old Maria was dying—destroyed by Indians!"

"What did he say?"

"He said that I should not weep, but feel blessed! And his words made me feel blessed. Anatsa, I love him," Maria whispered. "And I love his son."

Anatsa smiled, her face radiant. "We both love, and have never lived before!"

When they reached the lake it was deserted. Surprised that it was so late, Maria felt uneasy because they were alone. They had not met one Mutsik upon the trail.

"There is no one here," Maria said. "Perhaps we should not go in the water."

Anatsa smiled. "It is so peaceful and will be warmed with the day's sun. I will bathe in it."

They bathed quickly, Maria watching the rapidly darkening shores. As they were dressing a wood thrush called out from the trees near them. "That was the voice of a man!" Maria whispered, frightened.

"No," replied Anatsa.

Maria shivered, sensing danger.

Anatsa looked around them. "I would know of a presence that would destroy me," she said confidently. "I would feel the coldness of the burial grounds, and the light of the day would change."

"It is changing," Maria said tersely.

"The sun is setting." Anatsa laughed. "And it is beautiful." The orange sky was perfectly reflected in the tranquil waters. "It is such a peaceful time," Anatsa said, "when the sun is gone and its light and warmth remains."

"I hate it," Maria said. "The sky bleeds with the blood it has drawn from earth."

"Was it at this time that your wagons were destroyed?"

"Yes. And ever since, I have hated every sunset!"

"I am sorry for your grief," Anatsa said.

Suddenly a scream came from the burial grounds across the lake. It was a horrible cry, too unnatural to be the cry of a human and yet too human to be the call of a wolf. "What was that?" Maria whispered.

Anatsa's face became terrified. "It was the death cry!" she said.

"Before night ends someone is going to die. Go back to the village quickly, Maria. Do not wait for me."

"Anatsa, we will go back together," Maria answered, and the two girls went back to the village as fast as Anatsa could walk. The darkly shaded trail seemed endless. In the deepening gloom hawks and owls called hoarsely and flapped away from them; a huge bird swooped down and momentarily touched Anatsa's face with its shadow. "Tonight death rests in the trees where our dead lie upon the burial platforms," Anatsa said.

Maria felt such relief when they reached the village that it was a while before she noticed the change there. There was no noise. No children shouted in play, no dogs fought and barked over meat scraps; there was not even the sound of low conversation. Men, women, and children stood in silent groups, and most of them looked off in the direction of the burial grounds. Upon every face was fright, unashamed fright, even upon the faces of the Mutsik warriors.

"Who utters the death cry?" asked Maria.

"It is one of our dead calling to us. Before the ending of this night, or the ending of another day, one of us will be over there—with her!"

"Oh," Maria sighed, relieved. "Anatsa, the dead do not cry out!"

"That was the cry of Sokskinnie; there is not a person of this village who does not know the cry of Sokskinnie—and she is dead and buried, over there!"

"If she is dead, she can do you no harm."

"There are forces that do not die. Her voice has already reached us from across the river!"

"What will be done?" Maria asked.

"The dead do not like light, and so outside fires will burn until sunrise. The medicine drum will beat. Though the dead cannot cross water, all of our doorflaps will be laced tightly closed."

Apikunni strode rapidly toward them. "I will take you to Onesta's," he said to Anatsa. He looked at Maria. "First we will take you to Atsitsi's. Stay in her lodge tonight. The Mutsik will keep the outside fires going."

Near Atsitsi's tipi, numerous fires had been lighted. Maria left Apikunni and Anatsa, and when she entered Atsitsi's lodge the old woman almost knocked her down. "What is the matter with you?" Maria growled. Atsitsi put down her piece of wood.

"Close door and close mouth." Atsitsi had a fire going inside of the lodge, and now added more wood to it.

"It is hot!" Maria complained.

"You like dark, go to burial grounds!"

"Well Sokskinnie couldn't be worse than you!"

Atsitsi flung a piece of wood at Maria, narrowly missing her head. "You—not bring Sokskinnie to this lodge! No talk of dead. No talk of her!"

"Who was she?"

"No talk of dead when sun gone! Shut mouth or leave lodge quick!"

"You really are mad."

Atsitsi looked at Maria, her little eyes gleaming like coals. "Sweet Maria no believe dead walk?"

"Sokskinnie isn't going anywhere!"

Atsitsi grinned, and she looked as evil as any witch in a childhood story. "Open doorflap and say so Sokskinnie hear! Talk more of her with smart tongue!"

From outside they could hear the beating of the medicine drum. "See?" panted Atsitsi. "Whole village crazy! Only Maria smart, cause so fat on self. Why not fat Maria go to burial grounds and see if Sokskinnie make cry?"

"Oh, shut up."

"Why not go to door and tell Sokskinnie that she dead and make no cry with her voice? Tell Sokskinnie to leave Indian alone and walk with smart Maria instead!"

"You cannot frighten me! And I will open your door! It is so hot in here, I can't stand it!" Maria unlaced the doorflap and looked outside. The fires burning around them had already begun to die, and the tipis cast almost human shadows upon one another. Except for the medicine drum, the village was still silent.

"Speak to Sokskinnie with smart tongue now," Atsitsi said softly.

Maria laughed at the old woman's frightened face. She looked out into the night and called merrily, "I say there, old girl, aren't you going to sing us another song?"

A sudden wind came and shook the bells upon the ears of the tipi. In spite of the warm night, its touch was cold, and Maria shivered.

Atsitsi grinned. "Laugh again, fat Maria," she said.

The bells were still, there was now no sign of a breeze anywhere. "What was that?" Maria asked.

"Sweet Maria know. Little west wind."

"There hasn't been any wind today."

"Then you feel touch from burial grounds. Sokskinnie kill you. Maybe she kill others first, but she kill you."

Maria lay down upon her couch. "The dead cannot hurt me," she said.

"Go to burial grounds and see," Atsitsi answered. She sat by the fire and fed its flames with more wood. "One day, big Maria, go to burial grounds and see!"

Chapter Twelve

Maria went with Anatsa to the river the next day to bring back wood. The ceremonial drum was stilled. No one had been harmed the night before. Anatsa was strangely withdrawn, and Maria felt reluctant to intrude upon her thoughts. A Mutsik patrol rode behind them, and a group of women walked ahead. Maria was deeply thankful that they were not alone upon the prairie.

"It is not finished," Anatsa said suddenly.

"Anatsa, why are you so certain that this call was made by Sokskinnie?"

"Sokskinnie had a peculiar sound to her voice. This is what gave her her name."

"Her name?"

"An Indian is often renamed for a quality he has when he is older. Sokskinnie was renamed when she became a woman with a carrying tone to her voice. Sokskinnie—Loud Voice. We all know the sound of her voice."

"I mocked your belief in this last night," Maria said seriously. "Atsitsi goaded me into it. I opened the doorflap and asked Sokskinnie to sing us another song."

Anatsa looked deeply troubled.

"Anatsa! I frightened myself last night, but today, in the daylight, I can find no ghosts!"

"In the daylight you find no stars, but at night you see them."

"The dead do not walk, or call, or . . ."

"I do not know the barriers that are gone with the body. Look ahead of us, Maria. Do you see the women upon the trail?"

"No. They have followed the bend to the river and are out of our sight."

"But they are still ahead of us. And they can come back to us if they want to, and if we have the sight and the sound to hear and see them."

"Anatsa, it is not the same!"

"Do we all see and hear in the same way? What is at the end of the Wolf Trail? How long does the sleep of the body last?"

"No dead person made that cry yesterday!"

"I have heard of hot sands where there is no water and the sky is a furnace with the burning sun. I have heard that in these sands men see water and trees when they are not there. Are they water and trees that lie elsewhere? Was the call we heard one from a different place or time?"

"Anatsa, you will go crazy talking like that. Even if this cry was an echo of Sokskinnie's real voice, how can a faded echo do anyone harm?"

"It is the cry of death before the death, mixed up in time."

"Now you are talking like I dream!"

Anatsa smiled.

They had reached the river, and Maria looked across it at the shadowed burial grounds. "Now it comes back to me that I dreamed of that place last night. I dreamed of black trees and long knives hanging from them."

Anatsa looked startled. "You saw the skinning knives which we bury with the dead?"

"Then I saw a yellow river—much wider than this one, and across it I remember a black trunk. I crossed the river on a dead tree trunk."

"You crossed the river in your dreams? Why?"

"I heard a song. It came from the graveyard—your burial grounds—with the knives moving from the trees—long, long knives—"

Anatsa began hastily to gather scrubwood. "It is a hateful place, always in shadow and with the skinning knives always moving in the wind. I do not look there."

Helping Anatsa gather the wood, Maria noticed that the other women were leaving. The river rushed noisily beside them and from the trees of the burial grounds came the call of a gambel sparrow, three little notes, usually repeated once. Maria reached for some more wood and then noticed that the bird had not called again.

"It is back," Anatsa said softly. "The sky is yellow but without light, as when the sun is suffocated with thickening clouds."

"Anatsa, what are you saying?" Maria whispered.

"Something is choking the sun. Its light and the warmth are gone."

The expression on her face frightened Maria. "Anatsa! Anatsa! What is it?" she asked.

"It was like this when I was with Apikunni, when we rode to the meadow. Now I know, and it is death. That is why Sokskinnie called!"

"God help us!" Maria whispered in English, looking frantically around them. Where was the Pikuni rider? Where was the Mutsik patrol? She dropped her wood.

"Do not move," whispered Anatsa. "It does not know."

"Know what?"

"Whether to kill us. Do not move!" The urgency and conviction of her voice held Maria still, though her heart hammered wildly in her throat. The forest seemed serene, but she believed with Anatsa that death stood near them.

"It is gone," Anatsa said finally. "It has moved away. Now we will gather the wood and leave."

They picked up the wood, and walked toward the open prairie. "Anatsa, why do you say 'it'?" Maria asked.

Anatsa turned back to her, and Maria saw sight in her eyes beyond her own. "Because it is not man and it is not animal."

"Why did it not kill us?"

"I do not know."

They were upon the prairie now. Golden sunflowers and purple vetches nodded along the trail. Maria looked ahead of them in all of that lonely land and thought, "Dear God, where is that Pikuni rider?"

Around the first bend of the trail and still very near the river, they came upon him at last. He was lying upon his back and looking up into the summer sky, his head almost decapitated by the violence with which his throat had been cut.

Maria screamed. Death had swept silently from the hills again; the Snakes rode them down and Ana and her father and Anson would die horribly once more. Against a twilight sky Ana's long yellow hair gleamed in its last life, and night would come and never end. Maria screamed and screamed, the same long cry that could never be shattered. She was in the pit, falling, falling—Anatsa shook her with violence.

"Maria! Maria! Stop it!" she said. Apikunni and some of the riders of the Knatsomita stood over her. They looked at the dead man at their feet. Maria turned away from them all.

"Did you see who did it?" Apikunni asked Anatsa.

"No. We found him like this. But what killed him was with us first—at the river!"

"How do you know this?" Apikunni asked.

"It was the same as when we rode for the otsqueeina!" Anatsa replied. "It was the same! There was the sun, but no light! Yellow color like thick clouds were suffocating the day! It watched us—and then killed Kominakus!"

Maria's eyes were drawn to the body at her feet. So the thing still had a name, this inert form with its head askew and its eyes staring when sight was gone. Then she noticed what they had already seen. The corpse had not been scalped, and this was the strangeness that lay before them in final silence. No man—Blackfoot, Snake, Dahcotah, or Crow—would ever kill without scalping; only a woman would do this, and how could a woman slit a man's throat with such violence?

"Maria and I were watched from the burial grounds," Anatsa said.

"If we were watched from there," Maria replied, "why wasn't the sparrow disturbed? Why didn't it fly away?"

"You heard a bird call out from the burial grounds?" Apikunni asked her quickly.

"Yes. Just before Anatsa felt we were being watched—a gambel sparrow called out three times."

"Yes," Anatsa repeated. "It was the sparrow. It was not a man."

"Then why wasn't the bird frightened at a strange presence?" Maria asked.

Anatsa looked at Maria. "Because the presence was not a new one. Sokskinnie is no stranger to the burial grounds."

The men said nothing and followed Maria and Anatsa back to the village. Kominakus's body was left where it was. A travois would be sent back for it later.

In the village it was the same as it had been the night before, but now crowds gathered to meet them. The promise from the burial grounds had been kept; Kominakus would lie there before another sun. A pall lay over the village like a great shroud; these people, fearless before ordinary death, were numb before the unknown. Fear reached even to the camp dogs, who followed their masters anxiously, whining low in their throats. Maria fully felt the terror around her now. Nothing but a crazed animal would kill like that, and when she thought of the blood all around the severed head, she became ill.

Apikunni and Anatsa left her at Atsitsi's but the old woman was nowhere around. Maria lay upon her couch, still sick and completely drained of all energy. When she closed her eyes, she could see only Kominakus's severed head; she opened them again and stared at the skins of the tipi. A black shadow approached noiselessly and stood motionless by the door.

"Who is it?" Maria called out, frightened.

"It is Natosin," came the answer. "I have come to speak with you."

Maria went outside.

"My son has sent for you," the old man said simply. "You are to leave tomorrow for the buffalo camp."

The thought of being with Nakoa so soon made Maria's heart leap with joy. Near him death would be gone, and all fears would be nothing.

"You are glad for this?" Natosin asked.

Maria turned away, embarrassed.

"You are eager for my son," he said.

Maria felt her face redden.

"Pleasure from mating should not bring shame," Natosin said.

Maria looked aghast. "I had not thought - " she said, and stopped. Dear God, why hadn't she realized? He had changed his mind, and in sending for her to sleep with her, didn't intend to keep her now! Maria's eyes filled with tears. "He said he would not trade me! He said I was to be his second wife! Natosin—Natosin—" She stopped, not knowing what to say.

"My son must walk in his own way. I cannot stop him from taking you or leaving you, my daughter."

"How could he want me this way?"

"You want him in the same way."

"I could not bear the shame of it!"

"You feel shame, because it can be harder to accept what we want than what we don't want!"

"No! No!" Maria said. "I will not be traded to every man in this village!"

"I believe your words," Natosin said.

"Oh," Maria said in despair. "Dear God, have I not suffered enough?"

"Pain cannot be measured, and pain is the mother of joy. Let my son know you before Nitanna comes to be his wife."

"To you—and to Nakoa—I am nothing! I am nothing!"

"I have called you daughter," he said quietly, and left her alone.

Stricken, Maria looked numbly around her. Riders were going toward the burial grounds, their women and children following to wait silently for them from the other side of the river. She did not care that the widow of Kominakus had begun her wailing, and was probably slashing herself and mutilating her flesh in her suffering. When the wounds of the flesh finally healed, the heart would still be left bleeding; once despair came it revisited boldly, no longer a stranger. They would burn Kominakus's lodge, and bury him in the trees too. Then maybe he could take his skinning knife and scare off Sokskinnie! No, being a man, he would take her instead. Rage flamed within Maria; hatred for Nakoa possessed her. Going back into the lodge, she flung herself upon her couch. The world was depraved and provided food only for maggots. The sun warmed stench, and all moonlight was a deception. Waters purified nothing and just carried their own pollution around and around in endless circles.

And, dear God, in her terror she thought she was going to Nakoa's strength.

Every sunrise ended in bloody sunset, and she would never know a spring rain again.

Atsitsi came into the lodge. "It dark soon!" she screamed. "Why no by-damn fire?"

"Build one yourself!" Maria said angrily.

Atsitsi rapidly built a fire, and almost frantic, laced the doorflap closed. "Big Maria stay inside tonight," she said. "Already talk to Sokskinnie!"

Maria moaned.

"Why you scream big head off when you find Kominakus? Why you want anyone to come and help big Maria? Why not sit on holy ass and hold Kominakus's hand?"

Maria didn't answer.

"'Cause full of four selves so damned scared! Scared now, too! Now big Maria think Sokskinnie death cry not so silly!"

"I'm not going to talk to you."

"Who care? Who care what you do?" Atsitsi began to eat.

The medicine drum began to beat again. Nervously, Maria ate too, finally casting her half-filled bowl down in agitation. "Why is that drum beating? There was no cry today!"

"There was yours."

"No one is supposed to die!"

"You mean you safe cause no new death cry? Ha! Where Sokskinnie, sweet Maria?"

"In the burial grounds!"

Atsitsi grinned evilly. "Mutsik and Knatsomita warriors search grounds—all over. Sokskinnie gone! Burial platform empty!"

"That doesn't mean?"

"She leave tracks! Heel fringe and toe from her moccasins! She walk in grounds. Laugh at that, big Maria!"

"I am not laughing," Maria said. "But if she walks in the grounds, she is not dead!"

"I take care of Sokskinnie when she die!" Atsitsi said in a rage. "I see her die! I with her when medicine drum stop beating! She die—and she alive—once more!"

Maria felt a coldness again, and a prickling of her skin. Atsitsi stirred the fire. "Now no more talk of dead. When dark, no talk of dead."

They sat in silence, listening to the beating of the drum. The wailing of Kominakus's widow could be heard at intervals, and Maria looked at the flickering shadows of herself and Atsitsi upon the tipi skins. How little of themselves their shadows were, what a dim reflection, an incomplete part of the whole. In another light could what she knew to be herself be just another distorted shadow?

"Nakoa has sent for me," Maria said bitterly.

Atsitsi looked up in joy. "I know he never marry big Maria! Too much fool!"

"Thank you."

"I know all time! He screw you when Nitanna not here to get mad!"

"I wouldn't want to upset Nitanna!"

"You won't. You be gone to Siksikai then. Ah, sweet Maria dance such nice dance for sweethearts of Mutsik! And when Siksikai all through nice Maria can tell old Indian whore why all Pikuni women stay away from him!"

When Atsitsi finally fell to snoring, Maria lay upon her couch watching the fire. The wind stirred, shaking the little bells of the tipis; to Maria they tolled for the ending of human life. She saw Kominakus lying upon the prairie, and then she saw Ana, her father, and Anson, and she wondered how much of them was left. Was there a soul that the wolves could not reach? Was there anything that was not in the end devoured? Was the soul a last vanity, the Bible a dream?

Oh, it was terrible to think this way! She wanted a real father separate and apart from herself to end her pain, and to make her good and then to reward her goodness! She wanted a father to punish her badness, so she would know what to do what to seek!

Great walls had to be built against grief and loss and despair, and she was not old enough, nor strong enough, nor wise enough to do it herself! The floods came, the great tidal waves swept over the highest mountain, and her feet were upon sands! But her father's feet stood over all, for he was the creator! But her father would never taste new fruit of Oregon, and her mother had died and had left her father the warm breasts of Meg Summers. Whore! Harlot! The autumn leaves grow sodden, and with their own weight they fall and drift nowhere in the wind. Who is to light the evening lamp to shine upon them?

The wind was not quiet this night. It came down from the mountains, moving the little bells of the tipis. It crossed the Pikuni burial grounds and there it picked up the lament of the dead. It crossed the moving river and swept across the prairie grass, ruffling the manes of the nervous horse herds. It mingled its cry with that of the white wolf, both of them calling mournfully for the past.

The wind sucked against the closed lodge skins. Don't you know me now? Mine was the hand that touched your face tenderly, and cared for your wounds; my lips were those that returned the eagerness of your kiss. It was I who carried the seed of our new life. Could you want the river between us? How could you fear me when I have been gone for such a little while? Let me stay here, among the sights and sounds I knew so well. How could the medicine drum beat in prayer for my life and now beat in fear of the same life? Do not drive me away. I supplicate and if my hands are dust, is my soul only an idea that cannot last beyond tomorrow?

Maria began to sob, turning on her bed and clutching at her ears. She couldn't bear the mournful cry of the wind. "God, help me!" she prayed.

Maria slept at last, and while she slept, she dreamed. She heard her mother singing a Spanish lullaby, but she was seeking Nakoa. She stood alone in deep mist, and she trembled at the unknown that lay hidden in the fog. She called to Nakoa in fear; she called to him in deeper need, but only her own voice came back to her. She pushed the fog away with her hands, seeking Nakoa in the center of the mist, but there she saw only a shrouded reflection of herself. She gazed forlornly at herself. Was this the purpose of her life—this veiled reflection? It was Nakoa she wanted, Nakoa she had to have. She wanted his strength, the freshly killed meat he would bring, the warmth and the shelter he would create. As she gazed at herself she changed into a little girl, a fat sticky little girl sucking upon sweets. Maria turned to go and the little girl followed her. "Go away!" Maria shouted at her. Furiously, she knocked the sugared candy from her hands. The little girl sat down in the mists and cried. "I want my mother!" she wailed.

"You little fool, your mother is dead!" Maria said.

"Then why have you taken my candy?" the little girl wept. She sobbed and sobbed, way down in the mists, and Maria grew weary of her sobbing. With terrible effort, she walked away from the little girl. Now she saw herself upon the open prairie, and all around her grew luxurious bunch grass. It was full moonlight and the earth smelled warm and sensuous. Her vision widened and she could see all of the prairie, way over and beyond it, and it was as if she stood on a little island. Before her she cast a long shadow, and when it suddenly began to move, she was forced to follow it. "Stop!" she called after it, but it glided on through the luminous grass. She tried to stop, but she was a part of her shadow and where it went she was forced to follow. She heard the tolling of church bells around them— her shadow was leading her to a funeral! "Stop! Stop!" she pleaded desperately, for she could not bear to see another person die. She hid her face in her hands and began to weep.

"Maria," a voice said tenderly. "Do not weep. It is our marriage!"

It was Nakoa and he brushed back the hair from her forehead and kissed her there. Then his lips met hers and all of the mists suddenly parted and became her wedding veil; she looked down and saw that she was dressed in shimmering satin. "I am beautiful!" she exclaimed breathlessly. "Yes," he whispered, and the billowing veil gently enclosed them both. He removed the veil and then her dress and when his lips touched her naked flesh she was in rapture.

"There isn't time," she murmured.

"No," he replied. "There is no time!"

In the absence of time, she lay with him and accepted him, and his caress was the caress of the whole world.

When they had made love, they drifted off into languid sleep, and from a great distance, Maria could hear that the church bells were still tolling. "They wait for us," she said.

"There is no waiting now," he replied, and then they were walking up a pathway together. It was a long path bordered with white flowers that went all of the way to the church. She was dressed in virginal white again, but he wore Indian buckskin and carried a scalping knife. When they entered the church door together Maria heard a fluttering of excited whispers. "Look at him! He is handsome!" Gently, Nakoa led her to the altar, and the sweet smell of the prairie followed them. The flowers that had bloomed along the path bloomed within the church. At the altar the minister appeared to marry them, and, surprised, Maria looked up into the eyes of her father.

"Do you take this woman for your lawfully wedded wife?" he asked Nakoa.

"I do," Nakoa replied.

"He does not!" a voice said wrathfully. It was Meg, and she came to Nakoa, her lips red and moist. In front of them all she unbuttoned her bodice and exposed her full white breasts. Maria recoiled away from the sight, but Nakoa moved toward Meg. "Stop it! Stop it!" Maria screamed in agony. The people all became the white flowers, their petals scattering nervously in the wind.

"Maria!" her father said sternly. "Do you take this man for your lawfully wedded husband?"

"No! No! No!" she cried hysterically, and ran away from the church, stumbling to the ground and lying there sobbing. The church bells stopped their pealing. All of the little noises of living things in the prairie grass became stilled. The bright moonlit sky became clouded, and the wedding veil melted from her shoulders and became mist again. At the end of her dream she groped for the petals of the white flowers, and when she found them they had become dead and brown.

Chapter Thirteen

At daylight Maria wakened to the sound of the camp crier calling out that it was time for those going to the buffalo grounds to move. Snatches of her dream came back to her. The memory of her union with Nakoa was so real that her heart raced at the thought of meeting him. She bathed in the tipi, putting on a dress Anatsa had brought to her. It smelled of meadow rue berries and was beautifully decorated with red quills. The quills enhanced her vivid coloring, and as she carefully brushed her hair with a quill brush, she saw frank envy upon Atsitsi's face. Maria felt a sadness for her, for this fat sweating creature who so craved a man and was called a whore, but would sleep alone until she died.

"Are you going to the buffalo grounds with me?" she asked her gently.

"What matter with sweet voice?" Atsitsi asked grumpily. "Of course I go! What you think I be waiting for, ever since white virgin come to dirty Indian camp? Big head shrink a little now that Nakoa not keep it!"

"Why don't you get out of bed and put some clothes on?" Maria said, and went outside to wait. Few people in the village were up; the tipis still lay smoky gray in the dim light. The crier called again. "It is the word of your chief! Those who go to the grounds—move! move!"

Two men rode toward Maria leading four saddled horses. So four women were to leave, for the Pikuni did not saddle horses for men. Atsitsi came quickly out of the door, running her hands carelessly through her greasy hair. She looked up at one of the Indian braves. "I go with big white woman!" she shouted. "I need horse now!"

They moved out of the village, Maria's horse behind Atsitsi's.

The hunters had changed their camp, moving after the buffalo herd, and it was not until late afternoon that they rode within sight of their tipis. Great buffalo birds filled the sky, a sign that the herds were near, for the birds lived from the ticks upon the backs of the animals.

When they arrived Atsitsi greeted every woman she saw in a friendly fashion. "Ho!" she shouted. "Who Atsitsi stay with? Atsitsi not bring lodge, and white woman sleep with Nakoa now."

Maria ached to fly at the old woman and choke the life out of her. "Stop it!" she insisted.

Atsitsi got down from her horse and squatted by one of the lodges. "I eat now, and I sleep here."

The owner's woman looked pained.

Maria dismounted and sat in the shadow of the deserted tipi. Soon Atsitsi returned, agitated and carrying fresh meat. "Nakoa give this," she said. "He say we go to hunt tomorrow with rest of women!"

"He isn't coming here?" Maria asked incredulously.

"No. And he not send for you either! Say we to use lodge." She saw the disappointment upon Maria's face and squinted up at her against the sun. "Now poor Maria no find out man enter woman with sweet bird song!"

"Be quiet—please be quiet!" Maria said.

"Now go bang head on dirt. Not my fault Nakoa not screw you right away!"

Just after daylight the hunters rode out of camp, and the women followed, Atsitsi and Maria among them. Great clouds of dust rose in the prairie where Maria knew the buffalo to be, and before any of them could see the animals, they heard the hoarse bellowing of the bulls, like muffled thunder.

When they rode within sight of the herd, it presented a magnificent view. The shaggy backs seemed to cover the swelling prairie. Buffalo birds skimmed the sky, and below them the buffalo moved lazily, one huge bull rolling in the dust, the others following the cows, roaring their deep and hollow sounds. Around them the silent Indian hunters began to move. They divided into two groups. One group rode into a ravine that divided the women from the herd. As they rode into it they urged their horses into a lope, bending low over their horses' backs so that the gully sheltered them completely from the buffalo. Each rider had changed to his buffalo horse, leaving the horses they had ridden before in the care of the Tsistiks, the first and youngest society of the Ikunuhkahtsi. The hunters had stripped to breechcloth and moccasin, and some wore a robe around their waist. Each carried a bow in his left hand and five or six arrows in his right and had a heavy quirt or knotted bull hide fastened to his wrist. From the back of his pony he dragged a thong some fifteen yards.

Maria studied each of the riders that came into the ravine, but Nakoa was not among them; he had to be one of the riders waiting upon the hill. When the last of the hunters had disappeared into the hollow, Nakoa's group divided, and worked to surround the herd. Lazily they rode toward the herd, slowly driving the buffalo toward the ravine. At first the old bulls watched them curiously as they approached, but when they were only about a mile away, the bulls turned uneasily and joined the rest of the buffalo. As the riders began to close the gap between them, the bulls broke into a gallop, their hoofs flying and their shaggy heads down. Alerted, the whole herd was running now, going crazily toward the ravine. They boiled toward it like a giant thundering river, and when the first group of hunters emerged from the hollow, they wheeled from the ravine in terror, and choked themselves in hopeless milling confusion. Around and around they careened, trampling, goring, crushing, and climbing over the falling and weakening. High clouds of dust rose to the sky. Wherever the buffalo sought refuge, new groups of screaming, shouting hunters would emerge, and the circle of their terror became tighter and tighter, smaller and smaller, as their thundering hoofs continued to shake the prairie.

Then came the twanging of bows, and shadowy forms on horseback darted among them and separated the bulls from the cows. An Indian rode upon a cow from her right side, and shot his arrow into the soft spot between her hip bone and last rib. At the twanging of the bow, the pony wheeled away as the cow charged and attempted to gore horse and rider. The arrows went into the cows with such force that they sank to the feather and sometimes passed through their entire body.

Maria saw the shadow of a hunter left horseless and running for his life. A bull charged him, and the hunter snatched the robe from around his waist and threw it over the horns of the bull, blinding him. In an instant he drove an arrow into the animal's heart and worked his way clear of the herd. Another hunter, thrown violently from his horse, grasped the thong that trailed his pony, and checked the animal's flight. He mounted again, but he was now so thickly surrounded by the buffalo that he could not work himself free. The beasts crowded him closer and closer, and the women moaned to see this unknown rider crushed to death. But he leaped from his pony, and with marvelous skill, jumped from one buffalo's back to another, until he reached safety.

The clouds of dust now drifted to the women. They could see the buffalo still moving frantically, but slowing down, blood pouring from their mouths and nostrils. Their tongues lolled as their hearts and lungs labored, and some stopped and stood still, their sides feathered with arrows. They would gore feebly at passing riders, but soon the dust that they had kicked up settled to their shoulders, and the riders dismounted and began claiming their kill by the markings of their feathers. Drawn by the disaster, some of the cows and bulls that had escaped, returned, and stood stupidly gazing at the flaying and cutting of the carcasses before them, until they too were killed.

To Maria, Nakoa was the hunter who had defied death in the dust. There was no other hunter in the world that day, and when the women finally moved onto the bloody field, she looked for him eagerly.

As the dust finally settled, the shouting and calling of voices began. Women aided each other in finding their husband's kill; the Tsistiks joined them in the butchering and excitedly argued who was the best hunter; the dogs began to yap and growl furiously over the discarded meat.

Maria saw Nakoa far away from them.

"Nakoa always kill most by-damn buffalo," Atsitsi growled. "So you have most work."

"You too," Maria said grimly.

"Nakoa your man, not mine."

"You're still eating!"

"Atsitsi old and tired."

"You'll make me cry."

Nakoa had butchered three buffalo and continued to work far ahead of them. "Why not bury silly cows, and catch up with him quick?" Atsitsi asked, knowing Maria's eagerness to be with Nakoa.

All day long Maria and Atsitsi carried meat back to the camp, leading the burdened horses and carrying what they could. The sun grew hotter above them and the flies more tenacious in clinging to the darkening meat. Lines of women and loaded horses passed and repassed each other, all stained with blood and sweat, and Maria became too tired to care whether they ever met Nakoa.

They had taken the meat from thirteen butchered cows back to the tipis, and the afternoon was going. The dogs had gorged themselves and fallen asleep in what shade they could find. The field still lay strewn with carcasses and swarms of buzzing flies. As they walked through it, Maria thought she could not take another step.

Nakoa had butchered his last cow and rode to them without Maria's knowing it. She just looked up and he was there, studying her with his black eyes. Her hair straggled around her perspiring face and when she looked down at her new dress with its bright quills she saw that it was stained with dried blood. She hung her head, not wanting to look at him.

"Maria is tired," Nakoa said to Atsitsi. "I will take her back to the village. You can bring back the rest of the meat."

"You crazy, by damn?" Atsitsi screamed. "I old woman!"

"Who still must eat," Nakoa reminded her gently.

"I no eat fourteen cows!"

"Try her," Maria said.

"That sweet!" Atsitsi raged at Nakoa "You be with Maria and I prepare meat of half buffalo herd. Why I have to die so soon?"

"Sikapischis will be here tomorrow to help you," Nakoa replied and lifted Maria to his horse. As they rode away, Atsitsi broke into a frenzy of cursing.

Nakoa held Maria close, yet he did not embrace her. At his touch her strength returned. She wanted to go to his lodge; she just wished she could go to him clean and dainty in her new dress. He left her at Atsitsi's borrowed tipi, helping her from the horse and riding away without a word. Maria looked after him dumbly. Completely exhausted, she went to her couch, and without even taking off her dress fell into immediate sleep.

Atsitsi woke her up with a cry of rage. "What? What? Why you not in Nakoa's lodge? Why you here?" She had picked up a piece of wood, and Maria got off her couch in alarm. Atsitsi heaved the wood into the ashes of the fire pit. "God damn!"

The next day, preparing the meat from the hunt, Maria worked harder than she had ever worked in her life. The meat had to be cured before it spoiled, and although this large kill made it unnecessary for the men to seek another herd, there would be at least five days of curing before the camp could break and return to the main village.

There was much to do. Maria started working on the *depouille*, the only animal fat the Blackfoot ate. This special delicacy was tender and sweet, an Indian bread to be eaten with lean and dried meat, and was always carried by war parties. Nakoa had taken from the cows the fat that ran along the backbone from the shoulder blade to the last rib and weighed from five to eleven pounds. Maria dipped it in hot grease for about a minute and hung it inside a lodge to smoke for twelve hours. Once smoked, the *depouille* would keep indefinitely.

Pemmican was another essential for war parties; one pound of it was equal to five pounds of meat. To prepare it, marrow fat was boiled out of the bones, tallow boiled with it, and both were stored away in buffalo bladders. Then the choice parts of the cow were boiled and set out to dry in the sun. When these pieces became hard and dry they were heated until they became oily, and then were pounded with a stone hammer. A paste already made of cherries or other berries, including seeds, would be added to the meat and mixed with the marrow and tallow. The combination was stirred in a trough of buffalo hide, and then stored in parfleche bags. Pemmican could later be eaten from the bags without cooking; it would keep for years. Pemmican and depouille were usually eaten together, and Maria remembered them as the only food she had eaten when Nakoa and the Mutsik brought her from Snake land.

Sikapischis and her family arrived that afternoon. Maria greeted them warmly and then left Sikapischis to work with Atsitsi while she went to the river for more water. She knew how heavy the water paunches would be on the return trail, and she walked along the path out of the village dispiritedly. She could see nothing ahead but dismal days of work, without Nakoa seeking her out even once.

"Maria," a man said. Startled, Maria looked up at Siksikai. She flushed with embarrassment at seeing him for the first time since the Kissing Dance.

"It's you," she said.

"I thought you might know me," he smiled.

She did not smile in return. "Siksikai," she said, "I must speak to you with a straight tongue. I am sorry for what I did to you at the Kissing Dance. I am new to the ways of the Indian, and I was blind with rage at Nakoa. I did not mean to choose you as my lover."

He frowned in anger. "You did not know the meaning of the dance?"

"Anatsa had told me. But I acted in anger at Nakoa. I was foolish, and I am sorry."

"Why were you feeling anger at Nakoa?"

"Because he had been ignoring me."

"You want Nakoa?"

Maria began to feel fear of the man. "You know that it is announced that I am to be his second wife."

"You cannot be his wife if he takes you to his couch here!"

"I am sleeping at Atsitsi's."

His mouth tightened and he grasped her shoulders. "You lie," he said.

"I do not. Nakoa is keeping me for marriage. He would not make me unclean."

"In front of our warriors you promised yourself to me."

"I am sorry."

"You have made a fool of me. You pledged yourself to me!"

"I unpledge myself now!"

He stepped away from her, and Maria looked up into his face. In a different vision Siksikai's face became a mask of death. A coldness crept into her limbs, paralyzing her, as if she were slowly dying from the bite of a venomous snake.

"You will keep your promise," he said.

In the black depths of his eyes she saw herself extinguished. "You are a monster!" she whispered.

"Whom you have invited to enter you," he replied, and walked swiftly away.

Maria caught her breath. It seemed that in her terror she had ceased to breathe altogether. Never had she felt so frightened, so alone. She thought of Nakoa and knew that she would die before she would ever feel the caress of his love. This warm flesh that ached for him at night would be cold prey for the worms because of her foolishness at the Kissing Dance. She stood still in the warm sunshine of that afternoon with the coldness deep in her heart. Slowly she walked to the river. It was all now past her reach. The shadows that dappled the ground had moved beyond her; the birds were calling happily from another world.

Women were working around her getting fresh water and scrub wood. Their soft chattering and happy laughter were alien to her. They filled their water vessels and left. She was as alone as she would be when Siksikai killed her. In her rage, she had chosen oblivion instead of love. The pattern was set; the clay molded.

Grieving at what she knew was to be, she sat down by the river. The moss near her was cool and pungent. Weeping in loneliness, she put her head near the water that moved swiftly by, not pausing to give her the sustenance she had to have. She saw her own reflection swimming in its dark depths. Her long hair and pale face peered up at her.

The shadowed eyes continued to watch her. This was the harlot that had pledged her to Siksikai! This was the whore who would take Siksikai to get Nakoa's attention!

The woman below her moved seductively. "Go away!" Maria said. "Go away!"

"It is you who will be gone!" the woman in the waters whispered.

"I am real, and you are the reflection! You are hiding my view of the drifting clouds, of the sun! Who are you to cast me in shadow?"

Furiously, Maria struck at the waters and her image shattered in a flurry of bright bubbles, only to return again when the water calmed. She wanted Nakoa but she had seen the disapproving look on Ana's face when he had first kissed her with love, and she had slapped him. In her dream, she had seen Meg try to seduce him and she had run away from them both in terror. Yet she had to have him. Her body and soul craved union with his. When she had run away from him and their marriage, all of the beautiful and fragrant white flowers of the prairie had died. Every sensual sound in the moonlight had become silent. Then she would marry him to the tolling of funeral bells! Before her father and before God she would accept him! She eagerly bent over her image again. "You are wrong," she said. "I am the one who lives!"

A water ouzel skimmed merrily over the water and began to sing from the shadowed bank. A gust of wind shook the cottonwoods and the woman at her feet. When the wind quieted they looked at one another, each lost in the lonely expanse of the sky. "Nakoa," Maria called and filling the water paunches turned to go. A shadow lay immovable in her path. She looked up and saw that she was standing face to face with Nakoa.

"You were calling for me," he said, his voice soft.

"Yes," she answered.

"Why?"

"Because I am alone." From the river came the sound of soft mocking. "Dear God," she said bitterly, "she is back!"

"Who is back?"

"The whore! The harlot! The other part of myself that you all want me to be!" More tears slid down her cheeks.

He took her trembling hands and held them strongly in his own. "Where is this woman?" he asked her gently.

Maria went to the river, and pointed down at her reflection. "There!" she said in agony.

He came and stood by her side. "I have a reflection too," he said.

"Mine isn't just in the water!"

"We all carry many reflections of ourselves, Maria."

"But mine is real!"

"Why not? You are real!"

"You don't understand!" Maria sobbed, hiding her face from the woman at her feet. "She is a whore like Atsitsi, and I hate her!"

"How could you hate such a beautiful woman?" he asked. "Look at her again, Maria!"

She sat upon the bank, looking fearfully down at her image. Its long dark hair seemed to caress the pale face tenderly, its eyes were again mysteriously shadowed. "I don't know her," Maria said, recoiling.

"Yet you call her a whore."

"Look at her wiggle, and move her breasts for you! Look at her beg–"

"It is the effect of the wind. The man beside her stirs too. Do you think that in the touch of the wind any woman would remain untouched?"

"I am clean. I am not like her!"

"How can water remain always clean? Does it not absorb the earth?"

Maria pressed her hands to her face. "I am a virgin," she said stubbornly. "That bitch in there would accept anything!"

"That bitch in there accepts the universe."

"I am good," Maria wailed. "I am untouched!"

"To be untouched is to be unborn! This is not the woman who tried to ride back to the Snakes to save the girl with yellow hair. Did you think then of remaining untouched?"

"No," she said.

"Do you think of remaining untouched by me?"

"No," she whispered, feeling her face flush.

"Then do not think being untouched is being good! You are a woman of blood and warmth," he said. "Drain them away—give them to the woman at your feet—and what you will not know will rise and destroy you!"

He took her within his arms and kissed her. Then passion grew until she did not know that he had taken off her dress. When she felt his lips against her bare flesh she reached for her clothing.

"I want to kiss you, not your dress," he whispered.

"Someone will see us," she gasped. He smiled and moved her to thick ferns, and when they lay in shadow all modesty left her. She kissed his lips wildly, covered his face with kisses, his cheeks, forehead, and closed lashes. She closed her own eyes, blind to everything, for here was feeling beyond what she could bear. She would be gentle; she would be wild; in every way that she could, she begged him, begged to be close to him in all of the time there was on earth.

She was beautiful, beautiful. She had been created for him. Her breasts were soft and white for his touch. The roundness of her hips, the tapering of her legs, the full lips, the dark eyes so thickly lashed, the long dark hair, the white flesh, all were treasure for him— for this moment when the craving emptiness within herself would be filled. She moaned almost in agony.

He drew slightly away from her. "Where is the woman who wants me inside of her?" he said softly.

She fiercely pulled his lips back to hers.

He drew away from her again, finally. "Where is this woman, Maria?"

"Here! Here!"

"She is not a whore? A harlot?"

"No! No! No!" Maria sobbed, waiting for his penetration. "She is a woman—deeply blessed—in loving you!"

Their lips sought each other's again, and in their long embrace each could feel the violent emotion that shook the other. But Nakoa stopped the tide that swept them to total consummation. "Maria, Maria!" he said in pain, and wrenched himself free of her. "The agony of the Sun Dance I could bear," he choked. "I could do that—to become a warrior. Now I can keep myself from you—to keep you clean."

"I don't want to be clean," Maria cried. "I want you!" She reached for him, pulled him back within her embrace. "Nakoa, I love you. I love you!"

He kissed her lips, his touch more tender than it had ever been.

"Nakoa," she pleaded. "Love me!"

He kissed her still turgid breasts. He put his hand to her racing heart. "Culentet," he said. "The little heart beats so swiftly for me, blessing me with its life. I love you in my heart, and in my flesh I will love you too. But I will not make you unclean. Among my people, who are now your people, an unclean woman has no voice to the sun. An unclean woman can bring no children that stay with their father. An unclean woman has no lodge, no husband, and goes to the couch of any man who is willing to pay the price. Maria, do not beg me again. What I love so in my heart, I will not destroy with my flesh!"

Overcome, Maria bowed her head, feeling her long hair shielding part of her breasts.

"You have the most beautiful breasts I have ever seen," he said.

She turned away, flushing. Under his careful gaze she had begun to feel unclean again. He sensed this and gently kissed the side of her face. Her shame vanished, but with her quick response and the sight of her pink-tipped breasts so close to him a renewed passion shook him and he felt that he could no longer resist her. "Put on your dress," he said gruffly, and then watched her with agony as she covered her nakedness. He was ashamed. His strength might well have left him; he might have succumbed to his lust.

She walked back to him and kneeled over him, her face radiant. Her eyes shone with love. She kissed his lips tenderly. "Thank you," she whispered. He did not meet her smile, beginning to feel pain for having resisted her.

"Nakoa," she said softly, "I am a woman of heat and blood. I apologize now to that poor creature in the river—let her have the sky and clouds—let her have the universe—I have you!"

"Maria," he said seriously. "You will walk in my way?"

"Yes, yes!" she breathed, kissing him ecstatically. They lay in the lacy ferns, apart, so they could look at each other in wonder. "Before every sun in the sky, and every seed of the earth," she said soberly, "I love you."

"And before everything that I am, or ever hope to be, I love you," he answered.

They absorbed each other in long silence. Finally she whispered: "Has any woman upon this earth ever loved like this?"

"Has any man upon earth ever loved before?" he answered.

"How could there have been any time before now?" Maria asked.

The ferns rustled gently above them, and still feeling pain, he put her head upon his shoulder. "Maria, Maria, Maria, a white woman." He was testing her name, as if by saying it, he had magically made her appear.

"Nakoa," she said. "Nakoa."

"Maria, did you know that we met ten years ago?" he asked. She studied his face and his expression was solemn.

"When?" she asked, believing that they had always been close.

"When I was seeking my Nitsokan, my vision, or my medicine and sign from our Father. I was slow in finding it. I fought and gained coups without protection and with only luck. But upon my last fast a woman came to me, a woman shrouded in the morning mists that were thick in the forest where I had starved for five days. I could see her hair, it was dark but carried flashes of light, like yours. I could see a part of her beautiful breasts, and I went to her and although she did not touch me, from her breasts I drank—life."

"Is this the sign upon your lodge? The woman of the west wind?"

He turned her face to his and looked at her with all of the love of his soul. "Maria, I dreamed of you. You are my Nitsokan. You are my sign from the Great Spirit."

Maria felt tears come to her eyes.

"You are my touch with the sun," Nakoa whispered, and in spite of themselves they kissed, and while both wanted passion to remain dormant, it leaped to life in each of them, compelling them to break apart, shaken before its power. He rose for them to leave, and before she got up, she bent over her image in the water. Her reflection rose toward her eagerly, and Maria blew the shadowed woman a warm kiss. "Good-bye," she said tenderly.

"Where will she go?" Nakoa asked Maria, smiling.

"I want her to go to the villages where there is life and talk and the smell of cooking food. I want her to go where another Maria can meet her lover, and then let her sleep, and dream beautiful dreams."

"Sleep is not for such a woman!" Nakoa exclaimed, his image joining hers. "Do not sleep and remain in darkness," he said to the woman in the water. "You are the carrier of life, the reflector of the sun. You bring nourishment to the earth and to the man."

The two images in the water clung to each other in a long embrace and then with a sudden shaking in the river's depths, they seemed to be flung violently apart, and when the river calmed again, they were both gone, and only the blue sky with its drifting clouds shone upon its serene surface.

Chapter Fourteen

Nakoa came to Maria that night in great agitation. "You were seen talking to Siksikai!" he said.

"Yes," Maria answered. "I did talk to him."

"Why, Maria? Why?" he asked angrily.

She and Atsitsi were sitting by their outside fire, and Maria felt the old woman watching her closely. Embarrassed at Nakoa's anger with her, she began to feel anger of her own. "Why?" she repeated after him. "Well, why not?"

"Big Maria full of self again," Atsitsi growled.

Nakoa knelt swiftly at Maria's side. "I told you not to speak to him! That is why not!" His black eyes snapped in fury; how different he was now from how he had been at the river!

"Siksikai was in my path. I could do nothing but speak to him."

"If a mad dog blocked your path, would you stop and speak to it?"

"Siksikai is a mad dog?"

"Do not mock my words. Siksikai is a man, and a man can be more dangerous than a dog."

"I told him that I acted without thought at the Kissing Dance! I told him that I was yours and had no right to choose him!"

"What?" Nakoa asked her, his face incredulous. "What your words said is that you have to go to me! They said that you still want him!"

"They did not!" Maria answered hotly. "I called him a monster."

Nakoa turned to the old woman. "Go and help Sikapischis," he said to her.

"Now why old woman always have to leave lodge?" Atsitsi whined. "Sikapischis young and have fun fixing cows!"

"Leave, Atsitsi," Nakoa said firmly.

Atsitsi spat her food out, narrowly missing Maria's face. "Ha! See if you can fill sweet titty with milk!" she snapped, and lumbered away.

"Maria, Maria, when will you think?" Nakoa said despairingly.

"I talked to Siksikai that way because I am afraid of him!"

"Maria, if there had been no talk between you, he would not know your fear! Fear begs for more fear, and now he will seek you again! Napi—if I just could kill him now!"

"Nakoa, do not talk of killing!"

"I kill only with reason."

"Do not destroy Siksikai because of me! I will not talk to him any more!"

"Maria, do not go to the river alone again. Here, Sikapischis will go with you, and when we return to the circle camp, you can get water and wood with Anatsa."

"Anatsa?" Maria smiled. "I don't think Anatsa will have time to be walking with me. She and Apikunni are getting married."

"Apikunni is marrying Anatsa?" Nakoa looked surprised. "I didn't know they had even spoken!"

"Yes, they spoke coming back from the river one day. He even carried the scrub wood for her. It created much talk!"

Nakoa laughed.

"Then they rode together to the mountains to find otsqueeina for Apeecheken. The next night they rode around the village in courtship."

"I am glad," Nakoa said. "Apikunni is as close to me as blood brother. I am proud that he could see the beauty in Anatsa."

Maria smiled shyly. "Why didn't you love her?" she asked.

He met her eyes directly. "I had already been touched by you," he said.

"Nakoa," she said, "would you like to see the white man's land?"

"No," he answered.

"Why not?"

"Because I am Indian, and I live my life here."

"But when we marry."

"You walk in my path."

She felt almost overwhelmed with love. "It will be my pride and my pleasure," she answered softly.

He stirred the fire, and studied her face in that careful way of his. "Maria," he said finally, "talk to me of the white man."

"What shall I say?"

"Tell me of his power."

"The white man rules the world."

"No man can rule the great oceans."

"He rules all of the seas, and all of the land across them."

"All of the land?"

"All."

"No man can rule the land. No people can claim all of the earth."

"The white man does. He fights great wars and then the land is his."

"If he believes this, then the land owns him. He owns nothing."

"Your people fight for land, Nakoa."

"The Indian does not fight great wars. He fights to keep the enemy from his village and from taking all of the buffalo herd. We live upon Mother, the earth, but we do not own what has been given in grace. I walk this part of the earth now, and I feel the sun here in my youth and in my strength, but I cannot claim the spring or the winter of tomorrow. We cannot hold the sun, and we can hold no part of the earth it warms. It is like saying that wherever a shadow falls, the land will be mine and my children's children. But every man knows the pattern of the shadow changes with the movement of the sun."

"The white man keeps the land he takes."

"A people own nothing. A person owns nothing. At the end of his path, a man has only himself."

"You call this Blackfoot land."

"We live upon it now. But we cannot claim it in the years ahead when our hands have turned to dust. We cannot take what is greater than ourselves. Let your white man be the conqueror. Let him gorge upon what belongs only to the Great Spirit. Let him grow fat and sluggish, and sick on his own waste. Then slow and helpless, he will be devoured by the lean and the hungry. It is always the conqueror who becomes the slave."

"You hate the white man," Maria said sorrowfully.

"I would never walk in his way. But I do not hate what I cannot accept."

"Nakoa," she said, "Your father has been so kind to me. I know that in his heart he likes me. He has already called me daughter, and yet he does not want us to marry."

"I know this. All of the high chiefs oppose our marrying. I do not know myself if it will be a good marriage."

"Nakoa!" Maria breathed, stung by his words.

"When our touch is close I am not an Indian, and you are not a white woman. I ache to enter you until I feel pain from it. I look at you now in this firelight and I remember how you looked naked this afternoon. Upon my couch I have awakened in the middle of the night and ached to have you beside me. Twice I have almost entered you. I know that I have to do this. This is all I know!"

Maria kissed the side of his face tenderly.

"But how can such a love bring such pain of the flesh? How can a marriage be good with such an aching in its denial?"

"I don't know. But in my love for you I will bear all pain as I bear ecstasy," Maria said.

He gently brushed the hair away from her face and looked at her with tortured eyes. "Culentet, our way will be hard. I know this. I want you and I will have you, but if my feeling for you be love, you might prefer my hate!"

She kissed his hands. "Do you intend to bring me pain?" she asked.

"A man brings a woman pain when he enters her for the first time. And when the loved woman gives birth she may die from what love conceived. Maria, Maria, culentet, you are my sacred Nitsokan, the pathway to my Father, and the power of my feeling for you makes me shake in fear. I would shield you from every pain and I would feel every pain in my rage to have you." He stopped speaking, overcome with emotion.

Her eyes filled with tears. "I never dreamed that I would love like this," she replied softly. "It makes you so vulnerable."

"I know," he smiled. "My love for you has made me a stranger to myself."

They leaned back against Maria's couch, watching the fire. "The white man lives in houses of wood," he said.

"Yes. And of stone or brick."

"Can he see the sky as we do—through the smoke hole?"

"He has windows. He sees outside through glass windows."

"It is not the same. I would not like it."

"I know. You would not like a house."

"I would not feel the wind."

"In winter you might be thankful for this."

"Our tipis are warm in the coldest winter. Not even in the winter would I be separated from the earth. I love Mother, the earth."

"I know you do. And when the white man builds his cities he crowds out all of the wild flowers and the trees. There are carriages and wagons and so many people, and the earth that was, is lost."

"That is very sad that the white man has to live like this."

"Most don't live in cities. That is where the trading is done."

"Why does the white man move from his land of the rising sun across the prairie?"

"He seeks new land because he needs new soil for the food he plants."

"He hurts the earth?"

"The earth becomes tired from his planting. And he gets restless staying in the same place."

"Before he moves on he should nurse the earth back to the way it was."

"This is not important to him. He does not consider the earth sacred."

"Mother, the earth, is a part of the Great Spirit. The white man is stupid."

Maria smiled at him tenderly. "The white man rules the world."

"He does not. No man can rule the world if he can not rule

himself, and if he does not respect Mother, the earth, he does not rule himself."

"Nakoa, he has gold and guns. He has greater numbers than the Indian. He will take this prairie some day."

Nakoa looked sadly into the fire. "We have heard that they are without end. I have said that we do not claim this land. We follow the game of our hunting grounds. If your white man would not let the Indian remain upon the land that he does not claim, then the white man has no brothers, and he will be destroyed by this."

"Maybe you will be left your land. Our God has said that the meek shall inherit the earth. The people that covet nothing."

"Maria, do not say 'your God.' We have heard of the white long robes that come to us and tell us that there is a sun!"

"They want to teach—"

"All men are united with the Great Spirit. We know this. Let your long robes work with the whites. We have heard of your gold and guns. The white man worships the yellow metal and scars the earth to take it and then uses his guns to kill others who want what he wants. Your long robes should ask them why they have traded the fire of their soul for the fire in the ground."

"Indians fight."

"Not for the whole world."

She said nothing, watching the fire. Nakoa's closeness made her too happy for speech. He kissed her hair and with a little exclamation she turned to him, and he took her in his arms and kissed her deeply. He held her in his arms until Atsitsi returned. Before she finally dozed with her head against his breast, she heard him speak to himself. "I would never live in a house," he said.

Chapter Fifteen

In the five days that it took the meat to be cured, Maria learned what the buffalo meant to the Indian aside from meat for food and skins worked for clothing and shelter. The bull's neck was shrunk and used for a shield, so toughened that no arrow could pierce it. The green hides became kettles, cradles, whips, mittens, quivers, bow cases, and knife sheaths, and when the hide was braided, it became a strong and durable rope. Buffalo hair was used to stuff cushions and saddles; horns were transformed into spoons and ladles, hoofs into glue, sinews from the back and belly into thread, ribs into scrapers or runners for sleds; shoulder blades were fitted upon wooden handles and used for axes, hoes, or fleshers; and the buffalo tail was fitted to the end of a stick and used for a flybrush.

Skins took the place of cloth, for the Blackfoot women did not weave, and the dressing of skins was one of the main occupations of a woman; her worth was estimated by her output. The skins were given either a rawhide or a soft tan finish. The stiff rawhide skins were used for the soles of moccasins, parfleche bags, tobacco pouches, and bags to carry skin-dressing tools and sewing implements. The softened skins were made into clothing, the ceremonial buffalo robe, and the upper part of the moccasin. The skin for moccasins was tanned and decorated and then sewn to the rawhide sole. Buffalo hair was left on skin used for winter moccasins, as it gave much additional warmth.

The rawhide process took more strength than skill. Shortly after the hide was removed from the buffalo, it was stretched out upon the ground, hair side down, and held in place by wooden stakes.

Muscle tissue, fat, and coagulated blood were removed with a fleshing tool, and the hide was then cured and bleached in the sun for several days, being saturated with water to keep it from becoming too stiff. It then was scraped down to an even thickness. When this rawhide process was completed, the hair side was turned up and worked in the same manner.

The skins that required a soft tan finish were laid upon the ground and carefully rubbed with an oily compound of buffalo brains and fat mixed with liver. The rubbing was done in the sunlight, the fat worked in with a smooth stone, and when the hide was quite dry it was saturated with warm water and rolled tightly into a bundle. The skins then shrank and were stretched out again and rubbed vigorously with a rough-edged stone until they presented a clean-grained appearance. Then to further dry and soften them they were sawed back and forth through the loop of a thong. The Blackfoot darkened their soft tan skins by smoking them, then stored them away to be tailored into clothing later.

Maria worked hard but she enjoyed the days at the buffalo camp. Nakoa would meet her at the river in the afternoons when she was finished, and in sight of the other women they would talk long and earnestly; when they were alone she kissed him and was kissed in return, but it was he who held them from more intimacy. "I guess a woman just can't rape you!" Maria laughed, and he smiled.

"Many women could," he said. "But not you."

"Well, thank you." Maria pouted.

He looked at her dark face and laughed. "Maria! You are not just one other woman in the water. You are all along the prairie, behind each blade of grass! The first Maria in hiding says, 'I am a virgin and am clean and sweet!' The second says, 'I will protect this girl-woman and keep her a girl!' Another Maria shakes the grass in rage and says, 'You are a man, and why aren't you trying to rape me!' "

Maria smiled. "Well, Atsitsi says that I am sex crazy. And she says that she knows everything!"

It was a wonderful beautiful world. So deep was Maria's love for Nakoa that she told Sikapischis of it with wonder upon her face.

"Oh, what feeling has come to me that I have never known before!" she said. "There has never been a love anywhere like ours."

Sikapischis smiled. "I am sure that there has not."

"I have such strength from him! And yet before him I have no defense. He has parted my soul. I can almost see what is the center of my being."

"But how much will you finally long for the old ways of your people? The ways that are different from the ways of the Indian?"

"The ways of a woman and a man mating are the same all over the world."

"And the way of the child is always the same. To accept a man you must lose the child, and all of the child's memories."

"I have," Maria said soberly. "The child died along the Oregon Trail, back in the land of the Snakes."

"Marriage brings its own children."

"Oh, how I want to bear Nakoa's children! How I want to carry his son!"

"There are other children of marriage that cannot be born, or even carried. Sometimes the children of closeness make closeness impossible again!"

"Oh, I know the way you have of talking! I know that I must be part stranger to myself, and that Nakoa must be part stranger to himself, and neither of us knows how the unknown part of himself will accept the other! But we follow now the part of us that does speak. All I know is that Nakoa is mine. Everything else has been taken from me but Nakoa is mine—and will always be. My God made him, and made me, and has brought us together!"

"And your God can destroy you and destroy him and take you apart!"

Maria's eyes shone. "Not my God," she whispered. "Nakoa is in my heart and cannot be taken from me."

"Your two worlds can meet," Sikapischis said. "This can be, for it is like this even in our dreams. One time becomes a part of another time, and this is a truth to follow."

"Dreams are too silly to follow!"

"But not within the dream. I wonder how long our dreams are.

I wonder how long our life is. I wonder how long our time really is."

"How many dreams do we dream? Well, I do not want this one to ever end for me!"

"It will end in its beginning. My husband heard this from Natosin once, and told it to me. Everything ends in its beginning, and simple things show this."

Maria looked at Sikapischis sadly, remembering that her own husband was dead, and the springtime of love was gone for her. She felt a guilt in her own joy.

"You are wondering how the ending that has come between my husband and me is its own beginning. I have thought of this many times. When I was a bride I accepted my husband. As a wife I have accepted his death. It is the same: I have accepted. He is gone. The bowl might be empty, but I have been nourished. If the meat is gone, we have been nourished by its blood! I accepted my grief, and ended my grieving."

"How can this be?"

"When you accept, something does not fight to stay. Grief is hard to swallow, but when you accept you are nourished and you cannot wail for food that has filled your stomach!"

"Then we are not to mourn for the dead? We are to forget them as if they never were?"

"They were because we have accepted them as part of ourselves, and the part we knew is not gone, or we would not know it to grieve for what we believe to be lost."

"You speak only in words and they are still a long way from the emotion, the despair."

"And the spider weaves a web, and against the sky he climbs upon a thread that we cannot see, but he still climbs. Words do not have to describe the emotion. The emotion still is and can change as the spider climbs upon his invisible web. I have climbed from the pit of my despair that my husband's body rests back upon Snake land, and that now he does not come to my bed, or to the food that I prepare."

The meat had been hunted and prepared for the winter ahead;

the skins taken for new lodges against the winter's cold. When the day's work was done and the drying meat was covered upon its scaffolds, old Mequesapa played his deerskin flute, and the Indians moved to its sweet sound. Siyeh sat by his grandfather filled with pride, for when his grandfather played all the drums stopped, the dogs became still, and even the white wolves far away upon the prairie seemed to be silenced. In the long twilights after the early suppers old Mequesapa played on and on. The stars bloomed in the sky, a bloody sunset was replaced by a glimmering that went gently away; Mequesapa played a new tune, and the women of the village sang it.

> What alone can I call my own?
> What alone belongs to me?
> What is here I can never lose?
> What is here for me to choose?

Maria and Nakoa approached, holding hands. The night was filled with rich scents, warmed grass, and the petals of prairie flowers. In his blindness, the old man sensed Maria's presence, and began to play her favorite song.

> I accept,
> The love and the pain,
> The sunlight and the rain,
> I accept.

Nakoa stared at her, and Maria looked up into his sober eyes. Her dream came vividly back, all of the sensuous sights and sounds of the moonlit prairie, and she saw Meg again, and Ana, and her father asking her if she would take Nakoa for her lawfully wedded husband. That time fused with the present; the flowers of each moment bloomed with a common scent, and with tears coming to her eyes she answered both her father's words and Mequesapa's song. "I do!" she whispered, "I do!"

What alone can I call my own?
What alone belongs to me?
What is here I can never lose?
What is here for me to choose?

Love alone was all one owned; love alone was never lost. Maria thought of the song as she watched the slow fading of the coals of the fire pit. Except for the sound of Atsitsi's snoring, the camp was silent. The stars shone above the smoke hole and beneath their vast expanse she and Nakoa slept apart, but soon they would sleep together, and spend their time together, and the same stars would shine upon their children and their children's children, and their great thirst for life and love would remain unquenched.

She closed her eyes finally, and drifted into a deep sleep. Now her dreams were gentle. She and Nakoa were at the river and the green ferns rustled softly above them. Shadowed waters slipped languidly by. His hands began to caress her body, with their touch she waited for the meeting of his lips, but he did not kiss her. She tried to draw his mouth to hers, her fingers gently moving across his face, and in her touch and seeking a strangeness came, and she awakened with a violent start.

A shadow kneeled by her bed; the caressing and feeling beneath her dress had been no dream. "Aween?" she whispered. A hand clamped her mouth shut, and a knife was held at her throat. She lay still, and then the hand across her mouth moved and she could speak. "Siksikai!" she gasped, and at this sound her head was twisted and her hair pulled cruelly.

"Do not speak," he whispered.

Atsitsi had not stopped snoring. Dear God, if the old witch would wake up!

"Lie still," Siksikai said and quietly removed her dress. She attempted to cover herself with the buffalo robe, and at this, the knife at her throat drew blood from the skin's surface. "If you move or cry out, I will kill you!" he whispered against her ear. His mouth brutally covered hers, his hands hurt her breasts. Rigidly she fought her revulsion, her pain.

"You said you were virgin!" he hissed.

"I am," she sobbed. "Please—please . . ."

His hands moved from her breasts and at his exploration, she almost screamed in agony. "You are," he said and a new passion seized him that was almost a frenzy. "I will be the first," he breathed, forcing apart her legs, and looking at her pale body in the semidarkness.

He was lying upon her now. He would rape her and then he would kill her. What could she do to stop him? Nausea gripped her stomach; pain at his hands upon her breasts again almost made her cry out. But she made herself seek his lips, made herself move as if she were wild to have him too. Her nails dug into his back; she brutally pulled his hair. "Don't wait!" she gasped. "Don't wait!" He drew back to study her face for an instant, and in that instant let her move slightly. Immediately her hand went to her knife belt and before he could stop her, she flung it at the snoring form of Atsitsi.

The old woman gasped and sat up and rubbed her head. "What the big hell?" she said. "Something hit me on head! Something hit me on head!" she repeated excitedly, and before she was fully awake, Siksikai slipped from the tipi. "Big Maria!" Atsitsi screamed in rage. "You kill old woman?"

Maria heard the couch move. Atsitsi was straining to see her as she fumbled for the fire horn. "I light by-God fire!" she snarled, and Maria began to weep.

"Why you cry—I get killed!" the old woman raged. She started a fire and looked across at Maria who was sitting upon her couch and rubbing her aching breasts. Atsitsi saw the cut at her throat and then looked down at the torn dress upon the floor. "All right," she said finally. "Holy ass beg for this!"

"No, no!" Maria sobbed hysterically.

"Oh, stop cry. All done and anyway not enough blood for Siksikai to have finished. When all blood between legs, then Siksikai through."

"Oh, dear God!" Maria moaned.

"Siksikai mean 'Bloody Knife.' Not for killing men, but for using knife on woman while make love. Siksikai make love with knife!"

"Why hasn't he been killed?" Maria moaned, her body beginning to tremble convulsively.

"Other women just think and stay away from Siksikai. He bring back Snake woman and keep her until she bleed to death. I hear screams. When she die I go to body and find out why screams and where bleeding come from."

"Why didn't you tell?"

"Snake woman dead. Blackfoot women stay away from Siksikai. Why tell?"

"And Nakoa promised me to him!"

"You promised sweet self to him!"

Maria covered her face and began to cry wildly again.

"Oh, stop all damned noise. No get knife anyway! I tell Nakoa and he kill Siksikai."

"No!"

"What hell—no?"

"Siksikai might kill Nakoa! And—and—I don't want known what happened."

"Silly fool. Siksikai will try again."

"Not after I marry Nakoa. He would never come to Nakoa's lodge."

"You will never marry Nakoa."

Maria wept until she was exhausted. When she reached down for her dress and put it on she looked across at Atsitsi who had gone back to bed. "Atsitsi," she said furiously, "why didn't you tell me about Siksikai?"

"What to tell about Siksikai?" Atsitsi replied. "Sweet Maria already know man's stick is death!"

Anatsa and Apikunni were married five days after Maria and Atsitsi had gone to the buffalo grounds. Anatsa had been reluctant to marry in the shadow of Kominakus's death, but Apikunni was insistent.

It was July, the moon of flowers, or the moon of the ripened serviceberry, and it was a moon fraught with many changes. Heat of full summer came, and then black clouds skimming over the prairie, and there was light and darkness, one following upon the other.

The body of Sokskinnie could not be found. The print of her moccasin stopped where Korninakus had been killed. The river had been no barrier to her; she had crossed water. So every night, even in the heat, lodge fires burned until daylight, and the medicine drum beat to keep the dead away. If a shadow moved among the lighted lodges, it was not seen. The dogs scented a strangeness and whined to sleep within the tipis, but most of the doorflaps were laced closed against them.

Apikunni wanted Anatsa safe in his lodge.

"It is a bad omen to be joined when the medicine drum beats to keep death away," Anatsa whispered.

"It is sign for me to give you my protection now," Apikunni answered, and in the tradition of the Blackfoot they announced their impending marriage. They had ridden around the village in courtship, and had sung the Night Song together, and now the first processes of the marriage ceremony were begun. Apikunni, Mutsik, was permitted to take his chosen wife to his lodge. So he took many horses and picketed them near the lodge of Onesta, Anatsa's only adult male kin, in the practice of the Blackfoot male purchasing his bride. All in the village knew Apikunni's horses, and when they were seen tethered near Onesta's tipi it was known that Apikunni and Anatsa were now to be married.

In these five days of the announcement, Anatsa cooked for Apikunni and carried his food to his lodge. When she had served him and he had eaten she carried his empty plate back to Onesta's to be filled again, and her crippled leg dragged more than it ever had, as if it fought in last bitterness her desire to be whole. This was the only time that promised bride and groom were to see each other. There was no church aisle and there was no music but the call of the meadowlark, but there were the spectators, lined in a single row along her path, watching her pilgrimage silently and solemnly.

On the fifth night came the wedding feast given by Onesta for the bride and groom and the groom's closest male friends. The supper was a rich, savory one: meat from the choicest part of the buffalo sent back from the hunting grounds, crusted and juicy from roasting. Onesta's lodge in the circle of the high chiefs was bright with light and laughter, and the medicine drum beating near the entrance from the burial grounds was unheard and forgotten. Onesta, as head of the lodge, sat opposite the door with his wife, Apeecheken to his right, and Apikunni and Anatsa to his left. Anatsa wore a wedding dress of white antelope skin ornamented richly with elk tusks, a dress of great value and beauty which had been worn by Apeecheken upon her own wedding night.

Anatsa smiled shyly in the midst of the gaiety of those around her; the tinkling of the little bells upon the tipis was a song in her heart. Apikunni had been the desire of her existence, and now she sat by the fire as his wife. His hands would bring her and their sons food, and she would kiss them and wash the blood from them. She had not been born deprived if her crippled leg had led her to such a path. The moments of the marriage ceremony moved on, blessed in their holiness, this feasting during which she and the friends of her husband first took food together, when she and her husband were first recognized as united.

Apikunni was handsome in a fine shirt with stripes of white skin along his shoulders and the tops of his sleeves. He was gay and happy, for his wife was at his side and around him voices long loved and long familiar spoke.

Anatsa heard his laughter, and looked down at her thin arms, her flat breasts, her crippled shrunken leg. What could her nudity hold for her husband? Her presence was a promise that couldn't be kept, and in sacred marriage, she prayed inwardly and in silence. "Father, the Sun, here is a man strong with your light and warmth. Here is a man who will not be in shadow." What could she ask? For Maria's breasts, for such a face and body of beauty? If this would bring him pleasure, it would bring her more, and with her wedding wish she wanted to supplicate in his name only. Would she wish that their son be in his image? Again she would be supplicating in her name too.

So, inwardly and to her Father, the Sun, she asked only that Apikunni walk a path of his choosing, and in this moment his hand covered hers, and the power of prayer was silenced by the power of love.

"And now the dogs are scattered, having had their meal," Onesta said softly, an age-old custom meaning that the feast was finished. The smoking of the pipe ended. It came to rest with Onesta, the host, and there remained. The guests rose and silently took their leave. Apeecheken looked into her little sister's face, and tears came to her eyes. They shone in the firelight as Apikunni and his bride left to go to their own lodge.

Apeecheken sat long by the fire that night, even after her husband had gone to bed. The time of holy ceremony had remained in the tipi after the bride and groom had departed. It filled the cowskin walls with soft light, and in its presence, Apeecheken wept unashamedly while her husband slept upon his couch.

Apikunni and Anatsa walked away from the circle of high chiefs together. The medicine drum had stopped; only the tinkling of the bells on the lodges followed them sweetly. The night was warm and scented with the smell of prairie grass. Neither spoke. There had been no words of marriage ceremony, no prayer with the talking tongue to the Great Spirit. They had announced their courtship and then their marriage, and had shared food with the groom's closest friends and with the closest male relative of the bride. This is all that was needed, and it was done. When they entered Apikunni's lodge in the outer circle of tipis, they entered it as man and wife.

For just a moment, old doubts returned to Anatsa. She felt a rushing of tears and started to say, "Apikunni, you could have had so much!" but a magic came from the prairie, from the scents of the warm night, from perfumes of ancient lands and incenses, and she said, "Apikunni—I bring you so much!" and tears of joy in her giving came and touched his face.

Chapter Sixteen

The many drums of the Indian nation began to beat. One drum talked to another and that drum picked the message up and sent it on, and deeper and deeper into the prairie grass penetrated the sound of throbbing drums until the buffalo fled and the white wolves themselves slunk away to the mountains. This was the time that the sun was felt to be closest to the Indian, in the period of summer heat when the plains seemed to lie listless under its burning rays. Day and night the drums beat, summoning the Kainah, the Siksikauwa, the Sarcee, Gros Ventres, Kutenais, and Dahcotah to join the Pikuni in the great Sun Dance. The Pikuni lodges alone numbered over five hundred, its people over five thousand. Now dust began to rise beyond the horse herds as more and more visitors came, and before the dance, over sixty thousand Indians had arrived and camped with the Pikuni between the Marias River and the Red Deer Lake.

In the time of the longest days, when the grass was at its greatest height and the berries were ripest, when the running days of the buffalo were over and the meat for winter caught and cured, the Indian paused in his life and gave thanks to the Great Spirit. He gave thanks in his own voice, in the voice of the medicine man, and in the voice of Sacred Woman.

Sacred Woman had always been clean, had never given herself to any man outside of her marriage to her husband. Sacred Woman was a generous woman. In time of great need she had asked for help from her Father, the Sun, and had sworn to fast and mortify her flesh for Him at the time of the Sun Dance. In this year of Maria's captivity, it was her friend Sikapischis who was to be the Sun Dance Woman.

In the winter months before, little Siyeh had sickened with the coldness of the winter snows, and as each day passed on into earlier darkness the medicine drum that beat at his side became weaker with the weakening of his heartbeat. Then it was that Sikapischis, already gaunt with the death of her husband, left the sick lodge and faced the waning sun. Looking up into the pale sky, she crossed her arms over her breast. "I speak," she said trembling with emotion. "I speak to my Father, the Sun!" Others heard her voice and left their lodges, so that they could witness her vow to her Father, the Sun.

"I speak," she said, "to my Father who is separated from me now by clouds that hide His warmth! But I know that it is clouds that hide His warmth, and that He cannot be hidden, for every spring He warms the prairie again and melts the deepest snows that have been built in our winter. If in every sun for as long as we have known, He can bring to us new grasses, and the buffalo to give us life; if for every spring as long as we have known, he can bring life again to the earth, then He will give life again to my son! My son will grow again with the grass of the prairie, for if my Father so loves the grass, how must He love my son! I give my vow now to my Father with the deepest love in my heart. In the summer I will be the Sun Dance Woman. I will give for my Father the buffalo tongue; I will forsake food and drink and make for my Father an empty vessel of my body for the love that I hold for Him. For Him I will make myself a bridge to His suns and in my love for Him I will deny myself its transport. I, Sikapischis, the Sun Dance Woman of the summer days, have spoken."

Old Mequesapa left his grandson's sick lodge, and with his daughter, faced the directions of the four winds, north and south, east and west. And in the chilling and frozen land the winds bore Sikapischis's words to her Father, for in the spring, with the melting of the snows, Siyeh was well again, and ran with the other boys upon the green prairie.

Sikapischis began her collecting of the buffalo tongues. Some were donated to her, some were purchased, but when she was finished she had over one hundred tongues to be consecrated. She already had gained possession of the Natoas, or Sun Dance Bundle, from the Sacred Woman of the year before. And as she had come to like Maria so much at the buffalo grounds, she asked Maria's help in the consecrating of the tongues.

Maria accepted the great honor in spite of the strangeness of the ceremony to her own beliefs, and Sikapischis liked her even more. While they were working on the tongues, Sikapischis looked at her closely. "I have seen many times that a woman or a man has been born with a beautiful body and it takes from the spirit. It is as if there is so much to be given, and if all or so much is given to the flesh, then the spirit must be lacking. The weight of one takes from the other. Maria, I do not find this true of you."

"I am glad," Maria said happily. "But I have noticed too that ugliness from the spirit marks the flesh." She was thinking of Atsitsi.

With other women who were known to be clean, Maria and Sikapischis skinned and sliced the tongues, boiled them, dried them and purified them with the burning of sweet grass. While she worked, Maria suddenly trembled. How could she consecrate these tongues with hands that had fondled Nakoa, begging him to take her? What if the sacred tongues could speak and tell what she really was! It was Nakoa's will that had kept her virgin. She would have made herself unclean and been whore for the whole village in order to have his total caress at the river. Surely her fingers would slip and she would cut herself, revealing that she was unworthy of such sacred ceremony! Her hands remained steady but perspiration of guilt broke out on her forehead.

When the day's work was done she lay still at night upon her couch and wondered why Nakoa had not sought her out. Since their return from the buffalo grounds she had not seen him, and each night she grew more restive and unhappy. What if the Kainah had already arrived? What if he were with the Kainah girl who had come to marry him?

Early in the morning she would leave Atsitsi and seek out the new arrivals. She searched every pretty face of every young stranger with torture to her soul. He could not marry someone else. She would die before she would share him with another woman. She wanted to strike at the hurt and growing pain of his absence. Her love had reduced her to the terror of losing him.

One night she dreamed of his making love to Nitanna and she screamed out in her sleep. She awakened and saw Atsitsi sitting up, her hair standing on end. "No throw by-God knife again!" she shouted, peering terrified in Maria's direction. "Atsitsi old. Better you have screwing than Atsitsi knife in head!"

"Keep still," Maria said, deep in despair.

"Siksikai no here?" she asked.

"No."

"I be sure. No want knife later." Atsitsi rekindled the fire. She looked at Maria closely. "You ever tell Nakoa about Siksikai?" she asked.

"No," Maria said.

"You fool. Siksikai rape kill you."

Maria saw Nakoa lying naked with the Nitanna of her dream and thought she would be sick. "I don't want to talk about it," she said, and went outside.

The village was almost dark with a faint glow coming from the inner lodges of the high chiefs. The sky was moonless and the stars bright. Sadly, Maria looked at them. They were so cold and alien. Is this where her father and mother and Ana had gone? Was Heaven in one of those distant stars? How many worlds were there and how many dreams did a person have to dream out?

The sound of muffled drums came from the inner circle. The Mutsik was entertaining the braves from all of the visiting tribes every night. She pictured Nakoa as head of the Mutsik honored by them all. Her heart ached for him. She closed her eyes and tried to reach his thoughts, to will him to come to her. The drum beat on and on, and she stood by the door praying for him to seek her out. Then the drum beat ceased, and the village was completely quiet. In the great loneliness of the night a dog howled out to the silent prairie and then was still. No shadow came from the inner tipis to her.

In the days that followed Maria walked aimlessly around the

village. Nowhere did she meet Nakoa. She saw more and more strange women greeting one another excitedly as they unloaded their lodge poles, robes, bags, and the small children that had ridden the travois atop all of the household goods. The village was filled with strangers and happy confusion. Warriors who hadn't seen each other for a year greeted each other with joy, and their families spent the evening feasting together. Still the Kainah had not arrived. There was more and more talk of the beautiful daughter of their chief being late for her own wedding.

The ceremonies for the erection of the sweat houses began. Skulls of buffalo were now placed on top of the sweat houses, their empty eyes facing east. They faced the constant coming of new herds, and their ghostly eyes beckoned the thundering of hoofs, for in their skulls was placed fresh meadow grass so that the buffalo would always eat upon the prairie and bring the Indian life.

This was the thankfulness of the Sun Dance. The sun brought life to the grass and to the buffalo; the buffalo brought life to the Indian so that he could know the warmth of the sun. The circle of one began and ended in the other. The giant circle of the tipis upon the prairie reflected the greater circle of the sun. Man toiled like the ant upon the earth, but in his toiling his great distances could become small, and his small world become an unending distance.

The day before the erection of the Sun Dance pole the Kainah had not yet arrived. The great village was throbbing with excitement. The societies of the Ikunuhkahtsi had begun their ceremonial marches, painted and dressed in their regalia, followed by their drummers beating the rhythm of their chanting. Through the tipis they wound their way, each society led by its high chief. The last of the societies to march was the Mutsik in its position of highest honor, and when it passed through the village it was to enforce the silence that was traditional the night before the raising of the Sun Dance pole. Because its warriors were the greatest in the village, they were privileged to ride their horses, and leading them upon his horse as dark as the approaching night was Nakoa.

All of the other painted faces were nothing to Maria. She didn't see the scalp locks dangling from the war lances, the standards of eagle feathers ruffling in the wind; beneath his paint she saw only the face so beloved to her. He wore the shaved and polished buffalo horns that he had worn when he had met Shonka; besides his father, he alone among his people was honored enough to wear them. In passing, his eyes caught hers, and there came upon his face open recognition and love, and Maria thought she would burst with joy. Then he was gone, and when the last of his riders had passed, all chanting stopped, the last drumbeat was silenced. In the sacred silence Maria's heart swallowed all of the rest of her, and if she had tried, she could have reached up and touched the stars.

The quiet night was a night of full summer in the Indian moon of the homecoming days. A heat spell clung to the prairie; that night all of the silent tipis had their sides raised for ventilation. But there was no wind from the mountains; none of the little bells upon the tipis moved. The horse herds beyond the village grazed in peace; the warhorses of the high chiefs and of the Mutsik stood picketed by their masters' lodges and were tranquil.

The only sound allowed in the village was the music from Mequesapa's deer skin flute that rose plaintively from the inner circle; drawn to it, Maria left Atsitsi's lodge. Others were drawn by the sad little notes, and more and more silent shadows gathered to their source. Mequesapa was far from his daughter's lodge. Accompanied as usual by his grandson, he had come to play for the high chiefs:

What alone can I call my own?
What alone belongs to me?
What is here I can never lose?
What is here for me to choose?

Maria sat upon the warm earth and listened for the singing of the next verse:

All things go to ashes and dust,
All things go the way they must;
What alone is there for me?

What is mine for eternity?

The music stopped, and then Mequesapa played another tune, and this time no voices followed the music. The last words left Maria shaken, but all things could not go to ashes and dust. Love did not die. She felt a stab of terror in her heart, and she was beginning to live a nightmare of loss again when a hand clasped hers, and she knew without turning that it was Nakoa. Relief flooded through her. When she looked into his face, she saw that his black eyes were liquid with feeling. Their gaze was drawn to each other's lips, for they wanted to kiss, but instead they sat motionless and listened to the deer skin flute. Mequesapa's last note drifted to the stars, a benediction, and then all who had shared the earth with them began to leave. Old Mequesapa was the last to walk by them, and he paused by Maria, sensing her presence. "I did not play your song," he said softly.

"What you played was beautiful," Maria answered.

"Acceptance is the Indian gift to you," he said.

"I take it with deep thanks in my heart," Maria replied.

The old man looked sadly down at her. His hollow eye socket made him appear fierce, but to Maria he seemed the most gentle of men. "I will play for you again," he said. "Will you listen?"

"Yes. Yes!" Maria said.

The old man nodded and walked away with Siyeh.

"Did you know his words?" Nakoa asked Maria gently.

"I believe so."

"Do you accept?"

"I accept you. I have said it many times."

"There is more than accepting me, Maria."

They were alone now, and he had made no move to caress her. Impulsively, she flung her arms around his neck and kissed the side of his face. "Why have you stayed away from me?" she asked. "It has been seven days and six nights since we were together."

"Now I am free," he replied. "During the Sun Dance there are no Mutsik ceremonies."

Except the ceremony of your first marriage, Maria thought, and then in panic pushed the thought from her mind.

"Ride with me tonight," he said to her. "Ride with me around the camp circle and past the horse herds."

"I would love to," she said. When he brought his horse to her, she asked his name.

"He is called Kutenai," Nakoa told her. "He is my war horse."

"And is always kept picketed at your lodge so he cannot be stolen in coups," Maria added.

"Yes," Nakoa smiled, looking down at her tenderly.

"See!" she said, stroking the animal who was nuzzling his master's shoulder. "I know the way of the Indian. And I approach an Indian horse and he does not shy away from me."

"He is accustomed to your presence," Nakoa said. "As I am." His face suddenly became agonized and he held her fiercely, as if he were about to lose her forever.

Maria drew back in alarm. "Nakoa, what is it?" she asked him.

She felt a trembling in him. "Maria," he whispered. "I will give up everything for you." Their lips met and held, and in the ecstasy of their touch there was no room for Nitanna, the girl from a distant village.

Together they rode Kutenai out to the horse herds. With so many visitors the herd was vast, but neither the horses nor the young society riding guard around them paid any heed to their presence.

"I have never seen a night so still!" Maria said as they dismounted.

"It is sacred night," Nakoa answered, and released Kutenai to wander away and graze in the darkness. They sat upon the grass already damp with the night dew. Maria stroked some blades. "I love the touch of water," she said.

"Because you are the woman of the river," Nakoa said, smiling up at her as he rested his head upon her lap.

The thought of Siksikai came suddenly to Maria's mind. Pain and revulsion from the memory of his attack made her shudder.

"You have grown cold," Nakoa said.

"The night is warm," Maria replied.

"It is. But you are cold!" He sat up and studied her face. "What is the matter?" he asked.

"Nothing. But I am not the woman of the river! I could not have what a whore accepts."

"Of course you are not a whore."

"At the river with you, when I begged like I did, I was shameful!"

"No, you were the most beautiful and desirable of women. How can you call any part of what we shared shameful?"

"I was! I wanted to expose my nakedness to you!"

"Your flesh wanted to meet mine. It was the desire for our meeting. How can such a thing be shameful? Is it shameful to yearn to unite with the Great Spirit?"

"What does that have to do with my wanting you inside of me?"

"The drive of our existence is a yearning for union. It is in the male and female as one, that we are closest to the touch of the Father! Love begets love, and it is as one that we must return to the first fire of our creation! Of what would the Father create us but of Himself? If His breath is eternal, is not mine eternal? If His breath is sacred, is not mine sacred? A man seeks woman; a woman seeks a mate; it is an endless circle of seeking, and in all of the lives of yearning the union must finally be accomplished. If we came from our Father as one, we must return as one, and so both the male and the female must be close to the sun to find this light of truth."

"If we are all part of God, where is my Heaven and my Hell?"

"Within your heart and upon the path that you walk through your time."

"That would not be punishment enough. That would not be joy enough!"

He looked at her curiously. "Does the white man have a means of measuring joy and pain? Does the white man send his dead either to a place of eternal joy or eternal agony?"

"Yes. This would be the result of the manner in which he lived. He would go to Heaven with God, or to Hell."

Nakoa shook his head. "In Hell there is your great agony?"

"Yes."

"And in Heaven there is your great joy?"

"Yes."

"And your God would forsake those in agony and be with those only in great joy?"

"Those in Hell don't know God!"

"Oh," Nakoa said. "Then our beliefs are not different after all. Those in Hell have not found the sun, and do not know the light and the power that burns within themselves. They are in their own darkness and will have to live until they find their way to the sun. Our Heaven and our Hell, Maria, is our closeness to our Father, the fire that we know as light or as darkness!"

"Then Heaven or Hell is being yourself."

"What else could it be? The finding of the self is the finding of the center of our creation. What power we must reach! Think that the smallest flame could destroy the entire prairie!"

"Then you believe that there is hope for every man."

"Don't you? Is your Hell never-ending?"

"In life, every man can be saved."

"God lives in us and we live in Him. God knows us but we have to know Him. If in your life every man can find Him, then our beliefs are not different."

"They are, Nakoa."

"From where every man stands a mountain might appear different, but this does not change the mountain, and each man sees it just as clearly."

They fell into silence. "It is a strange world," Maria said, "and the only thing I really know is that I love you."

He took her hand. "And I love you," he said quietly. "In twelve days you will be my wife. Do you want this, Maria?"

"Of course! How could you ask me this?"

"Will you burn with your own fire and not be a reflection of me?"

"What do you mean?"

"The moon is beautiful but gives light with no fire of its own. Don't make yourself just a reflection of my love."

"Nakoa, I haven't!"

"You said that when you wanted me to enter you, you were a whore!"

Maria turned her head, remembering how she had caressed him.

"Do you look away from your memory of that day?" he asked.

"Yes," she whispered.

"The woman you were would take me anywhere, in the dirt—without marriage ceremony at all."

"I am not that woman! I am proud that you have wanted to keep me clean!"

He grasped her shoulders. "I have kept you clean so I could marry you. But Maria, I want your body. I want this woman you called a harlot. I want to enjoy the passion of this flesh you disown. I want to enjoy it and not have to give you up!"

"Your love is just sex?" Maria asked aghast.

"Maria! See this in yourself! See what you were at the river—you begged for sex with me!"

"Because I love you!"

"Because you forgot any idea of love and wanted me to enter you then, even if it made you the village whore! Maria, be what you are!"

"Why wouldn't you be satisfied with Nitanna then?" she sobbed.

"I want you more," he said.

"You talk so nicely about God and all of the noble things and sacred fires—and—and all of the time . . ."

"From the first day I saw you. If your body hadn't made me want you, I would not have saved you."

"God! God!" she moaned.

He tried to touch her face tenderly, but she pushed his hand away from her. "Maria, you know of my feelings. I have told you of them. I have told you of a tenderness I feel with my rage to have you. I want to take you in the dirt and worship you with the sun, but still I will not deny the heat of my flesh, for I live and am of the earth. I am not the pure man of your Heaven. And you are not in your white man's Heaven either. If my lips burn to seek your breasts, your breasts burn to be kissed, and if I ache to enter you, you crave my entrance just as much! As part of our Father's earth, it is our flesh that gives us transport, and the desire to mate comes before mating and comes before the birth of new life. It is through the mud of a riverbank that the life to the prairie flows!"

She did not answer him.

"I will take you back," he said shortly.

But they did not ride back to camp. Angry with each other, they were still reluctant to part, so they rode out upon the prairie, circling the horse herd.

"Tomorrow," he said finally, "the Sun Dance ceremony begins."

"Where did your people get the idea of the Sun Dance?" Maria asked coldly.

"In our legend the dance was brought to us from our Father, the Sun. But it was Morning Star who brought us the ceremonies and the dances, for Morning Star is half of the earth and half of the sun. His mother was an earth woman."

"How did a star come from an earth woman?"

"In legend, the Great Spirit lay with her when she was asleep, and she awakened and loved him in return, and accepted him for her lover. When she found that she was to bear his son, he took her to the skies, and there their son, Morning Star, was born. But the earth woman did not love our Father enough and wanted to return to the way of her childhood; she would watch the earth, and weep for her ways of the past. Even her lover and her son were not strong enough to stop her grief, so she was released and allowed to go back to earth and to her grave."

"Why her grave?"

"The past is dead."

"When she died, why didn't she travel the Wolf Trail and rejoin her lover and son?"

"Because she had been among the stars and did not want them. She had been with her lover and son and still had wanted the way of the past. She made her own darkness. She was a child. The wail of a child is so sad. How can one dream while crying? And how can one awaken without dreaming?"

"Another woman living in reflected light," Maria said. "That is why you told me this legend."

"You asked me to tell it," he replied. "But I do not want you to be a reflection of my passion, my feeling. You burn with your own warmth, and putting it in the deepest of waters will not extinguish it. Do not reflect me, for you do not know what I am. I do not know the life we will lead or the depth of waters in this world, for the depth of all waters anywhere depends upon a man's height. I do not know my height; I have not reached the center of myself, and neither have you. So how can I not say I desire but with my flesh? I would give all in the power of my hands and the power of my tongue to possess your body. But what can I pledge to you? I will bring you food; I will bring you our child; I will bring you shelter against the winters of our life, but I will also bring you pain, and anger, and sorrow. Yet how can I tell you that I will love you forever when I know that my flesh will turn to dust? When my spirit is freed I may not know what 'forever' is. Upon the Wolf Trail we may not even know the world! What sustains a small boy cannot nourish me; what sustains an old man cannot nourish me, so how can I speak with a straight tongue of forever? In what new ways will our hunger have to be met?"

All tenderness for him returned and Maria said gently, "Let us be fed in new ways; let us know hunger we have never known before; but if we return in awareness to the Great Spirit, then everything accepted by us has been accepted by Him, and if He is eternal, so will be our love!"

Kutenai picked his way noiselessly through the tall bunch grass, so still under the shining white stars. Maria looked up at them. "I do not like the idea of the Wolf Trail being up there," she said. "I would not like to be lost—in all of that!"

"Where is your Wolf Trail?"

"We picture Heaven as a beautiful city where there are fountains in the streets and song, and where all of the people walk with God."

"Our Wolf Trail goes through many suns. We do not think of what is beyond. We do not know what would be in the change and the growth, or even in the dreams of long sleep."

"We can never be separated!" Maria said, feeling a sudden coldness. "I can never be separated from you!" For the first time since their argument, he embraced her, and she felt his lips lightly touch her long hair. He stopped Kutenai and helped her down from him. This time the horse did not wander away, but stayed near them. Nakoa looked at her soberly. "Maria," he said. "Why haven't you mentioned my marriage to Nitanna?"

"You haven't married her!" Maria said quickly.

"You know I am going to. And very soon."

"I do not believe you will. I do not believe you can love me and marry her!"

He studied her face carefully. "The white man takes only one wife?" he asked.

"Yes," Maria answered. "We even have laws to keep him from taking another wife."

"Then he takes other women outside of his laws."

"No!"

"A white man never takes another woman?"

"Well, yes, sometimes—yes."

"So if another woman is in his bed, she is still outside of these laws."

"Nakoa, do not change my words. I could not accept your marriage to another woman! I could not!"

"Maria," he said sadly, "would you want me governed by what you cannot accept?"

"Nakoa, hear my words," she said, and couldn't keep her voice from shaking. "I love you, but I will not share you with Nitanna. I could not stand for you to love another woman and then love me. How could you want to love her when you love me?"

"I did not say I did," he answered.

Relief left her weak. She flung her arms around him, kissing him with trembling lips. "Then we are to marry?" she asked. "We are still to marry?"

"Yes," he answered.

"No one can stop our marrying?"

"No."

"Nakoa, you want this?"

"Yes, I want this. In twelve days we will be man and wife. In twelve days you will come to my lodge."

His lips found hers; here was the wine of the night, the well of being. In twelve days there would be no restraint between them and she could excite him without the wall of his will stopping them. In the warmth that flooded her, Nitanna traveled wraithlike and sorrowful, back to her people. A wolf howled out across the prairie, lamenting.

"The wolf song is our war song," Nakoa said as they rode back to the village. "The wolf is like the Indian, for we both follow the buffalo. The Indian who kills a wolf will never shoot straight again."

At Atsitsi's lodge they kissed goodnight. "Maria," he said softly as she clung to him when he turned to go, "I did tell you the legend to speak to you beyond its words. The past is a child's path, and can never be walked again. Your old ways are dead with your father and your sister with the yellow hair."

"I know," Maria said sadly.

"Think of the woman who wanted the past instead of her lover and her son. She had created the first star of the earth, but she wanted her grave instead."

Maria smiled and looked up at him tenderly. "I love you and there is no grave in this world for me," she said.

He caught her hand and put it to his lips. "I hope not!" he said with feeling.

"I will trade all that I am, to be your wife."

"I hope that you can," he said seriously, and mounting Kutenai, disappeared among the shadowed tipis.

Maria laced the doorflap tightly closed. She hummed softly to herself as she undressed. Atsitsi's great bulk was silent. For once she was not snoring. Maria felt a sudden pang for the old woman, who had never known a love like hers. How dismal it would be, how desolate, to live a life without Nakoa for a lover!

Soberly, she stretched out upon her couch. She prayed more deeply than usual. As she thought of her blessings, she thought of Ana who had never known a lover. She thought of her mother and her father, and of how they must have grieved at their separation. Pain that she had ever condemned her father for anything at all made tears run down her cheeks. But when she thought of Nakoa and remembered the feel of him and how he kissed her, warmth flooded her soul and her grief went off somewhere, a quiet whisper.

Chapter Seventeen

Early the next morning the camp criers announced the erection of the Sun Dance pole and the building of the Medicine Lodge. The blood bands sent young men of the tribe to bring in trees. Nine forked trees were needed for the lodge poles, branches for rafters, and green boughs to cover the lodge sides. The Mutsik went forward as a war party to bring back the center pole, counting coups as they cut it and broke off its branches. The pole was dragged back to the village by lariats and a travois.

Sikapischis had already purchased the Sun Dance Bundle and now in the lodge of Isokinuhkin, Chief Medicine Man, it was transferred from the former Sun Dance Woman to her. For the first time the village saw their Sacred Woman, now in her fifth day of fasting, as the ceremony of transferring the Sun Dance Bundle was witnessed by everybody who could crowd into Isokinuhkin's lodge. Sikapischis was still painted with sacred red, and she was dressed in ceremonial clothing of deer and antelope skins; singing in unison, her women attendants placed the sacred headdress upon her head. Then they put an elkskin robe upon her shoulder and sang the elk song, and those listening outside knew that it was time for Sacred Woman to emerge from the lodge.

The Medicine Lodge was yet unfinished, but a temporary shelter had been built for Sikapischis and Isokinuhkin. Maria watched her friend and the Medicine Man move toward it. Sikapischis was weak and could not stand without the help of a staff; leaning heavily upon it, she moved slowly toward the Medicine Lodge, faltering twice. Isokinuhkin waited for her in her failing, staying reverently behind her; she gained new strength and walked on, her eyes fixed upon the earth. In the ritual, it was not yet time for her to face the sun. Toward the unfinished lodge she walked, east to south, following the course of the sun through the sky, and finally she and Isokinuhkin entered the shelter.

Offerings were now brought to her from many warriors, and then women came, bringing their collections of sacred tongue. One woman came to Sikapischis, and faced with her the setting sun. "Father Sun," she said. "Hear my words, and pity me in my pain! I have lived straight, and I have been always a clean woman! I bring this tongue that my husband might live, my husband Wunnestou, messenger to the great Mutsik."

A strange look came to Sikapischis's face. She stopped looking at the sun and looked instead at the wife of Wunnestou. The woman became flustered, and bowed toward the sun. "You bow, when your words do not," Maria heard Sikapischis say softly. "Will you speak again?"

"Yes," the woman answered. "In pain I ask that my husband may live." Sikapischis nodded, and the woman departed. Natosin, head chief, entered the shelter, and with Sacred Woman and the Medicine Man, faced the sun. "It is time now for the raising of the Sun Dance pole."

Warriors already selected and dressed for the ceremony raised the pole with ropes; chanting, four lines of warriors raised the Medicine Lodge rafters. Green cottonwood boughs were placed against the lodge sides, and, in the deepening dusk, the Medicine Lodge stood completed. In a circle so large that its outer fringes were not within sight of the ceremony, the Pikuni sang the tribal hymn, and on its last notes, the crowds dispersed.

The village waited for the Sun Dance. Men were purified in the sweat houses; women had offered their sacred tongues; the Sun Dance Woman had mortified her flesh, and the next day could eat and drink. The boys who would become men ate that night in silence. The time for their suffering and their testing was at hand, and all of them knew the agony of its touch.

Caught in the crowds, Maria looked for Nakoa. She had not

seen him all day; yet he had said that during this time of the Sun Dance ceremony, he was free. She had not seen Anatsa since her marriage, and of course she could not talk with Sikapischis. Walking to Atsitsi's lodge, Maria felt lonely. The happiness that had lulled her to sleep the night before had vanished. She felt impending doom and death, and worked to shake both from her mind, but could not.

Atsitsi was eating when Maria arrived and looked as gloomy as Maria felt. Atsitsi bit into the meat, and Maria put her face in her hands and looked sadly into the fire.

"Why not eat?" Atsitsi asked.

"I don't want food."

"Nakoa leave you alone?"

"Nakoa will never leave me alone."

"Natosin stronger than Big Maria!" Atsitsi snapped.

Maria's head turned. There was a sound outside of the lodge. "It is Nakoa," she said happily to Atsitsi. "I said he will not leave me!"

"Man cannot keep pretty bird song or cloud in sky," Atsitsi growled, her face glistening with grease, and laced the door closed as Maria left.

Nakoa was outside, and the camp was light enough that Maria could see that he was smiling as they walked toward the circle of high chiefs. Many lodge fires burned, and the camp was almost as bright as day. They came to a group of boys dancing around a burning pine trunk. Two men with long poles scraped the burning wood, so that showers of sparks fell to the bare backs of the boys. They were being burned painfully, but not once did their circle break, nor did their singing or dancing stop. "Why do they do that?" Maria asked, repelled and shaken.

"They are preparing for the last day of the Sun Dance, and the pain they will meet."

"What will happen to them then?"

"You will see," he said quietly.

"I don't want to!"

He took her hand, and grasped it. "You must, and without pity."

Maria shuddered. "Is it that bad?"

"It is hard for the women to bear. They do not drift in the mists of pain, and they see."

"Did you do this?"

"Of course! You know that no boy becomes a warrior, or takes a woman, who has not borne the torture of the Sun Dance!"

Maria bowed her head. "Do any die?"

"Some have."

"I will not watch it!"

"Yes. You will be my wife. If I could endure the pain, you can endure the sight!"

"Oh, dear God!"

"It is done with reason. I have told you this."

"Is it just to test the ability to bear pain?"

"There is the thought of suffering for our Father, and maybe to some, of sacrificing."

"And being protected in turn."

"It might be. But the ceremony of this last day was first decreed so that the established warriors could pick new ones, so that men could be chosen among the boys."

"It is still terrible!"

"A part of everything is terrible. A part of every life is terrible."

"Birth is terrible," Maria said, thinking of Edith Holmes. "I saw a woman bleed to death having her baby, but her baby was never born. It came partly, and then could come no more. She just bled— and suffered—and bled—until she was like a pale rag doll—a doll with grass stuffing!"

He looked down at her. "You are strong," he said gently. "You will not die in birth."

"Edith Holmes was strong. That is why it took her so long to die."

He stopped, and caressed her shoulders with his hands, holding her still. "I would not let you die in this way. If you so suffered, I would take the child from you. I would take the son that I want with all of my heart in pieces before I would let you die!"

His solemn voice had carried, and a shadow stopping near them heard his words. Feeling the gaze, Maria and Nakoa turned toward him.

"Is it now that when I want words with my son, I have to seek him out?" Natosin asked quietly.

Nakoa said nothing. His father was looking at him sternly. "Were you and your white woman going to ride the camp circle again tonight?"

"Yes," Nakoa said.

"You speak just one word, but in that word lies anger. Is this anger for me or for yourself?"

"I did not know the anger in my voice. It is not for my father. I always welcome the words of my father."

"Then receive these. It is that you cannot ride the camp circle tonight in sign of courtship."

"It is that I cannot?" Nakoa repeated quickly.

"Defiance will rest until I have spoken. The Kainah have arrived, and with them my friend as close as blood brother, and his daughter, your promised bride. Both father and daughter wait for you now, at my lodge."

Maria's heart sank, and she felt her hands grow cold. What she had dreaded had come to pass. Nakoa saw her stricken face. "Maria," he said tenderly, "return to Atsitsi's."

"All right," she said stiffly. He now would send Nitanna away, and she could not tell what resistance he would meet from Natosin. She looked up at him pleadingly. Have courage, my darling, she wanted to say. Then she remembered that she had taught him none of her words for endearment—darling, dearest, my love—and she wanted to weep because he would not understand them at all. Their eyes locked, and in his she saw strength and a will that would not bend. And in them she read his love, and it was upon all of his face for his father to see too. "Do not walk in the camp tonight," he said.

"All right," she answered.

"Do not walk alone until after we are married," he pursued.

"All right," she said again and turned to leave him.

He looked toward the outer circle anxiously. Few people were moving among the lodges. Most of the Pikuni had retired for the night. "I will take the white woman . . . Maria," he corrected himself quickly. "I will take her to Atsitsi's lodge."

Natosin nodded in agreement, and left them. When he had gone, Nakoa took her cold hands and held them in his. "Why do you tremble?" he asked her.

"Because I love you," she answered. "I am afraid of Nitanna."

"Nitanna is nothing to me," he answered, and they walked toward Atsitsi's From a nearby lodge she heard the singing of the Raven

We fly high in the air,
Our power is strong,
The west wind is our medicine.

"I fly!" Maria answered to the song. "My power is strong, fresh from the mountains and the seas, for I am the west wind!"

He pressed the hand that he held as they walked together.

"Nakoa," she asked him softly, "what does your name mean?"

"It means Morning Eagle. I was named after the Nitsokan of my father."

Morning Eagle! How like a proud and untamed eagle he was. Oh, to marry him in a white man's church, to stand with him in front of all relatives and friends. How proudly she would stand with him for, among any people, white or red, his majesty would tower, and beside his strength the white man's cloth, the white man's churches and houses would be nothing.

At Atsitsi's they embraced briefly and parted without words. She watched his tall form until he vanished in the darkness. "Walk your own path, my beloved," she said to him inwardly. "Go with your father, but walk your own path!"

Nitanna meant nothing to him, and he would send her back to her people. Maria felt a pang for Nitanna and her great loss in losing Nakoa, but her own ecstasy swelled within her heart and banished any thought of sadness away. She looked up at the beautiful glittering stars; this was still Sacred Night to her, and she felt as if she and Nakoa were already married, having left the church of her dream, and walking together down the long path of white flowers that bloomed upon the prairie.

At dawn the next day Maria listened to the camp criers summoning the village to the great Medicine Lodge. She watched the Weather Dancers. To insure clear weather for the ceremonies they walked ahead, stopping on their way to the lodge four times and chanting to the beating of three drummers who walked behind them.

The sky was clear and blue; not one cloud marred the touch of the sun. Maria wore her best dress, richly quilled in red, and she felt herself beautiful. She would marry a king, so she was queen, and she was proud that her body had ripened for his caress. She walked in grace and beauty and dignity; every eye followed her as she made her way to where the Sun Dance would begin

Sikapischis, still painted but no longer fasting, waited for them in her sheltered booth, and by her side stood Isokinuhkin, the chief Medicine Man. Then from the lower societies of the Ikunuhkahtsi up to the Mutsik itself came dances and separate rituals to the sun. For two days the praying and war songs went on, and amid the beating of the great drums Maria sat in new dignity. Not once did she see Nakoa. Not once did she see or even hear sign of his bride to be, Nitanna. Natosin and the girl's father, Inneocose, sat side by side through all the ceremonies in majesty and pride, but they sat in no more majesty than did Maria. From the depth of her love she would make him proud.

Upon the third day the Mutsik gave ceremony alone, and Maria watched them file into the lodge and sit in the prominent places reserved for them. Nakoa, their high chief, was absent. The dancing began and fifteen Mutsik re-enacted their coups of the war path. A fire was started before the Sun Dance pole, and the Mutsik danced before it, and with each coup counted a stick dropped into the fire. "Where is Nakoa?" an old woman asked. "Where is Nakoa to make the fire blaze higher?"

Maria looked quickly to Natosin, but he gave no indication of hearing the querulous voice. Still, a silence fell, and the dancing stopped. Eyes turned to Maria, but she gave no heed to them. "It is dark," Natosin said, and he and Inneocose rose and walked from the lodge. Sikapischis followed, and then Isokinuhkin, the Mutsik, and, lastly, the spectators.

Outside, Maria felt the cool air of dusk and at approaching night was stabbed with loneliness. She would go to Anatsa. She had seen her every day, but they had sat apart at the ceremonies and had not talked. Now she had to have talk with her and be touched by her gentle eyes.

Maria walked to Apikunni's lodge and standing by the door, called Anatsa's name softly. Anatsa came out immediately, joy and pleasure shining upon her face at the sight of Maria. They clasped hands.

"Why didn't you come sooner?" Anatsa asked.

"I didn't want to intrude on the first days of your marriage," Maria answered. "Tonight, I have brought you a wedding gift." She unclasped a little golden locket of her mother's that she had worn around her neck from the day her mother had died. "This is all I have to give you. My mother left it to me—and I give it to you in love."

Anatsa took the locket and held it in her slender hand. She went inside the lodge and held it reverently up to the firelight. "It is beautiful," she said, her eyes filling with tears. "I know the feeling you must have for it."

"It is of white man's gold," Maria said, "but it carries the light and fire of my mother. I give it to you that you might have light and love in your marriage, and walk a long and happy path."

Anatsa looked down at the shining locket. "It shines with your light, not your mother's. I will wear it and never take it off, for it will carry your warmth."

"Anatsa," Maria said, "my heart is filled with such joy for you, for your love and happiness in a good marriage. Apikunni is worthy of your love."

"If all of the days left to me were to be filled with agony, I could pay their price with my happiness tonight! Maria, now that'Nitanna is here, when will you and Nakoa marry?"

A darkness came into the lodge. The fire flickered upon the

wedding gifts, the new robes, the backrests, and parfleches that Apeecheken had given her little sister, and suddenly the fire itself was without life.

"You do not answer," Anatsa said gently.

"I do not have a mother or a sister to bless my marriage," Maria answered.

"I am your sister," Anatsa said. "When is your marriage to be?"

"In eight days from now."

"I am glad for you. Nakoa's name is known in every Indian land, but he is gentle."

"I know," Maria said sorrowfully.

"Why do you grieve?" Anatsa asked.

Maria turned impulsively toward the fire, not wanting Anatsa to see the trembling of her lips. "Anatsa, why doesn't he come to the ceremonies? Why hasn't he sought me out? He said that he would be with me every night of the Sun Dance!"

"Nitanna is here. I have heard they are married."

"No!" Maria said in agony.

"I do not believe this," Anatsa said quietly. "They are too important to marry without ceremony."

"Anatsa," Maria said wildly, "we love each other so! Our worlds are one!"

Anatsa smiled. "I know."

"He does not want Nitanna."

"I hear your words, and I believe them."

"He will not marry Nitanna. He is going to send her back the way she came, unmarried."

Anatsa turned away, and put more wood upon the fire. Her face had saddened, and Maria felt new fear. "Maria," she said, "shall I speak to you with a straight tongue?"

"Yes," Maria answered in a small voice.

"Nakoa cannot do this. It would be deep insult to the Kainah."

"I know. But Nakoa cannot do what neither of us could bear!"

"Maria, that which cannot be borne is not known, for it has silenced the tongue."

"Anatsa, if they didn't marry, would the Kainah make war?"

"I do not think so. They are Blackfoot."

"Then why should he marry her if there would be no fighting?"

"There can be things worse than fighting. Even without fighting there is no peace. There would be nothing between us then but the empty prairie."

"I can't help it! I will walk in the Indian way, but I will not share my husband with another woman!"

"Then you are not walking the Indian way."

"Nitanna will love another! She can go back to her own people!"

"Maria—so can you."

Maria was stung, and showed her pain.

"Maria, we all carry the fire of the Great Spirit. If you put out the fire in another, you stand in coldness. I do not want this for you."

Maria bit her lip. "Anatsa, then I am weak and of little fire. I am not Indian and I cannot stand for the man I love—to . . ."

"If it is so close to your heart, I should not have touched it. I have spoken as I have, not for the sake of Nitanna, Indian woman I do not like, but for Maria, white woman as loved by me as my sister Apeecheken."

"I can't help myself!" Maria almost sobbed.

Anatsa touched the locket. "None of the white man's gold can measure what you have. How can you trade it in the name of Nitanna? How can you grieve because he would sleep with her? What is said and shared in sleep?"

"I don't want him making love to her!" Maria said bitterly.

"If he loves you, he can lie upon her and not make love to her!"

"I will not have him—after her! Would you want to share Apikunni with another woman?"

"It is the Indian way, Maria. If his love for me goes I cannot get it back, and if he loves me, ten wives cannot take love away."

"I do not believe this. I will not have it. We have laws against this. It is evil and wrong. Our Great Spirit says it is evil and wrong!"

"Evil?"

"Adultery! Adultery is against God's law!"

"We have strict laws against adultery too. If a woman is

adulterous once, she loses her nose, and if she is adulterous the second time, she loses her life. But we do not speak of adultery, for Nakoa and Nitanna will be married."

Maria clapped her hands to her ears. "Dear God," she moaned, "I cannot be a second wife. I will never share Nakoa with another woman!"

Anatsa took Maria's hand, and her luminous eyes were haunted. "Maria, you have the beautiful body that I always yearned to have. You have a spirit to go with your beauty, and your mind is quick and sharp. You are strong. I am crippled and weak. My face is thin and ugly. My tongue is slow. I do not have your fire. What I am has to be found with much patience—and no one but Apikunni knows me as I am. Beside you I am pale and cold. Yet going to Nakoa, you would hold nothing in your hands, if you would not go to him after Nitanna! Maria, with all that I am, and I see what I am, I would go to Apikunni after every woman in the world!"

The gold of her mother's locket shimmered through Maria's tears. "Then I am poor," she whispered. "I am poor and deprived, and am more crippled than you." She started to leave, for she did not want to be in the lodge when Apikunni returned. "I do not know my riches," she almost wept.

Anatsa gave her a parting glance and this was the only time she was ever to look at Maria fiercely.

"Then learn then!" she said.

Chapter Eighteen

The last day of the Sun Dance dawned hot and still. The time had come when the boys to be initiated into braves would bear the ordeal of torture. Crowds gathered slowly and quietly at the Medicine Lodge. The chief Medicine Man, Isokinuhkin, was already there, preparing the fire, the knife, and the thongs. Sikapischis, Sacred Woman, had not yet appeared. Maria walked to the lodge alone, and then was joined by Anatsa, who left her new husband this day and walked by Maria's side.

"This will be hard for you to watch," Anatsa said.

"I am prepared," Maria answered.

The morning was new; the prairie still shadowed, and the river in mist. Little Siyeh, tired with all of the days of his mother's fasting and praying, and bored with his grandfather staring endlessly at the sun in prayer, begged the old man to accompany him to the river to gather lodge sticks for a miniature village he was building. "We will be back for the ceremony," he pleaded, pulling his grandfather away from his mother's lodge.

"Yuh," the old man said gently, and let himself be led to the river trail. From far ahead of them, muffled by bunch grass, he heard faint voices. "There are women ahead?" Mequesapa asked Siyeh.

"I do not see any, Grandfather," Siyeh answered.

"I hear their voices. We will see them at the river. They come for wood too before the ceremony."

"When my time comes at the Sun Dance pole, I will be brave," Siyeh said.

"You will, my Siyeh. You will be very brave, and you will be very generous, for both your mother and father have brave and generous hearts."

"My father is gone."

"No. Your father walks with us now. I feel your father walking with us now!"

"Grandfather!" Siyeh looked around at the tall bunch grass bordering the trail, frightened.

"Fear is in your voice. If you are a little boy, you would know your father loves you with great tenderness. If you are a man, you would face any ghost without fear! Are you neither now, my little Siyeh?"

"My father is dead," Siyeh said in a small voice. "Do not feel him any more, Grandfather!"

The old man smiled, and took Siyeh's hand. "If he is here, he is here with reason, and I have never questioned the actions of your father."

"If we go back to the village, will he go away?"

"Siyeh! I have heard you cry many times for your father."

"Well, I do not wish to bother him! Is he gone and sleeping now, Grandfather?"

"No. He is not sleeping."

"Let's go back!" Siyeh almost wailed, looking ahead at the empty trail, and the mist-shrouded river.

"I hear the water. We are here, and I hear the voices of others. Women are ahead gathering wood, and you are not alone with your father and your grandfather."

"I will gather my sticks quickly," Siyeh said in a shaking voice. They came to the river and Siyeh peered into the mists but could neither see nor hear anyone else. He looked into the gray water and shivered. Moving upstream, he came to thick brush. Here were all of the little sticks he would need.

Mequesapa sat down, smiling, and looking around him with his blind eyes. His son-in-law had gone. So fleetingly had he stayed! It was strange that the dead returned for just a flashing of time. He had loved his son-in-law, and he had been warmed by his presence. But now he was not warm. A coldness struck him, though he felt no wind. Coldness flowed over him, like the cold water of the river. Had he slipped into the water? He was not in the water, but he still felt as if he were drowning. He gasped for air, then something seared his throat in white-hot pain. His throat had been cut; struggling, he staggered to his feet. He clutched at his wound, but to his amazement, his hands came away from it dry. He was not hurt. Nothing had touched him. Then revelation came, and his heart pounded in terror. "Siyeh!" he whispered. "Siyeh!" he shouted, when he found his voice.

From upriver where he had heard the sound of women's talking, a woman screamed. In his blindness he had a clear vision of blood flowing in running water, and he shook so he hardly could walk. "What is it?" he shouted, moving toward the sound of voices. "What is it?"

The awful coldness returned and touched tears upon his cheeks. He groped along his way frantically, wailing Siyeh's name like an old woman. Now he knew why his son-in-law walked with them no longer! "You can't have him!" he cried, falling to the earth and clawing his way forward. "You can't have him!" His hands clutched earth, rock, pebbles damp with the river, and then he felt a moccasin, a leg, and Siyeh's little back. Women sobbed nearby. With a strong jerk, Mequesapa pulled his grandson from the water. "Keep still!" he shouted to the hysterical women, and felt Siyeh's wet lashes and hair. His eyes were closed. "Siyeh!" said the old man. "Speak to your grandfather!" His hands groped to the throat and found that it had been cut. He looked in rage around him. "He will not die!" he shouted, feeling a pulse beneath the flowing blood. "He will not die!" he shouted again, after his son-in-law.

The women led him to the trail, and he carried little Siyeh cradled next to his heart.

Sikapischis, Sacred Woman, walked slowly to the Medicine Lodge. Paint was still upon her face on this her last day of fulfilling her vow to her Father, the Sun. The men and women of the village followed her in slow and dignified procession, but ahead of her she noticed some women wailing and wringing their hands. An old man was in their midst. He was burdened with something and his face was a mask of frenzy; she did not know it.

He carried her son.

His hands were red with her son's blood.

Sikapischis stopped walking—her legs had failed her. Her father carried Siyeh to a lodge before her, and from its interior came the beating of Sacred Drum. Again the drum was beating to the beating of her son's heart, but that was last winter when the skies were cold and gray and the strength of the sun had been hidden. That time had passed; the snow had melted from the ground and the earth was green with summer grass. How could time be one and the other—the sky storm-dark, and clear blue?

The drum beat on. When Sacred Drum beat, a spirit was seeking the Wolf Trail. Her son was dying—still dying and yet she had made famine and sacrifice in all of the ways in which she knew to give. Woodenly, she began to walk again. Her legs had not been taken from her after all. She had to walk to the Medicine Lodge and as Sun Dance Woman give help to the boys who were, in agony, to become men.

She stopped again. At her feet was the stain of her son's blood. What would the sun bring from its mark? What thing, what wonder beyond richness would spring unknown to the earth from her son's blood? Would it be endless food, endless warmth, endless light? Would all of the snows be gone and a bridge built with them to the stars? Napi—if there is such a bridge so conceived with the body of my son—I will never walk upon it. I will never walk, even to the Great Spirit, if I have to walk upon my son's blood.

Yet, she walked around the darkening stain, and entered the Medicine Lodge. The drum beat on. Siyeh lived still. Sacred Drum would save her son again. And she was Sun Dance Woman in her last day of voice to the Great Spirit; this day she would succor fifteen youths that would be braves. Her body was painted in sacred red, but she had not stepped upon her son's blood.

Isokinuhkin stood waiting for her by the fire, and she saw his knife, the thongs, and the Sun Dance pole. The fire burned brightly, in great strength, and she wondered if it could be shielded and never extinguished. Beat, beat went the drum, the sacred Medicine Drum, the last convulsion between life and the great Wolf Trail. Napi—let strength flow from these hands and light all fires, and banish the coldness from the prairie!

The fifteen boys waited quietly before her, stripped to the waist, with their heads reverently bowed. She touched their shoulders and with her hands gave them blessing. By twos they then walked to her, and she anointed them with black paint upon their faces and their wrists. When she had blessed the last one, and he had returned to all of the rest, the sound of the drum stopped. Sacred Drum stopped and its silence thundered out and froze the prairie. The world had died without color. All of the blood had drained away, and there was only the deepest snow and beneath it there would never be new warmth or another spring. The sun had gone, reeling behind the other fires of the sky; left in coldness they would die too, and the blackness of the earth and the darkness of the sky would be one, devouring each other in timeless death. Sikapischis held her hands before her face; from these fingertips the blood of her son had flowed and she had anointed the sons of other women. She had become the bridge to the stars, but without the eyes of a mother she could not see their fire or know their warmth. She was neither of earth nor the sky.

All the spectators who had come to see the ceremony of the Sun Dance heard the drum stop and knew that little Siyeh had died. Tears came to the eyes of every woman in the lodge, but no tears came to the eyes of his mother. Women clasped their hands in grief; men looked down in sorrow, but not his mother. Her face a mask of sacred red, she stood frozen and apart from them all.

It was time for the Sun Dance to begin. Drums in the Medicine Lodge began to beat, an echo of Sacred Drum. Other hearts lived. Still others would grow to bear the agony of this dance, to be men, to fight, to take women, and bring their sons after them. Other fires burned. All over the world other fires burned, and other hearts beat. There would always be others to touch the sun.

When the drums began, Maria felt a spasm that shook her body. By her side Anatsa sat with bowed head, weeping silently. Maria looked into the face of Sikapischis, and rage and despair shook her. Sun Dance Woman stood straight and as still as a statue. No emotion appeared to mar her stillness. Maria then looked to the widow of Kominakus, killed in the same way, and saw another Indian woman standing in deep calm. But this woman, Awasaki, wore her hair loose, no longer parted and neatly braided, as if she were saying, "I wear my hair in the manner of an old woman because my husband is dead, and with him is gone my desire for youth."

Maria moaned, seeing in her mind Siyeh with his grandfather as Mequesapa played his deerskin flute.

The fire was fed with fresh wood, and in its new flame Isokinuhkin cleansed his knife. The first two youths of the fifteen stepped forward to be prepared for the dance. Quickly Isokinuhkin made two Long deep gashes in their right and left breast. His bloody knife ran under the two-inch width of skin between each cut, and under each he ran a thong, tying the skin up tight. The boys stood with two rawhide thongs sewed into their chests, and these were attached to a longer thong hanging from the Sun Dance pole. Isokinuhkin thus mutilated all of the boys, and not one showed, by look or cry, a sign of pain.

"What are they going to do now?" Maria whispered to Anatsa.

"They will dance around the pole until they have pulled themselves free," Anatsa replied.

"Won't they rip away all of the skin and muscle of their chest?" Maria asked.

"Yes," Anatsa answered.

"How can you watch?" Maria asked. "How can any of them watch?"

"They bear the pain," Anatsa said. "I give them recognition for this."

The drums began the Sun Dance song, and the boys began to dance around the pole, straining to tear loose the heavy thongs. The smell of their blood permeated the lodge.

"They will be maimed for life!" Maria said.

"The scars of this agony are borne with pride."

"It is useless," Maria said.

"No," Anatsa answered, "pain is never useless."

The frozen woman of the sun watched the boys who moved in

a red haze before her. If she could take long steps backward and go back through the years, what would she do differently? To save her son's life she had vowed to make herself a vessel to the sun, and it was as an empty vessel, starved and still in fast, that she had suffered him to go with a blind old man to his death.

The sun still moved across the sky. It would follow the same path through the different seasons and through endless years ahead. Why then did their Father, the Sun, move crazily in guiding their path? Had the Great Spirit created a life with a tongue and a heart, and regretted not the heart, but the tongue? Was all of this blasphemy? Were the consecrated tongues, the bleeding flesh, the starved vessel, ugly profanities? Was there to be no crossing the heavens to the glittering Wolf Trail? If a man were to be but a bridge, he must be forever still, and not follow the path of the sun like the earth.

Maria watched the Sun Dance with growing horror. The boys began to strain violently in an effort to jerk themselves free from their torture. They danced faster to the increasing tempo of the drums, chanting while they moved, and their mothers and fathers and relatives who watched them chanted too. Sweat poured from the youths' backs, streaking down the muscles that stood out in ridges.

But the flesh upon their chests remained too strong to be torn loose quickly, and as they tried to work it free, it drew as far away from their bodies as their outstretched arms. At the sight, the sound, the smell of their blood, Maria became ill, and clapped her hands to her ears and closed her eyes to fight the waves of nausea that cramped her stomach. She bent over the ground at her feet and was sick. No one noticed her. When she looked up again the first boy at the pole suddenly threw himself from it with great violence, ripping his flesh and muscles away, and at the sight of him, mutilated, Maria became sick again. In time, the second boy freed himself in the same way, then the third and the fourth. The fifth youth could not tear himself loose, and as he struggled in desperation, in red and bleeding nightmare, the rest of the fifteen were freed. Dimly, Maria saw them go to Isokinuhkin to have their wounds treated with herbs while the fifth boy hung limply at the Sun Dance pole, unconscious.

"Are they just going to leave him there to bleed to death?" Maria asked Anatsa.

"If he becomes conscious they will tie the thong to his horse and let the animal pull him free. If he does not become conscious, he will not be touched until he is dead."

"Oh, dear God, dear merciful God!" Maria moaned, looking at the inert boy. The whole world stank of blood. Blood flooded the earth; there was no need for streams or rivers of rain. And Sikapischis watched it all, all of the torture upon this afternoon of her son's death without even a tremor. In rage again, Maria looked at the painted face. Behind its red mask lurked a woman animal, a woman who did not wail at her only son's death at but six years of age. The black eyes met hers, and Maria felt tears coursing down her own cheeks, but the regal head turned with no open recognition of a woman's suffering. Maria wanted to spring at her and claw her for her indifference, this spirit of the sun. Damn you! Damn you! Maria thought, her hands pressing each other until her flesh trembled. Then from behind the red mask, the expressionless black eyes that still met her own, she heard the singing of a woman's voice. Clearly and sweetly it sounded through her soul, and it would not be stopped.

I accept.
The love and the pain,
The sunlight and the rain,
I accept.

"No! No! No!" Maria screamed, standing and drawing every startled look in the Medicine Lodge. She had to end the woman's song; she had to staunch the flowing of blood; she could not remain still while Siyeh, her father and Ana all died. "I will not accept this!" she cried. "I will not accept!" She wept until she was weak, and except for the first glance, those in the lodge went back to watching the ceremony.

The last day of the Sun Dance was near conclusion and it was dying in bloody sunset. The boy hanging limply from the Sun Dance pole was left there, and the boys who had become braves filed solemnly outside and knelt upon the earth, facing the west.

They crossed their arms over their bleeding breasts and bowed their heads in prayer. Now the Sun Dance Woman and Isokinuhkin and Natosin left the Medicine Lodge followed by the spectators in absolute silence. Anatsa had helped Maria to her feet, and the fresh air outside drove some of the nausea from her. She saw the fourteen new braves kneeling in the light of the fading sun. In its last appearance it burned in greatest strength. All of them and all of the tipis, and all of the prairie as far as she could see seemed bathed in a red glow.

Natosin came forward and stood before them all. He wore the dress of the head chief: the polished horns that Nakoa had worn before his battle with Shonka; shirt, fringed from shoulder to hand with locks of human hair; and leggings, bearing scalp locks from hip to feet. The polished horns gleamed in the pale light above the ermine skins of his crown. He raised his right hand in sign that he would speak. "Hear me, Nokosaki," he said. "Hear me, my children. I speak, and what is upon my tongue is in my heart. This day ends in a fire that lights our mountain and our tipis and the prairie around us. But we know that night comes and that in its darkness we will have the light from our fires. Our hands bring the flame, and our hands have been nourished from the strength of the earth too. We have grown upon the earth, and we have walked forward in our lives. We chase the buffalo, but we still walk forward, and we have walked in our own path. Now we will look at the sun, and behind it, our Father will speak. Before the night comes the sun's greatest power, and in darkness its reflection is not gone. The Wolf Trail travels across the stars and because we see it in night does not mean it is gone in day. Know then that when the earth part of us rests in sleep, and the spirit enters a place of darkness, we know not in our wailing how many suns there are in the night sky."

Natosin looked at Sikapischis, mother who had lost her only child. She stood stiffly before him. His words were for her and at his feeling, the mask of Sun Dance Woman began to crack. The chin moved, the lips quivered, and then with a cry of anguish that smote all of their hearts, this woman who was supposed to bear the strength of the sun, crumpled in her grief and fell to the earth.

Maria turned away from the sight. Where rage had consumed her heart at the other's strength, pity now became an agony in her soul.

Natosin spoke again. "We must know that we feel the touch of the sun, but we are not the sun. The sun is light and warmth, and so are we. But we are also shadow and coldness. The sun moves in light. We move in light and darkness." Natosin looked down at Sikapischis, still upon the earth, her face colored with it, all of the sacred red of the sun washed away by the force of her tears. "We are not the sun," Natosin softly repeated. "But though we move in light and darkness, it is the sun that casts the shadow that stretches before us!"

Slowly Sikapischis sat up, and then rose to her feet, her eyes meeting Natosin's. Her face stopped its tortured working. "I am but a bridge to the stars," she said, her voice shaking. "I am an empty bridge between two worlds," Sikapischis wept.

"You touch both," Natosin replied. "In the last light you can be both the traveler and the bridge, as the last light of the sun flames upon both earth and sky."

"I hear your words," Sikapischis said, and her face was filled no longer with unbearable agony.

All became silence. Natosin turned to the rest of them in the still village. It was strange to Maria, this silence. Not even a dog barked, nor did the mountain wind touch the bells upon the tipis.

"I will speak now to all my children," Natosin said, "not just to a woman lost from herself in her grief. Today the Sun Dance ends. We have seen the young boys who have become braves; in becoming braves they become men. As men they will protect their women and children, their sick and their old. They will be a guide for the younger to follow and a source of pride for the old who have walked most of their path. Our nation will be fierce and proud with what began within them today.

"Men have smoked the Medicine Pipe together, and its smoke

has carried all bad feeling away that existed between our tribes. Women have felt the warmth of a pure heart, in sacrifice and in talk to the Great Spirit. In the winter ahead the warmth of this day will comfort us. Tomorrow our friends who have ridden here will leave, and another winter will lie between us. As the sun leaves the sky now, let us speak together to our Father."

Natosin turned from the Blackfoot, the Dahcotah, the Sarcee, Kainah, Kutenais, and the Gros Ventres, allies who had come to the Pikuni camp from across prairie and mountain. He faced the west and the last glimmering of the day:

Father, the Sun, I pray for my people.
Let them be warmed in their winter
With the burning of your fire.

Mother, the earth, receive the Sun,
And in your warmth let the grass and berries grow.
Give us the spring
And in our thirst
Let us know
That it comes from you.

Father, the Sun, Mother, the earth,
We come from your union.
Let us be humble in this
And not proud,
For we are of both and not one,
Neither of flame nor dirt,
Neither soaring nor still,
But crawling as babies, even as the small ant
You have created.

We have been created,
And will know your warmth,
And will burn with your fire.
Bless us in our struggling;

Let us walk a straight path
And at its end find ourselves.
But upon the great Wolf Trail let us remember,
Our mother was the earth!

Natosin had finished. Twilight was gone; the stars had come out above their bowed heads. A long "ah-h-h-h" came from them all, the closing of a prayer. Maria felt the touch of her own tears. The sound of Indian benediction was not unlike the last sad sigh that had escaped the doomed wagon train. And Nakoa was not with her, and where he was in the village she did not know.

There was a last hush before parting, the long "ah-h-h-h" still lingering, sacred. Sun Dance Woman slowly walked back to her empty lodge; Natosin left them, then Isokinuhkin and then the Mutsik and the new braves. The Medicine Lodge loomed black and silent against the bright stars of the Wolf Trail; in it a youth hung limply, losing too much blood to regain consciousness. All around Maria the shadowed forms silently dispersed and the last night of the Sun Dance ceremony ended.

By the next twilight the Pikuni camp had shrunk to its original size with most of the visitors gone. Out upon the prairie, by the restless horse herds, there was nothing to indicate that they had ever been there at all except the ashes of their fire pits now abandoned in brooding silence.

Chapter Nineteen

Nakoa's marriage to Nitanna was announced two days after the Sun Dance ceremonies. The five day announcement was made in the traditional manner. Nitanna made moccasins and took them to her future father-in-law, and for five days she prepared food and walked with it in ceremony to Nakoa's lodge.

Maria would not accept the announcement. She would not watch Nitanna take food to her future husband. She would not look at the Indian girl once. Let the others line up and watch her. Let the others exclaim over her beauty and her dignity!

She fled with Anatsa to the lake.

"I cannot believe this!" Maria cried to her, in anguish.

"It is true," Anatsa said quietly. "Maria, I have said this to you before, when you gave me this white man's locket of gold for a wedding present. For your wedding present I have no riches to give to you, but you have so many riches already. Know them."

"Know my body? Oh, yes, I have heard people say that it is pleasant to see. Even that old Atsitsi says I am beautiful. Is this my wealth? The way my eyes meet my brow, the size of my waist, and my breasts? Can I stand always before a mirror of this beauty and stare myself to sleep? Anatsa! Anatsa! What do I care what Atsitsi, or Nitanna, or anyone sees—but Nakoa! And if he is lost to me, and cannot be accepted, I am not rich in beauty! My body is my transport—to him!"

"Maria, think of Natosin's words, his prayer of this Sun Dance. At the end of your path, you will find only yourself!"

"No! No!" Maria was weeping, and Anatsa moved to shield her

from the other women at the lake.

"I have to have him!" Maria wailed.

"Have him. Love him. Be loved by him. Let his manhood enrich your womanhood. The sun brings life to the earth, but the earth stays the same!"

"He doesn't have to marry her! His father said that he would walk in his own way!"

"Then this is his way. You cannot change it."

"I will! I will! He will not make love to that—bitch!"

"Nitanna is a woman and not a dog in heat. Because she loves the man you love does not make her a dog and leave you a woman."

"Then we are both dogs in heat."

"No, Maria. No."

Maria clung to Anatsa's hand. "I love him."

"Then do not use your love as a weapon. Do not take his blood with the power of your love."

"Anatsa, this is only the first day of the announcement. He will come to me before it is finished!"

"He cannot. He cannot even seek out his announced bride these nights."

"He will come. He will come, and when I have seen him again, he will not marry Nitanna!"

"Maria, you will not speak with him until he has married Nitanna. You will not be alone with him again, until the consummation of your own marriage."

Rage lit and blazed with unholy strength. "I am clean, and untouched by men, and I will not have one crawling to me in the night like Siksikai!"

"Like Siksikai?" Anatsa's face paled. "Has Siksikai come to you in the night?"

"Yes! Yes! He tried to lie with me—but I could not accept with my body what I did not love with my soul. I—am not— Indian!"

Anatsa looked quickly away. Maria's face flamed. "And when will your great Nakoa consummate a marriage with me?" She had hurt Anatsa, hurt herself, and now she had to hurt more.

"When you sleep in his lodge you are considered married,"

Anatsa said.

"Ah! Will Nitanna and I sleep on the same couch? And when he wants a woman, how will he know which of us he is having? By lighting the lodge fire?"

"You will not sleep in the same lodge," Anatsa said. "Nakoa and Nitanna will spend four days in their marriage tipi, and on the fifth day, or the fifth night, you will move to Nakoa's lodge. He will come to you there."

"He will crawl to me like a dirty animal, weak with debauchery of a first honeymoon."

"I do not know all of your words," Anatsa said sorrowfully.

"And I do not know all of yours." Maria laughed bitterly. "But Atsitsi would. Atsitsi would. My good Blackfoot godmother would understand every one!"

"Why do you strike yourself? Why do you draw pain from this marriage you have to have?"

"I have to have?" Maria mimicked.

"You said that your body was transport to him."

"In love. Only in love! And if it is not in love, I would give this body to Siksikai to destroy."

Anatsa gasped, and held herself as in pain. "Maria! Maria!"

"Who is she?" Maria mocked. "She is a fool who would love an Indian who would destroy her and suck away her sweetness."

"You are made not of sweetness, but of blood. Blood is the sacred color of the sun."

"I know blood. The Indian has smeared my world with blood. There is none left in the world—for me!" Fury vanished in new pain. "Anatsa—Anatsa—you would not want Apikunni to seek another wife!"

"He is Mutsik. The day will come when he will take another wife."

"How will you greet this fine day, Anatsa? Will you meet this new wife happily? Will you share your husband with joy in your heart at his fine and new pleasure?"

"I have already accepted this."

"Accepted! We accept life! But how will you feel?"

"Acceptance is what I feel."

"No! It is not all! You will feel hurt and jealousy! You will feel lonely and cold! You will hate him, and you will hate her!"

Anatsa looked deeply into Maria's eyes, and her own eyes had never looked more beautiful. "I can not answer with a straight tongue what I would feel then, for I feel now Apikunni's love meeting my own. In the warmth of summer sun it is hard to feel the coldness of winter. In the midst of feast, it is hard to imagine famine. I love and am loved. I look ahead to this other wife, or these other wives, and I think not of them, but of the love between my husband and me."

"With other wives it would be gone!"

"It is not that way with us. It is not that way with Nakoa."

"I know. Your men take other women for wives so the first wife can have help with her sewing. Why don't you have other husbands, so they can have extra help with the hunting?"

"That is not needed. One man can hunt for his family."

"And so can one woman sew for hers!"

"The woman's work takes longer than the man's. Bringing the meat and the skins is done more quickly than working the meat and the skins for the lodges and clothing."

"Then I will struggle along with last year's lodge!"

"You cannot. The skins are worn from traveling on the travois, and they become worn around the lodge poles. Lodge skins have to be replaced after every winter."

"Then I'll be cold!"

"But you do not live in the lodge alone."

"Anatsa," Maria said quietly, "if this moon of the homecoming is our month of August, then I have already had my birthday, but I do not know my age. I have seen my father and my sister and my old life all die in blood. There is nothing left but the life here, because here is the man I love, the man who will make me complete. My love for Nakoa made the strangeness of savagery warm! I was no longer cold and apart. But when he marries Nitanna, I am alone again, all alone!"

Anatsa bowed her head, her eyes moist. "My heart hurts with your hurt, but for this my tongue will remain silent. You will not hear my words."

"You have said them and I have heard. You would have me go to Nakoa as his second wife, and be starved from him for the rest of my life."

"You will only starve when you refuse to eat."

"I will not do it. I will be a wife to him or nothing."

"What will you do?"

"I do not know."

But she did know. The announcement of his marriage would let her do nothing else. When Atsitsi slept, she would steal from the lodge and go to him.

A new moon had come to the sky on August thirteenth, the last day of the Sun Dance. By the fifteenth it lit the prairie faintly and promised to shine with full light upon Nakoa's wedding. Walking to Atsitsi's lodge, Maria looked at the sliver of light and remembered her dream of marriage to Nakoa in the moonlight. She was the one who married him in full ceremony when the prairie was silver with a full moon—not Nitanna!

When she reached the lodge she found it lit by a fire within, but the door laced tightly closed.

"Atsitsi!" she called. "Let me in!"

"Where big fool been?" Atsitsi growled, unlacing the flap.

"I have been walking," Maria said quietly.

"Now Nakoa take Nitanna, big Maria look for more Siksikai?"

"No. Have you eaten all of the food?"

"Little left. Has sweet Maria seen Nitanna yet?"

"No." Maria started to eat, her heart pounding in fear at the name.

"I watch Nitanna carry food to her lover. Still beautiful."

Maria cringed.

"Sweet Maria want to keep all beauty for little bird song! Nitanna know what to do with her beauty."

"You have already said," Maria said bitterly.

"Oh, Nakoa and Nitanna sleep together already. I know this. Last Sun Dance he on her all of time."

"Were you watching?"

"I hear she in his lodge. Meet by river too, 'cause Atsitsi see them there."

"I suppose you followed them to the bushes!"

"He take her to ferns. What need to see more? I know what happen then very well."

Maria's food caught in her throat. He had made love to Nitanna in the ferns, but he had restrained her when she had begged him.

"Sweet Maria unhappy? Sweet Maria want Nakoa pretty little virgin too?"

"I thought an Indian kept his bride clean. I thought this was part of sacred prayer to the Sun, and that is why you crawl around in the dark earth all of the time!"

"Nitanna Indian princess. Any man want Indian princess, even if known Nakoa get to her first."

Maria started to eat again. He had made love to Nitanna before he had ever seen her. Most of the pain of his taking the Indian girl left, and Maria pushed the rest of it away. "Why did you have the door laced closed?" Maria asked, deliberately changing the subject.

Atsitsi's expression changed. "Siyeh, little boy, killed by Sokskinnie. Sokskinnie kill anybody now! She friend to Sikapischis too!"

"Atsitsi, Sokskinnie is dead!"

"Moccasin right at where Siyeh found. Sokskinnie moccasin. Now I lace door closed every night, and if big damn fool walk around looking for more Siksikai, then she sleep all night with him! Tomorrow night big Maria in here before dark, or stay away!"

Maria yawned elaborately. "I am tired." She took her knife belt off and moccasins and lay down and closed her eyes.

She heard Atsitsi lie down on her couch. For fifteen minutes, she feigned deep sleep before she looked furtively over at the old woman. Her eyes were wide open, and she was staring at the door. She saw Maria watching her. "Why not drums beat?" she whined. "If drums beat, Sokskinnie stay away!"

"She is only wandering around by the river!" Maria said flippantly, and turned her back to Atsitsi and the fire.

"When you go to river to meet her?"

In seconds the old woman began to snore. Maria waited for a while, and slipped noiselessly to the door. She unlaced the flap and left the lodge.

The small moon cast a faint light upon the silent tipis. The camp circle was mostly in shadow as Maria made her way to the inner circle. Dimly she recognized Nakoa's lodge, south of his father's. Kutenai turned to her and nickered softly, and she would have touched him, but an iron hand seized her, and jerked her backward. She gasped and struggled, and in her terror all she could think of was Siksikai. An arm brushed her breasts, and then the awful grip loosened, and she was spun around, and Nakoa looked into her face.

"Maria!" he breathed. "I could have killed you!"

"For touching your horse?"

"You know that Kutenai would be sought in coups!" He was shaking. Maria trembled too. Why hadn't she thought of this? Why hadn't she remembered that they not only walked like cats, but heard like them?

"It is so dark. I heard you walking and I thought—Maria, Maria, why are you so foolish? Did you want me to kill you?"

"No," she moaned, touching his chest. "I want you to love me." It had been so long since she had seen him, touched him. It had been a century of five days. "My darling! My dearest!" she whispered in English. "I love you! I love you!" she said in Pikuni.

"Maria, you cannot stay here."

"I am not in your lodge!"

"I am to see no woman now."

Maria looked around at the silent and dark lodges. "The high chiefs sleep. We can whisper." She touched his beloved face, the tender lips. "Kiss me, Nakoa," she begged.

Wordlessly, he bent and kissed her. Their bodies met and clung, and through her excitement she felt greater passion in him. "You want me, you want me!" she whispered.

"I always have," he replied.

"But more—tonight!"

"Yes!" His face was wet. She moved against him, as close as she could press herself, and when he stepped away from her, she followed him and tortured him more with her closeness.

"Maria, why do you do this to me?"

She was wild. She was Meg. She was worse than Meg. Meg slept with her father on a bed, and she would sleep with Nakoa here, on the dirt, outside of his father's lodge—before Nitanna if she cared to watch! She began to caress him, and she felt all of his resistance go.

"I will take you—inside," he whispered, strangling with the defeat of his will. He was caressing her now, his hands under her clothing. He started to move her toward his lodge.

"No!" she whispered. "Here! A harlot would take you here!" His hands stopped their wild begging. She caressed him again, with her body, her hands. "Nitanna will not do this! Never again will Nitanna touch you!"

Violently, he shook himself free from her. Maria stood before him stunned. "One trade for another," he said to her in rage. "You would make yourself nothing—in trade."

"What do you mean?"

"You set fire to my flesh, to blind my vision. And that which inflamed me beyond reason you call a harlot! I would rather have your hate."

"I do not understand," Maria whispered, almost sobbing.

"You would have taken me here—in the dirt!"

"Yes! Yes!"

"To keep me from Nitanna you have to become to yourself the white man's word for a dog in heat?"

"I would do anything to keep you from her!"

"You can do nothing to keep me from her. Nothing."

Maria gasped, unbelieving. "Nakoa, you said you loved me, that you would deprive yourself of everything for me."

"Deprive myself. But not my people. Not my father. Not the Pikuni. Not the Kainah. If the Blackfoot tribes are not a nation, the white man will come and the buffalo will go, and if the buffalo go, the Indian goes with him."

"The Kainah would not make war if you didn't marry Nitanna."

"There would be neither war nor peace."

"You are not that important!"

"My father's word is that important. My word is that important."

"Nakoa, you want me."

"And I shall have you."

"No! I will never become your wife it you come to me—after her!"

He gripped her shoulders, tenderness for her gone. "You do not remember. You are my property as much as the horses I brought back from Snake land. I can do as I will with you."

"You are an animal!" Maria began to cry. "You do not love! You cannot love!" She was crying bitterly, and she sank to the ground, clutched at his leggings. "Nakoa my love, my heart, my soul."

Tender with her again, he picked her up and brushed her hair back from her forehead. "I am part of your love," he said gently, "but not your heart, and never your soul. This is my girl-woman talking; she will grow and know that she will not find me until she has found herself. I know what you will be Maria, fierce of spirit—do not keep what you are away from our marriage!"

"What am I?" Maria asked sorrowfully, looking up at him with trembling lips. "Do not speak of what I will be—or can be—what am I now? Do you love me?"

He took her hands and held them strongly within his own. He studied her pale fingers, and then he took each hand to his lips and kissed its open palm.

"Do you love me?" Maria persisted.

"Yes," he said, and a tremor of emotion swept over him. "Yes," he repeated, his voice deep with feeling.

Maria freed her right hand and slapped his face. "Marry Nitanna," she panted, "and what I am or will be—both of us— will spit upon you!" She turned and fled from him, running toward the outer tipis. Staying behind her, Nakoa saw that she reached Atsitsi's lodge safely. When they had both gone, Kutenai shifted restlessly. A shadowed form of a woman stood at the door of Natosin's lodge, and for a long time, looked after them.

Chapter Twenty

Early the next morning, Maria went to Natosin. Before she had eaten she walked to the circle of high chiefs, and walking boldly past Nakoa's silent lodge, approached Natosin's and called his name softly. He came to her immediately.

"I have come to speak to you," Maria said. "In pain, I have come to speak to you. Are you alone?"

"I am alone."

"May I enter your lodge?"

"Yes." He led Maria inside of the tipi, and motioned her to be seated on one of the three couches in the room. A lodge fire burned slowly. Maria could see that he had already eaten.

"Why is it, my daughter, you speak to me in pain?"

Maria laughed sorrowfully. "You call me daughter again, this woman whose marriage to your son would kill you."

"Your marriage with my son would not cause my death."

"It would mine!" Maria said. "Natosin, I cannot marry your son."

"Cannot?"

"I do not want your son—now."

"Now? Your feelings for him have changed?"

"I cannot become his second wife!"

"You are in pain because of his marriage to Nitanna?"

"Yes. I did not think that he would marry her. I cannot. Live with him now—after her. It is not my way. I cannot accept it. I cannot! Will you help me, Natosin?"

"My daughter, how can I help you?"

"You are head chief. You can give me my freedom. You can have some of your warriors take me south to the trails of the white man."

Natosin studied her face. She met his eyes directly.

"My son has said that you are a woman of courage," he said. "He has told me also that you are a woman of honesty. I will speak to you with a straight tongue. When my son first brought you here I thought he would sleep with you, and give you your freedom. But he came to love you and did not want to give you up. So he has kept himself from you, and now in less than ten days he has said that he will make you his second wife."

"No," Maria said bitterly.

"When he marries you, he will take you to his lodge for the rest of your days. You will be under his protection and his provision for as long as you and he live. You are a white woman. If you grow to dislike the life of an Indian woman, you will be unhappy, and this will bring my son unhappiness. Then there is what you could do to our people, to this Blackfoot village. A white woman among us could be a thing of great danger. The news of your captivity has already traveled on many tongues. White man's wagons have been destroyed in Snake and Dahcotah land, and those destroyed have more people who might hear of you, and think you might be one of them! White men would come to find you, and then my son and his society of warriors would fight to keep you here. This land would be fire; the prairie would be fire, for the rest of the Ikunuhkahtsi would join the Mutsik. All this could be because my son has not shown wisdom in whom he would choose for a wife!

"No, my daughter, I do not approve of this marriage my son says must be. Nothing can warm one man's blood enough to suffer the bleeding of others! I have told this to Nakoa in strong words, and because of his heat for you, the air has grown cold between us. But my son has brought you here. By our law, what he takes in coups is his, and you belong to him to do with as he will. He intends to marry you five days after he has married Nitanna. This is insult to her, to take another wife so soon, and to take a white woman; this is insult to the Kainah and to my otakayi, as close to me as blood brother— this is insult to Inneocose! But Nakoa will not heed my words. No one can make my son do what he does not feel in his heart. He knows the price he will pay when he marries you, but if he pays, you are more strongly attached to him than ever."

"What will—he pay?"

"He will walk alone in his foolishness."

"What do you mean?"

"If he does not lead, the Mutsik will not follow him if the white man comes for you."

"Natosin, set me free!"

"You know now that I cannot!"

Maria bowed her head and began to weep. "What then, can I do? You were my last hope. I cannot marry him now. I cannot."

"You cannot." Natosin's face became saddened beyond description. "The poor young. The poor wretched suffering young. It is better to suffer the torments of an old body than the anguish of a young mind. The young say they cannot when they can. The old say they can when they cannot. Why can't body and mind meet in this life? Why do they meet in just the last moments, the golden moments of dying?"

"Is death beckoned with golden moments?"

"Death is beckoned with golden moments and a kiss beyond sweetness, beyond tender flowing of a loving mother's milk! There is for every man two kisses. The first kiss is of the mother—the kiss of the new world with its food and light and warmth for growing. But it is the second kiss that is the golden kiss, for it is the kiss of the self, and its fire and its warmth is greater than all of the suns in the sky!"

"Why does it come with death?" Maria whispered.

"Because the world is needed no longer. Because the world is a child's toy, to be played with by the children yet crawling upon its surface!"

"What good is a kiss that comes with dying? In dying, how could you even feel it?"

"You have passed beyond feeling with fingers of clay. You do not feel. You know. In the last shimmering moments—you are!"

"Have you died, Natosin? Are you a ghost, who eats and sleeps, and talks in a voice from the human throat?" Maria was serious, her face just as sober as his.

"Yes, my daughter," Natosin said quietly. "I have died."

"But you are alive, Natosin!" Maria was scolding.

"I have yet another death to go through. But I have died once, and, in dying, I have felt the second kiss. My daughter, there is a different death for each man, and for some men, there are many deaths. Lucky is the man who can die, for it is the living who are the most dead!"

"I know that so many of us move blindly," Maria said.

"Blindness can have great sight. It is moving and not knowing what we are that is so sad. It is worse than not knowing our path— this not knowing what walks upon it!"

"What was your death like? What did this second kiss make you feel?"

"Complete stillness. Complete quiet. For the first time in all of my life, I was completely within my body. I looked through it and not at it. I saw with no eyes but my own and thought with no mind but my own. I wasn't what I was thought to be, or what I should be, I was myself. I had the second kiss, and I have known its fire ever since. There is no cold, no darkness, no struggling with strangers to myself. With my fire I meet the darkness and bring it light. With my fire I meet the snows and they melt. I meet any stranger and know that he cannot test me and try me as did the strangers within that I banished by accepting. My daughter, you have wept for those you loved who were taken from you by the Snakes. Weep not for the dead, for blessed are the dead, and they are not as dead as the living! If they were yet untouched by the second kiss they would wail for us, and their voices would be heard even from the Wolf Trail!"

"Yet we lament so for the dead."

"Daughter, you know that we grieve for ourselves. We know only that we are deprived and do not know where they have gone. We weep for what we see our empty hands and not theirs, which could be filled with new riches!"

"Natosin, in your stillness of death, did you leave? Did you travel from this world to another?"

"Maria, the Wolf Trail is not a world, another earth; I do not believe it so. I do not believe that travel is being. I think stillness is being. In the stillness, the long stillness when I searched for just myself, I found shimmering wonderful things—new worlds, new stars, new fires, and they were all within myself. In stillness I saw them, and when my stillness comes again, I will reach them. Men who have fattened and become rich from the kiss of the mother, shrink in terror before themselves, for that is what their death is, the kiss from the self. They came to the mother unknown to her, and she unknown to them, and they accepted and grew, but what they have known all of their lives and created themselves, they reject violently until the second kiss. Man is the real strangeness of the universe!"

"Merely, thou art death's fool," said Maria. "For him thou laborest by thy flight to shun, yet runnest toward him still." She had spoken in English, and now she translated in Pikuni.

"The man who said that is a wise man."

"He is dead. He was a great writer who lived far across the seas. He said many wise things."

"There are Indians with the written tongue. I have heard of this, and I am sad that we save our richness only in song and talk. Song and talk are too fast, and some words have to be accepted slowly, and they should be written down and seen and touched and caressed like the white man's gold. This shall be the Indian gold, and when he finds it he shall know new riches, and become a new people."

"Will he die as he is?"

"Of course. This is good. When he sees from his own eyes and not the eyes of the white man who will come among him once more he will have new life, and new fire."

"Natosin, you speak like a prophet. There is such a mystic quality to you."

"I have died, my daughter, and I have seen that time is not as we see it. Time is a whole, not cut up and portioned off into useless little pieces. That is why there is the last quiet, the last stillness, so we can put back into one piece all the little pieces of time we have mutilated. With our tiny hands, with our antlike bodies, we gnaw at the present and chip away at the past, and the busyness of our own reflection cuts us off from the future. We are our own mirror, and past it we blind ourselves."

"Natosin, how did you die?"

"My daughter, I have never spoken of this to any man. My own death involved the deaths of my wives and of all of my children but Nakoa. I died my own death but not theirs, and so theirs still causes me pain, for I lived and am human again. Talk of this draws fresh blood even now, but I look into your face, and I see your trembling suffering youth, and in my age I pity you. I cannot give you your freedom, but you will not leave my lodge this morning with your hands empty. Hear my words, Maria. I give them to you, in fresh blood of old wounds that brought death, as a new path to this freedom you seek. Hear me, daughter, and you will have your freedom, but not by the trails to white man's land."

"I hear," Maria said softly.

"I had five sons beside Nakoa, and three little daughters, and I loved them all, the fruit of my heart. I had three wives, and I loved them, each in her own way. The sun was warm on the strength of my manhood. I gained many coups, and I begot my children, and because my people were their people, a fierce pride and a fierce love for them seized me, and easily I rose to lead the Mutsik, and from there I became head chief to the Pikuni. The stories of my coups were riches to my people, and thus more so to my children, and my deeds were pictured upon the council lodge. I walked among the laughter of my children, the love of my wives; I soared above the Morning Eagle, my sign, my name, my Nitsokan, and my protection. Humble in my thanks, the scars of the Sun Dance on my breast were not enough, and I was dumb that I should be so many times blessed.

"I had a friend, a Mandan, and he was called by the name of Mahtatohpa. He was a great Mandan warrior with many coups, and he would ride to my village, and we would hunt and eat and smoke the Medicine Pipe together.

"One great sun, I took my wives and all of my children to visit him, in his village with the high wall his people had built all around their lodges. The Mandan is different from the Blackfoot. His heart is warm toward the white man, and he has done trade with him, but a white man has never been allowed in a Blackfoot village. In that sun I first saw a white man, for one of them was living then among the Mandans, and he was called by them Tehopenee Washee, because he was a white medicine man. He painted many images in color and not on skins but on your paper, and he painted the Mandan and me, so that he might take our images with him and show them to his people who had never seen a Mandan or a Blackfoot. He asked me for permission to visit my people, and I refused him, telling him that the Blackfoot heart was cold to the white man, and that when the white man came to the Indian land, he brought trouble."

"Did the white man speak Pikuni?"

"No. We talked through the tongue of Mahtatohpa."

"What was this white man like? Was he a priest? Did he wear black clothing?"

"No. He wore skins like the Indian, and he was a good man, for he and Mahtatohpa were friends."

"I have never heard of him," Maria said.

"He was interested in study of the Indian way. He drew pictures of Mahtatohpa's robe that told of Mahtatohpa's twelve coups, and he said he not only drew this but would tell of it in the words he would put on many sheets of paper. He wanted to write of all of the tribes on his paper with his drawings. When I returned to the Mandan village for another visit he was no longer there."

Natosin's face changed. It became suddenly lined and old. "That day is before me now. I live it now, as I lived it then. Again, I had my wives and my children with me. My oldest was Nakoa, who was then fifteen.

"It was ten suns ago. It was ten winters ago, and if I had not died too, the earth would still be hidden with snow!" Natosin bowed his head, and his face became older. Maria touched his arm.

"Do not go on," she whispered.

"I went on that day. I went on that day, and so I shall go on now —when the only person I bring pain is myself, and from my pain I can give you sight.

"It was summer, the sky was hot and cloudless, and against it circled the vultures. I knew these were the birds of death, and that death had come to some of my friends. I wondered if the Dahcotah had raided the village, for the Dahcotah is not ally to the Mandan, and we had met on the trail Dahcotah warriors painted for battle. The birds circled above us too, and seeing them and hearing their hungry cries I felt terror for my wives and children, and I made them stay on the trail behind me.

"Slowly, and in plain sight, I rode into the Mandan village. There was no sound of people. I heard growling of camp dogs, but no voices of people. There were no fires. It was early morning, but there were no cooking fires. The lodges stood quiet and seemingly deserted, and in the one before me I heard frenzied growling of many dogs.

"My horse felt terror. I fought to hold him still. I picketed him, and entered the lodge before me. The day was bright, but the lodge was deep in shadow. Before I could see, I smelled the dead inside, and then as in a dream where I could not act but only see, I saw the dogs eating them. There was a mother, a child, a baby and an old man, and I do not know how much more of them I allowed the dogs to devour. When I had driven them off, I looked at the mangled corpses, and I could see that they had died in an awful agony, and their bodies were swollen to three times their size.

"I went into lodge after lodge, and everywhere it was the same. The Mandans in them had died and were being eaten by their dogs. Now I noticed a different thing. Upon every corpse were strange marks that had come to the skin, as if the white man who had lived among the Mandan had painted each one in an evil and an awful way.

"There was no one alive in the village. I went to the lodge of Mahtatohpa, but it was empty. There was no sign of him or his wife and four sons. Despair for all my friends was in my heart, and I stood still with my sorrow, and I stilled my horse.

"Now I will explain that the Mandan village is different from the Blackfoot in that the Mandan builds a lodge of willow boughs with a clay roof, and he does not move his village to hunt. The

Mandan village had not been moved in the memory of any living man and had always been protected by its two walls, and the river. The river that guarded the other two sides flowed below towering bluffs, and it was from one of these bluffs that I heard soft and distant chanting. It was the death chant, and as I walked to the sound, I saw the figure of a lone Mandan against the sky. The sun faced me and hid the Mandan's face, and not until I got very close to him, did I know him to be Mahtatohpa, my friend. When he recognized me, he became quiet.

" 'Mahtatohpa,' I said. 'Are you the only one left?'

" 'Yes,' he replied, and his face seemed pitted and marked, though it was drained of all color.

" 'Where are your wife—your children?' I asked.

"He pointed to the base of the cliff upon which he stood, and when I followed his gesture with my eyes, I saw with horror that it lay heaped with corpses.

" 'They burned with fire,' he said. 'They became swollen and marked with thirst, and in madness they sought the river by jumping from here. Then those who knew they could not reach the river in this way went headfirst so they would know death sooner. It is those who did not have the strength to walk here who are left for the camp dogs.'

" 'How did this happen?' I asked.

" 'This sickness came from the white man's boat which traveled up the river to do trade with us. They took our furs, and they took our lives.'

" 'How? How?' I asked my friend, thinking that my disbelief could prevent this terrible thing from ever happening when it did.

" 'The boat came, and as we had done before, all of the chiefs and warriors of prominence went onto it for trade talk. On the boat two white men lay sick, and when we left, we were sick. Our bodies became large, and strange marks came quickly to our skin, but many died of burning and mad thirst even before their skin became marked. The Dahcotah had come outside of our walls and waited in a large war party, and if those who were not sick had fled from us, they would have been killed as surely as we were dying. A person just had to look upon our faces to die. This will happen to you now, Natosin, if you stay and speak to me.'

"I looked at my friend's scarred face. 'You are alive,' I said quietly.

" 'I was marked, and I burned and thirsted,' he said, 'but I did not die. This is my punishment, because in my sickness, I did not have the strength to prevent my wife and sons from jumping toward the river below. I watched, but I could not tell them that they would reach not the water, but death. Now I am glad in my heart that they lie there, beneath the waters, and that I did not awaken finally to the sound of their being eaten by my own dogs!'

"I took my friend's hand" Natosin continued. "I told him that he needed no punishment because sickness of the body is not a wrong that sickness comes unsought and is an invader and not a welcomed guest. I sought to talk him from jumping from the cliff and dying like his family. It was no use. Before he jumped, he walked with me through the village, weeping, and stood long before his deserted lodge.

" 'They wait for me,' he said brokenly. 'They cannot travel upon the Wolf Trail alone. My wife is an easily frightened woman, and she fears strangeness. My sons are little boys, and are not yet men. They wait for me and call piteously.'

" 'No. No,' I entreated, 'there are many things yet for you to do.'

" 'There is nothing left for me to do,' he answered. 'I am a ghost, and so I will leave this world of living men, and walk quietly to my family and my people.'

" 'You stand before me, as I stand!' I replied. 'You speak as I speak!'

" 'No, my friend,' he said. 'From me life is gone. I have not eaten or drunk for nine days. I am starved already, and nowhere, now, is there water for my lips!'

"With these words," Natosin continued, "he walked away from me, wearing his robe in ceremony, and standing tall and straight, as if he entered the council lodge for the bestowal upon himself of the highest honor. I felt tears upon my face, for I wept for my brother. I saw him walk toward the precipice, and once more, I heard his death chant, and then there was nothing but the still frenzied growling of the dogs in the lodges."

"Natosin, Natosin, why didn't you stop him?"

"I could not stop what he had already done in his heart."

"It is horrible! Horrible!" Maria exclaimed.

"Yes, my daughter. The horrors are for the living. It is the brave man who suffers life, and the coward who seeks death in glory."

"Did you think your friend a coward for killing himself?"

"Mahtatohpa's path had ended. He had walked as far as he could. He knew this and accepted it. I speak of the coward who seeks death in frenzy because he so dreads it. It is easier to rush toward death blindly than to accept it in light. There are cowards who die great warriors but remain cowards, because they would rather be destroyed and be nothing without life than wait quietly in the sun and receive what they are!"

"Natosin, life is so hard!"

"And you are so young for these words. A loving mother does not give to her child all of the time. Punishment and denial bring strength. My daughter, perhaps your mother, the earth, is being generous to you in your youth."

"No," Maria said, shaking her head.

"I will go on with my story. I did not keep the dogs from the rest of the dead. Why suffer the dogs, I thought, and feed the lower worm? The dogs were of the master, and let them feed thereupon."

Maria strangled, seeing the white wolves after Ana, her father, and even Anson. She hid her face in her hands.

"I went back to my family, and we ate and slept together, and there was laughter and good feeling between us. Early in the morning, long before even the seven brothers in the sky touched the prairie, I awakened. I had heard ghost voices. Two thousand Mandans had died, and it was the end of a proud tribe, a proud way of life. I felt great sadness for this, not for the bodies becoming part of the dogs, but for the passing of the last Mandan village.

"Then I heard a sound, a difficulty in breathing, a crying for drink, and then, in that moment, in my detachment of bodies returning to worms and dogs, every one of those two thousand Mandans rose, and led even by my friend Mahtatohpa, struck me in the heart. Two thousand times I was struck and suffered the deathblow with each one, and I reeled and gasped and clawed blindly at death, but could not die. My wives and my children except Nakoa died before me instead. They died because I had brought them the disease, because I had marked them and tortured them, and drained the juices from their body. My innocent little daughters who had loved me hours ago before the cooking fires, were mutilated, swollen, and gasping in thirst that could not be filled. My sons tried to die in silence—because their father was such a—great warrior!"

Natosin shuddered. His strong muscular arms became frail, his broad shoulders bent, his face marked beyond any age. Maria could not fight her tears, and wept with the old man as he lived this time again.

"My wives died last," he went on. "They died last, and saw their children dead before them. Then it was my time. I burned. I was on hot dry sand with no life and no water, and nothing but the blazing sun. The sun was in the sky, and I thought, 'Can the Great Spirit burn with such heat to destroy one of his children?' The sun burned closer and closer, and my flesh cooked, my eyes were seared with blindness, and in my first blindness I felt wild panic for I could see nothing, not even the burning sun which had left the sky to destroy me. Then, in my blindness to the earth and the sky, came sight within myself. I thought if the Great Spirit would bring the sun to earth to burn me, he cared; he had moved and he had toiled for me, and I would accept his torturing sun. I would turn to ashes and accept what was left.

"In my searching within I felt coolness, shadow; I had reached a sanctuary, green and safe from fire. A part of me thus burned, and a part of me thus rested, soothed and comforted in deep darkness, and in the deep shadow rose a spring, for I could hear its waters bubbling upward to the earth's surface. The water went to the earth and then to the sun, and new rains came to replenish the spring, to feed the earth, to find the sun, and I saw the circle, and was charmed by the simplicity of it, the sweetness of burning heat, the shadow, the spring; and I loved them all, accepted them all, tasted them all, and felt a richness that cannot be described in my poor words.

"The sun in destroying me had brought torture and blindness. The blindness had brought sight and had made me find the shadow that allowed me to live in the heat. In shadow and in light, in coolness and blazing death I lay still, and my long quiet began. I went deeper and deeper within myself, and there were distances, greater than those that separate the fires of the Wolf Trail; there were worlds that shrink ours and make it a leaf upon a sea. Food and drink lay abundant but unneeded; love and companionship surrounded but was unsought. The sky could be touched; the heavens could be spanned; the newness was of the present and the past, and the future no longer blind.

"And so I lay in death. Nakoa buried my wives. He buried his mother, and he buried his brothers and sisters, and above him the silent Mandan village looked down, and the black birds of death darkened the skies."

"How horrible it must have been for him!" Maria whispered.

"I lay in death, and I knew Nakoa's suffering, but so contented was I in my exploring, in my glimpsing of the worlds that led one into another, and so silent were they, that Nakoa's anguish was softened and became a muted thing that would soon pass, for these worlds lay ahead of him too."

"Didn't you seek your children and wives?"

"They did not have to be sought. The richness was theirs too."

"You were with them?"

"Time is the divider. Our bodies are timepieces ticking with our heartbeat, and when we are free of the time watcher—when we are free of the clock, we are no longer separated by time."

"How do you know about clocks?"

"Mandans had white man's timepieces which they regarded as having great magic. They are nothing. The beating of our heart is the timepiece."

"Natosin, I am cold! I am chilled!"

"The coolness within me let me live, my daughter. Nakoa had placed me in water when I was on fire, but it is the coolness within that saved his work from failure.

"I felt his efforts, and gradually I realized that the sun that burned so hotly was not within the sky, but within myself, and from its heat and life I could feel the shadow and the spring that fed the earth. The sweet circle of spring, earth, and sun was within me too. Deep within myself, I had felt the second kiss."

"I am so glad that you lived! I am so glad, Natosin!"

"Then your hands are not empty. This morning, I have given you something."

"Yes. But I will not know your strength, Natosin."

"You know nothing, daughter. Outside of the worlds of the self the wind is strong and blows the grasses and changes the sands into shifting patterns. The wind changes even the seas that march forever onto the land. You do not know even what you see, for you can only feel the wind.

"Now that I lived, what would I do with my life? Had I walked to the end of my path, and remained on earth a ghost, as Mahtatohpa had refused to do? I knew this was not true. I knew that I lived with reason. I had felt the second kiss for a reason, and I saw from within myself, and not through the eyes of my people, that I could be their leader. I would know my last son, and in my dying days he would lead, and take my place as head chief.

"Ten winters have passed since this day of my death. My son has become powerful and leads the Mutsik three years earlier than I did. His voice has been strong in the council lodge: His path has been straight and his heart is warm to his people. His voice to them could have been louder than mine—but now, it will never be."

"I have destroyed your wish," Maria said sadly.

"No. Nakoa walks his own path. His path is not my path, and I accept this. His path is not your path either, my daughter, and you too will accept this."

"No," Maria said. "You were touched by the white man's disease, but left unmarked. I am touched by your words and think you a great and a good man, Natosin, but I too am unmarked. I am weak and my hands are still empty. I will not accept Nakoa's marriage to Nitanna." She rose to go. "Kennyaie ki anetoyi imitaiks—" she started gently, in age-old custom among the Pikuni that a friendly conversation had ended. "And now the dogs are all scattered . . ."

Natosin interrupted her. "Your hands are not empty. You do not see them with your eyes, but with those who live in the land of the rising sun."

Chapter Twenty One

The day of Nakoa's and Nitanna's marriage dawned bright and clear. It would be a beautiful day, and the night of their ceremony would be a beautiful night, with the moon just twenty-four hours from being full.

It had been four days since Maria had gone to Natosin, and every hour of that time Maria thought that Nakoa would come to her and tell her that he would not take Nitanna for a wife, that the pain in her heart did not have to be. But now her suffering was the only real pain; the sun burned her without pity. Before another dawn he would take this awful Indian woman to his bed and in his lawful right he would make Maria an outcast, a perpetual mistress, a whore to be used and not caressed.

That morning she tried to bead moccasins, but she soon put them down, for her tears would not let her see the beads. She walked with the other women to the lake. Anatsa saw her but let her walk alone. Maria's agony was too great for any words. Even the warmth of the sun was a cross, for it would be gone soon and in the night he would mate with another. The lake lay cool and placid beneath her touch, and in its reflection she could not stand sign of her nakedness. The long hair with its touches of the sun, the breasts that he said were beautiful: What good were they when she would be trapped forever in a pit of shame and rejection? Walking back to the village she passed Siksikai, but she passed him without thought, looking at him indifferently.

The sun burned on, hot and relentlessly. The dogs ate and dozed: Did they know their own emptiness? Atsitsi was gone. Inside Atsitsi's lodge Maria sat upon her couch alone, looking at the light of the afternoon against the cowskin walls. She covered her face with her hands, and shrank deeply into the pit of herself, seeking, seeking the spring that Natosin had found in his long death. "Dear God," she moaned. "Give me help."

"The white woman calls to the Great Spirit," a voice said softly.

Maria turned toward the door and, seeing a tall, slender woman in its light, sat up in surprise.

"Who are you?" Maria asked.

"I am Nitanna," the slender form said. With slow dignity, as if she were hostess instead of intruder, she moved to the other couch, and sat upon it, facing Maria. They studied each other carefully. "You are a beautiful woman," Nitanna said.

"So are you," Maria replied, meaning her words. Nitanna was indeed beautiful. Her form was more slender than Maria's; her build was boyish, but they were of the same height. Nitanna's hair was worn severely in the Indian fashion; her nose was straight, her teeth even and very white. Her eyes were large, long lashed and very beautiful, and if there was any flaw in her face at all, it was the slight thinness of her lips. In studying her, Maria saw that there was a cruelty to the mouth, a lack of softness to the body.

"Why does the white woman call to the Great Spirit?" Nitanna asked.

"My name is Maria. Do not call me the white woman."

"You called to your God."

"He is not my God. He hears my tongue as He hears yours."

"I have seen you before," Nitanna said. "I heard of your capture and your beauty even before we left for this village."

Maria grew uncomfortable under Nitanna's appraisal. "We have looked at each other," she said. "I thought it was not the Indian way to stare. You look at me as if we were creatures apart!"

"We are," Nitanna answered. "We are women apart. Let us look at each other and know this."

"Why are we women apart?" Maria asked angrily. "Are we not to have the same husband?"

Nitanna revealed anger herself and then her face again became a smooth mask. "I have heard that this is not the white man's way" she said.

"It is not," Maria said hotly.

"You do not want to be second wife to Nakoa?"

"No!"

"You have already lain with him," Nitanna said bitterly.

Maria felt shock and then sudden rage.

"You beg him with your body. Do you not know you are different? It is only the difference he wants! He will hate what attracts him now!"

"Will he?" Maria asked. "Well for all the times I have lain with him—he isn't tired of me yet."

"I knew he had not kept you clean. Where have you lain with him?" she asked, looking at Maria wrathfully.

Maria remembered Atsitsi's description of Nakoa's and Nitanna's lovemaking. "His favorite place is by the river," Maria answered candidly. "He loves to lie with me upon the cool green ferns."

Nitanna rose and paced the floor, her eyes flashing fire. "I thought this!" she said in rage. She stopped her pacing and stood over Maria's couch looking down at her with open hatred. "Tonight I will be his wife. When a man has eaten, he is no longer hungry."

"It depends upon his appetite!" Maria taunted. "And the diet he has become accustomed to!" Maria rose to confront the Indian girl and suddenly felt shame. "Nitanna," she said, "my words were not straight. I have not lain with Nakoa."

"I do not believe this."

"All right. But I speak with a straight tongue now. I do not want to be his second wife. I cannot share him with another woman. It is not my way, and I could not bear it."

"You do not have to accept this," Nitanna said softly.

"I do not? What do you suggest I do? Kill myself?"

"You can escape. You can go free."

"How?" Maria asked sorrowfully. "Even Natosin could not set me free."

Nitanna sat down upon the couch, and her eyes became lit with an unholy fire. "I do not want to share my husband," she said. "I will not share Nakoa with a white woman. I will give you your freedom."

Maria began to tremble. "Nitanna's how could you set me free?" she asked.

Nitanna grasped Maria's arm. "Tonight you can ride to the land of the Nez Perces! They are warm to the white man and do trade with him all the time. They can take you south to the white man's trail. I can hide a horse for you, and upon it I will have food for three days."

"It will take me three days to reach the Nez Perces?"

"Yes. Only three days. The horse I will hide for you was stolen from them, and it will know the trail back to their village. Upon him I will have robes, pemmican, a knife, and a fire horn. You will have to ride all of the first night, but the next night you can have a fire, and no animal will harm you. Upon the trail there will be no other Indians until you reach the Nez Perces. They speak your tongue. With promise of a reward, they will take you back to your own kind. You will be free."

"I cannot ride as fast as a Blackfoot," Maria said slowly. "I will be followed and recaptured."

Nitanna stood again and silently paced the floor. "There is one way you will not be followed," she said finally.

"What is this way?" Maria asked.

"You can leave at night."

"Your hunters ride at night!"

"Not through the burial grounds."

"What?" Maria asked, aghast.

"The trail to the Nez Perces is reached only through the burial grounds. And you know the grounds are forbidden to the Blackfoot at night."

"I do not want to go through them either."

"Why? Is it your belief, too, that the dead walk?"

"No. But two people have been killed without reason!"

"They did not die in the burial grounds. They died on the path that you still walk every day to the river." Nitanna looked nervously toward the door. "Think upon this quickly. Atsitsi will be coming back, and I do not want it known that I have been here."

"I do not know what to do."

"Do you want to escape or not?"

"Yes!"

"Then I will have a horse waiting for you at the entrance of the burial grounds tonight. You can ride through them quickly—upon the horse nothing will be able to harm you."

"No, I will not leave tonight. I will see you and Nakoa marry, and then I will seek the freedom you offer."

"Do you think we will not marry?" Nitanna asked, surprised.

"Yes," Maria said.

"Then come to the ceremony and see us as man and wife," Nitanna said.

"When I have seen this then, I will go," Maria said quietly.

Nitanna went to the door and looked out of it. "I have more words," she said. "I am Indian, and I do not speak with a forked tongue. Nakoa marries me tonight. But he will not wait even the five-day period to take a second wife. He has told me that you will go to his lodge tomorrow night. This is pain and outrage to me!"

"It is outrage to me also," Maria answered. "After he has married you, every ceremony with me would be false. I do not want your husband. As you have said, I am not his kind."

"Then you will leave tomorrow night?"

"If you marry him, my wedding gift to you both will be my escape."

"Then hear and remember my words. Do not approach the burial grounds until after dusk, for they are patrolled until then. I will have your horse picketed at the entrance, and it will be as white as winter snow so you can see him easily."

"How can you bring the horse there?"

"I can do it easily. But remember if you enter the grounds before dusk, the Mutsik will just bring you back, and you will have to belong to my husband!"

Maria looked into the black eyes alive with fury again. "You do not accept the Indian way either, do you Nitanna?" she asked.

Nitanna moved her head haughtily, the white pendants at her

ears almost flashing. "Not with a white woman!" she said scornfully.

Maria smiled, her full lips and beautiful eyes sensual. "Not with me!" she amended softly, and Nitanna turned quickly from her and left the lodge.

The moon rose early upon the prairie. The marriage tipi of Nakoa and Nitanna had been erected and stood near the great council lodge where the wedding feast was to take place. Crowds had gathered by it already. Few wanted to miss the sight of Nakoa and his bride and the dignitaries of both the Kainah and the Pikuni in their finest ceremonial robes.

Mequesapa was invited to attend the banquet with his daughter, Sikapischis, but he did not have the heart for a marriage dinner; he did not have the heart for any joy. He sat near the lodge upon the warm brown earth, and in his hands he held his deerskin flute, but he would never play it again. The last note of music had left his world.

The blind old man searched vainly around him, listening to the voices of the waiting crowd, straining to hear in each boy's voice the voice of Siyeh. He listened to the stirring of the little night creatures in the grass. The night was warm and fragrant, and in its deep sensuality, he wondered if the mists still lingered by the river. He did not want a shroud to hide the moon from little Siyeh, for he remembered how, as a young boy, he himself had thrilled to its pale majesty upon the prairie and the mountain, how he had loved to watch the river divide the living from the dead with its line of molten silver.

The wedding guests were beginning to arrive, and he could tell how magnificently they were dressed by the sudden silence of the men around him, the gasping of the women. Atsitsi passed him, moving closer to where Nakoa and Nitanna would walk their wedding path. The white woman whom Siyeh had thought so beautiful was not with her, and the old man grieved that she could not see this marriage. He wondered how deep her acceptance was, how unknown her depths were to herself.

He heard Apikunni's voice and knew his little bride walked with him, Anatsa whose crippled walk he knew as well as the thunder upon the prairie. They would be honored wedding guests, for Apikunni and Nakoa had always been as blood brothers. Then in a hushing, he heard the step of Inneocose, Iron Horn, and Chief of the Kainah, as proud and regal as his beautiful daughter. But Natosin did not walk with him, and this must be a strangeness to everyone, because it was always custom for chiefs to enter the lodge together. Now Isokinuhkin, Medicine Man, passed, and Mequesapa's heart lurched in bitterness. Of what use was his sacred drum, his voice to the Great Spirit? Was the Father so unhearing that the drum had to beat loud enough to drown out a boy's feeble heart? Siyeh was dead, and he would never know music again.

All the guests had arrived, and the spectators grew restive. Where were the bride and groom? A strangeness grew in the air. Something was wrong.

A woman walked toward them alone; a beautiful woman dressed in bridal white. All eyes turned toward her. In the moonlight the long tushes that fringed her dress and sleeves caught flashings of silver. Her hair was neatly braided in its Indian style, and in her quiet hands she carried a single flower of white. There was awe for Nitanna's beauty; never had she looked so lovely. But it was not custom for a bride to approach the marriage banquet without the groom; as an Indian princess why would Nitanna go to the wedding in such a strange way?

She walked slowly and regally. Long pendants gleamed from her ears; elk teeth shone at her slender throat, enhancing the vivid beauty of form and face. Dimly, they could see the smile upon the lovely lips, the love in the shadowed eyes. It was not Nitanna, but the white woman.

Maria walked between them all, and stood waiting by the door of the council lodge. Shocked silence settled over the spectators. Some of them could see the petals of the white flower shaking in her hands and knew that the serene face masked fear. All eyes were on her, so Nakoa and Nitanna's approach was known only by Mequesapa.

Maria was the first to see Nakoa, and she did not see Nitanna who held his arm. Here was the moonlight, and the long path of white flowers; here was the warm night with all mists gone, and the sound of animals moving in the sensuous grass. A tolling came to her mind too, and her white skirt was not of animal skin but billowed out in gleaming satin. This was the way it had been in her dream, before her father had even asked her if she could accept him. Dear God, in his towering strength and dark majesty, she could accept him! Let Meg claw at him and smother him with her breasts—she would accept him!

But Nakoa was not looking at her with love but with anger. Nitanna still held his arm; he did not free himself from her in any way. He did not even step away from her, and when Maria lightly touched the buckskin over his breast, no recognition came to his black eyes.

"You do not know me!" Maria whispered.

He did not reply, but when Nitanna impatiently tried to move away from her, Nakoa held her still.

"Nakoa," she said in a low voice. "Hear my words. I love you, but I will not be a second wife. Choose between us now. This is the only marriage for me." She kept her voice steady, but she could not keep the tears from her eyes. They all could see them shining as they ran down her cheeks. The little white flower in her hands was trembling violently.

In fury, Nitanna broke away and walked into the lodge. Without a word to Maria, Nakoa turned and followed her. They were both gone from sight. No one around Maria said a word, and she stood still and saw the white flower fall to her feet. She bowed her head under the most crushing blow she had ever known. All dreams were ultimately nightmares. He had never known her.

Finally she walked away from the marriage lodge. Its gleaming skins stretched up to the sky. From the inside came the sounds of soft laughter, the revelry of a typical wedding dinner. She could see his beautiful smile; she could see the look exchanged between bride and groom. She had become hollow and had difficulty walking erect. She could not think of the time this night when they would be alone, Nakoa and his wife, Nitanna, Kainah princess. Maria, whoever she had been, was already gone, swept away, useless, and a ghost of the past that walked through the tipis like the lost souls from the burial grounds. The wind rose and moved the little bells of a tipi near Atsitsi's, making a sweet lilting sound that was the requiem to her heart's love.

"I know it of no use to ask sweet Maria why she want so much pain," Atsitsi said.

"I was seeking Nakoa," Maria said, as she and Atsitsi ate the next morning.

"How you do this by being fool?"

"I wore the white dress to show him that last night would be my wedding night, or it would not come at all."

"You show nothing but your hurt, and now your wedding night come with him anyway."

"Does it?" Maria asked.

"Now you stop sun in sky?"

Maria smiled. Her eyes were haunted.

Atsitsi looked at her thoughtfully, and began to scratch. "Big Maria not so big any more."

"No." It was hot and sultry. Off toward the mountains a storm threatened. "It looks like it will be raining by tonight," Maria said. "Happy is the bride the sun shine upon!" Tears stood in her eyes.

"Maria never believe Nakoa's marriage."

"Yes. I believe now. I saw it."

"Well, I never believe yours either, so we both wrong."

"Neither of us knew Nakoa."

Atsitsi wiped sweat from her face. "I hate summer heat. I will be glad when we break camp and move to mountains."

"Why do you move to the mountains?" Maria asked indifferently.

"For new lodge poles and herbs."

A low peal of thunder came from the west. Maria put down her food. "I will go to the river for water."

"I go too. Nakoa say."

"Nakoa say what?"

"That I not leave you alone today."

Maria laughed. "Does he think I will escape?"

Atsitsi started to eat more food. "All right. You go to river. Plenty women on trail with heat of prairie making thirst. But I go to lake with you when you bathe."

"How do you know that I will bathe?"

"Sweet Maria have to wash and wash for Nakoa."

"Big Atsitsi know everything. Maybe she stop sun in sky for me."

Maria went into the lodge and got the water pouch. In it she concealed another dress. "When I come back we will go to the lake," she said quietly. Atsitsi looked worriedly after her as she walked away. "Something wrong," she said to herself, and belched.

Maria followed some women she did not know to the river, and once there quickly walked from their sight. She left the brush and snowberry bushes of the river banks and headed toward where she knew the lake to lie. She entered a thick forest of cedar, pine, and spruce, and even in the light of morning, the area was shadowed. Ferns were thick and untrampled, growing almost to the height of her shoulders. Taking the first step of her escape, she found that her heart was beating wildly. She grew suddenly cold with fear. Sickness came to her stomach, and she wanted to vomit the food that she had just eaten. She had to ride for three days upon a strange trail, to a strange people. And in the deep dusk she had to enter the burial grounds, untread at night by even the Pikuni braves. She hated the nights and loneliness. Then before her eyes was Nakoa spurning her in the moonlight. The trembling left and the nausea vanished. Nothing would keep her from that white horse. Sokskinnie with her loud mouth and sharp knife could ride with her all of the way! She walked resolutely on, not even making an effort to walk silently.

She came at last to the northern shore of the lake. Across from her, on the other side of the water, she could see some women bathing. From that shore she would swim to this one, and Atsitsi would not even know what she was doing, until it was too late for her to be stopped. When the fat old whore waddled back to Nakoa, she would be on the white horse, and Nakoa could be damned, Nitanna could be damned and the whole world could be damned. Maria looked carefully around her, so she would remember where she stood now. Near her a straggly pine had been hit and scarred by lightning, and in the hollow of its burned-out trunk she hid her extra dress. Quickly she returned to the river, filled the buffalo bag, and walked back to the village.

It was about four hours before dusk. Clouds moved across the sun, but still it was unbearably hot. She wanted to see Anatsa once more, but in the close heat most of the warrior's horses were picketed outside of their lodges, and Apikunni was probably dozing on his own couch. The thought of going to Anatsa's when she slept with her husband repelled her, so she headed toward Atsitsi's. Tonight was to be her wedding night, but no one would watch her take food to Nakoa in a five day ceremony. In his lust, he would not even wait five days for her, in his dirty animal lust that he had to parade before the entire village. Ahead of her, in the inner circle of high chiefs, she imagined she could see the form of the marriage tipi. Did they lie within it yet? Did he lie on top of Nitanna yet? What difference? What difference? the iron heart said, and once more the sickness and the trembling was stopped. She was iron. She was cold strong iron, and she needed no food, no light, no warmth, no man; she would escape from them all. Nakoa could crawl to an empty lodge this night and then he could go back to Nitanna.

When she reached Atsitsi's, her face was wrathful.

"Big Maria's face like red sun," Atsitsi said.

"It is hot."

"Heat in big Maria. Sun cool little breeze beside big Maria now. Big Maria burn up all prairie because Nakoa still in bed with Nitanna."

"You don't know a thing about my feelings."

"Well, in happy time, we go to lake together now. Little girl has to get clean so can be sweet in her couch tonight."

Maria felt a pain in her heart. "Yes. Tonight I am united in holy ceremony that will take place as soon as my husband has the strength to climb off another woman and crawl on me."

"Nakoa young. He take care of you fine tonight."

They met Sikapischis. She was walking toward them. Some small boys, running and shouting, threw a ball at her feet. When one ran to pick it up, she turned away from them, and her back bent in the agony that shook her body. Maria reached out from her own black world to touch her, but Sikapischis was too far away. The song came to them both, the thought, the words, the melody:

What alone can I call my own?
What alone belongs to me?
What is here I can never lose?
What is here for me to choose?

All things go to ashes and dust,
All things go the way they must,
What alone is there for me?
What is mine for eternity?

Sikapischis turned, and her stricken eyes wandered over the village blindly. She did not see Maria. Atsitsi had walked on, and now Maria passed Sikapischis without a word of good-bye. To her left, from the side of her hurting heart, loomed the marriage tipi, and in the crashing desolation of despair the unfinished verse came to her, and its bitterness was benediction.

What alone is there for me?
What is mine for eternity?

God alone is all I own,
God alone is all that's mine.
What is reaped is always sown,
I am the cup to bear
His wine!

She was going home. She walked after Atsitsi toward the lake and the great mountain that towered over it. Beyond it lay the villages of the Nez Perces. Beyond it lay freedom. God was all she had. God was all she owned. She looked up at the great mountain, and its shimmering grew to shadow the whole prairie. Ana and her father were gone. Her mother had died long ago. Nakoa was dead, but she had her God. She walked toward the mountain, and from its towering heights came a long and ominous pealing of thunder.

Chapter Twenty Two

The lake had never looked more beautiful. The sky, although rapidly becoming clouded, was serene. All of the earth around Maria seemed suddenly to have an exquisite loveliness. In her despair a wonder touched her too, as if something, long beckoning, were about to be reached.

Two women were bathing, and Maria watched them emerge from the water and dress. It was strange. She died and the people who were around her went on. Slowly taking off her clothes, and no longer self conscious of her nudity, she walked into the water. Its cooling touch was another thing of beauty. With swift clean strokes she swam rapidly toward the other shore. As she started walking out of its shallow water she heard Atsitsi howling in a frenzy of cursing. She waved to her in a gesture of farewell, and saw the fat old woman turn and waddle desperately toward the trail that led back to the village. In the shadow of the trees Maria shivered, then walked through the lush ferns toward the straggly pine where she had hidden her clothes. It was farther than she had ever walked naked before in her life. The forest was quiet, and at last she found where she had cached her clothes. She dressed rapidly, and noting the quickly gathering dusk, began again to feel fear. She paused, for a last lingering look at the lake. "Good-bye, Nakoa," she whispered. A thrush called mournfully out near the still waters, and very clearly, to Maria, its last notes were a farewell to life.

The sky turned yellow, and the earth below it reflected its eerie light. The earth suddenly seemed strange, expectant, and hostile.

Anatsa, leaving her lodge to start the evening cooking fire, stood still at the strangeness and shuddered. It was the same. It was the same light that she had seen smother the earth when she and Apikunni had sought the otsequeeina. It was the same! She began to shake. Death was threatening, close to the village, and she hoped fervently that no women were yet on the trail from the river.

The fire was burning, and she prepared the meat for cooking. She grew colder in the ghostly twilight. Apikunni slept inside of the lodge, and she knew him to be safe. Apeecheken had not gone to the river; she was with her husband and son. Maria, readying herself for her marriage night, was with Atsitsi. Why then, the fear that death was going to strike and leave her bereft? Why the terrible restlessness, the looking up at the sky and the clouds that were sweeping down from the mountain as if they would destroy more than the light of the moon?

This was the night for the medicine drum! This was the night for its beating, and the night for outdoor fires to burn until sunrise! Suddenly, something cold slid across her throat, and she strangled in terror. She touched her neck. Maria's locket was gone; its clasp had broken and it had slid to the ground. She thought immediately of Siyeh, and Kominakus, and how each had had his throat cut. She had felt an omen. A sign had been made in warning, and with trembling hands she desperately sought Maria's locket. She found it at last, not by sight, but by touch, for its goldness had not shone; even in firelight it seemed to lie in shadow. The locket seemed as cold as the deeply frozen snow. She debated what to do. This was Maria's marriage night, but even so, the Great Spirit had spoken. She would go to her white friend and tell her that the pulse of her life was threatened with a knife.

Maria felt growing terror as she neared the burial grounds. The twilight still held, but thickening clouds would hide the moon. As she moved to where Nitanna had said she would leave the horse, the ferns seemed more and more reluctant to part for her. They rustled as she passed, as if scolding her for disturbing their shadowed peace, and Maria thought, "Do not scold; I will soon be gone." Then she began to see Nitanna before her, as if Nakoa's wife were actually leading her to the Pikuni dead. Deep in the shadow she saw her fleeting form, but even so far away, she still seemed to see clearly the Indian girl's cruel mouth.

At last she reached the river, the last barrier, and she walked north along its shore, looking for a crossing. The waters were turbulent— almost silver in the dark forest—and rushed beside her noisily. The smell of rain was thickening in the air; there would have been no moonlight for her wedding. She would be glad when the storm came, for it would wash away all sign of her trail by morning.

She had come to it. She had found a crossing, though Atsitsi had said there was no natural crossing to the burial grounds. Yet here it was; a fallen tree made a perfect crossing; black across the churning waters it was her bridge to her old world. It was even an old and a familiar bridge; she had seen it and crossed it in another life. Behind her lay the smell of food upon the cooking fires, and the talk of other voices, and for a long hard minute she wanted to turn back to them, and flee from the forest that was building more fear in her with each moment that passed.

She made herself cross the foaming waters, and when she had walked beyond their sound, she heard a faint noise from the trees up ahead. She stopped, her heart pounding, but then she recognized it as siren song, sweetly and tenderly sung. It was a Spanish lullaby, and Maria stretched pleading hands ahead of her, a little girl searching among the wheel bands and white ashes of a burned wagon train. She walked more rapidly, searching each thicket desperately, and the deeper the shadows grew, the clearer her mother's song became.

Then suddenly, the sound of the loving lullaby stopped. Maria was stunned by the complete silence. Why would her mother lead her into deepest darkness, and abandon her—alone? Why did she have to be alone, without light? Dear God, she had forgotten about the horse, forgotten to look for the entrance to the Pikuni graveyard! Where was she? How far into the forest, how far away from the trail to the Nez Perces had she wandered? Night had fallen; darkness was complete, and still there was that awful silence and penetrating cold. There was no wind. Did the wind die too in a graveyard? Her hands began to shake; she didn't know where to go. Desperately she looked closely around her. She could see only a small part of the pines and firs that rose somberly ahead of her.

Softly, from close to her, came the call of a gambel sparrow. She listened to its three notes. This was the call that she and Anatsa had heard before the thing that had murdered Kominakus threatened them. She saw Kominakus again with his throat slit and the grass bloodied and violently trampled all around him. Dear God! she prayed in panic. How could a night have become so black? She ran until she was exhausted and still she did not see any sign of a white horse. When she stopped, she heard something else stop, and although she knew that her own tortured breathing could be heard in the distance that separated them, she did not hear a sound from where she knew someone to be standing. Her body was covered with sweat, but still the coldness almost numbed her. Had she reviled the old ghost woman Sokskinnie? Had she mocked this restless spirit back behind the river and among the burning fires and the medicine drum? "Words all come back!" Atsitsi had leered. "Words grow— and all come back!"

Now she moved as silently as she could, and just as silently, footsteps followed her, but in the darkness she could still see no sign of what it was. What kind of an insane thing would murder a little boy?

When she had laughed at Sokskinnie, hadn't a wind come from nowhere and furiously shaken the bells of the tipi? "Go and walk in the burial grounds!" Atsitsi had said, and now she was in them. Would the sweet sound of her mother singing a lullaby lead her to death? Would she die rather than be Nakoa's second wife?

Sobs constricted her throat. She did not want to die. "Our Father, which art in Heaven," she whispered, and her body shook so that she had to finish her prayer inwardly. "God," she pleaded, and hearing nothing behind her now, stopped to listen and convince herself that nothing had really followed her after all. But when she stopped suddenly, there was a soft cessation of sound behind her, and she slipped away from it as rapidly as she could. She wanted Nakoa to save her. She had done them both a terrible wrong, and in her dust and in Atsitsi's there would be no separation of whore and angel.

Directly above her she could see the dim outline of the burial platforms. There was no wind, yet the skinning knives hanging from the branches near the dead moved restlessly.

So, I am in the graveyard of your people, Maria addressed her thoughts to Nakoa. Here I will die, and here I will be buried. In time you will lie here too, and if the winds are kind there might be a touching in death of what couldn't meet in life.

The footsteps pressed closer. The time had come for her murder. Why the delay? You do not follow me so quietly to leave me untouched? Tears began to course down her cheeks. It was a wicked and a terrible thing to give Nakoa her corpse upon their wedding night.

Maria faced the shadows behind her. There was no sound from them, not the slightest rustling among the fallen leaves. Why did death wait?

Everything around her remained still. Then, God, I am to live! Maria clasped her hands in prayer. She was weak with gratitude. Breathing deeply in relief, she turned to leave the burial grounds. A motionless figure crouched before her. She was looking into the face of a dead woman. Little wisps of gray hair curled all around the unseeing eyes, and from the open mouth came a long train of crawling ants. Maria screamed in horror, and as panic seized her she screamed again and again, running blindly back toward the river. "Nakoa! Nakoa!" she called wildly.

Sokskinnie would follow her and slit her throat as she had done to Kominakus and Siyeh! Her God had not saved her; a corpse would sever her head from her body. Running now completely by instinct, she plunged into a thicket of balsam and scratched her face and hands. Smarting with pain she ran hysterically on. A crashing came down from the skies, and for one moment the full moon broke through the clouds. Gleaming palely before her, she saw the form of a white horse. He was picketed to a clump of small firs and was prancing nervously upon fine slender legs. Sobbing with relief, Maria ran to him. Upon him were provisions, a robe, a knife and food, all of the things Nitanna said would be there. She would ride him back to the village; nothing could catch her now! She mounted the horse easily, but two hands seized her and dragged her back to the ground. The white horse wheeled, shied, and fled in terror.

Chapter Twenty Three

Nakoa had been summoned that night before a council of the high chiefs. He knew why he had been summoned, and he reached the council lodge early, when thunder was first rolling out across the prairie. His father was already seated in his customary place, and for a while they were in the lodge alone, but neither spoke to the other. In the pit a fire burned with great light, and Nakoa could see his father's face, and for the first time his father seemed old.

Others entered quietly and were seated. Nakoa stood and looked down upon faces beloved to him since childhood, his father beloved to him, Onesta beloved to him, Itamipai, high chief of the Emitaks, beloved to him. Ninaistako who had taught him to hunt the redtailed deer entered, and as high chief of the Is'sue, sat near Natosin; Maka, Short Man, and high chief of the Raven Bearers, entered and was seated on the other side of Nakoa's father.

No one spoke, and the medicine pipe lay untouched. Nakoa stood before them all and waited for the three high chiefs of the younger societies. They came together: Kinaksapop, Little Plume; Imitaikoan, Little Dog; and Sistsauna, Bird Rattle. Only one of these men that headed the societies that led to the powerful Mutsik was younger than Nakoa. The chiefs of the Little Birds, Pigeons, and Mosquitoes looked at Nakoa strangely, and their faces said they could not believe why Nakoa stood before them. To trade any woman for the leadership of the Mutsik—to trade a white woman above all for this—was a sickness, yet it did not show upon the calm and unruffled features of Natosin's son.

Natosin began to speak.

"Tonight I am old, and my age rests upon me heavily. The winter of my life numbs my bones, and my flesh aches with their stillness. I could be a young and vigorous man again, and this same path would be walked, and this same end met. My heart is heavy with the words I will say, but before the Sun, I will say the words that are in my heart. I will speak the truth as it appears to my eyes.

"My son who stands before us now is high chief of the Mutsik. It is known by us all that he earned this chieftainship with his many coups, and with his acts and deeds of warmth toward his people. In this lodge, and many, many times, his voice has been raised strong in wisdom."

"Yes," said old Itamipai, chief of the old men's society. "Your son has long shown the wisdom of his father, and the story of his coups covers most of the skins of this lodge. He has never been selfish with the fruit of his bravery, whether it was meat from the hunt, or what he has gained in coups."

"This is true," said Onesta, and the rest of the chiefs murmured in assent.

"Now it is," Natosin went on, "that my son will marry a white woman tonight, without even five nights spent with his first wife, Nitanna. Is this not true, my son?" he asked Nakoa.

"It is true," Nakoa answered. "The white woman will sleep in my lodge tonight. She will be taken as my second wife."

"She will be your wife," Natosin said softly, "even when there is no sweetness in love unreturned, and she herself does not want this marriage."

"She will be my wife," Nakoa said, his voice tightening.

"And so it will be," Natosin said. "In this marriage, there is no wisdom, but so it will be."

"And why is there no wisdom in this marriage?" Nakoa asked his father angrily.

"The anger in your voice says that you already know this, my son."

"Tell me, my father. Tell me what I already know."

"You are Indian. She is white. You have walked different paths."

"This will not end our marriage. You feel anger in your heart, my father, because I do not walk in your way."

"I feel sorrow, but no anger. I feel age, and coldness, but not the heat of anger. There is sadness because I have to speak to you of this before the council of high chiefs, because you would not let me speak to you of this thoughtfully and quietly, as father to son. Take this woman, then, but in taking her you will not take from others! Walk your own path, but it will not be one that will bring fighting and killing to your people!"

"I know what my father's words will be, but speak them, my father, so the others will know, and will understand why I say here and now that I am no longer high chief of the Mutsik."

The lines upon Natosin's face deepened. "Or head chief of the Pikuni," he added. "Or head chief of the Pikuni when I am gone, and my body is dust."

"Or when my father is gone, and his body is dust."

"All for this woman?"

"All, for Maria, my woman."

Natosin bowed his head, and then he looked up at his son, and then the high chiefs. "My son's woman is white," he said quietly. "The white man enters Snake land and crosses the prairie in growing number. More and more of the white wagons will come and then the buffalo will go, and the prairie will be fire between the red man and the white man.

"My son's woman came from wagons burned by the Snakes. There were many whites in those wagons, killed and already grieved for by their blood bands back in the land of the rising sun. In their mourning they might hear of my son's white woman, for news of her capture has already traveled on the winds, and they will come here to seek her. There will be many, for many will hear, and all will think that this white woman is of their band. The Dahcotah who came to our Sun Dance saw the white woman, and the white man's drink makes the Indian talk, and the white man's warriors will learn of her, and then fire will come to Pikuni land. White warriors will come for my son's woman.

"And I will meet them alone. I will not spend another man's blood for a woman living in my lodge!" Nakoa's voice was as quiet as his father's.

"The woman by being here will make the Blackfoot land become fire!"

"I cannot see what lies ahead, my father. But if I am not chief, no man will have to follow my path. When I see the white men come, then I will speak to them, and if my wife has accepted her marriage to me, so will they."

Father and son looked at each other.

"Then so it will be," Natosin said quietly. "Is there any one among us who would speak?"

"I speak," Onesta said. "When Nakoa no longer leads the Mutsik, he walks his own path."

"Nakoa will marry the white woman, and I will be silent," said Itamipai.

Ninaistako spoke, "Nakoa walks alone. He chooses his own path." When the third high chief had spoken, a long terrified scream came to them all from the direction of the burial grounds.

"*Weekw?*" someone asked.

It came again and again, chilling, and something in the quality of the voice struck Nakoa, and he felt a violent coldness, and a strangling. "Maria!" he said. "Maria!" he shouted, and ran from the lodge.

The chiefs looked after him in long silence. There was not another scream, but they all listened intently as if there would be. Soon thunder rolled out strongly from the mountain.

"The voice of Esteneapesta is loud tonight," Natosin said tonelessly, and looked into the fire. Quietly, all of the chiefs assented to the marriage of Nakoa to the white woman and the relinquishment of his leadership of the Mutsik. There was a long silence, and at last Natosin spoke. "Then, so it will be," he said, and continued to look into the fire. Without another word spoken the high chiefs left him alone.

The fire flickered and burned. It seemed as if a wind had come up. Natosin looked at the west wall of the tipi that lay toward the burial grounds. Painted upon it were all of the coups of his son. Now the little stick figures moved to the dancing fire, moving and suffering and bleeding again, fighting and killing again, all for this night when their courage and agony would be traded for a white woman.

When she could, Maria turned to see her assailant. "Siksikai!" she gasped. "You have done these killings!"

"No," he replied. "Someone walks these grounds wearing the moccasins of Sokskinnie to make our graveyard more feared. I did not kill Kominakus and Siyeh."

"Then why are you here?" Maria asked.

"To make you keep your promise of the Kissing Dance. Nitanna told me where to stake the horse and that you would come to it."

"She meant you to kill me. She knows what you are," Maria said. "What am I?" he asked, gripping her chin and turning her frightened face to his.

"A monster!" she cried. "You rape and you kill!"

"Yes!" he said. "Yes. But as long as you satisfy me—you will live. I want you to scream—cry. I want your pain." His face was wild. His eyes were as hollow and as black as the eyesockets of a skull.

This was the escape Nitanna had arranged; this was the way in which Maria was to be kept out of her marriage! Maria shuddered, for already Siksikai's hands had gone to her breasts, hurting. If she were raped, how long could she live? It would not be the rape but the knife. Would she still be alive by morning? Could her trail be followed or ever found? Her mind raced on and on frantically, and she struggled against the pressure of his hands.

"Don't fight me," he gritted. "If you struggle, I will kill you—first."

I will bear it, Maria thought. Dear God, let me bear it! Already he was inside of her, plunging like a wild animal, and the pain, repeated and repeated, was an explosion against everything tender and female that she had ever been.

"Cry—cry!" he panted, but Maria bit her lips in agony and remained still.

"You tricked me once when I started to do this—trick me now!"

He would never be through—he would never be through.

Impaled beneath him she saw a flash of lightning rend the sky, and the searing light didn't end there, but reached the earth and cut burning into her flesh. "Cry!" he repeated, pulling her hair back from her face until she thought that he would pull it out of her head. He bit into her breasts and when she screamed, he withdrew from her and watching her convulsed body, straightened her out and entered her again in maniacal fury. Now she moaned and could not stop, and did not know the rain that began to beat strongly against her face.

His lips covered hers, bruising them, and then over her lips she was startled to feel the pounding of his pulsing throat. With violence equal to his own, she was determined that he should die. Summoning strength she had never known before, she bit deep into his throat. He cried out and beat her face with a rain of blows. In mud, rain, and blood they struggled, and soon he forgot his pain and exulted in her struggling. With her arms held behind her back he forced her legs apart again and held his knife in his free hand and cut deep into the already outraged flesh. "Now enjoy Nakoa!" she heard and then she had had enough and spun away into unconsciousness.

The rain was steadily falling. It was a cold dreary rain that beat upon her mother's grave.

The rain was gently falling; it was a tender sweet rain and beat against the lodge of her husband, upon this, their wedding night. A fire burned low in the firepit; even in its last embers she could see the gentle line of his lips.

But there had been a bloody god who had straddled her and raped her and then gone back to an orange sky. No, he was the lightning who had seared her and burned her so that she could not enjoy a man. She was not to enjoy a man. She was not to accept her husband upon this their wedding night, when a summer rain beat against the lodge skins so softly. "I am sorry," she said with bruised lips, her hair wet and dark in the mud.

What had she done? She was sorry and in the flowing of her tears and in the scarring of her body she could not think of what awful thing she had done. She would remember later. She might come back to the pale form lying inert in the rain and remember.

Of course, she was Earth Woman. The sun had brought to her womb Star Boy but she wept for the way of her past. Lover and son were in the skies above her and she tried to open her eyes to see them; why had they suffered her to choose her own grave? Why did she have to remain and feed the crawling things of the earth?

Serenity returned, the spring wonder of the rain blessed her spirit. She was not consigned to the earth. She was of no distance, no time. Joy permeated everything like the most brilliant of sunshine. She departed, but was called back in doubt. Hovering over the still white face she wailed in denial, "Dear God, who am I?"

Nakoa found her lying upon the wet dark earth. Her flesh was naked and cold; he could feel no sign of life within her. Lightning lit the sky, and he saw the extent of her bleeding.

"Maria!" he called in terror. He covered her with his shirt, and wept over her inert form like a child. The wind howled over them both, the pines brushing the unholy sky, the rain slashing the unblessed earth. "Maria! Maria!" he called hopelessly. This was not what should have been. This was their marriage night. On this night she was to find his love and protection; he was to love her tenderly, to cherish her and make her forget all past grief. Gently he lifted her and placed her upon Kutenai. Holding her in his arms he rode slowly back to the village.

Her screams had been heard by the village, and the news of his riding to the burial grounds had raced among all of the tipis. Crowds lined his path. Impervious to the rain they watched him silently as he carried her home. Her face was beaten beyond recognition; blood came from her nose and mouth, coloring his naked chest so that it looked as if he, too, were bleeding. Those who could see her clearly bowed their heads in sorrow; their hearts were touched. Above the storming clouds the full moon shone serenely, but the prairie knew it not.

At Atsitsi's, Kutenai halted, and the old woman came quickly outside and helped Nakoa take Maria from the horse. Anatsa appeared, and followed them inside. They placed Maria upon her couch, and taking away Nakoa's shirt, they saw in the bright firelight what Siksikai had wrought.

Nakoa looked at her and began to tremble, as if in convulsion.

"She will die, like the Snake woman," Atsitsi said.

Isokinuhkin came into the lodge with Sacred Drum, his herbs, and hands of healing. With Anatsa's help he attempted to stop the bleeding. Nakoa held the cold hands and never took his eyes from the swollen face.

"We cannot stop the bleeding!" Anatsa said, bursting suddenly into tears. She left Isokinuhkin's side and began to sob helplessly. Atsitsi joined the medicine man, and the two of them worked without words.

The fire burned silently, consuming all of the wood. When it had sunk into embers, Anatsa put more fagots into the fire pit. Pressing her hands against Maria's locket, she rocked back and forth in agony. She could not look at the still, tortured form and she could not bear to watch Nakoa's suffering.

"We cannot help her," said Atsitsi.

"Yes, we can," replied Isokinuhkin. "We can!"

Nakoa watched her labored breathing, too frozen from himself to pray.

The wind howled, sucking at the skins of the lodge, and sending a scurrying of sparks up the smoke hole.

"She is my wife," Nakoa said. "She cannot leave me!"

"She still breathes," replied Isokinuhkin.

"She cannot leave me!" Nakoa repeated.

The new fire began to die too. All of the shadows in the tipi grew and moved helplessly with the changing caprice of the wind. In time Isokinuhkin removed the robe that covered her and examined her closely. "The bleeding has stopped," he said in triumph.

Nakoa made a strangled sound and went to the door. "I am going to kill Siksikai," he said. He looked back at Anatsa. "None of you leave her."

"Yuh," Anatsa replied, turning away from him in embarrassment. He looked as if he might weep and never in her life had she seen a man cry.

In the driving rain Nakoa walked to the inner circle of the high chiefs, where he knew Siksikai to be. He passed his marriage tipi and new pain almost smote him to the ground. He saw Maria as she had been in the moonlight of his marriage to Nitanna, begging for him with the petals of a white flower trembling in her hands. He saw Maria's tear-streaked face, and he looked up at the storming sky in agony.

He had been raised upon acceptance. He knew the night must come, the darkness and grief of sorrow beyond any hurting of the flesh. But where were the gods now to give their strength to man? How dared the clouds hide the moon when she loved it so? How dared the stars move in the sky when she might never look upon them again? He saw Maria in her Indian wedding dress, with bone pendants flashing from her ears, and as he walked on, Maria's face begging for him was all that he could see. Every thrust that he had made inside of Nitanna had brought the knife into Maria. Napi, Napi, where was the strength of acceptance?

He walked on, pushing against the wind that was raging against him. He heard the Medicine Drum begin its sacred beating to keep that beloved heart alive. Over the howling of the wind he strained every nerve to hear it. Maria was clinging to the rainswept earth, and he knew how feebly she grasped it.

Beat-beat-beat, then thunder rolled out from the skies and in panic he couldn't hear the drum. Napi, my Father, the Sun—but the beating had not stopped, and in the falling rain, he began to sweat. He had put on his shirt, and some of her blood still clung to it and to his leggings. Crowds began to follow him; every male in the village wanted to see him kill Siksikai. Ahead, blurred in the wet night, Nakoa could see the fires of the Council Lodge.

Beat-beat-beat, but the drum beat more feebly. Without her he would not know the secret of union. Without her he could enter every woman in the world and find only emptiness. He looked frantically back at Atsitsi's lodge.

The drum stopped. He stood still and waited for it to resume its feeble beating, but it did not. He saw Maria trying to save her sister with the yellow hair. He remembered her face as he almost raped her in Snake land. He saw her when she asked him to make love to her by the river, and then he saw her again upon his first wedding night, and he almost collapsed under the driving rain. "Live! Live! Live!" his thoughts raged against the night. She was his touch with the sun. But the drum remained silent. She was gone from him. She had left him. The only sound in the village was the howling of the wind.

He had reached the door of the Council Lodge. He did not know that he was there. He was still crouched in agony.

Natosin felt his son's pain. Although the white woman had died and now his son could walk his path as head chief of the Pikuni, the old man would have traded all of his dreams and every moment left of his life to make the white woman's heart beat again. How foolish he had been to speak against union. When one believed himself to be in the pit, then the Great Father had only to reveal greater agony to show the smallness of sight.

Beat-beat-beat so softly that it seemed an echo, the drum began again. Beat-beat-beat, it went on, picking up strength.

"*Aio nochksiskimmakit! Nochkochtokit—*" Nakoa choked, straightening and standing tall before them. Tears were streaming down his face. Flowers would bloom in another spring. The moon would rise over the prairie in beauty again.

Siksikai sprang at him, his knife seeking his throat. Instantly a hand stopped his and held it still in a grip of iron. Siksikai looked into the enraged face of Apikunni. "Dog!" Apikunni shouted. "Woman! You would kill a man asleep?"

"Nakoa is the woman!" Siksikai shouted back. "Look how he shakes before me with a woman's tears upon his face!"

Everyone around Nakoa was a stranger. His thanks to the Great Father flooded his soul and in his Father's waters no hatred existed.

Siksikai was lunging to be free, and Apikunni pushed him toward the fire. "Nakoa," he shouted. "Let me kill him!"

Nakoa stood motionless, the woman's tears still touching his cheeks.

Natosin looked at his fine handsome son and thought, "He will be killed." His son was a man asleep in his soul's radiance. It seemed such a short time ago that Natosin had seen his son born in blood; must he see him die in blood too? "I am very old," Natosin thought. "I cannot live through another winter."

The drum beat on. Natosin stared intently at his son. "Do not listen to it! Do not listen! Kill Siksikai now!" But the head chief of the Pikuni sat perfectly still, his tongue silent, and his face bearing no sign of anxiety.

"Nakoa!" Apikunni was shouting again. "Let me kill him!"

"No!" Nakoa said harshly, as if he resented any sound that muffled the beating of the drum.

"Then kill him!" Apikunni said furiously. "Kill him now!"

Siksikai sprang away from Apikunni and moved at Nakoa, his face a mask of hate. Murder was in his moving hands, circling like a snake about to strike. Nakoa appeared to be seeing him for the first time. "A woman's tears are gone," Nakoa said. "Now you will have no time to feel yours!" Nakoa drew his knife, and the crowd in the lodge moved as far away from them as possible.

Siksikai lunged at Nakoa and drew some blood.

Siksikai attacked again, and Nakoa retreated. "*Omaciociccaak!*" Siksikai hissed, and spat into his face. Another of his blows just missed its mark. Apikunni struggled against the hands that restrained him. "Nakoa is still asleep!" he shouted.

Now, as head chief, I will stop this fight. I will raise my hand in sign for it to end, for I will not let a snake strike down my son when my son has no heart to fight. How could my own death have tasted so sweet when I choke upon the bitterness of my son's?

"*Meqneken-Eekimaawisa!*" Siksikai was taunting, his face shining with triumph. "*Wekimaawiw!*" Burning with boldness he came in close to Nakoa to lunge at his heart, and they all heard the sound of his knife as it bit into Nakoa's shirt and down his leggings. They saw the blade draw an immediate path of blood, but in that instant, Siksikai's knife was spent, and with his left hand Nakoa held it stilled. Fiercely, he looked into Siksikai's face and whispered, "Here is a man who uses a knife upon a woman! Now he will have a knife used upon him!" Nakoa's knife moved and Siksikai screamed and

Nakoa's Woman

writhed in the shock of his own castration. "You will not have another woman!" Nakoa hissed, his face lusting at the agonized form that was convulsed at his feet. Siksikai screamed again, and Nakoa kicked at his mouth. He kicked the face again, and there was a gasp of horror around him, but out of control, Nakoa kicked at the face until all of its life and shape were gone.

In time, he stopped. His own blood now covered his shirt and his leggings. Breathing deeply, he turned toward the outer tipis. The drum was still beating.

Natosin gave sign that the lodge was to be cleared, and except for the high chiefs, the crowd went out into the rain. Natosin then spoke softly to his son. "You did not finish your words of earlier this evening."

"I will speak them now," Nakoa replied. "When the white woman is moved to my lodge she will be my wife. I alone will speak for her presence. I will move my lodge from the circle of the high chiefs and never seek to live there again."

"The woman may yet die," Natosin said.

"I have still taken her. I will move out of the circle of the high chiefs."

"You can never follow me as head chief."

"I have accepted this."

"There are no more words to be said?" the old man asked softly.

"There are no more on this subject, my father," Nakoa answered, his face suffering.

"Then so it will be," said Natosin. "*Kenny aie ki anetayi imitaiks*," he said in traditional sign the feast had ended, and then his voice broke, and he did not go on. Silently the chiefs departed, but Nakoa remained.

"My father," Nakoa started with great tenderness, but Natosin raised his hand for silence.

"I have accepted your words," Natosin said. "I do not want to hear them again."

"All right, my father," Nakoa said with emotion, and left the lodge.

Sacred Drum continued to beat. The old man put his head into his hands and wept. As the fire died, his shadow grew along the council wall. The wind had stopped and the village was silent except for the beating of the Medicine Drum. Natosin listened to it beat-beat-beat, and then the thing lying so grotesquely at his feet shuddered in its last coldness, and kicked out convulsively at the glowing embers.

Chapter Twenty Four

Limping heavily, and bone weary, Anatsa walked slowly toward the lodge of her husband. It was not far from daylight, and the storm was clearing. Esteneapesta, the thunder maker and voice of many drums, had stilled, and to the east a false light gleamed. In her tiredness, Anatsa thought it to be the sun, and she stopped walking, and crossing her arms over her breast, faced it. The Medicine Drum still beat, caressing the night.

Tears slid uncontrolled down her cheeks. Maria had not died, but an awful emptiness enveloped Anatsa. She touched the gold locket at her throat. She saw Maria's face, smiling and happy, and then she saw it haunted and tear-streaked when she could not accept Nakoa's marriage. Then she saw Nakoa as she had just left him, sitting with head bowed at her couch. Beside him was the beautiful face beaten and swollen, the thighs bruised and mutilated, the body that stopped bleeding, only to start again. Every movement brought fresh blood and new agony to Nakoa, and it was his suffering and not Maria's that had driven her from the lodge. "Napi, Napi—help them both! Help them both!" she whispered to the glimmering sky. "Whatever it may be for them—whatever it may be—help them both!"

Sadly she moved on.

And as she moved on, the evil thing, the insane thing that had followed Maria to where Siksikai had waited, moved out from the burial grounds and crossed the river near which it had already taken two lives. In the smoky gray of ending night it thought of the silent tipis and the dozing horses tethered to the lodges of the Pikuni

Mutsik.

Anatsa walked on, and as she did she imagined that the drum weakened. Ahead she could see Apikunni's lodge, and his warhorse picketed to it. She thought of her husband and of her marriage, and unbearable pity for Maria smote her. She had so much. She had everything, and now Maria struggled even for her life. Once more she halted, and faced the eastern sky in position of prayer. She spoke aloud:

> Father, the Sun,
> hear my words.
> You know that I have lived straight,
> that I have been pure.
>
> Hear my words, Father, the Sun.
> If the white woman lives,
> I will for you become Sun Dance Woman.
> I will starve my body of food and drink.
> I will suffer my body,
> if this white woman lives!
>
> Father, the Sun, Behold me! Hear me!
> Let the white woman walk a long path filled with
> happiness and love.
> Let her have strength of body and heart,
> and for you I will humbly make sacrifice!
> I will make sacrifice, Father,
> I—will—make—sacrifice!

She finished her words and shuddered, shivering and cold. The coming day seemed to bring strange light, the yellow suffocation she had felt in the mountains with Apikunni, and at the river before Kominakus had been killed. The Medicine Drum beat, and now she knew that it would not stop, and even with the yellow sky a serenity came to her. She smiled, and smiling reached Apikunni's lodge. Because she had stopped to pray, she reached it the same time as did the Crow who had hidden for so long in the burial grounds.

She did not wholly grasp his presence. She saw the strangeness of his deerskin bleached white, of his long hair, of one forelock cut and trained to stand erect in a most terrifying manner. *"Aween?"* she whispered. "Who is it? Why are you dressed in the manner of the— Sahpo!" She cringed. Quickly she raised her arms before her, but he stabbed her in the breast, and she looked at him in amazement. He stabbed her again, and as she doubled over he cut the thong that held Apikunni's horse picketed, and rode away.

She tried to straighten, but couldn't. Some unbearably heavy force pulled her to the earth. A man in shimmering white had stabbed her, but it was poor Maria who was cut and bleeding, not she! She smelled fresh rain on the wet earth, gentle rain that she had always loved so much.

"Apikunni! Apikunni!" she called, and to her amazement, he was already with her. From far off she heard the beating of horse's hoofs. Death had ridden out of a yellow sky after all. All of her coldness had not been wrong.

"Anatsa! Anatsa!" her husband moaned, and gently tried to move her. Her chest, white hot with pain, stabbed her again in mortal agony, and he put her down, and pillowed her head with his hands. Tears from him touched her face, for surely she was not crying!

She clenched and unclenched her hands. "I will not die!" she whispered, but she saw in her husband's face that she would. "I did not even reach you," she said, mourning that she had not even reached the lodge and lain with him in their bed. "I—did—not— reach you," she said again, with great effort, for now she was too tired for talk.

"You reached me!" Apikunni answered, and then great silence began to grow between them.

In silence she smelled the rain of the earth again, and skipped through warm meadow grass to the glen. There Apikunni waited by the pink swamp laurel, and she was whole and beautiful, and her breasts were warm and full for him. They walked into the autumn of smoky mists, and then into the frozen winter, and clasping hands they sat before the council fires with flames crackling red and orange. Outside, spring bands from the sky were driven away in summer wind. The glacial fields had melted, the snow crept silently into streams and rivers, and on the new earth their son walked ahead of them, and shafts of the sun came through the trees and caressed him with light. The circle was completed, and the world at last lay whole and beautiful.

Upon the twenty-first day of her marriage, Anatsa lay quietly in death, her face more beautiful than it had ever been in her life. Her husband released her still hands. In agony he looked to the eastern sky where the sun was beginning to show. Above it a star shone steadily, and involuntarily he watched it, for it was as if she were already there, lost to him as he stood bound to earth, and frozen forever as a part of the great and final silence of the skies.

Beat—beat—beat, sounded the drum, and the moon, full that night, moved reluctantly across the prairie, as if it would stay in its full beauty. Two women had lain sorely wounded, and one had lived and one had died, and the new day came tenderly, with the last of the storm clouds gone.

The sun shone warmly upon the refreshed land, cooled and comforted by the summer storm. Women went to the river for wood and water. Cooking fires were lit, and smoke from them curled lazily into the blue sky. Someone found Apikunni and his dead bride. Someone carried her slight form away from him. Wailing then came from the lodge of Apeecheken, the long Indian lament for the dead, and more fires were lit, and in the afternoon sun the dogs fought lazily over discarded meat.

Apeecheken would shun all public gatherings, all dances, and all religious ceremonies of any kind. She would wear old clothes and not paint herself, and shun the wearing of ornaments. She would do this, and then when slow time had moved, she would give birth to a new son, and in his growing, and in her love for him, the thought of her sister would come less and less, and Anatsa would be a memory absorbed without grief.

But it was not so with Apikunni. And it was not so with Maria.

She heard the drum too. It throbbed and beat against her suffering flesh, an anvil pinning her to pain. With the drum she heard Nakoa's voice. "Culentet," he said. Little white bird; he called her little white bird, as he had done when he had first kissed her outside of the Indian village. Nakoa, why did you do that? Why didn't you just take me then—as you did later? What did you do to me?

Hurt! Hurt! Hurt! She became suddenly rational, and saw him. He was trying to still her agonized thrashing. She looked up into his black eyes. "Hurt!" she screamed. He gently touched her face. "I am," he said quietly, and she was off again, linked to him only by that awful drum.

Ana, Ana, help me! "We are all dead now," she sobbed and in her moving, pain stabbed her so deeply that her face became wet with perspiration.

But the drum wouldn't stop. The awful drum wouldn't stop.

Ana, this is a Blackfoot village. See all of the tipis with their black bands at the bottom and the top, and the little white circles did you know everything is a circle? I want you to meet Nakoa. Isn't he handsome? Ana, I love him, but he wanted that dirty Meg! Anatsa, were you really Ana all the time?

Look at those Shawnees, all ragged and dirty. The poor miserable Indian! But Father, the Blackfoot are different! Look at the land. It is wild and savage; only a strong people could live here! All right, Father, let me present Nakoa. He is the man I love. He is my husband already. Why is Nakoa dressed like a white man? He would never do this—walk the path of a woman! Father, make Meg get away from him! Dear God, I have to leave! Where is the white horse Nitanna said would be in the burial grounds?

She tried escape again. She sank into darker waters; she saw shadows weaving against the sky above her. Great hands came into the waters after her. Great hands held her pinioned against the hot dry air. There was no way she could escape him. Upon the seventh day after Siksikai had mutilated her, Nakoa brought her back from death. Around her now was the warmth of the sun. She opened her eyes and knew only him. "We had such a beautiful wedding," she whispered. "Nakoa, why did you take me to give me such pain?" His hand gently covered her lips, stopping her words.

Apikunni refused to burn the lodge they had shared together. In this way he broke tradition. He also carried Anatsa to the burial grounds himself, and he placed her upon her burial platform, gently putting all of her sewing and tanning instruments by her side. He held her cold hands, and kissed her serene lips, and then he left her alone in shadow under the summer sky. For eight days he disappeared, and remained neither at their lodge nor near her body.

When he returned to the village, the Medicine Drum was silent, and he knew that Maria had died, or was no longer close to death. Insulated from the world, he made no effort to find out which it was, for he was still apart even from the man as close to him as blood brother. Instead he went silently and unnoticed to his and Anatsa's lodge, and sat upon their couch, and for minutes was crushed by inner desolation and emptiness.

The belongings that he had not placed with Anatsa had been removed. He looked at the ashes still in the firepit; she had started the last fire that had burned there. She had brought warmth to their lodge, and now it was lifeless and cold. He wanted to kneel and touch the ashes, to bless them as a part of her, but he could not. He could not slash himself, or cut his hair; his grief had to be silent. And so he painted his face in the fashion of the Indian for killing, and he marked his new warhorse, and in the next dawn, when the sky was red with sunrise, he left the Pikuni tipis and followed the long trail to Crow land.

He left silently, but a blind old man unable to sleep sat outside his daughter's lodge and heard him pass. He knew that the warrior rode toward the rising sun and that the warrior was Apikunni who would ride until he found his warhorse picketed outside a Crow lodge. And then he would kill the murderer of his bride. The old man dropped tears upon the flute that had been silent in his hands since Siyeh's death.

In time he heard the passing of another horse. Another warrior followed Apikunni. It could be no one but Nakoa. So the white woman would live. Fresh tears came and ran down the old man's face. He wept for both the dead and the living.

For five days Nakoa and Apikunni rode toward the eastern sky, and then they saw smoke rising from many wood fires. In front of a lodge they saw Apikunni's horse picketed. Apikunni did not wait for the new day, but rode boldly through the village, stopping near his horse. The Crow left his lodge, and in front of his people, Apikunni killed and scalped him. Dogs awakened and barked frantically and a crowd began to gather around the dead Crow. Apikunni stood surrounded by his enemies, but before a Crow could issue a sign of challenge, Nakoa, painted for war and known to them all, rode out of the shadows. The Crow watched silently as the two Mutsik left the village, Apikunni leading his warhorse, the bloody Crow scalp dangling from his belt. Women and children watched them fearfully. Warriors followed at a distance, and when the Blackfoot had gone, there remained a respectful silence.

For five days Nakoa and Apikunni rode back to their village, and when they reached it, they parted, Nakoa taking the extra horse to the herd. Apikunni rode directly to the burial grounds. On the trail to the river he saw her slight body ahead of him, and with a wild plunging of his heart he quickened his horse, but saw instead another maiden, another face.

The river flowed strongly on, shining in the sunlight, winding its way into cool shade. She would never bring vessels to it again. Its empty waters would never reflect her image again.

In the shadow of the dead, a light wind moved gently in the trees. He stopped his horse beneath her platform and looked silently up at her still figure. Her skinning knives were moving beneath her. With tears falling unashamedly down his face, he touched the scalp at his belt. It did not lessen his pain. "Anatsa," he said sorrowfully, "this is all I could do!"

She remained silent, deep in sleep.

Apikunni bowed his head, and his horse pawed at the earth impatiently.

He left her finally, and never again returned to the burial grounds. From the earth she had come and back to the earth she was returned. All of the elements would seek her, the four winds, the rains, the winged of the air; and together with the earth, each would take a part, until she again became one with them all.

Chapter Twenty Five

The first thing that Maria felt when she had fully awakened was the gold locket at her throat. She touched its cold metal, and knew that Anatsa was dead.

She did not want to face this. Here then was one more death. She was a tree, and all of her loved ones leaves, and in the coming winter she was to be stripped of all of them and left barren and naked. Sunlight moved to her face and was warm and comforting. Still she would not open her eyes. Maybe she could drift back to long quiet sleep, and in a new awakening, Anatsa would be alive. She touched the locket again, and opened her eyes. Natosin sat near her.

"Anatsa is dead," Maria said painfully.

"Yes."

"How? How?" Maria cried, trembling with grief.

"She was killed by the Crow that had killed Kominakus and Siyeh."

"When?"

"When she returned from Atsitsi's the night you were attacked."

"She had been caring for me?"

"Yes."

"Oh, dear God!" Maria moaned. If she hadn't been caring for me . . ."

"She would have met the Crow upon another path."

Maria began to weep. "Where is Nakoa?"

"He was always beside you until it was known that you would live. He slept by you. He, and not Atsitsi, has cared for you. You are his wife, my daughter."

"I need him now!" She struggled to sit up. The old man restrained her.

"It is only eleven days since you almost bled to death again. Do not sit up now."

"I want Nakoa!" she said helplessly.

"He is gone. He rode into Crow land with Apikunni. He will come to you as soon as he returns."

"Everyone—I—love dies!" she choked. "Everyone!"

"My son will not. My son will live more suns than I have."

"Where is Nitanna?" Maria asked suddenly. "Where is your other daughter?"

"She is back with the Kainah. She has returned with her father to her own people. My son sent her away."

"Why?"

"In your sickness you talked of many things, and one of them was of the white horse that waited for you at the burial grounds. He asked Nitanna of this, and she said that she had meant you to be killed. My son said their marriage was ended. He could not have a woman for a wife that would kill another who was innocent."

"What about you—and her father?"

"It was agreed upon. Nitanna did not want to stay."

Maria looked searchingly into the kind eyes watching her. "Natosin," she said, "I am proud to call you 'father.'"

"I am glad for this. You are my son's woman."

Maria turned away. "How can I be any man's woman?"

"You are young. You will heal."

"Will I?" Maria asked with sudden bitterness. She saw Nakoa walking past her with Nitanna. She saw Nakoa rejecting her outside of his lodge, and she began to shake. "He did not want me enough," she said.

"Should he have wanted you with the passion of Siksikai?"

"Atsitsi says all men rape!"

"Siksikai was not a man. He was killed by my son and dumped out on the prairie for the wolves, because he was not a man. Live with my son, Maria, and know a man!"

Time passed, slow days and long nights, and before she rose to walk again, he returned. One dusk his tall form shadowed the doorway, and he came to her. She called his name, and he sat upon her couch and gently touched her face.

"You are the most beautiful of women," he said. "You are the softness of all women!"

Maria smiled and touched his hands.

"I did not let you go," he said seriously. "You wanted to leave me, Maria, but I did not let you go!"

"You are a stubborn man," Maria said.

"I had the strength of the sun behind me."

He tenderly kissed her face. "Culentet, my culentet, my little culentet—"

Maria began to sob, and he held her in his arms and kissed the tears on her lashes.

"We can never have a marriage," she wept. "Never!"

"Never," he pretended to agree.

"Now you mock me!" she wailed. "How can you be so cruel? The pain . . ."

He kissed her lips. "Pain is not lasting. Life is. Pain, culentet, is always the introduction to life. Life without pain is a toy for children."

"You sound like your father."

"Do you like my father?"

"Very much. I have love for him. He has given me much comfort."

"I am glad."

"Did you find Anatsa's murderer?"

"Yes."

"Did Apikunni kill him?"

"Yes."

"How can I bear it without Anatsa? How can I bear to think that she is dead when she had Apikunni?"

"I had no words for Apikunni. There are not words for everything."

"Nakoa, we cannot have a marriage. It is not just my body and what Siksikai did—"

"No, it is not so. The woman in the river that you feared so much —she will come to me again. I know it. And then we will have our marriage." He kissed her again, gently, but lingeringly. "I will prepare our food, or have it prepared."

"Please, not by Atsitsi!"

He smiled. "Sleep, my wife. I will bring the food to you when it is done."

She lay back, and sat partway up again, thinking of something. "Nakoa, did you lose the chieftainship of the Mutsik?"

"Yes," he answered.

Tears came to her eyes again. "And you did this—for me."

He looked almost angry. "No, Maria. For myself," he said, and went outside.

The day after Nakoa's return, the village moved to the mountains. Nakoa carried Maria outside, and she watched the dismantling of the lodges, Natosin's first, and then all of the other tipis, like giant mushrooms swept away in the wind. Most of the morning, the horses stood patiently during the loading of the travois. The old and the young who could not ride a horse sat atop the loads, and the Pikuni moved out, scouts in the lead, then the high chiefs, the societies of the Ikunuhkahtsi, and last, the women and children.

Natosin came and said good-bye to his son and Maria. Sikapischis, more gaunt than ever, called on Maria for the first time since her sickness, and neither of them mentioned Anatsa or Siyeh in their brief farewell. Atsitsi, even dirtier than Maria had remembered her, halted at Nakoa's lodge as the camp was leaving. "She woman again soon," she said cheerfully to Nakoa. "Maybe Siksikai get rid of silly bird song!"

"I'll stop being bird song if you take a bath!" Maria said grimly.

Atsitsi laughed and leaned toward Maria. Her horse shifted unhappily. "Winter come soon and why wash in by-damn cold?"

Smiling to himself, Nakoa slapped Atsitsi's horse, and the animal moved dispiritedly toward the other horses leaving the village. "Can Nakoa take big surprise if find wife a woman?" she shouted back at them.

"Do you suppose she ever was human?" Maria asked Nakoa.

He looked at her seriously. "She saved your life as much as did Anatsa and Isokinuhkin."

Maria saw Apeecheken pass, dressed in mourning, her head bowed in grief. Maria remembered Anatsa's words: "I shall rest on the burial platform, and it will not be my time. The sky is yellow, and voices from the grounds call to me, and I am afraid of the coldness there." Maria waved to Apeecheken, but Anatsa's sister did not wave back.

The scouts were already lost in the rank grass of the prairie. She and Nakoa watched them leave in silence. When they were gone from sight, they heard faint cries from the children, the barking of dogs, and then nothing but the wind moving through the desolate village site. Never again would Nakoa's lodge stand in the circle of the high chiefs. It is such a waste! Maria thought bitterly.

In darkness that night when they had eaten and she lay quietly watching the fire, she missed the drums, the voices, the sounds of dancing and chanting.

"I am so lonely," she said. "It is so lonely here, all alone."

"You are still apart from yourself," he said quietly. "That is why you are lonely. It is not because the village is gone."

She smiled. "The two women again?"

"You are apart from them both."

"Both? What am I?"

"The shock from Siksikai's act. You are unknowing."

"Nakoa, your words are so strange."

"You will know them to be true. It will take time for you to change from numbness to feeling, to become a woman, to become my wife."

Maria looked quickly away. If he talked of physical contact between them, she could not bear it. He had kissed her lips in sweet ness, but if he kissed her in hunger she would become sick. He saw her expression, and his face looked haunted. "I accept," he said softly. "I was a glutton, so I will accept my hunger. Maria, Nitanna is gone, and Siksikai is gone. Let not their names be mentioned between us again. We build our lives without them."

"Build our lives?"

"First in your healing. Your healing is first, so that you will live again—as two women—as one woman—and my wife."

He was right; she was numb. Though her body grew in strength, though she could walk, she wanted to lie still upon her couch. She wanted to stay within the lodge. She wanted to turn her face to the wall, and look at nothing else. She relived her past. She suffered all of her old griefs, and even when moods of sadness left, she sought them, and was disappointed that they didn't stay constantly. Nakoa brought her food. He built the fire, brought the wood, and the water for bathing and drinking. In her moods he did not speak to her, and absented himself from her in her self-inflicted pain.

Then came the evening he decided she was to remain numb no longer. He had returned to the tipi with freshly killed deer. He stood for a long moment at the door, looking inside at the shadowed lodge with its fire unlit. "Maria!" he said sharply. "Maria!"

Dozing, she sat up, surprised at the anger in his voice. "What is it?" she said weakly. "What is the matter, Nakoa?"

He put the deer down and strode to her, smelling of blood, of pines, of the outdoors, and he was so strong and powerful that his strength was sickening to her. "What do you seek in sleep? What do you see upon the walls of this lodge that, when you are awake, it takes all of your time to watch it? Maria, get up!"

"I can't!"

"You can! Stand up, Maria!"

"I am sick."

"I say you are not! You are sick no longer!"

"And who is saying this—God? Are you the voice of the Great Spirit, Nakoa?"

You are taking a life! Stand!" The violence in his voice drove her to her feet.

"All right," she said bitterly in English. "Now what do you want me to do? Go butcher that awful deer?"

"You are my wife. You will speak in Pikuni."

"Do you want me to butcher the deer?" she asked, still sarcastic.

"I will cut the meat. You cook it, and then you will have the hunger to eat it. The blood in it will make you strong."

"I have no hunger. I will not eat."

"I have hunger, and you will cook the meat for me."

She glowered at him but cooked the meat he cut for her. When it was broiled, tender and juicy in the inside and crusty on the outside, she could not resist it, and ate with him. When she had finished she looked at him for approval.

"And now," he said, "we will walk."

"You are mad!"

"We will walk and then you will sleep tonight, and not lie awake and watch the lodge fire."

"It will hurt me to walk!"

"It will hurt you not to. We will walk tonight, and then you will ride the bay. You will heal, Maria."

"I will not!" she blazed.

He smiled. "You will not?"

"No!"

"How will you keep yourself sick? By lying on that couch?"

"You just want to climb on me and rape me!"

He was incredulous.

"You will not rape me!" she almost screamed.

"I would not rape you."

"You tried once!"

"And so you did with me," he said.

Angrily, she threw a robe over her shoulders and left the lodge. She walked in such fury that she forgot to be in pain.

He joined her. She walked far from their lodge, and would have walked farther but he restrained her. Without speaking to him she went to bed that night, and was so tired that she fell asleep. She woke up furious with herself and was so ravenous that she ate. "Dear God!" she said, when her stomach was satisfied, "now what do you have planned for me today? Do you want me to hunt a little deer?"

"We have meat," he said seriously.

"Then we can take a nice long horseback ride!"

"All right," he said simply.

"No! You fool! No!"

"It will not hurt you."

"Of course not! Then tonight, you can climb all over me!"

"Maria," he scolded, "can you think of nothing else?"

She kicked over the water paunch.

He smiled. "We will ride to the river for water. You see, your strength is returning!"

She hid her face. "I am a fool!" she whispered.

"Yes," he agreed.

"You don't understand English!"

"I understand you."

"Dear God, what will I do?"

"Ride to the river."

He helped her mount the bay, and he mounted Kutenai, and the two horses walked easily to the river. In the fresh running water they filled two paunches, and then rode back along the deserted trail. The land was so quiet, so fearsomely, awfully quiet. The shadow of the burial grounds stretched out from behind them, and weighed heavily upon Maria. She looked sadly at the ground, at the abandoned prairie Anatsa would not walk again when the new camp was made.

"You can go and see her," Nakoa said. "You can see how peacefully she sleeps."

"I don't want to see her dead."

"If that is all there was, this sleeping—then you would see how gently it came to her. If there is more than sleeping, then do not feel sadness at what you cannot know."

"You said that when the medicine drum stopped for me, you were just a vessel to hear it beat again. Why would it be different for you than for Apikunni?"

"We were unmated. I was not whole."

"You could lose me then, after . . ."

"When the circle is completed, wholeness can take loss with more strength. Until we have met, each of us will be empty."

"What if we cannot meet?"

"We both will suffer and wail at our denial."

That night they slept again upon separate couches, and she

watched the lodge fire flicker lazily upon the shadowed walls. "Nakoa," she asked, "when will we join the others?"

"Before the first snows. We will join them as they are ready to seek the prairie again. The camp stays in the mountains all the moon of the falling leaves, and then the camp divides, and separate blood bands seek the winter shelter that cannot protect a whole village."

"Where is this?"

"Usually along the river bank, where the land offers protection from winter wind."

"Then why do we ride to the mountains at all? If we are just to return to the prairie . . . ?"

"I thought you would be lonely and would want to hear the drums and see Apeecheken and Sikapischis before we were alone for the winter. We can visit your friends and stay in the mountains if you would like. I know a beautiful warm and sheltered valley. We could spend the winter alone—there."

"All right."

"It is a beautiful valley," he repeated softly. "I would like to be there with you when the snows leave it, and spring comes again."

In the spring, would she be carrying his child?

"While we wait for you to grow strong," he continued, "we will walk and ride together. I will show you how to find the camas root, and how to cook it. I will show you how the Blackfoot builds snares for the deer and the antelope, and how the Indian makes caches. We will gather roots and berries, and you can ride with me when I hunt, and learn the dressing of meat."

And so it was. He was adamant about her working. He made her move, walk, ride, and she became so tired that she accepted each night's sleep immediately.

The old Maria emerged from the shadows and relished the rich earth, the wind, and the sun upon the long prairie grass. She gained weight. Her breasts became full again, and her face bloomed with beautiful color. They became good friends. They laughed together, and talked. He sensed her moods with fearful omniscience, and stood firmly between her and the pathways of the past.

He was friend and teacher. He showed her how to roast entrails

Indian fashion, turning them inside out before stuffing them so that the sweet fat covering the intestine was confined to the meat in roasting; how to cook meat with wild parsnip to bring out its natural juices; how to gather the camas root and to cook it in deep pits lined with sweet grass; how to start a fire without coals by using rotten touchwood and rubbing it up and down a sinew bow until an ember was started. She helped him build snares, rubbing the rawhide rope with buffalo tallow to disguise human smell, and they made caches for food by digging a hole four feet deep, lining the bottom with stones, and covering the top with a heavy slab. They cached food in trees, with rattles tied to the parfleche bags to keep small animals away, and they used parfleche bags as caches in water, and anchored them securely with heavy stones. They made fresh pemmican, adding peppermint leaves and wild cherries to the meat Nakoa hunted. He showed her the difference between game and war arrows, and taught her safety and caution upon the trail. He showed her how to read sign of man, the stirrings of the forest animals, and how to make camp in the open and still keep it hidden from a distance, for a lodge must be erected where no enemy could approach it secretly, and still be hidden as much as possible. They lit their cooking fires in the midday, for the wind was strongest then to dissipate the smoke, and there was no glare to serve as guide in the darkness. Their trails followed sheltered ravines and avoided hilltops even in Blackfoot territory.

More than a month had passed since they had been left alone in the village. The moon had grown in size and had become full again, lighting the prairie like day. Indian summer clung to the land, but sometimes in the mountain wind Maria thought she felt the first touch of fall.

One night when the moon had risen early they walked after their meal. He held her hand as he had done long ago. There was an urgency in his touch, and he allowed himself to study her.

"You are contented," he said. "You have finished seeking shadows.

Maria looked at the abandoned village site, and the warm quiet prairie. "I feel at peace," she answered.

"I am grateful for this. Numbness is gone if your feelings have returned."

She smiled. "Tonight I am even content with both Marias. You said I would have to accept two the lady in the waters—whichever one of us was the image."

"You do not have to destroy what you accept. And fighting within the self is fighting an unmatched foe. You do not believe the woman who wanted me was a whore?"

She immediately became wary. "Whatever she was, she was the loser. Her begging did her no good."

"The victorious one led her to Siksikai."

"No! Nakoa, you rejected me! I did not reject you! Do you think I will ever forget that night? In the moonlight before my Father, you took her."

"I could not take what I did not want. Do not speak to me of Nitanna, Maria. She is gone."

"No," Maria shuddered. "I will see my own wedding dress, and I will see you walk by me and follow Nitanna all the rest of my life."

"You will limit your vision to this one incident?" he asked her angrily.

"Yes."

"Then you have vision as limited, the one patch of sky, as the warm and beautiful woman you assigned to the river. You are then not at peace, and you will never know serenity."

"I would among my own kind!"

He looked stunned. "This is the first time you have wanted the white man."

"Why was I in the burial grounds?"

"You were following the path of a child. You were not seeking escape from me, but from growing up."

"To grow up, must I become a whore?"

"I was not making you a whore. I was taking you as my woman. Not all women are whores."

"I was to wait for you after you had been making love to Nitanna. That would make me a whore. Nakoa, I was so wild to have you. I loved you so much!"

"Is that why you went to the burial grounds rather than to my couch?"

"I told you I would be your only wife. I told you, you had to choose between us."

"No. I had told you that my marriage this moon was not one of my choosing. I told you that Nitanna meant nothing to me beside my feeling for you. You fled from the woman you keep buried that has more blood than you. Because you tried to deny her life she rose and almost destroyed you. Maria, you have not accepted anything. How could you ever become a whore when you cannot even accept yourself?" His black eyes were searching hers earnestly. "This other woman you will not know, Maria, would go to her love even after ten wives. She would follow her feelings past every rule that had been sacred to her heart." Now desire for her was plain upon his face.

She stopped walking and looked up at him. "You expect to sleep with me tonight," she said tonelessly. "You think I have healed enough for this."

"Yes." His voice was just as flat as her own.

"You will bring me pain!"

"No. I will be gentle."

She trembled violently. "I do not want this. I cannot bear to be raped again!"

"I will not rape you. We love each other. We are man and wife."

They had reached the lodge. She bowed her head. "I will not," she said softly. "I can't."

She walked away from him, back toward the river. The moon was rising in gentle majesty, and she wept bitterly before its poignant beauty. This was the most beautiful of all nights when she was to become a bride to Nakoa. The moon should be shining for them in holy grace. Such a short time ago she had exulted with unbearable happiness at the thought of becoming his bride. Anatsa had loved Apikunni so deeply and now she was dead, lying dead beneath the tender moon, and Maria was alive and yet she could not accept the man that loved her.

It was dark when she returned. He had started the fire; it gleamed through the lodge skins even in the moonlight. She wished that he had left the lodge dark. She did not want him to see her, and she did not want to see him when he possessed her. She opened the doorflap and went to him neither in chastity nor lust. She entered the tipi without innocence or desire, to receive the man she had wanted more than anything in the world before all feeling had been taken away from her.

Chapter Twenty Six

She stood uncertainly by the lodge door. "I don't like the fire," she said.

"Does all warmth bother you?"

"I do not like its light. If you are going to have me, I do not want to see it."

"Then close your eyes. I do not seek darkness."

Fury suddenly choked her. "Do you want me to take off my clothes?"

"Do you want me to start undressing you too?"

"That is not what I meant!"

He removed his shirt and leggings and lay upon the couch. He stretched contentedly and closed his eyes.

"What are you going to do?" Maria asked, still unable to make herself leave the door.

He opened his eyes in annoyance. "I am trying to go to sleep."

"You said I was to sleep with you!"

"In time," he murmured. "In time you will."

"You said now! Tonight!"

He opened his eyes again. "I have changed my mind," he said. He turned away from her and fell asleep almost immediately.

Maria went to the fire and looked into the greedy flames. When they died, she went to her couch. He slept with his face as happy as a child's. She lay down and tried to sleep, but his peaceful breathing almost drove her insane. How could he have said such a thing and then go to sleep? He had fallen asleep right away just to make her feel rejected. Never, never would she give him gratification. The fire had sunk to coals and she couldn't see him clearly. She sprang out of bed and replenished it. At the noise she made, he stirred and a smile settled upon his lips.

"Beast!" she snarled.

She went back to her couch and turned coldly away from him. The wind had come up, and she echoed its wailing. She wanted to go home. She wanted her own kind. She wanted to follow the lullaby of her mother, to put her head upon the soft leaves of her mother's grave. There was no disgrace in this. Forget Atsitsi and her silly sugar titty. Forget Nakoa and Mequesapa's song of acceptance. What had it brought to Siyeh?

Here, upon her couch, within the sound of her husband's breathing, death would be sweet. Yet in the burial grounds when death had been so close, she could not accept it and had wanted only Nakoa. One can see the same thing as another, but from where each stood, the same thing was not the same at all.

Tears slid down her cheeks. Why couldn't he know her loneliness? Why didn't he hold her and give her comfort?

She stretched out flat upon her back and felt her breasts pushing against the buffalo robe. "Beautiful body—all waste!" Atsitsi had said. Maria felt her body cautiously, running her hand from breast to thigh. She remembered how beautiful he had made her feel at the river, how unashamed of her nakedness. Her face grew hot; she threw off the suffocating robe. Nitanna stood before her in the lodge, her lips curled in disdain. Her mouth was cruel and thin, but he had taken her. Maria saw him holding her, caressing her, kissing her lips as he had kissed her own.

"Whore!" Maria said to the tall and beautiful Indian girl.

"And what am I?" she asked herself, for she felt a growing desire for Nakoa she could not restrain. He had said that she would have to free the woman of the waters. Then rise from the muck and mire, and feel cool rain upon your eager lips! Let the rain wash the hair back from the pale face and slide unchecked from naked breasts! Reflecting waters cannot return the heat of the sun, and her heart was hammering against her flesh.

"Nakoa!" she called softly, but he gave no sign of hearing her. In the firelight he was handsome. His face, his naked breast, his long hands were handsome. Never was a man more a man than this Indian who would die bound by nothing. She had sought the escape of deep waters, but with his strong hands he had blocked her way to them.

At the river she had lain naked with him and had asked for his lovemaking, but he had stopped and left her craven.

Outside of his lodge she had made his face wet and agonized with desire, but he had resisted and left her empty.

Beside his marriage tipi he had walked by her and had gone to Nitanna's bed.

"Nakoa!" she said again, and saw that he was awake. In a rapture of rage she threw the robe to the floor. The burning fire made the lodge a violent red, the walls, the floor, the ceiling. She moved to the fire and standing near it took off her dress. Firelight danced upon her breasts, her hips and thighs. He lay as still as sculptured stone.

Maria moved seductively, her hair partially hiding her breasts. He sat up.

"No," he said. "It will not be this way."

She laughed, her long black hair catching the red of the flames. "Nitanna was nothing!" she said scornfully. "Look at me—and see a woman!"

"I do not want you like this!"

"Like what?" she asked and went swiftly to him. Before he could answer, she covered his mouth with her own and caressed him with her hands. Is the male stronger? Does the male have all the strength? Let the male crumble and fall before a woman, and she will have all the power in the skies!

He was no longer protesting. He trembled beneath her touch, and then his body became as seeking as her own. "I will be gentle," he whispered, kissing her face, her eyelashes and her throat. The air shimmered all around them; the fire burned against the torrents raining from the skies. "Culentet, culentet, my beautiful"—but she stopped his words. "I will be gentle," he promised again, but already she was defeating him, driving him wild with the unchecked force of his passion. His awful strength led him blindly on; the months of painful abstinence rose within him and riding the crest of blinding desire, he came brutally into her. In holding her and loving her so deeply he uttered low cries of protest, but he could not stop. He possessed all of her; she was so swept up in his caress that at first she did not know the pain of his penetration. When she felt the throbbing and the agony from Siksikai's knife again, she looked up into her husband's face in triumph. She had proved that all men were like Siksikai that in their love they mutilated. She lay pinioned beneath him in pain, and if blood came again she would be in complete victory.

When he had finished and saw what he had done, he looked at her still and suffering face in disbelief. He moaned and pressed his head against her breasts. He said nothing. He was a stranger to himself, and now they were neither friends nor lovers. But no bleeding came. He held her tenderly in his arms and once when she thought him asleep she saw tears touching his eyelashes. By cold dawn no word had passed between them, and still she did not bleed. Where was the proof of her suffering?

In the morning he prepared their food and fed her. With his face still tormented, he treated her with herbs and warm water, and she lay too inert for modesty. Her pain was strong, and it was the only thing she had to cling to.

But she healed rapidly, and the pain was of short duration.

"Nakoa," she said one morning. "Let me go."

"Go where?"

"Back to my people."

"Your people are dead."

"Let me go back to my old life."

"That is impossible."

"Let me try!"

"I cannot."

"You want me here to rape again!" she said furiously.

"You were not raped."

"You hurt me!"

"You used me to hurt yourself."

"Aren't you sorry that you caused me pain?"

"Yes. But the price has been paid." He looked at her tenderly. "Maria, even in your seeking of revenge for my marrying Nitanna, do you not feel the force that brings us together?"

"What do you mean that I sought revenge?"

"You seduced me into taking you the way I did."

She laughed scornfully. "I seduced you?"

He became angry. "Maria, do not make me a fool! Twice you have begged for my penetration in rage. Outside this lodge, before my marriage to Nitanna you almost dragged me down in the dirt to lie with you. And what did you do before the fire? You awakened me so I could see you take off your clothes. How did you move when you were naked—where did your hands caress me when I was kissing you?"

Maria turned away from him. "I did not mean to do those things," she said.

"You speak softly now. The woman who begged for me last night did not speak softly, and she did not speak with only her tongue." He began to stroke her hair, and she warmed to his gentleness. He kissed her lips and began to hold her so that she knew he meant to make love to her. There was no way of refusing him. She was his wife and was no longer virgin to him. Yet she would not be ready for him. With her rage gone, so was all passion and when he could postpone his entry no longer she remained passive within his embrace. Now he made love to her tenderly, with all lust stemmed, all savagery masked; the victorious male could lie hidden and subdued. When he could postpone shuddering climax no longer she still remained apart from his lovemaking.

He tried to awaken passion within her again. Many times he desired her, but she never knew his pleasure. Upon her bed, in the forest in the shadow of the trees, she could not refuse him, but neither did she accept him. He could not restrain himself to tenderness all of the time. She felt the growing wildness in him, the depth of his seeking. "Meet me, Maria," he cried.

"I can't! I can't!" she sobbed, and at his withdrawal, turned away from him. "I can't help it," she said. "Siksikai drained me of my womanhood. There is nothing left but a shell. How can you ask me to respond to another bloody knife?"

"My love is not an instrument of destruction," he said simply, and put on his clothes. "If you cannot meet me, I will leave you alone until you can." He then abstained from her. Again they slept separately. They rode together, and even bathed together, for he would not give her privacy at the lake. He watched her nakedness with obvious pleasure, but in no way did he suggest that they resume lovemaking. The weather suddenly turned stifling hot, and on one burning day they sought sanctuary in a mountain meadow. While the horses grazed in the open they slept together where shade from thick trees and high ferns cooled them from the hot afternoon. They slept together long and peacefully and both awakened at the same time. Maria looked up above them at the moving of the ferns. Light filtered softly through them giving her an illusion of resting in deep water.

"I wanted to die," she said to Nakoa. "But you wouldn't let me. I was sinking into a beautiful shadow like this."

"I will not let you die," he said firmly, as if she were still fighting to live.

"And you will not let me go?"

"I am not able to do this."

She sighed and lay still.

He studied her face. "You have grown even more beautiful," he said.

She looked quickly away.

"Why do you not like your beauty?" he asked.

"I do not know of my beauty," Maria said shortly. "It is of no importance anyway."

"If you do not know of it, it is very important."

"I know. That which is not accepted is haunting."

"Yes."

"The two women again. Tell me about them—they seem to interest you so!"

"I want the girl and the woman to be one. Your beauty awakens a man's desire and acquaints you with the power of your breast.

You do not want this, for breasts belong to a woman. Maria, see yourself as a woman! The part of yourself you starve will be fed. What you reject in love will rise in hate! Maria, how can you be such a fool about yourself?"

"I am not a whore! I am not a slut! Do you think I am dirty Meg?"

"Who is this woman?"

"A slut my father had when my mother was dying!" Maria sat up, her chin quivering in spite of herself. "I saw it!" she cried. "Every filthy part of it—when he first climbed on her—and I was horrified, I ran away to our orchard—where I was sick."

Nakoa sat up and gently touched her lips. "This Meg might have been a strong woman, Maria. She might have given your father strength to bear your mother's dying."

"By sinning like that?"

"What is sinning?"

"Doing the work of the devil!"

"Your devil helped them both at that time. Your mother would have died harder knowing your father's grief. Did she like to bring your father pain?"

"Never!"

"Did he like to bring her pain?"

"Not before my mother became ill."

"Then this Meg worked with the devil and helped them both."

"You don't even know the devil."

"Is this another god only the white man knows? Do you think we do not know evil and hurt to others? Must every man talk with the white man's tongue? Because he has such a big mouth must the whole world use it?" His eyes were snapping with fury.

"There is beauty and sacredness in holy marriage! My father defiled my mother and their marriage by making love to Meg!"

"Does any man have the power to do all of that?"

"Nakoa, by taking Nitanna you defiled me! I wanted you in sacred marriage because I loved you with all of my heart." Her voice trembled with emotion. "I had a dream of our marriage. We were married in the white man's church, the place where he seeks closeness with the Great Spirit. I wore white because I was pure of any man before you, and we walked down a long aisle together—a long row of white flowers that stretched from the prairie into the church— it was so beautiful—so close to my God—" She put her hands over her face and wept. "I thought my love was met—but look at the way it was! You walked by me to crawl upon another woman! How could my God have any part—how could He ever know sacred marriage between us!" Weeping harder she rocked back and forth in utter desolation.

He said nothing. When she looked at him finally and turned away, he turned her tear-streaked face back to his. "The Indian knows the Great Spirit, too, Maria," he said quietly. "The Indian feels love, too. In your moments of deepest love, were you not met by me?"

"At the river! At the river!"

"So close to the woman you would keep upon her back so she can see only the sky!"

"You crawled from Nitanna—to me!"

"We see in love the joy of giving. Is that not true of you?"

"Yes," she whispered.

"In love, barriers are gone, doubts are gone, two become one in a union to conceive of themselves. Does this not happen?"

"Yes. It could have happened to us!"

"But only in the white man's way! Maria, I am not a white man! I am Indian. A man must walk his own path. It is the woman who accepts change, as she accepts the change in her body from mating! Cannot life speak to you in its wisdom? Is all the love from the Great Spirit blessed only in a white man's church? If you really love me, Maria, you would not demand you would accept!"

"I am tired of struggling," Maria said brokenly. I want to live in my way, and you will have yours and the only thing for us to do is to part!"

"Or for you to grow into a woman. The female is eternal and bears the fire of creation too. If you do not accept her in love and in pain, you will be destroyed!"

"Nakoa, I cannot do it!"

"You have already. By the river you were a woman."

"When we rode around the horse herds you said I was a reflection of your burning, like the moon is to the sun."

"That is what you would like to be now. The moon, Earth Woman, who wanted death more than her husband and son, the little girl who weeps eternally at her mother's grave! I know that when it became time for me to first enter you, you invited me in rage. You drove me beyond my restraint so you would feel pain and I would feel guilt in your agony! Maria, it is also the woman in you that did this, the woman that sought revenge against the child that would keep from her the touch of the sun!"

"Send me away, like you did Nitanna!"

"You see—you kill too!"

"Let me go!"

"Maria, how could you have had such a beautiful woman's body?"

"For you to climb on!" she burst out.

They looked at each other in fury. A little breeze rustled through the ferns and touched Maria's hot face. "Let me go," she said again.

He grasped her shoulders and looked at her somberly. "Maria, hear my words, and do not speak until I have finished. Before you became my wife I denied you to myself. I did not hold myself from taking Nitanna. The thought of this did not even meet my mind. I wanted to keep you clean. I thought it was because I wanted to keep you in marriage, but I know that you could be carrying my child for the whole village to see, and my power would be strong enough for me to take you as a wife. My denial of what I wanted since the first day of your capture—this was so you could speak to the Sun! I would know—you would know—our Father would know that I had held you sacred in my love and could not see you defiled! Maria this is as sacred to me as your path of white flowers, your dress of white, your sacred ceremony in the white man's church! In the tradition of my people, keeping you clean was deep ceremony to me! This was love, Maria, not lust. You are the woman I love."

"I am sorry for what I said," Maria replied, suffering at the hurt in his eyes.

"I accepted you as my sacred vision that came to me in my days of fasting. You would be my voice to the sun. Now do not tell me ever again that I wanted you just to sleep with. There are many women among my own people with beautiful bodies."

Maria looked again into the fine handsome face, the full tender lips. His eyes still bore pain at her words. She suddenly wanted to kiss him.

"When I brought you to my lodge we became man and wife," he said. "In a dream, we had the white man's marriage ceremony. You are more than my wife. You are the other part of my whole self that, parted from me, will leave me bereft and grieving. For me, to know the fullness of myself, to find the way to my Father, I seek union with you. Maria, strong within my heart, I know that I am the man for you, that without your acceptance of me, you will be craven and empty, too, and never know the growth of your life. Have you heard my words?"

He was so close to her, she smelled his clean buckskin smell that once excited her so much. She thought of the way it had been when he had made love to her. "Yes," she said, "I hear you."

"What do you feel?"

"I feel a desire to kiss you. To kiss you just once."

"Then do it. Kiss me just once, Maria."

She pressed against him and kissed his lips gently. He was impassive beneath her touch.

"Was that enough?" he asked her when she had finished.

"No," she said truthfully, and kissed him again. He didn't respond. "Don't you like this?" she asked.

"Not at all," he smiled.

She smiled, too, and kissed him again, lingering against him this time, and waited for his hands to seek her breasts.

"You still don't like this?" she flirted.

"Do not stop. I will bear it with Indian strength," he replied.

She laughed for the first time since Nakoa's marriage to Nitanna. She had aroused him; there was a leaping of passion in his eyes.

She lay upon her back and looked up at the gently moving ferns. "It is a beautiful day," she whispered.

"Yes," he said, stretching out beside her.

"This is a beautiful place," she said.

"Now life is beautiful," he said, looking down at her. Their eyes met and held. She drew his mouth down upon hers and they kissed long and lingeringly. Still he masked the passion that was in his eyes. In growing excitement she began to kiss his face, moving his hands to her breasts herself. Her heart was beating wildly against his palm. "Take off my clothes," she breathed.

Naked, fire consumed them both. He still held himself from her. "Maria," he said. "Accept my love—meet my lust!" She caressed him in rapture and exulted when he came into her and fought wildly against every withdrawal. The cool green shadow became the red heat of day. She was finally drained by her first orgasms, but the fire continued to burn and the tall ferns glowed in its light. It was a sacred light, and she turned so that he would take her again, and she was caught so strongly in her own satisfaction that she did not know the shuddering power of his. When she was suddenly spent, he looked at her tenderly, and brushed her hair back from her face as he had so often done before. "My wife," he said lovingly, and let her sleep. In time he closed his eyes and in the deep shadow of the ferns they slept together, their marriage consummated, each deeply tranquil.

Chapter Twenty Seven

The next morning, Maria awakened upon Nakoa's couch, and remembered that she had gone there herself, seeking him again. Something had awakened her; one of the horses had nickered, a white wolf had called from the prairie—or a newly awakened voice within herself had cried for him to possess her once again. She had tried to resist and go back to sleep, but she could only think of the way it had been that afternoon—and she had to hold the pulsating life of Nakoa within her again.

So she went to her husband, no longer in fury, but in hunger, and when he felt the touch of her kiss his response was immediate. He stroked her body, kissing her breasts and tantalizing her almost beyond endurance before his entrance. When he came inside of her they both ached to postpone what had to end. She moaned in ecstasy as she drew him deeper and deeper into herself. He brought her into climax after climax and during them he lay still to catch the heart of her inner trembling. At her last convulsion he finally allowed himself fulfillment and then tenderly kissed her lips and the tips of her softening breasts. He cradled her in his arms. "Now sleep, my culentet," he whispered, and never had she seen his face so contented.

He slept almost immediately, but she did not. She began to fear the awful force that had driven her to him. Now she was more his captive than ever; she would toss everything to the winds to lie beneath him again. She watched the stars through the smoke hole of the tipi, and the fear within her grew. He was right. The female had been mastered in her body; this was the simple truth he had told her to learn. She began to cry softly, and when sunlight touched the skins of the lodge, her lashes were still wet.

In the daylight she looked at his tranquil face. In his sleep his arms were still around her and she cautiously removed herself from them and bathed herself with the water in the lodge. He awakened once and smiled at the sight of her bathing and then went back to sleep. Maria dried herself and dressed rapidly. She went outside into the morning air and started the cooking fire.

She was now a vessel to be filled by him in his need and desire, but always to be empty again. He used her, but he did not really need her. She could never entrap this wild and free man. He would walk in his own way and her life would be an agony of dependence upon him. He would take other wives and kill her with separation.

By the fire she knelt and prayed for strength, and it came to her like iron. She felt the same strength that had led her to the burial grounds even when the woman within shook and trembled to return to the warm fires of the village.

She had to mate with a man who would give his life to her, as she would to him, who would not be complete without her, and who would make her complete in his giving. The freedom of a wild eagle could not be fettered. She could not try to keep the morning eagle from the sky.

It was that simple.

He came to her while she prepared the food, and kissed the side of her face. While she moved, he watched her quietly, and never had she seen such light in his dark eyes. When she brought him food he kissed her hands. "Thank you for last night, Maria," he said, as if her going to him in the middle of the night were a beautiful and wondrous thing.

She withdrew her hands and sat beside him. "Nakoa, I have to speak what is in my heart."

"I listen," he replied, eating with relish.

"I am going back to my people," she said.

He looked thunderstruck.

"Nakoa, I have to walk in my own way. I have to walk my own path. I am sick for the white man's food, his clothing, his books and his music."

He dropped his food bowl, his hands shaking. She rushed on, "I want to walk again upon streets and see lights shining from houses. I want to see carriages, and boats and trains. I want to be with my own kind."

"These are playthings. You do not know what you are sick for. You are sick because you felt the emotion of the woman and you want to remain the child."

"Don't tell me of last night!" she almost shouted. "I do not want to hear of what I did!"

"Last night is speaking to you in powerful voice."

"I will not hear of it! I will be free!"

"You do not know what you will be because you do not know what you are!" He paced before her, his lips twisted. Finally he stopped and his face became smooth and devoid of agony.

"All right," he said calmly. "I accept. You cannot, but I can accept. I never saw you as you are, but as I hoped you to be. Napi forgive me—in my love—in my lust—in my blindness, I struck out at my father for nothing."

Maria bowed her head. "Then you will let me go?" she asked.

"You forget that you might be bearing my child. If the time comes when you know you are not—then you will go. Even now you are forever free from me, Maria. I will never seek you again. You will not come to my couch again. If after what we felt together last night, and yesterday at the meadow—if after these moments you ask to go free, then every word I could utter the rest of my life would be useless. I am silent. Everything between us is finished. I accept it."

"What if I do have a child?"

"The child will be left with me. When you are well enough for traveling, Apikunni and some of the Mutsik will take you back to the white man's trail."

Her throat constricted and she ached to tell him she was sorry. "Nakoa—Nakoa—" she faltered.

He looked at her grimly. "Do not say that you are sorry. There shall be no more words between us—of what we were or might have been—together!"

She started to weep.

"Dismantle the lodge and pack our things," he said. "We will ride to the main camp when you have finished."

He left her and, taking the water paunches, rode to the river.

Maria did what he asked. When their tipi was down and all of their possessions packed, the desolation of the empty camp was appalling. She looked out at the silent prairie and remembered the way it had been. She saw where the entrance of the village had been, where he had kissed her and first called her culentet. She saw Anatsa walking the path to the river, and she saw where Mequesapa used to sit, playing his deerskin flute for Siyeh. Winter snow would cover it all, and she looked out toward the burial grounds and wept.

He was standing over her, saying nothing. She helped him pack the horses and they rode silently from the deserted camp. A meadowlark called out from the grass and was answered. The fragrance of the prairie grass warming in the morning sun smote her and she breathed deeply in unbearable pain. Purple finches and the white crowned sparrow were flushed from their nests, but were seen by neither of them. Behind, the ashes from their cooking fires remained deep in the fire pit. That afternoon the wind from the mountains rose and scattered them away. A brilliant sunset came and went and the full moon rose late. Across the silver river Anatsa rested quietly, mated and murdered, and in the pale moonlight her face was still serene and beautiful.

In the mountains, a fierce wind swept down upon them. Maria felt terror from its strength and from its roaring through the pines. Cones tumbled down from the trees. In the deepening gloom she sensed the stalking of death. They had intended to stay at the old campsite; she had changed this plan and now the breath of hell was loosed.

The horses bowed their heads into the wind, and Maria shivered upon the bay. Her long hair was whipped away from her face; dust stung her eyes and lips.

Far ahead of them two trappers left the trail and sought the shelter of a ravine.

"Goddamned wind," one said.

"Forget it," the other replied. "We have plenty of time."

The bay stumbled. "Nakoa!" Maria shouted, and he looked back at her. "I want to stop! I am cold!"

He nodded and signed for her to assemble the lodge in a grove of spruce near the trail. He had watered and picketed the horses before she could even organize the possessions he had unloaded. He left her again when she assembled the tipi and because her hands were stiff with fear, she silently cursed him for deserting her.

Night rushed down upon her like a wild thing. When she finished the tipi, she could not start the lodge fire. The flames blew out repeatedly.

She cried out in despair. When Nakoa came in he adjusted the doorflaps, dug a larger fire pit and started the fire.

"Thank you," Maria said in wrath.

He didn't reply.

"Are you never going to speak to me again?" Maria screamed.

"I have brought fresh game. I have prepared it for cooking."

"Go eat your horse!" Maria said in rage.

He looked at her calmly. "I need my horse," he replied. "We will eat the meat you will cook. I am tired of pemmican."

"'Go Kutenai! Stop Kutenai!' I am not Kutenai!"

"No, but you can prepare food."

"Yes, I can do that."

"It is something," he said coldly.

She cooked the meat and they ate it with fresh berries. "You are sulking like a child," she said bitterly. "You are the child!"

He looked at her directly. "You speak again without thought. I have said there are no more words between us."

"Then make some!"

"Why? Is silence so terrible?"

"I am lonely."

"Both of you?"

"Nakoa, why must you be so bitter?"

"I did not take my marriage lightly."

"You mean your marriages."

"I took neither lightly. You did not accept even one."

A gust of wind shook the lodge, making the fire move as if to seek escape from them.

"Nakoa, I feel such fear! Be kind to me, please be kind to me!"

He shuddered.

"Nakoa, I loved you—I did not lie in the way I loved you."

"At what time? When was this time when you did not lie?"

"Before your marriage."

"You lie now, after our marriage."

"I am speaking about Nitanna."

"Stop speaking of her. She had no part in our marriage."

"Didn't she?" Maria asked.

He rose and faced her wrathfully. "I said there were to be no more words. Do you want to sleep in this lodge alone?"

"No," she said sorrowfully. "I do not want your anger. Please, Nakoa."

"Do not weep."

"I won't. May I speak?"

"Not about Nitanna."

"All right. But do not hate me!"

"You have the love of your mother."

"Nakoa, I have no one. You know my mother is dead!"

"No, I don't. She is alive to you. Let her die and rest in peace."

She hid her face. "I wanted to love you," she whispered. When she looked up he had lain upon his couch and had turned his back toward her.

"Don't go to sleep!" she said, panic-stricken.

"Lie with your mother," he said.

She went to him and shook his shoulders. "Nakoa, have pity upon me!" He turned toward her. Her teeth were chattering.

"Maria, what is the matter with you?" he asked angrily.

"I feel death. I have felt it ever since we left the old camp."

He sat up, studying her face thoughtfully. "Have you not heard my words, that without each other we will exist but not grow? Of course you have felt death, for that is what we are meeting. I have accepted. Now let the woman in you die in silence."

She put her head upon his lap. If he would only touch her with his strength!

"What do you want of me?" he asked.

"I want your comfort, your touch. I want your touch! Dear God, I would even—"

"You would make that sacrifice? How lonely you are in your dying!"

"Help me, Nakoa." The wind surged mightily against them again. "There is so little time," she sobbed, "we will soon be parted." He gripped her hair, holding her eyes to his own.

"How closely am I to hold you?" he asked. "How closely for just this moment?"

"I don't care!"

"I do!" he said in a rage, and flung her from his bed. She fell to the floor and he stood over her in shaking fury. "I told you not to come to my bed again! I will not be beaten with your body! I will not let the present increase what I cannot have! Go back to your mother's singing! Just give me my son and the blood in him from me! Go back and leave some room upon my couch for a woman!"

He became frenzied. "And if silence sickens you so, we will have talk. We can speak of my horse, Kutenai. We can speak of the bay, who was also blessed with coming from the white man! We can speak of food, of the lodge fire, of the possessions we carry and pack and unpack. We can speak of the lodge, of the earth and the stars, and the noises and sign of forest animals. But we will not talk of you, and we will not talk of me, or of women and men, and the feelings they are said to have! Do you hear me, Maria?" Tears shone upon his cheeks, and she was amazed at seeing them.

"Yes," she said quietly.

"We will say nothing of real men or real women!"

"All right."

"You will sleep alone, and I will sleep alone until I take another wife. You will never show yourself naked to me again! You will never touch me again—in any way!" He paced in front of the fire until he was calm. "I wait for my son, and that is all. That is all you have to give." He turned his back to her. "When our child is born, I return you to your mother, and may she shelter you and love you in your agony of not being able to do these simple things for yourself!" He turned to her finally and at the sight of the suffering upon his face she sprang toward him, and without thought, reached to touch him. He slapped her across the face and sent her spinning away.

"I do not know you!" she sobbed.

"No," he replied. "We have already parted."

Chapter Twenty Eight

In the next two days of their traveling, Maria did what Nakoa asked. She kept all talk between them impersonal. She slept in clothing, and when she bathed herself, he left the lodge.

When he spoke to her, it was as if he were not speaking. Upon the trail, in Indian custom, he was silent. At their evening fire he told her more about the tribe she was leaving, that the Pikuni moved to the mountains every fall so that the men could hunt elk, and the woman gather medicines—gray leaves for stomach pain, black root for coughs, sticky weed for the liver, blueberry for bleeding, and yellow fungus from the high pines for drying and placing upon fresh wounds. That in the mountains men procured new lodge poles chosen by their women from the lodge pole pine, and the women prepared them, and finished the new lodge skins for the coming winter. New lodge poles were needed every year, for they were used as travois in traveling, and so became worn and rough, breaking holes in the lodge skins and causing them to leak.

So close to her, and yet far away, he explained that in the mountain camp, men cut the red willow sticks they mixed and smoked with their tobacco. That, for ceremony, a man's pipe was always passed from right to left except in the ending of a war. In sign of reconciliation the usual order was reversed, and the pipe was passed from a man's left hand to the right.

He told her the Pikuni hunted horses from the wild horse herds in the spring when the horses, hungry from winter, had eaten too much grass and were weak from dysentery.

He talked to her quietly in his deep voice and Maria was lulled away from her fear. The wind still blew, but it did not seem a personal rage directed against her.

Ahead of them the two trappers were joined by a third. "We'll follow this path until we hit water," one said and the others agreed. The pelts would be plentiful and when night came and they built a fire, they all sat near its flame dreaming of what their trapping would bring them.

The next morning Maria and Nakoa started early upon the trail, eating cold pemmican and the last of the cooked meat while they rode. But there was a difference in the way he rode his horse; always alert, he was now as taut as a bow. Above them the wind was still roaring in the pines, the cones still tumbling down to the earth. They passed overturned rocks, sign of a grizzly looking for insects and ant eggs; they passed the fresh tracks of the coyote and the timber wolf, the tracks of elk, and Nakoa saw to it that their horses walked silently. "What is it?" Maria wanted to ask, but upon an Indian trail talk was dangerous. A white wolf sprang out at them suddenly from some bushes, and the bay reared and neighed excitedly. "Silence him!" Nakoa hissed, and subdued the animal himself. Some loosened rocks went crashing down the mountain. He held the horses still and looked carefully around them, listening for the slightest repetition of noise. It was late afternoon, the light of the day was rapidly going. "We will sleep here—away from the trail," he said in a low voice.

"We haven't come to water," Maria complained.

"There is a large stream ahead. We can fill the paunches again in the morning."

They moved quietly away from the trail, Maria looking for a place to assemble the lodge.

"We will sleep in the open tonight," he said.

"It will be too cold!" she replied.

"We have robes."

"We will have no fire either?"

"No." He led the horses away, watered and picketed them so that they were well hidden in a thick clump of trees. Silently he returned and they ate without words. They each fixed their beds and prepared to sleep.

"Nakoa, what is it?" Maria asked, trying to speak over the rising wind.

"I feel death too," he said quietly.

"It is the awful wind! I hate the wind!"

"Tonight it is sad and wailing, like a lost woman's cry. The wind goes back, Maria, around and around the world, and it still wails."

Maria had started to doze when suddenly she heard a terrified scream. "Nakoa!" she called, sitting up and looking around her in panic. She could see his face in the moonlight. He had not stirred from his bed. "It is a mountain lion," he said quietly. The eerie noise remained in the darkness around them. She was cold with terror. He turned his back to her, and she tried to calm herself and go to sleep again. Above them the pines brushed against the sky with the same madness they had upon the night of her rape. "I cannot sleep," she whispered, more to herself than to him, and when he turned back toward her, she was almost numb with relief.

"You want talk," he said.

"Yes. I am so cold!"

"I cannot warm you."

"Can't we build the lodge?"

"No."

A star streaked across the sky, and Maria imagined it falling to the earth in a shower of sparks. "What does a falling star mean to your people?" Maria asked him.

"That is Smoking Star," he said. "He comes to bring the death of an Indian warrior."

"Do you believe this?"

"It is Blackfoot legend."

"Smoking Star has not come to take your life!"

"If my path is finished, I do not want weeping, even in my father's heart."

Maria felt sorrow constricting her throat. "Nakoa," she said gently. "Nakoa . . ."

"Speak tenderly to me when my ears are deaf and my tongue

silent. Look up at the stars, like your woman of the river. Look at the north sky; you will see six stars bunched together. We call them the six lost children of the prairie. They are there because they did not want to be different. They alone had no skins from the spring buffalo hunt when the hides are yellow. They felt that they were unblessed with the touch of the sun, because they wore skins of brown. But it was they alone who felt this, for the children who wore yellow skins were not saddened by their brown ones. The brown skins did not keep them from walking in the sun, or finding food and drink, or from finding even those with lighter skins. Still the difference in their own eyes was too much for their hearts, so the six little children left the earth and their home seeking the yellow skins though it made no difference whether they had them or not. As they would not be of this earth, they sought the Wolf Trail and the fires that burn there, and they were lost in light, for those of the earth have to be of both light and shadow.

"There they are, all six of them," he continued. "The legend is that they only show themselves in the fall when the skins of the buffalo are brown. They are frozen there because they did not want to be different, but all of the children they knew are gone and would not know their difference anyway."

"In this legend you have another lesson for me."

"No, Maria, the lesson is for me," he said sadly. "The six children who were afraid to be different remained children through the first time, past the burning and falling of new stars—their fear is frozen in the sky now for me to see!"

"I have never heard your voice so sad," Maria said.

"Sadness weighs heavily upon my spirit. You are searching Maria, as the wind searches for the sound of its own voice, but there are those who seek and never find, for in the seeking alone there is no change! You have remained a little girl, frozen in your innocence, so far from the earth that you can never know a first spring." His voice deepened with emotion. "I said with my tongue you are free. Now I say it with my heart. I release you—and my woman—my woman."

Tears came to her eyes and touched her face. She could not speak, and for a long while they both listened to the hopeless wailing of the wind in silence. "Nakoa," she said finally, "if we have a son he will be of my flesh and of my heart too. What if I cannot leave him? What if I cannot give him up?"

"Then you may stay near him, in the village of my people."

"But not with you?"

"No. But you should return to your people. You will take another husband from among the white man and have another son."

"It would not be the same child!"

"Nor would it be the first love."

Maria sat up. "Nakoa," she said. "I smell smoke!"

"That is because someone burns a fire ahead of us on the trail. They are camped by the stream. They are three white men. We have been following their trail all day."

"Dear God! What does it mean?"

"Smoking Star has come for my life."

"Nakoa!"

"I feel this. I want your word upon one thing, Maria."

"What is it?"

"If I am to die before our son is born, I want your word you will still leave him with my people. I don't want him to know the way of the white man."

"I will make no such promise because of some legend!"

"It is not the legend. It is the knowledge in my heart. One of the three men will be the instrument of my death. It is clear to me now."

Maria's heart began to hammer in fear. "How do you know they are white?"

"By the mark of their horses."

"They could have been traded from the white man!"

"No Blackfoot or their allies trade with the whites."

"Then it could be Crow—Snake . . ."

"No Indian would light an evening fire in enemy territory. They are whites and do not know the land. They do not know they are traveling a trail into a Blackfoot camp!"

Maria sprang from her bed and went over to him. "Nakoa, they cannot kill you if you stay here, if we hide!"

"I will not hide. I will not stay here and wait for them to surprise me upon the trail. Following an enemy from a distance means death. I will go to their camp and kill them. I will try before they kill us."

"Nakoa! Nakoa!" she exclaimed horrified. "They are my people! Are you as savage as the Snakes? They came to do you no harm!"

"They would kill me on sight."

"No!" she said, clinging to him.

He pulled himself free from her.

"Nakoa," she cried. "They have guns. If there are three of them, you would be killed."

"Then Smoking Star would have come for my life."

"I won't have it!"

He looked up at her curiously. "Why?"

"I don't want you dead."

"What difference would this make, when you are safe in the streets with the lights shining from windows?"

She shuddered. "Why are you so cruel?" She wiped her eyes and pushed her hair back from her wet face. "All right," she said. "We will make a bargain. I will leave your son with your father if you are killed."

"I am glad," he said.

"But I will promise this only if you do not seek out the white man. If you show yourself to them, if you try to kill them, then I will seek my freedom if I have to crawl all of the way back to the Oregon Trail and starve both myself and my baby! Without your promise, if they shoot you down, I will escape with them if I can, and your father will never know your son!"

"Your words are foolish."

"They are straight! I will follow them. I will."

"All right," he said wearily. "But I want a chance for my life. Before daylight, I will go to their camp and see where and when they go. Stay here, off the trail, with the horses hidden. Do not follow me. Wait here until I return. You can wait here until the pemmican is gone and then ride ahead to the village. You have food for three days or longer."

"My God, I can't stay here alone for three days!"

"You won't have to. But do not follow me do you hear?"

"Yes," she said and went back to her bed. Soon she could tell by his deep breathing that he slept, but she could not. The wind quieted and she watched the stars move across the sky. The smell of smoke drifted to her more strongly, and when she turned to close her eyes another falling star streaked to the horizon. She shivered and finally, slept.

When the moon was low in the west he awakened her. "I am leaving now," he said. She looked mutely up into his shadowed face.

"I will not try to kill them. I give my word and you have given yours."

"Yes," she whispered, wanting to touch him just once.

They looked at each other, each seeking the depths of the other's eyes, but darkness was between them.

"Good-bye," he said, and she watched his tall form as it silently vanished in and out of the patterns of soft moonlight.

Bright sunlight awakened her. It shone warmly upon her face. The wind was gone; it was a clear and beautiful day filled with the scent of pine. The mountain seemed to stir with the long life of summer. Maria rose, and, finding the food and water paunches, ate and drank. She went to see the horses and they were grazing contentedly.

Should he not be back? If the white men were close enough for them to smell the smoke of their fire, should he not be back? She walked noiselessly to the trail and looked ahead into its shadows. Above her, birds sang and squirrels loudly scolded each other. There was no sign of any person.

The sun climbed steadily higher and shone in noontime strength. If the trappers were alive they would have broken camp. If Nakoa were alive he would have returned. Would he leave her to bear a long night alone? She was frightened of the wilderness. In the full sunshine she was frightened of the forest with its strange secretive noises. She went to the horses again, and stroked their inquisitive faces. She packed the robes and food, expecting him back shortly. There had been no shots. Except for the sound of animals, the forest had remained quiet. Why, oh, why, had he not returned?

He had gone before daylight! She walked about restlessly, panic pulling at her stomach and making her sick. She listened for his step. She went to the trail and hid and watched it in shadow.

The sun would soon be moving toward sunset. The awful wind would rise again, and she would be alone. The mountain lion screamed again in her mind, and then she thought of Smoking Star and Nakoa's premonition. He could be lying wounded and bleeding with the trappers long gone. They could have killed him silently. Oh, God, Nakoa could not die! He could have been knifed—he might have been shot and she might not have heard the sound. He could be lying still upon this trail with neither fire, cover, nor the protection that a woman could give him.

She clutched desperately at her stomach. If he were not hurt, he would be back. But darkness would come and he could bleed to death before she could find him! With sudden resolution she followed the trail he must have traveled. Carefully she watched the ground. She saw no sign of his tracks, but she could not read a trail like an Indian. The birds stilled as she glided silently past; there was only the screeching warning of the blue jays. Nakoa, Nakoa, her mind called, desperately searching his for an answer. All around her were thick shadows as the trail became more and more wooded. Still there was no sign of a living person. Now she could hear the murmuring of a stream, where Nakoa thought the men would be camped. She became cautious and moved more slowly.

"Well," a voice said. "Look what we have here!" Maria recoiled as a grizzled red headed man stepped out upon the trail ahead of her and pointed his rifle at her heart. Maria stood still in terror.

A lean, sandy-haired trapper joined him. "Why don't you let her pass?" he asked quietly.

"Look at her," the redhead answered. "Aint you got eyes? Hey, Louis!" he called, and a third trapper stepped out from some trees. He cocked his gun and looked frantically around them. "I said this was a goddamned Indian trail," he said.

"Look at that pretty little ass," the redhead said.

"This is one you better not touch," said the third trapper. "She's probably Blackfoot."

Nakoa's Woman

"Let's git," said the sandy-haired one. "She couldn't be alone."

"Yes, she is," replied the redhead. "I watched her come up the trail. God, look at them tits!"

"Shut up, you damned fool. Let's get out of here," said the third trapper.

"She's alone." growled the redhead. He moved closer to Maria. "God damn, she's pretty enough to be white!"

There was a slight rustling around them. Maria held her breath in panic. Nakoa, Nakoa—be still—still—

"You speak English?" the redhead asked her. "*Savez-vous* English?"

"The Blackfoot don't trade," the sandy-haired trapper hissed. "They don't know English. And with her here we have to be near a village."

"Shut up! Shall we take her with us? She would be good company," the redhead grinned.

"You son of a bitch," the third one said, looking around with less fear. "You just want to screw her."

"And her husband can watch!" said the sandy-haired trapper grimly, and, getting his horse, quickly mounted him. "You two can set up housekeeping with the little lady," he said. "I'm leaving."

"Ain't you going to read over us with the good book?" the third trapper laughed and without answering the lean trapper left them, abandoning the trail and riding his horse straight down the slope of the mountain.

"He's chicken shit!" said the redhead.

"Blackfoot ain't good playmates," said the third trapper. "What you going to do with her?"

"Come here, you little bitch," said the redhead.

She would cause Nakoa's death. There were still two guns against him, and he would not see her raped. If she could speak! She could say, "I am Maria Frame from St. Louis. Take me back!" But then, he still would die, for he would not allow them to take her. So she remained silent and still while the redhead came closer to her until his breath almost touched her face. She was so terrified that Nakoa would be killed that tears slowly coursed down her face.

"Goddamn it!" the third trapper said. "She is bawling. She'll be yelling next! I'm gittin too!"

"I never seen a more beautiful woman!" said the redhead stubbornly.

"They're all the same where you want her," said the third trapper. "You gonna trade your hair for that?"

"If I could talk with her! She might come with us. Ain't we got any more beads?"

Be still the wind, and be still my heart, for they are scared crazy and would fire at any movement. Smoking Star, streaking across a night sky, you will not have this warrior's life!

"Talk to her in sign," said the third trapper. "She's scared, but she ain't running. Ask her where the village is."

The redhead signed for the nearness of tipis.

Maria signed back immediately. *"Ehelwisi ka ki,"* she said, indicating that the camp was close by.

"Jesus Christ! I ain't staying to meet no one else!" said the third trapper, getting his horse and the redhead's too. Both men mounted and looked silently around them, with their guns primed.

Be still—be still—let them go! She cramped forward in pain. When she looked up, they were gone, riding down the slope of the mountain as fast as they could. "I am Maria Frame," her heart beat dolefully. "I am Maria Frame from St. Louis and what difference does it make now?"

She stood bowed and still. All about her the forest life moved again, the wind moved again. Nakoa gently touched her face, he who had said he would never touch her again.

"Maria," he whispered. "Maria." The word was a caress. She looked up into his face. It was suffused with joy and in his eyes burned a thousand lights. "You could have gone with them," he said. "You could have gone—and I could not have stopped you."

"I made a promise," she said. "You kept yours. I kept mine."

"Is that all?" he asked her steadily.

"I would never buy my freedom with your death!"

"That is right," he said quietly, with all of the light going from his eyes. "You want no part of me. Not even my life."

She could not answer him.

They walked back to the horses and reached the main camp before dusk. In the outer circle now, Nakoa's tipi was pitched, and out of respect for their newly married state no one came to see them. They ate together, and, separately, they went to bed. As usual, he fell asleep first.

In the morning she knew she was not to have a baby. She stood over his couch triumphantly. "I am free now," she said. "I am not going to have your son. I bear no life that belongs to you."

He got up and rapidly dressed. At the door he looked back at her sadly. "You bear no life," he said and left her alone.

Chapter Twenty Nine

He did not come back. Why didn't he return and at least tell her his plans for releasing her? In a growing fury she ate alone, inside of the lodge, so the whole village would not know that he had left her before they had eaten together. She washed, and then tried to sleep some more, but could not.

Finally, she went outside. Smoke rose lazily to the clear sky; she walked among the outer tipis and no one even looked in her direction. She gathered meadow grass for the floor of the lodge, for the camp was situated in a wide and beautiful meadow with the tipis pitched in the same order as they had been upon the prairie, with the exception of hers and Nakoa's lodge. She returned to it, but there was no sign of him. She put down the grass, and put away their possessions. It was afternoon. Where did he eat? She washed again, and combed her hair. She would go to the inner circle and see Apeecheken; maybe she could find out if Nakoa had passed the time with his father.

Women were peeling the bark off new lodge poles, cutting off twigs and branches, leaving them smooth so that no rough places would tear the lodge skins. Near all of the tipis the poles already prepared were stacked neatly together, to dry and harden in the sun. Men were bringing in fresh poles to be worked, but among them Maria saw neither Nakoa nor Apikunni.

Apeecheken sat in front of her lodge, large with her pregnancy. When she saw Maria, joy shone upon her face, but remembering she was once always with Anatsa, tears came to her eyes too. "Maria, you are well," she said, signing for her to sit beside her.

"Yes," Maria said.

"I am sorry for the tears that came to my eyes," Apeecheken said. "It is that when you walk, it should be that Anatsa walks with you. We miss her so."

"I know," Maria said disconsolately. "There are tears in everything. I think tears must be the fountain of our life!"

"You are young to feel this, but so was Anatsa. She spoke in such a manner too. I did not always know all of her words, and now that there are to be no more, it hurts my heart that I did not know them. I have always been more a mother to her than a sister and so, there could not be as much time between us—do you understand?"

"Yes. The mother has to be the root, and the sisters are the leaves that can feel the wind together."

"And the leaves bring to the mother the sun."

"Yes." Maria bowed her head. Nothing would ever bring her the sun again.

"My little Anatsa, so frail in her body and so great in her spirit!"

"How close to the birth of your new child are you, Apeecheken?"

"Less than two moons."

"New life always comes. Without the life we wouldn't have the awful dying!"

Apeecheken looked at her closely. "I am sorry that you have known so much of death."

"I did not mean to bring you more sadness. I just felt a great loneliness for you—and Anatsa." Suddenly she put her head in her hands and wept. I have no husband! I have no husband! she wanted to scream, but she remained silent except for her weeping.

"Maybe you have a child too," Apeecheken said, wondering at her distraught face.

"No," Maria said. "I bear no life."

"Do not grieve for this. You have just been married!"

Maria moaned.

"You have a strong man for a husband," Apeecheken said in comfort. "My heart is so sad for Apikunni. I do not see him. He has shunned us all, even the Mutsik. He could probably follow Nakoa as their high chief, but he leaves his lodge and is not seen for days at a time. The loss of Anatsa has made him a man so apart from himself."

"They had such a deep and beautiful love. I can't understand. I can't understand the whole crazy pattern of anything!"

"In this life we must see just a pale reflection of ourselves. If the spirit has the strength to go on without the body, there must be great powers of the two combined that we have left untouched."

"I do not know. I do not know anything!" Maria rose to leave. "My heart is too troubled for talk," she said. "When I can bring to you comfort or joy from myself—I will."

"I feel great warmth toward you," Apeecheken said. "It will always be with gladness that I see you."

Maria walked slowly toward the outer tipis. In the inner circle she had seen no sign of Nakoa. Suddenly a hand lightly touched her arm. It was Sikapischis. The last time they had met was when Maria had been on her way to the burial grounds. "Sikapischis!" Maria exclaimed warmly, clasping her hand. "My friend of wisdom."

Sikapischis smiled at her, but Maria sensed a withdrawal from their former closeness. "I have seen your husband," she said. "He has told me to tell you that he has gone to hunt with Apikunni. He will be gone from your lodge for a while."

Maria was left breathless. If he were going to free her, she should leave before fall turned to winter. Did this mean that he would not free her now, that it was already too late to avoid the first snows before the southern trails could be reached?

"I am sorry if there is trouble between you," Sikapischis said. "I have taken fresh meat to your lodge for tonight's cooking. I will bring you food every day until he returns."

"He did not say when this would be?"

"No," Sikapischis started to leave.

"Sikapischis . . ."

The Indian woman turned to her, and never did Maria see a face become so suddenly old and filled with suffering.

"I am nothing!" Maria exclaimed in grief.

"Siyeh said that you were a beautiful woman. He thought this. And my father, though blind, has seen this. Beauty is a gift, for it is given, and when seen, brings its own joy. I have no more words for you, Maria. I am sorry for this. We have many gifts and never know them, and when a gift is not shared, it becomes a burden." Sikapischis walked from her, her carriage erect and beautiful.

Maria returned to their lodge, his lodge, and began to prepare the meat. She was bending over the fire when an awful force struck her from behind and sent her sprawling. Dumfounded, Maria looked up into the sweating face of Atsitsi.

"What are you doing?" Maria screamed at her.

"Kicking holy ass," Atsitsi said.

Maria lunged at her, but the old woman moved out of her path. She sat down upon Nakoa's couch and glared at her in fury. "Now," she said, "why you drive Nakoa from here?"

"Get out of here!" Maria shrieked.

"Shut big mouth. I stay. You tell me to leave and I hit you with a big stick!"

"I have nothing to say to you!"

"I have words! That why I here. You think I come to see big Maria? Ha!"

"I won't listen!"

"Then I kick holy ass again!"

Maria ran for the door, but like lightning, Atsitsi was there before her, blocking her way. "You dirty Nakoa's lodge—why not leave it quick? You take him from Indian woman who live, for white woman in sky?"

"You do not know."

"Don't sing baby song to me! What you do to Nakoa? We lose second Natosin because of you! Feeling between Pikuni and Kainah less because of you! Nitanna feel deep grief because of you! Now what have you done to Nakoa that he leave you to seek warmth of cold forest?"

"I have asked for my freedom!" Maria screamed.

"What Nakoa say?"

"He has agreed to let me go."

"Good! Good! Why not now? Why fool go off when could send you away before too late when snows come?"

"I don't know," Maria said.

"It awful if you not leave quick!"

"Thank you," Maria said bitterly. "Now, will you leave?" Maria asked her.

"I leave," Atsitsi said. "And I say good-bye to sweet Maria now, so old Atsitsi can stay on Indian earth in peace!"

Her huge and sweating form was gone, and Maria took the meat that she was cooking from the fire. It had burned beyond eating. Smoke from it curled toward her. She didn't eat that night. She sat long and held the burned meat. It was charcoal. Like her—it was lifeless.

The pit of the night is dark and still. The pit of the night is black without sound or color. The pit of the night smothers life, chokes dreams, and allows only a drifting that is terrifying because it has no purpose and no goal. It is the time that the body awakens, too rested for sleep, and too early for the tasks of the day. It is too soon for fires and food, and too late for rest and the warmth of the couch.

The first night she was alone without him, she touched it, this black time of nothing, as the wolves howled out across the mountains in their loneliness.

The second night she knew it too. It awakened her from sleep, and let her know her nothingness. It stretched ahead, deep and endless, never to be lighted by a morning sun. Was it because she had accepted him, lain with him, been possessed by him, that she felt such a craven emptiness? Because he had brought freshly killed meat, was all other food to be forever tasteless? What good would be the white man's salt, the white man's sugar?

The air grew colder. Would they live without contact all through the white winter until the trails south were open and free once more? Autumn leaves were falling, and back in her own land, were gently covering her mother's grave. Blinding tears came, and fell uselessly upon the Indian buffalo robe. And from far far away, down the mountain and across the green prairie, came the sweet lingering lullaby.

She heard steps approaching the lodge. She sat up, wiping her eyes, her heart leaping to her throat. The door flap opened, and she saw a giant form silhouetted against the glimmering stars. "Nakoa!" she said, throwing the buffalo robe over her shoulders, "Nakoa!" She went to the fire pit, and built the coals into flame with fresh wood. She turned to him. "Apikunni!" she breathed, stunned. "Where is he? Where is Nakoa?"

"He did not return with me, Maria."

"Why? Why Apikunni?" Her voice had risen, and hastily she motioned for Apikunni to be seated. He sat away from her, upon Nakoa's couch. His face was drawn and tired, and Maria saw that he had lost all of his boyish look since Anatsa's death.

"You are free. Nakoa has given you your freedom. In the morning, two Mutsik and I will take you south. We will reach the white man's trails before the first snows."

"Why did he not tell me this? Why did he send you?"

"He will not see you again. You do not carry his child. You are free."

"Oh!"

"You speak in pain. You do not want this?"

"Yes. But what we want brings pain too."

Apikunni said nothing, but his face expressed coldness. Maria put her face in her hands, and the tears came again, unchecked. "I am sorry!" she said finally. "It seems that all I have done since I have been here is weep!"

"That is why Nakoa is letting you go. He does not want the grief in your heart."

"Among you I have so many friends. I loved Anatsa. I love Sikapischis and Apeecheken and Natosin, my Indian father. I have love for you, Apikunni, husband to Anatsa."

In the firelight, he looked at her shrewdly. "With so much love for the Indian, there must be some for your husband."

"There is. Of course, there is. But not the love for a marriage. Not that—any more!"

"Love does not come and go like the day and like the night. Anatsa told me that your love for Nakoa was as hers for me. Could you ever have felt a love so deep, so sweet?"

"The scorn in your words and upon your face hurts my heart.

Of course I had a love so deep and so sweet. But I cannot be wife to him now. I know this."

"Siksikai . . ."

"Oh, do not tell me of Siksikai. I know myself, Apikunni! I know my feelings. I will speak to you, and with the straight tongue of the Indian." She huddled close to the fire. "Once—so very much—I wanted Nakoa. I loved him so! My love for him was pure, beautiful, and so my lust was not lust, and there was no dirtiness!"

"Dirtiness?"

"My body was beautiful because it was for him." She looked away, fighting the shaking of her lips and her chin. "To exist, Apikunni, a love has to be met. I met Nakoa, but he took Nitanna to his bed instead. He dirtied himself in Nitanna!"

"And you were dirtied—and wounded—and knifed—by Siksikai."

"I could not help that."

"You could help that more than Nakoa could help his marriage to Nitanna."

"No! No!"

"Maria," he said softly. "Was he not punished enough with what Siksikai did to you? I have never seen a man show so much agony."

"I do not know! But my love is gone, and I stand in night, and in this darkness I want my own kind!"

"You are not in night. You are in blindness!"

"Whatever it is, my love is passed, and I want to walk now in the white man's way!"

"You will walk alone. You will flee in shadow. Maria, have you thought of life without the sun?"

"My sun is not Nakoa. My sun burns within myself!"

"Your sun burns within the two of you, joined as one. And such a sun would melt the highest snows and bring light for growing."

"It is done," Maria said miserably. "It is all done."

"All right. We will leave after dawn."

"Yuh," she said softly, using a Blackfoot word that in the years ahead would be a stranger to her tongue. She did not go back to bed. She went instead to the fire, and building it up, huddled the

Nakoa's Woman

rest of the night in its warmth.

The next morning they were delayed in their departure. Natosin came to his son's lodge to tell her good-bye.

"I would not let my daughter leave in silence," he said, his face much like Nakoa's in the early morning light.

"I am glad," Maria whispered. She looked toward the lodge of the west wind. "There is great sadness in my heart that your son's lodge is no longer in the inner circle of high chiefs. If I am gone—and he did this for me—it is all a waste."

"No. Something happens as we would not wish it, but its happening keeps it from being a waste. Time is wasted in other ways—in the sweetness of content. When all is content then all is the same, and all is nothing."

"He will never again be high chief?"

"My son has not shown wisdom. It is unlikely."

"Love does not always tolerate wisdom!" Maria said with spirit.

Natosin smiled. "Wisdom comes with the greatest love."

"All right. Then we did not love each other, for neither of us was wise."

"Love grows as wisdom grows. We walk through the foolish years, but we are not time."

"Natosin, whom will he marry? Will he have many children and many wives?"

"Why would your thoughts dwell upon this, when you have chosen to walk different paths?"

"Can we choose different paths, when once we were . . ."

"Why do you ask this, daughter? You wait now to mount the bay; you wait now for three Mutsik to return you to your land."

"I know I am doing the right thing."

"Everything is neither right nor wrong. The right or wrong is in the choosing, the keeping, the losing. All paths are light and shadow, and every path is a different thing to each man. The right and the wrong; the good and the evil lie not upon the silent pathway, but in the man that walks it."

"Natosin, I told you long ago a stranger had come to me, and you said that I should feel blessed. How could I be blessed when I have lost so much? I have lost my family, my friend Anatsa, my husband —your son. I have lost everything!"

"And you are deeply blessed. A stranger met is not a stranger. The dead are gone but not lost. The stranger to yourself has come and has brought the turmoil, but you know the storm, and you feel the storm, and after every storm comes peace."

"Where? How?"

"You will see. You will know. You will climb my daughter, and in great height and great silence, you will know!"

Maria smiled now. "It will be the silence after the storm?"

He looked at her intently. "You will have accepted. And then you will be free to marry."

"I do not know your words, but behind them I know love and kindness. You are a great and a good man, Natosin."

"I wish I could give you more than words. I know my son's love for you. I was an old old man the night he said he would marry you, the night the head chiefs agreed that he walked alone as your husband. This morning you leave; my son has set you free, and again I am an old, old man. Good-bye, my daughter. Your Indian father wishes you well. May your path lead upward toward the sun. May you walk a long and a straight path, and at the end . . ."

"Find myself. Thank you for speaking to me, as you did to your own people when the Sun Dance had ended." Tears stood in her eyes. "Thank you, and may Napi travel with you always."

Apikunni had come and had saddled the bay. She mounted the horse swiftly, and as she and Apikunni rode away, she looked back at Natosin once more. Straight and tall he stood, his long gray locks moving slightly in the wind.

Cooking fires had already been started. It was long after dawn, and many women moved about the tipis. Two other Mutsik joined them; Maria did not even look at their faces, but searched instead for Sikapischis and Apeecheken; Apeecheken had left the inner circle, and Maria saw her and rode over to tell her good-bye. Sikapischis was with a large group of women talking together, and she left them, and came to Maria and Apeecheken. "You are leaving us," she said, reaching up and taking Maria's hand.

"Yes. Nakoa has set me free. I return now to my own people."

"I thought that Nakoa had done this. That is why my heart had no words for you yesterday."

"Maria," Apeecheken asked. "Do you want this freedom?"

"Yes. I have to be free. I could live no other way now."

"We will always remember you," Sikapischis said. "We will always remember you, and this time that we shared together."

"I am proud in our friendship," Maria whispered, stung by the sadness in their black eyes. She saw Nakoa's eyes again, black, luminous with the light of a thousand candles that had gone out, one by one. *"Amba wastayeh!* Good-bye, good-bye!"

She turned the bay toward the three men who quietly waited for her. Apart from the group of silent women watching her, stood Atsitsi. She looked up at Maria, her little black eyes squinting against the bright sky.

Maria turned quickly away, but her eyes were drawn back. Atsitsi began to scratch, and their eyes met and locked.

The bay walked back to her, and Maria took the fat woman's unwashed hand and clasped it within her own. "Good-bye, Atsitsi," she said softly.

Atsitsi sucked and gummed her meat, and finally spat it out. "Leave fast before Nakoa have time to change mind. Who need you?" She scratched harder, watching Maria defiantly. Still scratching, she went into her lodge.

They rode from the village. The bay moved ahead eagerly; he could hardly be restrained to a walk. Good-bye, Nakoa. She had said this before, when she had crossed the lake on her way to the burial grounds. Before they left sight of the camp, she turned back one time. She looked at the inner circle of the high chiefs, and the brilliant colors upon all of the lodges ran together like paint, colors that she used to play with as a child. Tears came again. Good-bye! She used the Blackfoot word, even in her mind. *Amba wastayeh! Amba wastayeh!*

Chapter Thirty

The trail was cool tree shadowed and soft with fallen leaves. The hoofs of the horses moved over pine needles, rustled the brown and gold leaves of the oaks to brief activity, and then in deeper shadow, moved noiselessly through leaf mold. Leaves were constantly drifting down under the oaks. Maria looked up at them and thought of her father's orchard, and of how as a girl, she loved to run among the trees in the autumn, and catch their falling leaves. Each one, she had pretended, was a life, and by catching it and keeping it from the ground she allowed that life to continue. Happy, and worn out finally with her goodness, she would walk home, and through the quiet dusk see the lamp lights burning. She forgot what she had done finally with the rescued leaves. She must have dropped them upon the path from the orchard. So she had not saved them after all. She had tried so hard to be good. She had to try extra hard, for she had something that sweet Ana did not; she bore a wicked shadow that, from early days, made men turn and look at her.

One day a man had come to the farm and had visited for a long time with her father. Helping her mother in the kitchen, she caught the man's eyes upon her bodice several times; when she had finished with her work, she had gone to the cellar, and with cold hands touched her burning face, for the man's looks had made her ashamed of her young breasts.

She remembered the smell of apples cold in the cellar, and her heart lurched to go home. Gone for her now was the springtime, the time of youth; gone for her now was even the summertime, with bees buzzing lazily in summer flowers. Gone now was everything but the blue cold winter.

Maria looked at Apikunni and the two men with him, Opiowan and Ahkiona. They were three of the original five Mutsik that had brought her from Snake land. Siksikai was dead, his carcass already eaten by the wolves, and Nakoa was in the winter forest.

"I leave you a virgin but for two meetings," he had said. She thought of the first meeting, their mating in the shadow of ferns, upon earth, meadow grass. They had met like animals, and yet there had been a trembling sweetness with the wild ecstasy, the shaking ecstasy, that made everything else move out of existence.

She had to stop thinking of their lovemaking. She looked up at the sky. High thin clouds were coming to it. The day was growing cold. Apikunni came to her side.

"The warm days are gone," he said. "Look, the geese are flying high. It is sign of a hard winter."

"Coming back, won't you be caught in the snows?"

"We can camp. We can pitch our lodge in a sheltered place until the circle camp meets in the spring."

"Apikunni, why did he send me away on this—this verge of winter?"

"Waiting is too bitter. Nakoa is my friend, and friend to Opiowan and Ahkiona too. The feel of a blizzard would be nothing to us to the feeling Nakoa would have if you lived with him until spring. You have departed one from the other and must separate at the time of departure."

"My heart is heavy at this leaving of your people."

"How will you remember the Indian, Maria?"

"With respect."

"With liking?"

"Yes. With very much liking."

Ahead of them, Opiowan stopped his horse and pointed up to the sky. Maria followed the direction of his hand and saw strange bright crosses of light shining near the sun. "What are they?" she asked Apikunni.

"Sun dogs. They mean that a great storm is coming down to us from the north."

"Are we going to stop and make camp?"

"No. The storm will not reach us before nightfall. We will ride until it is dark and then we will camp."

"When will we be able to go on?"

"When the storm passes."

"Will we not be snowbound?"

"No. The chinook will come, and will melt the snow."

"The chinook?"

"The warm wind from the west. It fights the cold-maker, and melts heavy snow in less than one day."

They rode silently on. After they had stopped and eaten, the sky grew more and more threatening. Over the mountain, black masses of clouds piled up swiftly from the north, and bands of mist drifted ghostlike against its dark shoulder. The winds grew, roaring through the pines, deafening them all. At dusk they were suddenly stung with a furious blast of hail and sleet. Maria shrank into the warmth of her buffalo robe, blindly following the others as she bent low over the bay's neck. The horses became covered with white frost, and icicles formed on their muzzles and matted their tails. Snow fell, and began to drift through Maria's clothing, sifting coldly down her neck, and filling her eyes and her mouth with its thick white pall. Darkness would not come, and Maria thought that she would suffocate. There was no air, no sky, only thick white, drifting down from the treetops and burying them all.

"Here," she heard Apikunni shout, and in this known camping site, the men assembled the tipi and put a large supply of wood in side. They dug the fire pit, adjusted the doorflaps of the lodge to suit the wind, and built a large fire. To hold the lodge anchored against the growing storm outside, they weighted its pegs down with stones, tied a lariat around the apex of its poles and anchored it to stakes driven in the ground. Near the skins of the lodge, the horses huddled, heads down, as if they could feel warmth too from the fire within.

Around the dancing fire they ate, and finally they slept. All night icy pellets lashed against the lodge, but inside of its double skins and by its fire it was warm and comfortable. There were other shelters besides white man's wood.

For three days and three nights snow continued to fall, and the wind howled crazily. The lodge poles creaked and groaned under its mighty onslaught, and great gusts swept down the smokehole and sent them all into spasms of coughing.

The men left the lodge when it was necessary, and in time Maria had to do this too. Even after her long period of living among the Blackfoot, this still caused her embarrassment. Oh, the body, the hated troublesome body! The body that had to be fed and had to be clothed, and went on and on with its disgusting animal functions.

Nakoa, you loved my body naked. Why could I not love my body naked? Atsitsi, forgive me! Forgive Maria—big with herself! Forgive the two Marias that had not the courage to accept each other!

Gentle Anatsa, my frail crippled friend! To you I turned, but did not hear, and now your tongue is silent and will not speak again! Anatsa—Ana—I lost you twice, and when I thought I was saving the leaves, I was only keeping them from nourishing their mother.

Upon the fourth morning the storm ended, as Apikunni said it would; then the warm chinook came, melting much of the snow. The fifth day they broke camp and traveled the thin trail once more that wound down the mountain to the prairie below.

The sky was bright and clear, and the wind cold enough to crust the snow again so that it crunched beneath the horses' hoofs. They rode to a valley, deep with powdery drifts that had been rippled by the chinook and frozen into lapping little waves by the north wind. It seemed a frozen sea, and through it the horses pranced spiritedly, arching their necks and blowing in the brisk air so their breath clung wraithlike to them.

They crossed the valley and came to a small glen when Apikunni, who was leading the party, signaled for them to stop. He stayed away from them and sat his horse without moving or speaking. While the rest of them waited, they ate and looked after him curiously. High in the snow-covered trees, the wind moved out strongly and sorrowfully.

He had almost not seen Anatsa's glen. He had almost ridden by it, covered with its first snows. His heart gave a violent wrench, as if with his unseeing eyes he had hurt her. He listened intently to the forest sounds around him, but in winter there were no sounds of spring. His horse moved, pawing at the ground and nuzzling the cold earth.

If the stream were moving again, between its banks of moss and swamp laurel she would be alive. If the stream were flowing down into the river again, from its waters she would drink.

He bowed his head. In the cold air he felt tears cold upon his cheeks. *Napi-mi notchokeaman!* Where is my strength? A shadow darkens all of the land and hides the sun! Spring will come again and the water frozen into silence at my feet will flow again—but the winter of my heart will remain. Anatsa, my love, my bride, I cannot bear the pain of a knife in your heart!

The wind moved more sadly through the pines and Apikunni remembered their day at the glen so vividly that he shook in agony. He would wail her name to the end of his days but it would do no good.

Gently, chidingly she came to him. Swiftly, suddenly, lovingly, and shy no longer, she entered his soul. In their love they were joined, closer than man and wife; death had not torn them asunder. She was too close for words; he felt her love, and the solace of her own deep serenity. Her joy was a flame in the blackness of his desolation. In the radiance of her being he saw the endless limits of his own. He would never accept her death again except as illusion. He did not know how long she stayed with him, for time no longer bound them. She had freed him from the agony of thinking her lost.

The swamp laurel bloomed a delicate pink; the green moss shadowed the moving stream and the deep pool that had caught her image. Tears were gone from his face; the wind no longer mourned at the coming winter. The world was a toy for them both; their meeting was not confined to its limits.

His horse was moving restlessly. Apikunni saw that the others had finished eating and were waiting for him. He led them forward on the trail again. Maria rode to him and looked anxiously into his face. "Do you not want to eat?" she asked him.

He turned to her, his eyes burning with a radiance. "I have eaten," he said. "I am sustained."

"And now I will speak to you," Apikunni said to Maria as he rode beside her. "I was going to say nothing and lead you to the white man's trail without words of love, but now I will speak."

"I listen to your words."

"At this glen, where we halted, I stopped in agony and grieved for Anatsa. It was here that I saw her for the first time. It was last spring when we rode to the mountains for the otsqueeina."

"I remember the morning you left for the mountains. The day before Atsitsi and I met you coming back from the river together."

"It might have been that my seeing her started that day. I do not know. But all my life, Anatsa was before my eyes. I think of her now, see her now, running as a little girl, running in such a strange manner, trying so hard with her crippled leg. I laughed at her trying to run, and wondered why she did not just walk."

"She heard the laughter and ran no more."

"I do not know. She might have stopped running in the village, but I feel that here, in these mountains, she could run like a young colt, tasting the wind of her running, the passing sky, and loving it."

"How can you speak so lightly of her crippled leg that brought her so much suffering?"

"She is crippled no more. Beauty has died, and is whole and complete, because I have seen what I cannot see, and in my blindness have accepted. That day at the glen the banks bloomed with swamp laurel, and the flowing stream became an island against the heat of the day. On the way up the mountain trail, she rode with me in such shyness. Talk between us was painful even when we halted for the otsqueeina, but there, at the glen, she drank from the pool and she changed, or I changed, and I saw her—really saw her. And today— how can I speak of today? My tongue struggles to say what I would, but my heart has reached so far beyond it!" His voice shook. "Today Anatsa came to me; she became a part of me. Her feelings were my feelings. We did not need talk. Our hearts were one. The winter of my grief is gone; she brought spring to my soul." Again Maria saw the radiance of his eyes, of his whole face.

Gayle Rogers

"I am glad for this, Apikunni. I am so glad in my heart."

"I cannot keep this shining love to myself. You must feel it too; I will tell you of the love between Anatsa and me."

"I hear, Apikunni."

"Maria, there is sight without seeing. I saw Anatsa today when she was a part of me. All of my life I had seen her, but in blindness. Anatsa to me was her crippled leg—her run that brought laughter to us all. I remember now, at the Kissing Dance, when I saw Anatsa enter with you, I was afraid that she might choose me for a lover."

"Oh, Apikunni! Apikunni!" Maria said sorrowfully, and tears flowed unchecked from her eyes.

"Eyes, awake and open, yet seeing without sight! I curse their blindness that kept me away from her for one day, one hour before our marriage! If I could have had her for my bride one full moon. If the moon could have come to the sky and grown into fullness just one time with Anatsa—my wife!"

"Do not grieve, Apikunni."

"I do not grieve for her now. I grieve for blindness that kept me from seeing her until that afternoon at the glen. I remember she bent over a pool there and when she arose she was like a water spirit. She was free and she told me that she used to dream of me as a lover there. She held some swamp laurel to her face and her eyes glowed with love for me. I thought she had risen like a magical spirit of both earth and water, for she was suddenly the beauty of both, and I wanted her and felt pain at my long self-denial. She was trembling when I touched her hand; and when I held her and kissed her, it seemed to me that she was shaking white foam, of neither land nor stream. I would shield her with my hands, but she would soon be gone. I knew this, Maria, I knew this!"

"Six notes of a gambel sparrow, a song of neither earth nor air."

"Why do you say this?"

"This is how she saw her life. She knew that she would die soon. She said she would rest in the burial grounds before her time."

"She rests not. She parted the skies for me and brought the sun to my soul."

"I am glad that she did this. She loved you so."

"Loves," Apikunni corrected. "Death is an illusion. She has changed the world for me twice. When I first saw her at the glen and we rode back to the village, the afternoon became golden and shimmering. This afternoon she showed me that there is no death. When we do not see with our heart, we walk in terrible blindness. What do you see ahead, Maria?"

"What do I see—where?"

"Ahead of us, upon the trail."

"I see untouched snow, white beneath a sky that is darkening with the coming of night. I see a day ending in sadness."

"I see snow that will be touched by us, that will yield to the hoofs of our horses, our lodge and the warmth of our fire. I see snows that will melt even in the light of a winter sun. I see change. I see growth when the snows melt and nourish spring grass."

Maria watched him closely. The wind sighed behind them. The sky had become overcast, and a light snow fell, and the horses walked softly through it, their manes blowing forward. Suddenly the setting sun broke through the clouds. Gleaming particles drifted brilliantly against the somber pines and then the light faded and they became pure white once more.

"You see," Apikunni said, "even the falling snow takes the color of the sun."

"What are you saying to me, Apikunni?"

"You have mated with Nakoa. You at least have reflected light."

"Then I live with just reflected light."

"I asked you before, in the lodge of your husband, have you ever thought of life without the sun?"

"You are saying that without Nakoa I am nothing."

"I am saying that without rebirth you are nothing. Anatsa did not come to comfort only my grief. Anatsa loved you as her blood sister; Anatsa loved Nakoa. I have love for Nakoa, as close to me as blood brother, and I have love for you. Let our love be joined. Love is the true circle of our creation." He stopped talking, overcome with emotion. "I do not grieve," he continued, "I want you to see beyond your vision. I want you to see with your heart!"

"I have felt with my heart. I have suffered so from the pain in my heart."

"There are so many worlds, Maria. The pain in this world is a shadow that skims across the prairie to bring rain to the parched earth."

"Pain has made me die many deaths," she whispered.

"Then rise nourished from your suffering. See that this world and everything in it is a child's toy. See that whatever is a part of you can never be torn away, any more than you can pluck out the heart of your body and expect it to live. If you deny a part of your soul, the vessel for the Great Spirit is cracked and cannot give you sustenance."

"Nakoa told me this. This thought is part of your religion?"

"No, this is not a part of our religion. Anatsa revealed this to me. She is a part of my soul and we were once one, and will never be separated now that we have mated. What was once one will seek itself through all eternity, and if you destroy this part of your spirit, the seeking goes on and on."

"Only the spirit of man and woman rejoined can seek the Great Spirit?"

"We all seek the Great Spirit because we are of the Great Spirit and seek our source. Only man and woman joined are His children."

"I do not understand."

"You say you have died many deaths with your grief at losing those you love. Be born again and see with your heart."

"The world is so dark and cold. The clouds hide the sun."

"The clouds hide the sun, but the sun is there. After every night the sun is there. Anatsa's body lies in the burial grounds but she did not remain still with a knife in her heart. She did not sleep in peace without knowledge of my pain or sorrow for my suffering. The eyes are blind, Maria. Hear my words."

"I hear, but what can I do?"

Apikunni stopped his horse, and signaled for the two men behind them to make camp. Maria's horse huddled close to his. Dark had fallen and in the coming night the snow particles above them still drifted, white and untouched.

"Here, Maria, the trail divides."

Maria looked ahead and saw that a path led below and another above them.

"The path that we are to take in the morning leads down to the prairie, and to the place of our circle camp. It goes through the burial grounds. Here, Maria, you can sit still. You can remain with the dead and seek those who did not seek the ghost trail."

"I do not want this... I want to go back to my own land."

"It is the same."

"And where does the other path lead?"

"It goes to your husband. It goes to the valley where Nakoa is camped, and where he has erected a lodge for the winter."

"I cannot go there."

"You cannot travel toward the sun?"

"Apikunni," she sobbed, "why do you do this to me?"

"Because Anatsa brought me warmth through even the ice of my grief; through my deepest blindness, she brought me sight. Go to Nakoa, Maria, and meet yourself."

"I must go home! I must go home!"

"You have broken into the white man's tongue. You cannot say these words of refusal in the language of your husband."

The lodge had been erected. Still weeping, Maria entered it and Apikunni remained outside alone. A cold wind blew against him steadily; next to the new moon a single star shone in brilliance, and Apikunni stood still in deep silence and watched it.

Chapter Thirty One

The snow continued to fall gently throughout the night. The clouds came and went. The sky would momentarily clear and the stars would shine through the smoke hole and then more clouds would come, bringing more snow. The west wind rose, pushing against the tipi and the creaking lodge poles. They had eaten, and now the three men slept, but Maria could not sleep, and lay still and listened to the wind high in the snow-covered pines.

Back at the circle camp she had heard the wind mournfully reach out from the burial grounds. Never had she heard such a sad song, this eternal seeking after itself. She thought of Apikunni's words. Was going home a search for the dead? Among the whites her mother was dead; the old farmhouse was either empty or inhabited by strangers. The same lamps would not be burning in the windows; the same foods would not be cooking upon the stove. The cellar might be empty of apples or cool cider, and her mother's orchard would now be barren against the sky. In the softness of civilization could there be another man for her?

She sat up and covered her face with her hands. Nakoa had said that their souls were once joined and now she knew it to be true. As Anatsa had entered Apikunni's heart, Nakoa had entered hers, and eternity without him would be an agony of desolation.

She rocked back and forth in the silence of the tipi. Nakoa would never taste milk or toil in the fields. Nakoa would never sleep under a white man's roof and smell the scent of lavendered sheets.

Maria got up and dressed warmly and left the tipi. The clouds had vanished and the new moon shone in the sky. Tears touched her face again. Then it must be good-bye to the feel of silk, the taste of salt, and milk cooled in running water. Go then the lamps shining behind windows, the sound of the violin and church bells tolling on Sundays. Go then the Christian marriage, and come my love to me, for the night is beating in beauty!

Above her on the dimly lit trail he camped. In his hidden valley, his new lodge stood, and around them the first snow had made the land bridal white. This was the night of her dream, of her marriage, and now no power on earth could keep her from going to him.

Apikunni joined Maria by the lodge door. She reached up and kissed the side of his face. "Tonight I will seek the path leading to the sun," she said. "I do not seek the burial grounds. I want the dead to sleep and wail for me no longer."

He took her hands and held them warmly within his own. "You are going to him tonight," he said.

"Yes. Tonight. Now!"

Apikunni went to the horses and led back the bay. She mounted him and tenderly looked down at Apikunni's face. "I love as Anatsa loves," she said.

"Yes, Maria," he replied. "And that is the difference between us and the animals we hunt for meat. We touch the sun, and in their dumbness they do not, and so we feed upon them!"

"Apikunni, I feel blessed."

"I know," he said softly.

"We will meet in the spring when the circle camp forms again. Think, Apikunni," she said in wonder. "I might be carrying his child!"

He reached up and touched her hands again. "I hope it will be," he said, his face suddenly haunted.

"Good-bye, Apikunni," she whispered.

"He is not too far upon the trail that leads back up the mountain. Do you want me to take you to him?"

"No. I will find him. Wherever he is, I can find him. Tonight I do not need the vision of my eyes, for I see with my heart."

She nudged the bay, and waving to him in farewell, set out upon the smooth white snow.

The trapper rode cautiously along the trail. His cache had delayed him a week in leaving the mountain, and though he was a good distance downslope from the Blackfoot, he still felt uneasy. He did not know what had happened to his two companions, and he didn't care. They had probably screwed the squaw and lost their hair for it.

He was cold and sleepy, but he kept riding. He would stop and make camp at daylight, well hidden, in case any Blackfoot were out hunting. While he was still in their land, he would continue to sleep days. Then he'd cut east, over to Crow territory where a white man could breathe a lot easier. He had the forest to himself, and it was a good thing since the snow had fallen. During the storm his tracks had been covered, but now nagging fear persisted that there might be someone following them.

The trail ahead led into complete shadow. His horse went leisurely on, sensing nothing strange. The trapper glanced at the silver thread of the moon before it was hidden by the thickness of the trees. He remembered how as a boy he had told a girl he loved her under just such a moon, and now even with all the years in between, the same sight brought her to his thoughts. It was not just the girl he felt nostalgia for—it was the excitement of first love, youth, the first stirrings of manhood. All women were that young girl to him, for she was the only woman he had known intimately.

Suddenly, deep in the total darkness before him, he sensed movement. Then a shadow came toward him, and in his terror his vision widened and he saw the vague outline of a tipi. Without another thought he fired his gun. It was a goddamned Indian! He kicked his horse wildly and the animal left the trail and careened down the powdery slopes. He ran the horse until he reached the prairie, and light was threading into the eastern sky.

He found shelter for himself and his horse. There was no sign that he had been followed, but cold sweat still stood upon his face. He would have to hit Crow land in a hurry, for a war party would soon be upon his tracks. He was certain that when the Indian had come to him, he had shot the bastard right between the eyes.

The trail wound ahead untouched, unmarked by any sign of man. An owl hooted softly from the trees above her, and a soft flurry of snow fell suddenly to her shoulders. Maria brushed it free. There was no sound except the plodding footsteps of the bay.

Around a bend, gleaming somewhere ahead, would be his lodge. There would be the warmth of fire, the touch of her husband.

I will love the hands that touch my breasts, and when the hands are gone, I will love the breasts still.

The love and the pain,
The sunlight and the rain,
I accept.

The mystery was unfolded, the flower of my creation. Deeply I would know him, to drink deeply of myself. His hands brought me from the farthermost shadow.

The day and the night,
The blindness and the sight,
I accept.

Sleep my mother and my gentle little sister, I am humble. I am the cup to bear His wine.

The love and the
glory, The end of the
story, I accept.

Across the virginal snow her father spoke.
"Maria, do you take this man for your wedded husband?"
"I do."
"Then walk to the altar."
Maria looked ahead, but saw only the gleaming trail. The bay walked on, pricking his ears in curiosity and moving his head from side to side.

Suddenly a woman in white appeared. Shimmering, she moved

phantom-like, not touching the snow. Another woman waited for her by the side of the trail, hanging her head in deep sorrow. Her long black hair covered her face.

"Who are you?" the bride asked her.

"I am your father's mistress," came the answer, and Maria saw that when she raised her head, her breasts were naked.

The bride touched the suffering face. "I am glad that you could accept my father when I could not," she said, and walked on.

Now she was struggling, for the snows had deepened. Her veil became torn, her skirts became shreds and clung wetly to her legs. She was hiding her face. She did not want to look up, for ahead of her stood a tall man in shadow. It was Siksikai. "You can only pass me in nakedness," he said.

"I will be naked only for my husband," the girl replied.

"Your husband is in me. We are all of each other."

"For my husband within you I will be naked," the bride said, and took her clothing and cast it from herself. Siksikai bent in agony, and upon the snow he melted and became nothing. The bride then turned and faced Maria without shame, and Maria looked upon herself.

Atsitsi stood by them both with her hands upon her fat belly. "Now where big Maria from?" she asked sarcastically.

"Our Mother, the Earth," Maria said proudly. "I know my father, but I am of my Mother, the Earth!"

Atsitsi grinned and vanished.

The bride had vanished too. Maria bowed her head and wept. Living and dying were never apart. The eye of final wisdom was the circle.

Nakoa came to her, not from the lodge but from the side of the trail where he had gone when he heard the sound of her horse.

"Maria," he said, reaching up and touching her face.

"I came to you in my dream of white moonlight," she said.

In his old way he tenderly brushed the hair back from her forehead. "From out of your dream of mists you have come to shame all the waters to silence."

She leaned toward him, and they kissed deeply. "With my body and soul, I thee wed," she whispered.

He lifted her from the horse and held her tightly. "East is west, for the wind touches both and knows neither," he said.

Tears of joy coursed down Maria's cheeks. "Nakoa, Anatsa returned to Apikunni. There is no death. And when you are mated, there is no separation."

He smiled tenderly, tears touching his own eyes. "I know," he said. "I know."

She put her head against the clean buckskin smell of his breast. "Nakoa, I don't want this moment to end. I want the stars to stand still."

He drew away from her and cupped her face between his hands. His warmth was the warmth of all of the suns. "Maria," he said softly, "we just said that when lovers have met there is no time." Then like all the other phantoms, he vanished.

"Oh, no," Maria protested. It was too much to lose him even in a dream. She urged the bay on, terrorized that she would not find him. She had become sick with fear when she saw the dim outline of his lodge. The fire in the fire pit had sunk to its last embers. She was cold, bitterly cold, but she had reached him. She held the bay in and savored the night. A little animal bounded swiftly over the trail, disappearing in the black and white patterns wrought by the moon. Above her the highest branches of the trees were frozen white, gleaming palely against the twinkling of the stars. It was the most beautiful of all nights. "Nakoa!" she called out and leaped eagerly from the bay. Over the smooth snow she ran to him; from east to west, from paved streets to meadow grass, past Meg, past the innocence of Ana, past the burning wagon train, past the little girl crying for sugared candy, and every good-bye was the beating of her triumphant heart.

Bibliography

Catlin, George. *North American Indians,* (volumes I and II). London: Egyptian Hall, Piccadilly, 1841.

Grinnell, George Bird. "Early Blackfoot History," *American Anthropologist* 5, no. 2 (April 1892).

Hafen, Le Roy, and Rister, Carl Coke. *Western America.* New York: Prentice-Hall, Inc., 1941.

Hofsinde, Robert. *Indian Sign Language.* New York: William Morrow and Co., 1956.

McClintock, Walter. *Old Indian Trails.* Boston and New York: Houghton Mifflin Co., 1923.

"Four Days in a Medicine Lodge." *Harper's Monthly* 101 (September 1900): 419-31.

Old North Trail. London: MacMillan Co., 1908.

"The Blackfoot Tipi," *The Masterkey* 10 (May 1936): 86–96.

"Painted Tipis and Picture-Writing of the Blackfoot Indians," *The Masterkey* 10 (July 1936): 121-33.

"The Blackfoot Beaver Bundle," *The Masterkey* 9 *(May* 1935): 77-84.

"Dances of the Blackfoot Indians," *The Masterkey* 11 (July 1937): 111-21.

"Blackfoot Warrior Societies," *The Masterkey* 11 (September 1937): 148-58.

Parkman, Francis. *The Oregon Trail.* New York: Longmans, Green and Co., 1910.

Steward, Julian H. *The Blackfoot.* Berkeley: National Park Service Field Division of Education, 1934.

Wissler, Clark. *North American Indians of the Plains.* New York: American Museum of Natural History, 1912, and Duvall, D. C. "A Mythology of the Blackfoot Indians," *Anthropological Papers of the American Museum of Natural History* 11 (1908): 1–163.

Biography of Gayle Rogers

Gayle Rogers was born on May 17, 1923 in Watsonville, California. U.C.L.A. graduate, with graduate work completed at U.C.L.A., Northridge University and California Lutheran University. Schoolteacher for twenty eight years. Author of The Second Kiss, Nakoa's Woman, Gladyce with a C, and Dark Corners. A death experience at age seven left author psychic and open to the power of the soul, its core of divinity, its eternal seeking of growth and the power of human love to inspire that growth. The window opened into the soul through the death experience expanded further and expands with each book written and is considered by the author to be the jewel of her life.

Other Books by Gayle Rogers:

Gladyce With a C
Dark Corners